GUARDIANS IN BLUE
BOOK TWO

KEN BANGS

For John T. Johnson a friend for life.

Ken Bangs

BLACK ROSE
writing™

The final approval for this literary material is granted by the author.

First printing

This is a work of fiction. Names, characters, businesses, places, events and incidents
are either the products of the author's imagination or used in a fictitious manner.
Any resemblance to actual persons, living or dead, or actual events is purely
coincidental.

ISBN: 978-1-61296-976-3
PUBLISHED BY BLACK ROSE WRITING www.blackrosewriting.com

Printed in the United States of America
Suggested Retail Price (SRP) $23.95

Guardians in Blue: Book Two is printed in Book Antiqua

DEDICATION

"…David said to Saul, "Your servant has been keeping his father's sheep. When a lion or a bear came and carried off a sheep from the flock, I went after it, struck it and rescued the sheep from its mouth. When it turned on me, I seized it by its hair, struck it and killed it. Your servant has killed both the lion and the bear; this uncircumcised Philistine will be like one of them…" (1 Samuel 17: 34-36 NIV) *

In this passage of scripture David is addressing King Saul who can find no man willing to go out and confront the giant who had come to kill, steal from and enslave the people of Israel.

David was but a shepherd boy with no training as a warrior. But he had heard the call to protect and serve.

When the giant came against those who David served, he did not hesitate. He stepped up and did that which he knew to do and brought the giant down. His sole thought was to protect those he was responsible for. David was a *guardian*.

This work is dedicated to all the modern day David's whom face that which we fear and keep us safe from the giants of life who come against us. They are worthy to be called *GUARDIANS*.

*See Victory's Hand, a poem by the author describing this event in full, at the end of the book.

WHAT THE GUARDIANS SAY

"I found *Guardians in Blue* by Ken Bangs to be both entertaining and enlightening as he places his audience in the shoes of a young rookie policeman learning to serve and protect the citizens of Dallas, Texas. Set during the late 60's and early 70's, Officer K.W. Bangs relives some of his most memorable experiences as a street cop, field-training officer and investigator for the Dallas Police Department. I think readers will come away with a better appreciation for the challenges that all Police Officers, both then and now, face daily."

David Elliston
Deputy Chief of Police Retired
Dallas Police Department

"Guardians in Blue is an action-packed book about actual crimes from the Dallas Police files. These cases, as retold by Ken Bangs, come alive in a format that makes you feel like you are at the location and involved in the investigations."

Gary Holly
Retired Police Officer

"After spending over 46 years in Law Enforcement, it didn't take long for me to realize that only one who has walked the walk could have written *Guardians in Blue.*"

Terry G. Box
Sheriff
Collin County, Texas

"As a man who was privileged to work the streets with Ken Bangs, I can tell you that he was the Guardian. If you want to understand police work at the base level, then *Guardians in Blue* is a must read. It goes beyond the violence and the sensationalism and gives you a window into the hearts and souls of those men and women who ride toward danger when everyone else runs away."

Doug Sword
Captain Of Police (Retired)
Dallas Police Department

"*Guardians in Blue,* authored by Retired Officer Ken Bangs, gives us a look at what it was like growing up poor and fatherless in a small Texas town during the 1950's and '60's. Police officers became his father figures and instilled in him a determination to take control of the circumstances and chart his own course. He chose to follow their example. His heart's desire was to be like them, to be a *guardian.*

I too grew up in a small Texas town and like Ken; my life's ambition was to be a guardian. Again, like Ken I became a big city police officer and served 37 years with the Dallas, Texas police department. Maybe that's why I found *Guardians* so compelling, why the story evoked such a raw emotional response. The story is so realistic; it so reveals the rawness of life experienced by a police officer that any who have ever worn the badge will be drawn in as they see themselves in the *Guardians in Blue.*

If you are a guardian, there are no x-police officers, this is a must read for you. It is reality at its finest. We are *Guardians in Blue* and this is our life."

G. David Payne
Lieutenant of Police (Retired)
Dallas, Texas Police Department

If your question is "How do the police really do their jobs?" this book is your answer.

Television and movies paint fantasifull pictures of cops solving complex cases in the running time of the film. But that is Hollywood. *Guardians in Blue* and *Guardians In Blue ~ Book Two* takes you to the street where those who choose to stand between the flock and the devourer face the grim realities of their commitment to serve, protect and defend on a daily basis. The reader is given insight to investigative techniques employed by law enforcement investigators, informatively interspersed with dialogue that conveys the guardian's thoughts and feelings as he pursues justice for the victim.

Curtis Green
Former Texas Police Officer (Highland Park & Plano Police Departments) - Investigative Manager (Retired)
Medicaid Fraud Unit, Texas Attorney's General's Office

Tender, tense and tough. Ken takes the reader through his experience of growing up in a small town to seeing his dream of being a police officer come true on the mean streets of Dallas. A riveting story of real life crime fighting by a masterful and dedicated Guardian In Blue.

Jim Green
Former Chief, Commerce Texas PD
Retired Texas Peace Officer

WHAT THE READERS SAY ABOUT BOOK TWO

I have known K.W. Bangs since we were kids. Love his passion for serving his fellow man as a police officer, then judge, and then from the pulpit. We need more like him.

His experiences, as outlined in his two *Guardians in Blue* books, are an eye-opening tribute to those called to protect us.

John T. Johnson III
Arlington, TX

Ken Bangs has written a book about real life as seen through the eyes of a real Guardian. The description of the facts is as chilling and real as the officer who is telling them. Kens attention to detail has you feeling that you are right beside him and on the scene in the cases he describes.

George A. Cox
Fort Worth, Texas

Guardians in Blue ~ Book Two is fast paced and keeps you wondering what is next. The book defines the roll of the Guardian in varying aspects of our lives. We all should be thankful for the Guardians.

Carl Grey
Dallas, Texas

GUARDIANS IN BLUE

BOOK TWO

CONTENTS

CHAPTER 1
THE CLOUD OF WITNESSES

The tension twisted each man's gut as they stood silently waiting for the Captain. K.W. chewed his bottom lip and reached down to caress the Colt forty-five strapped to his hip. He ran his hand over the rough checkering of the grips, down along the cool metal of the slide and back up to the hammer. It was *'cocked and locked'* with a two hundred and thirty-grain hollow point Super Vel waiting in the chamber. The Colt was ready for action, and so was K.W.

He glanced at the clock on the wall just above the squad room door. The second hand swept up and passed the big red twelve, the minute hand ticked up, and it was now four thirty and the Captain left everyday at five o'clock. *'Come on Captain, I want to kick that door no later than five o'clock tomorrow morning, and I need your approval before you leave today,'* K.W. mumbled to himself.

Captain Jack swept into the room and ran his eyes over the detectives. "K.W. do you have the warrant?" he asked.

"Yes sir, right here," K.W. pulled the arrest warrant from his shirt pocket and handed it to the Captain.

The Captain reviewed it carefully and then asked, "You have his picture?"

"Yes sir, and I have given each man a copy of it," K.W. answered.

"Have you double-checked the address, are you sure of the apartment number?" the Captain asked.

"Yes sir, and Elmer confirmed it also. We are good to go," K.W. said.

The Captain locked his gaze onto K.W. and said, "You are good to go when I say so."

"Yes sir," K.W. squirmed under that piercing gaze.

Looking at the raid team, the Captain said, "All of you have done this before. You know how quickly things can go wrong. K.W. here is young and in a hurry. I want you old heads to slow this down and be sure that it goes right.

Elmer, this is K.W.'s case but you are senior, and I want you in charge. Do you understand me, K.W.?"

K.W. nodded and looked at Elmer.

"I didn't hear you answer the Captain," Lieutenant Gus said.

K.W. pulled his gaze from Elmer and turned slowly to his Lieutenant. "I heard him Lieutenant. Yes sir, I understand Captain.

Elmer is in charge, and I will follow his lead. But Cap, I would like to be the first through the door. It is my case," K.W. said looking from the Captain to his Lieutenant."

"I just put Elmer in charge, so that is his call," the Captain replied.

K.W. nodded and said, "Yes sir."

The captain left the room, and the Lieutenant said to Elmer, "Take over and get this done safely."

Elmer nodded at the Lieutenant and turned to address the team, "Okay, we want to hit that door no later than five tomorrow morning. Let's assemble here at four. K.W. you draw a car before coming to the office. Millie, you get one too.

Johnny and I will ride with K.W. He has driven by the apartment complex several times and knows the way better than I do. He will drive our car and Mille you will drive the second car.

When we get to the complex, follow us in. Turn your headlights off and keep the noise down.

K.W. stopped by the office and got a copy of the floor plan of the unit we are going to hit. The apartment is on the second floor. It is unit two zero nine. It is an open concept unit, with one bedroom, a kitchen, and one bathroom.

As you enter, there will be a door on the immediate right. That is the bedroom. The master bathroom is to the left as you enter the bedroom.

Directly in front and opposite the front door is the kitchen area. There is no door, but there is a four-foot high counter.

K.W. will lead the way as we climb the stairs. I will be next and then Johnny. Millie, M.G., and Forrest you will follow. J.B., I want you to stay with the cars. Leave the motor running so the radio is powered up and ready in case we need to call for assistance.

The apartment faces the landing. We will fan out along the wall on either side of the door, and K.W. will kick it. He is first in, and we will follow.

K.W., Johnny and I will go in with pistols. Millie and M.G. will have shotguns, Forrest you will stay on the landing for security. Choose your weapon.

I will stay with K.W. Johnny, you will secure the front room. Millie and M.G. you will sweep the rest of the apartment. Bring anyone you find to the front room, cuff them and sit them down on the floor with their backs to the wall. Do not put them on the couch or in any stuffed chairs until those seats are checked for weapons. Johnny, you will maintain control of those they bring in.

Finally, remember that this is a violent felon. This man has pistol-whipped customers and staff in three other robberies. Newton and his gang are responsible for the killing of the guard during the robbery of The Big World Liquor Store. The rules of engagement are that you free to fire on any hostile action without the requirement to issue a warning. Are there any questions?"

The detectives were quite for a few seconds, and then Forrest asked, "Any chance the office personnel might have tipped them off about K.W. picking up that floor plan?"

Elmer looked at K.W. and waited. K.W. shifted his weight and said, "I don't know. I didn't ask for the floor plan to that particular unit, didn't tell them I was police. I just asked if they had any one bedroom second-floor units available.

None were available at that time. But the manager said that one was due to come open in two months. She told me that all the one-bedroom units had the same plan. I told them I would get back with them."

"What kind of weapons can we expect to be up against," Millie asked.

"Pistols, shotguns and a sawed off twenty two rifle is what they have used in the robberies," Elmer answered. Our target this morning, Issac Newton, is the last of this bunch. The rest are locked up. Newton carried the sawed-off rifle during each robbery," Elmer answered.

•   •   •

K.W. led the caravan of unmarked police vehicles through the predawn darkness. He cut the headlights on his car as he pulled into the parking lot of the *Lemon Avenue Apartment Homes* complex. He looked into the side view mirror and saw that the trailing cars did the same.

He stopped at the foot of the stairway leading to unit two zero nine. He stepped from the car and closed the door without making any noise. He walked to the foot of the stairway, paused and looked back at Elmer and the other officers assembled in a single file.

Elmer nodded, and K.W. eased the forty-five Colt from its' holster and clicked the safety off. He mounted the stairs and then sprinted up to the second floor landing.

K.W. stepped aside and let the team fan out on either side of the door. He turned to face the door and waited. He felt Elmer place his hand on his shoulder, holding him in place.

Time seemed to have stopped. Everything was happening in slow motion, and he saw only the door, standing at the end of a long tunnel directly in front of him. There was an acrid taste in his mouth, and his heart was pumping so hard and fast that the pulse in his throat was choking him. Then, the barking of a dog in the unit next door shattered the silence. 'Damned dog,' K.W. thought.

Elmer tapped his shoulder and said, "Go."

K.W. rocked back and exploded forward crashing his right foot just to the side of the doorknob. The cheap lock gave way, and the door slammed inward, bounced off of the wall and swung back toward the charging officer.

K.W. lowered his shoulder and pushed through. Movement on his right caught his attention, and he swiveled to see Issac Newton running toward the bedroom doorway.

Newton tried to close the door, but K.W. used his momentum to force his way through. The edge of the door struck Newton's face, and K.W. heard the bone shatter as the nose was flattened. Blood splattered across K.W.'s face, and he felt it flow across his cheeks and down over his mouth. He fought to resist the impulse to lick the blood from his lips.

Newton had fallen across the foot of the bed. K.W. quickly kneeled with his knee on his chest and placed the Colt between his eyes.

"Dallas Police, don't move or I will scatter your brains all across this bed," K.W. growled, his voice thick from the rush of adrenaline.

Looking into Newton's eyes, K.W. saw that he had no fight left. He holstered the Colt; flipped Newton onto his stomach and Elmer handcuffed him.

K.W. wiped the blood from his mouth and stood looking down at this man who had brutalized so many. He didn't look so mean now, lying there in handcuffs with his blood pooling on the bedspread.

The pounding in his head began to subside. His breathing was no longer audible, and things were happening in real time again. K.W. looked at Elmer and nodded.

It was over. Newton was the last of the Big World bunch. They were no longer threats, no longer would they prey on the innocent.

He grabbed a corner of the sheet and wiped the blood from Newton's face. He lifted him from the bed and moved toward the front door. As he stepped onto the landing, he heard the little dog barking again. "Did you hear that dog bark just before we came through the door," he asked Newton.

Newton nodded and said, "I heard him. I looked out the window and saw you in front of the door, and the others lined up along the wall. My rifle was in the kitchen, and I was headed for it when you kicked the door. I generally sleep with it right beside me. You are damned lucky that I left in the kitchen last night. I would have shot your white ass right through that front door."

K.W. just kept him moving forward. No need to argue with a dead man, and he fully intended to do all he could to see that Newton got the death penalty for killing the guard at the Big World robbery.

Garth Binkle had been sixty-six years old. K.W. had kneeled beside Binkle's dead body, laid his hand on his chest and promised to bring to justice those who had murdered him. They were all in jail, but justice was not fully served. Not until they forfeited their lives for the one they had taken from Binkle.

He looked back as the detectives came down the stairs behind him. Their faces were beginning to relax as the adrenaline rush faded. *'They are Guardians, proven many times over. I will ride with anyone of them, anywhere, anytime,'* K.W. thought.

"Watch your head as you go in," K.W. said to Newton as he placed him in the back seat of the squad. He closed the door, hitched up his gun belt and smiled up at the sun that was peeking over the roofline of the apartments.

There, now visible in the morning haze, was a cloud filled with light. But, it appeared that there were figures of men within that light, peering down at him.

K.W. nodded his head and smiled. There had been a cloud of witnesses watching.

'Not all Guardians wear blue. Some are clothed in light,' he thought as he settled in behind the wheel and turned the vehicle toward downtown Dallas.

CHAPTER 2
THE SKULL ~ THE ROLEX ~ THE RING

Bobby woke and lay in bed gathering his thoughts. He glanced to his right and saw that Eugene had left a note on the bedside table. He tried to sit up but the sheets were wrapped around his legs, and he had to struggle to free himself.

He kicked out of the tangled mess and stood up. He grabbed the folded paper and saw that there was no money in it. "*Damn you, Eugene. You promised you would leave my money when you left for work,'* Bobby flopped back down on the bed.

He opened the note and read, '*Sorry that I lied to you Bobbie; I think of you as Bobbie rather Bobby. I am as broke as you are. I get paid Friday, and I will catch you up. Hey, you showed me a great time last night, and I won't forget it. See you later. Eugene.'*

Bobby wadded the note up and tossed it across the room. Hunger pains pinched his belly. He stood again and moved to the bathroom. He pulled the false eyelashes off and laid them carefully on the side of the sink. He took the stud earrings out and placed them beside the eyelashes.

He looked at the tub and grimaced. '*I am not getting in that vat of filth. I bet Eugene has never cleaned it,'* Bobby said and opened the tap on the sink faucet. He opened the towel cabinet and grabbed the last clean cloth. He held it under the cool water and then began to remove the makeup and lipstick from his face. He ran the cloth over his head, across the back of his neck and then down and under his arms.

Finished with his morning cleansing, Bobby pulled on his jeans and then took a shirt out of Eugene's closet. He pulled it over his head and settled it around his waist. *'I'll keep this as an advance on what you owe me, Eugene,'* he mumbled. He grabbed an empty envelope off of the table and put his eyelashes and ear studs in it. He looked around the room and walked out.

Bobby stood in the shade the canopy provided. He could feel the heat radiating off of the sidewalk. *'Hot as hell and it is only the middle of July. What will August be like?'* he wondered. He looked both ways along Forest Avenue and could feel the increase in tempo as the sun began its' westward slide.

He heard the click of high heels on concrete and heard his name called, "Bobby, what's up my man or is it going to be Bobbie again tonight. I saw you leave with Eugene last night. Bet he didn't pay you, did he?"

He looked at the woman standing before him. She was at least six foot tall in those platform shoes. Her red hair swooped back and swirled around her long, slender neck. She had just the hint of makeup on, light blue eye shadow, pink lipstick, and eyelashes that had to be a half-inch long. She was wearing a gold lame dress that stopped at mid thigh, dangling gold hoop earrings, a gold chain necklace and a pink hat that sloped down almost touching her shoulders.

"Well look at you! Girl, you look like Eleanor Rigby herself. I have to admit, you are the best looking woman on the block," Bobby smiled.

"Don't forget Bobby; this is real. *I am a real woman.* Why do you try to compete with this Bobby? You know that given an option the men are going to choose me every time," Eleanor laughed.

"They will tonight for sure. You are always beautiful, but tonight you are hot," Bobby nodded his approval.

"Well thank you, Bobby. I see that you aren't made up yet. Are you going to work Forest Avenue tonight? If so, let's agree on what part of the block each will work," Eleanor said.

"I'm not working Forest tonight. I am broke and hungry. I am going to call my white man and meet him downtown," Bobby said.

"I wish you good luck getting a whole sack of sugar from that daddy," Eleanor said as she headed for her corner.

Bobby stepped out of the shade and walked down to Harwood and turned north. He stopped at the '*Rack Em Up*' Pool Hall and asked Joey if he could use the phone. He dialed the number from memory and waited for his meal ticket to answer.

•   •   •

"Anyone have anything else to add," Jeremy asked as his team continued to gather their papers and push back from the table.

No one answered and he said, "That's it then. Have a good night, and I will see you all tomorrow."

He gathered his papers and walked to his desk. He glanced at the clock and saw that it was nearing six o'clock. He shuffled the papers and was tempted to sit down and work through the issues that had been raised during the meeting.

'*Nope, it will wait until morning,*' he thought as he turned to take his jacket off of the rack. He reached for the door, and his phone rang. He hesitated with one hand on the doorknob and looked at the phone. He sighed deeply and walked back to the desk. Picking up the phone he said, "This is Jeremy."

"Can you come out tonight?" Bobby said softly.

Jeremy said, "Wait one," and stepped back to close the partially opened office door.

He walked around behind the desk and sat down in his chair. "I don't think so. I have been working late every night this week. I should go home tonight; maybe I can come out tomorrow night," he said.

"I need to see my man," Bobby whispered.

Jeremy felt a surge of excitement. He swiveled around in his chair and looked out of the window. He knew he was going, so why drag it out, "I'm leaving the office now. Meet me at the Greyhound Station."

"I'll be waiting in the usual spot," Bobby said.

Jeremy hung up the phone and then picked it right back up. He dialed his home number and waited.

"Hello," Sally said.

"I will be late again tonight. Don't wait up," he said.

"Why do you even bother to call? You know I don't care anymore. Just go do your thing and leave me out of it," Sally said and hung up the phone.

Jeremy dropped the receiver back onto the hook and hurried out the door. He made good time and was soon circling the Greyhound Bus Station looking for Bobby.

Bobby saw the tan Lincoln and stepped to the curb. Jeremy pulled up and stopped. Bobby slid in and reached for Jeremy's hand. "You get Bobby rather than Bobbie tonight," he said.

Jeremy squeezed his hand and said, "That is just fine with me."

Bobby winked and said, "Hurry baby. I'm ready for you."

Jeremy turned onto South Ervay. He drove to Forrest Avenue and turned back to his left.

"Jeremy, why do you always want to go to South Dallas? Why don't you ever take me to a nice hotel up North," Bobby asked.

"I like the motel at Second and Hatcher. Besides that is closer to your projects, isn't it?" Jeremy asked.

"What does that have to do with anything? But if you insist on going that far, stop at the Williams Chicken on Second and Hatcher and get me a snack pack. All this driving has made me hungry," Bobby said.

"Okay," Jeremy said.

Bobby fingered the Rolex on Jeremy's wrist. "You shouldn't wear such expensive jewelry down here. Somebody will take that away from you," he said.

"No one is getting my watch. They would have to kill me first," Jeremy said.

"Whatever. There is the Williams Chicken. Don't go through the quick lane. I want to go inside so I can get the pieces I want," Bobby said.

Jeremy parked the Lincoln in front of the big glass windows. He handed Bobby a fifty-dollar bill and said, "Hurry."

Bobby stepped inside the restaurant and drooled at the smell of frying chicken. He stepped up to the counter and said, "I want a custom order. I want two thighs, two legs, and two wings. Put some fries and a couple of rolls with that. Hurry it up please."

"Why Bobby? Is your *white man* in a hurry?" the clerk asked looking out the window at the Lincoln.

"Don't give me trouble Gaston. I have to make a living just like you," Bobby said.

"Yeah, I hear that. But listen Bobby, what's he going to pay you? I bet he doesn't give you any more that that Fifty-dollar bill you squeezing.

Look at that Lincoln. I bet he has four or five hundred in his pocket and he is going to give you fifty. You ain't his whore; you are his slave," Gaston said handing Bobby, his snack pack.

Bobby hesitated a minute and then said, "What would you do?'

"I would kill that white son of a bitch, take his car, his money and leave Dallas. That's what I would do Bobby," Gaston said.

"How much do you think a Rolex watch is worth Gaston," Bobby asked.

Gaston's mouth dropped open, "He has a Rolex? Bobby those watches start at five thousand dollars. Don't let that man penny ante you. Take his stuff and start a new life. What has Dallas ever done for you?"

Jeremy honked the horn and Gaston glanced at him, "Better run now Bobby. The master is calling for his slave."

Bobby walked to the car thinking, '*Gaston's right. Jeremy has been treating me like a slave. That is why he likes to come to South Dallas. Bring his Black Slave down here among all the other colored folk and use him. Well, tonight that all changes Jeremy. I bet he has enough cash on him for me to get all the way to St. Louis. You can give it up Jeremy or I'm going to take it. St. Louis here I come.*'

•   •   •

The fan squeaked as it oscillated back and forth. It was fighting a losing battle against the heavy heat. The afternoon sun had climbed over the pitched roof and now beat against the backside of the apartment, driving the last vestige of comfort from the small family room.

Emma wiped the sweat from her face with a wet towel and glanced at the thermometer propped up in the kitchen window. The Black Hand was pointing at ninety degrees. *"Lord, this place is an oven,"* Emma sighed.

She placed one hand on the tabletop next to her chair and the other on the arm of the chair. She pushed, propelling herself up and out of the deep comfort of the chair. She waddled over to the screen door and looked out.

"Well, the sun has finally moved behind the house so I can go out front and sit in the shade," she said to the empty room.

She pushed the door open and grabbed her chair from the concrete slab that served as a porch in the projects. She went down the steps one at a time, letting the chair bump along behind her.

Emma settled the runners of the metal lawn chair in the ruts created by the daily ritual. She sat down and wiped her face with the towel again. *'This heat is drying my towel out,'* she mumbled.

She dropped into the chair and looked to where her grandsons were playing in the sandbox. "John, Jason; you boys get out of that sun. You are going to get heatstroke," she yelled across the yard.

Both boys came running over to their grandmother. "Momma, can we have some money for a snow cone?" Jason asked.

Emma looked at her grandsons' dirty faces and pulled them close to her, "Yes, I will give you some money for a snow cone. But first, I want to clean your faces."

She wiped the boy's dirty faces and handed them two dollars. "Now you boys go straight to the snow stand. Don't get distracted and start messing around. Get your snow cones and a strawberry one for me. Then you come right back here so I can have mine before it melts. Do you promise?" she asked with a smile.

"We promise," John said racing after his brother who was half way to the stand. Emma love listening to her grandsons giggling as they anticipated the sweetness of the cold treat.

A rancid smell floated by on a wisp of wind and Emma turned to see where it came from. She saw her dog coming out of the wooded creek area that ran beside the projects. He was dragging something along behind him.

Emma laughed as she watched him struggle with his trophy. The little dog's legs were too stubby to allow him to pick it up, but he was determined to wrestle it into the shade. As soon as he made it into the shade, he lay down and started to chew on the object.

"Whew, Shorty! What are you chewing on boy? My word, that stinks," Emma said.

Shorty looked at her and wagged his tail. He turned back to his chewing and Emma said, "You had better enjoy that now Shorty. Because as soon as the boys get back I am going to have them drag that right back to the creek."

She heard her boys and turned from Shorty to see John and Jason running up with the snow cones. "Here you go, mama. Strawberry just like you wanted," Jason said.

"Thank you, honey. Now you boys go over there and get whatever that stinking thing Shorty is chewing on and throw it down by the creek," Emma said.

"Yes mama," John said running toward Shorty. The boy stopped and took a step backward. He turned and ran back to stand behind his grandmother's chair.

"Mama, that is someone's head Shorty is chewing on," John whispered.

"What? A head? Do you mean a human head?" Emma asked.

John nodded and said, "Yes mama and the eyes are gone."

"You boys get into the house," Emma said as she stood. She took a few steps toward Shorty and leaned forward to get a better look at his prize.

"*Lord have mercy!* It is a skull," Emma said. She turned and said to Jason who was standing on the porch watching her, "Jason you run up to the office and tell Mr. Smithson to come down here," she said.

• • •

K.W. looked up as his sergeant walked into the squad room. He eyed the yellow notepad that Bill Senkel was holding in his hand. He watched as Senkel scanned the note. Senkel extended the note to K.W. and said, "The patrol units out of Southeast are calling for a detective to meet them in the Projects on Second Avenue near Scyene Road. A dog has dragged a skull up into a yard of one of the apartments. Dispatch has ordered crime scene and the medical examiner. Go see if you can help them."

K.W. had worked patrol out of Southeast and knew the area where he was headed. The projects were built in a low area surrounded by woods and White Rock Creek.

The creek that ran alongside the west side of the projects fed into a lake, a large pond really. The pond stretched from the point where Second Avenue and Scyene Road met back north and west to the Trinity River bottoms.

It was an urban forest and a favorite place for the dumping of bodies, stolen cars and other trophies of nefarious activities. He sighed knowing that he was about to go tromping through the area looking for the body, or body parts, which went with the skull.

He smiled remembering what his old sergeant used to say, "*Off your ass and on your feet, out of the cool and into the heat. This is what you boys signed up for, and today you get your wish.*'

K.W. drove the Ford up the ramp and picked up the microphone and said, "Eleven-forty eight is switching to channel three."

"Eleven-forty eight is gone to channel three. Fourteen thirty-three hours, KKB-three sixty-four, Police Department Dallas," came the response.

"Eleven forty-eight is on channel three en-route to Forty-four hundred Second Avenue. Ask the Park Police if they have a couple of mounted units they could send to help us search the wooded area adjacent to the crime scene," K.W. asked the dispatcher.

"Ten-Four, Stand by one, Eleven Forty-Eight," the dispatcher said.

"Two mounted units of the Park Police are en-route to meet you

Eleven Forty-Eight," the dispatcher advised.

K.W. parked his cart at the project office and followed the pointing of the manager toward the scene. He could see an object on the ground and figured it was the skull.

He noticed that everyone was standing upwind of the skull, *'Bet this heat has made it rather ripe,'* he said as he walked toward the collection of blue suits.

Sergeant Tommy Breedlove stepped out of the crowd and came to meet K.W. "Good to see you K.W., " Tommy said.

"Same here Tommy. What do we have besides a skull that a dog brought out of the woods?" K.W. asked.

"The Crime Scene techs have photographed the skull. The medical examiner is ready to bag it, and I have J.R. standing at the spot the witnesses saw the dog come out of the woods with the skull," Tommy said pointing to a uniformed patrol officer standing at the edge of the woods.

"Great, let's get a look at the skull," K.W. said moving forward.

"You go ahead K.W. I've seen and smelled it as much as I care," Tommy said as he stood still.

K.W. walked around the skull. He could see that the eyeballs were gone, the lips, nose and the ears had been chewed away, and a few tufts of hair remained. K.W. could tell from the hair that the skull most likely belonged to a Caucasian person, but there was no way to ascertain any more without a forensic laboratory examination.

"Well, the elements and the critters didn't leave us much to work with. But the teeth are present, so if we have dental records to compare with, we will be able to identify this person," K.W. said as he made notes.

K.W. heard the horses and looked up to see four mounted Park Police Officers approaching. "Hey, we got four of you! That's great. Thanks for coming," K.W. said.

The Park Officers were staring at the skull, and one said, "I take it you want us to ride these woods looking for the rest of this person."

K.W. nodded and said, "That would be a great help. The witnesses say the dog dragged the skull out of the woods over there, where that officer is standing.

I am going to put these men into the woods there, form a line and move them East searching for more bones. If you would start a hundred yards to the West of that entry point and work a circle around and across that creek so that you will come out a hundred yards East of where we enter, I believe we will stand the best chance of finding the body."

"We are on it," the officer said and moved his men out.

Tommy said, "I heard you. If you are ready, I will put this crew in and start the sweep."

"Let's do it. I am going to walk straight to the creek and check the banks in both directions," K.W. replied.

"Do you want us to wait here?" the medical examiner's agent asked.

"Yes please. Go ahead and bag and tag the skull but give us a few minutes to see if we can find any more of this body," K.W. said.

He stepped into the woods and made his way through the vines and brush to the creek. The bank sloped down sharply, but the bed of the creek was only about six feet wide. There were eight to ten inches of water running slowing down toward the pond. *'I hope none of these bones ended up in that pond if so we will never find them,"* he thought as he trudged along scanning the bank and the bed of the creek.

Half an hour into the search K.W. heard a horse galloping through the woods. He stopped and waited as the officer approached. "Found him. The animals have scattered him some, but there is enough left to tell it is a white man," the officer said.

K.W. turned and whistled to the line of officers working in the opposite direction. Tommy Breedlove turned, and K.W. waved and pointed in the direction the Park Officer was riding. The line of officer reversed their course and came to meet K.W.

"They found him," K.W. said to Tommy.

As K.W. approached, he saw that the officers had dismounted and were standing at intervals in different locations. *'Each officer is marking a set of bones,'* K.W. reasoned.

K.W. approached the first officer who pointed toward the creek and said, "His torso and most of his legs are there in the water. The animals have taken his feet, one hand is gone and all of the flesh in gnawed off of the other."

K.W. walked to the edge of the bank and looked down. He saw the skeletal remains of the upper torso of a body. The bones were gouged where it appeared the flesh had been chewed away. The arm bones were mostly present, some of the ribs had been carried away, and all the internal organs were gone.

Below the waist were the shredded remains of what appeared to have been a pair of blue pants. A black leather belt was still in the loops around the waist. As his gaze moved down the legs, he saw that huge chunks of the flesh and muscle had been ripped away.

In the water, just past the body, K.W. saw a shoe. Moving closer he could see that the foot had been chewed off of the leg, but the part of the foot that was inside the shoe was still there. The other shoe was missing. *'An animal got the foot off of the leg, or ankle, but could not get to the flesh inside the shoe. The animal carried the other shoe away to chew on it,'* K.W. guessed.

He moved away and stopped to look at the remains where the officers had marked the spot of discovery. *'There is one of the ribs, here is what looks like part of a hand, ah what a mess!'* he stopped and called for the field agents of the medical examiner and the crime scene techs to join them.

"Process this whole scene. I want a video in addition to still shots. Do a diagram of showing the exact spot where each bone was found and cross reference it with a table of contents correlating the identifying number or symbol with the location of each body part noted. Then bag all the evidence and tag it with the service number. Send me an inventory in CAPERS," K.W. told the senior agent.

K.W. cleared the scene and started back to the office. He picked up the microphone and said, "Eleven Forty-Eight to Five Five one."

"Go ahead Eleven Forty-Eight," Susie Mason answered from his office.

"Susie, call General Assignments and ask for a list of all white males reported missing within the last three weeks," K.W. said.

"It will be on your desk," Susie said.

•   •   •

K.W. scanned the medical examiner's report again. *'The skull is that of a white male approximately forty years of age. From the markings present on the skull it appears that the head was torn from the neck and the flesh chewed away by scavengers. Decomposed brain matter is present inside the skull, the ears, lips, nose and eyeballs are missing,'* he had read it all before so he skipped down to the conclusion.

'The time, cause and manner of death cannot be determined due to the decomposition of the body,' he read.

He laid the autopsy report aside and picked up the list of missing persons. He ran his finger down the list to the one he had highlighted in yellow. *'Jeremy Willis Spurgeon, w/m/42, reported missing July 29th by his wife, Sally Timmons Spurgeon. Home address is Fifty-Two Forty Nine Limestone Court, Richardson, Texas,'* the summary read.

'We found the remains on August eighteenth or twenty days from the day he was last seen. His wife says he left for work that morning, called her at six p.m. to say that he was going to be late and she never heard from him again. She told the reporting officer that he had left home wearing a blue suit, white shirt, and red tie. Our guy was wearing blue pants, is about the right age and the time frame works,' K.W. sorted through his notes.

He reached for the phone and dialed the phone number listed for the Spurgeon's residence in Richardson. She answered on the second ring. "Hello," she said.

"Mrs. Spurgeon, my name is K.W. Bangs. I am a detective with the Dallas Police Department. I am working a case where we found the remains of a white male in a wooded area in South Dallas. I would like to come by this evening and talk with you about the possibility that our body might be your husband," K.W. said.

"What makes you think it is my husband?" she asked with hardness that K.W. found interesting.

"The age, the time found when compared with the date of your husband's disappearance and the fact that our man was wearing blue pants," K.W. said.

"Did you say the remains were found in South Dallas?" she asked.

"Yes, near the projects on Second Avenue," K.W. replied.

"Is that part of town populated by predominately Black people?" she asked.

"Yes, does that matter?" K.W. asked.

"Yes, it does. Maybe you do need to come by the house. I will expect you at seven this evening," she said and hung up.

K.W. was surprised by the neighborhood. '*These homes run from half a million to over a million dollars,*' K.W. thought as he parked in front of the Spurgeon residence.

The front lights came on as he approached the front porch and the door opened as he stepped up onto the columned porch. "Are you officer Bangs?" the woman standing in the open doorway asked.

K.W. extended his credentials for her inspection and said, "Yes I am. Are you Mrs. Spurgeon?"

"Yes, please come in and call me Sally," she said standing aside and waving him inside.

K.W. looked around at the palatial surroundings and then at the beautiful woman standing before him. '*This woman is beautiful, wealthy and poised. But she is also very calm for a wife who is about to discuss her missing husband with a police detective,*' he thought.

"Mrs. Spurgeon, Sally, I am sorry we meet under these circumstances, but I need to ask you some questions to determine if we might have found your husband. Some of these questions will be personal, intrusive even, and I apologize in advance," K.W. said.

"Well let me see if I can save us some time. My husband and I met in college. We both come from wealthy families and shared common interest. It seemed a perfect match.

We married in June after graduating in May. That was ten years ago. We have two children, a boy eight years old and a girl six years old.

Jeremy is an electrical engineer. He is a Senior Vice President at Texas Instruments in charge of Research and Development. I stay at home and take care of the kids, and he works, that is our deal.

I will tell you right away that our marriage is strained. It is because about five years ago I found out that Jeremy is bi-sexual. Once I found out about his liaisons with men, Black male prostitutes are his preference, I moved out of our bedroom.

I live upstairs, and he lives downstairs. We agreed to remain together until the kids graduate high school and then we will divorce. Does that help you officer Bangs?" she asked.

K.W. had been busy making notes and took his time to finish and gather his thoughts. "Well, it certainly provides me with more information than I had before," he answered.

"Would you like to see his bedroom, to look through his closet or to have a photograph of him?" she asked.

"Why do you ask that Sally," K.W. said.

"I asked that because the officers who took the report asked to do that," she answered.

"Do they know about his propensity to engage in sexual liaisons with male prostitutes?" K.W. asked.

"I didn't tell them. I told you because of where you said the body was found. Again, Jeremy prefers Black male prostitutes.," she answered.

"How do you know that Sally," K.W. asked.

"Because, when I grew suspicious that Jeremy was seeing someone else, I hired a private detective. His name is T.O. Spearman and he used to be a Dallas Police Officer. I have his number in the event you need to talk with him.

But back to your question, I would contact Mr. Spearman every time Jeremy called to say he would be late getting home. Mr. Spearman would follow him as he left work.

He photographed Jeremy 'trolling' as he called it around the bus stations downtown. Jeremy always picked up Black male prostitutes and took them to motels in South Dallas.

When you told me that the remains were found in that part of town, I thought the information would be relevant and important to you," she said.

"Okay, well that is helpful. I read the report about how Jeremy was dressed the day he disappeared, but it said nothing about jewelry. Did he have any unique pieces of jewelry that a thief would take?" he asked.

"Yes, he wore a Rolex Platinum Pearlmaster. The dial and face of that watch is encrusted with custom cut diamonds. Jeremy told me the diamonds cause the watch to be valued at two hundred and seventy thousand dollars. It has his full name, *Jeremy Willis Spurgeon*, engraved on the back. It was a gift from his father. He never wore rings," Sally said.

"Are you sure he had that watch on the day he disappeared and do you by chance have a photograph of it?" K.W. asked.

"Yes, I am positive he was wearing it. He never took it off; it was a vanity thing for him. Our insurance agent will have a photograph of it," she said.

"Thank you, Sally. Will you give me the name and phone number for Jeremy's dentist? I need to get a copy of his dental records," K.W. asked.

"Yes, his dentist is, or was, James Sully. I will write his number down for you before you leave. What other questions do you have?" Sally asked.

K.W. closed his notebook and sat back in the chair. He looked directly into Sally's eyes and said, "Mrs. Spurgeon, I have been doing this a long time now. It is very seldom that I see a woman so composed as I interview her about the possibility that I have found the remains of her husband. Frankly, your demeanor causes me to wonder if you have anything to do with your husband's disappearance.

The thought has crossed my mind that you might know the remains *are indeed* your husband's because you had prior knowledge of where his body was dumped.

So, I'm going to ask you straight out. Did you kill, have killed or play any role in your husband's death or disappearance?"

Sally smiled widely revealing perfect teeth. She leaned forward and said; "Now why didn't the other officers ask me those questions. I know they were thinking them, but why didn't they ask? I suspect because they were more impressed, or maybe intimidated, by the *'splendor and wealth'* we live in.

But that does not matter. No Officer Bangs. I did not have my husband killed nor do I know anything about my husband's disappearance or death, if he is dead.

I had anticipated being asked these questions. So I had our attorney arrange for me to be polygraphed on this matter. I passed, and my attorney will be happy to share those results with you."

K.W. nodded and said, "Last question. Will you provide me with a copy of your husband's life insurance policy and will?"

"Yes, I will. But Officer Bangs, when you check our finances you will find that my wealth far exceeds that of my husband's," she smiled and stood.

K.W. thought about the interview as he drove back to the office. *'I believe my skull belongs to Jeremy Spurgeon. I don't think his wife had anything to do with killing him. The odds are that he picked up a male prostitute who robbed and murdered him.*

If the dental records show that I am right and this is Jeremy, that watch will be a key to finding the man who killed him.' K.W. knew he was going to find Jeremy's killer.

●   ●   ●

The gusting wind found its' way through the foliage where Bobby Gene Williams was squatted. He pulled the stocking cap down further over his ears and dropped to his knees. He was growing stiff in the cold, and now it had started to snow.

He heard a noise and thought, *'that sounds like the garage door going up. Maybe they're leaving.'* He moved deeper into the foliage and turned his face down toward the ground. His forest green coveralls blended in perfectly with the evergreen foliage.

He heard the car as it came around the house and stayed still as it left the drive and stopped in front of the gate at the end of the lane. He heard the whine of the electric motor and then the creaking of the metal gates swinging open. He did not move until he heard the car drive through and the gates close.

He stood and ran across the lawn and around to the patio and pool area. He had been here many times, cleaning the pool as an employee of Cardinal Pool Services.

He knew that the owner of this house was a member of the St. Louis Cardinals. They had chatted many times, and Bobby knew that the owner trusted him. He had allowed Bobby to look at his World Series Championship ring and had even allowed him to try it on.

Bobby peered through the patio doors and saw the kids and their nanny sitting on the couch watching television. He looked at his wristwatch and saw that it was seven o'clock. He had been 'casing' the house for ten days and knew the family's routine. *'The kids don't go to bed until eight thirty. They will be down here until eight when they go upstairs for their bath. That gives me plenty of time,'* he reasoned.

He eased away from the doors and jogged around to the side of the garage. The ladder was still there, just where he left it.

He hoisted the ladder and moved to the side of the patio. He leaned the ladder against the house so that the top of it was next to the second-floor deck. He climbed quickly and stepped over the railing onto the deck.

The French doors were closed but unlocked. He opened them quietly and stepped into the master bedroom. The carpet was plush, and its' thick pad allowed him to move noiselessly across the room.

'Where would I keep a ring like that?' he wondered looking around the room.

He saw two dressing areas. *'That one is obviously for a woman, so that would make this one his,'* Bobby mouthed.

He tiptoed into the dressing area and began to open drawers. *'Nothing,'* he fumed.

Frustrated he moved into her dressing area. Sitting on the counter was a large oak box. He lifted the lid and there it was. *'Look at that beauty!'* he sighed.

Bobby lifted the ring out of the box and slid it into his pocket. *'What else might I find? Maybe Bobbie would like some of her lingerie,'* he smiled.

Bobby resisted the urge to prowl through her intimate wear and started sorting through the woman's jewelry. The size and quality of the stones, the beauty of the design and the purity of the gold mesmerized him. *'She does not have one piece of silver, no rubies, no sapphires and no costume jewelry. There is nothing here but gold and diamonds. I can work with that,'* he moved to the bed and grabbed a pillow. He pulled the case off of the pillow and dumped the jewelry into the case.

He looked around the room but then thought better of further exploration, *'Do not be greedy Bobby. Take what you have and get while the getting is good,'* he laughed and headed for the deck. *'Wait,'* he stopped and hurried back to the jewelry box. He closed the box, wiped it down with a hand towel and then straightened the bed.

'Maybe they will come in, jump in bed and not discover anything amiss until tomorrow morning. That will give me time to fence this stuff. Good as it is, I might get a quarter on the dollar,' Bobby had a spring in his step as the hurried out of the room and down the ladder.

He put the ladder back beside the garage and made his way over the brick wall and down the street to his Buick. Forty-five minutes later and he was sitting at the Ace of Spades Club sharing a cold beer with Damien Cutter.

"So, Bobby, my man. Where is this product you called me down here to appraise?" Damien asked.

"Outside in my Buick," Bobby said as he slid off the stool and headed for the back door.

"Why we going out back?" Damien asked.

"Because I parked next to the dumpster. Gives us more privacy," Bobby said.

They slid into the Buick and Bobby reached under the seat and pulled the pillowcase out. He handed it to Damien and sat back with his beer.

Damien opened the case and looked inside. He looked up at Bobby and asked, "Where did you get this and when?"

"Up on the north side about an hour ago. Folks aren't even home yet. They won't know anything until at least midnight and maybe not until morning. That gives you plenty of time to take the stones out and melt the gold down. By the time the sun comes up no one can prove anything about this stuff," Bobby said.

"What do you want for it?" Damien asked.

"I figure there is a couple hundred thousand worth of diamonds and gold there. I will take ten thousand. That leaves you a nice profit for a quick deal," Bobby said.

"If all of this stuff is real it might be worth two hundred thousand. But I have expenses. I will give you five thousand if you take it now, so I have plenty of time to re-work this stuff," Damien said.

"I figured it to go for a quarter on the dollar, so it is a deal," Bobby said. He turned the beer up and looked at Damien. "If you want, I can switch from Bobby to Bobbie. It will be just like we were cell mates again," he said patting Damien on the leg.

Damien jumped from the car and opened the back door. "Get in this backseat Miss Bobbie," he said as he was taking his shirt off.

•   •   •

He waited until he saw the proprietor walk to the front door and turn the sign from open to closed. He stepped up to the door and tapped gently on the glass.

The proprietor turned and saw that it was Bobby. He smiled and opened the door. "A midnight caller is usually holding something special Bobby," he said locking the door and moving to the back room.

Bobby held out the World Series ring and asked, "Is this special enough Walter?"

Walter whistled softly, "Wow Bobby. That is a beauty. Not as good as that Rolex you brought me the last time, but still nice. How hot is it?"

"I've had it three months Walter. I know that means it is on all the lists and I am willing to let it go at a deep discount," Bobby said.

"I would love to have it, Bobby. But there is no way I can sell this. Not in this town. It even has the man's name and uniform number on it. This is a police magnet if I ever saw one," Walter said handing it back to Bobby.

"Hold onto it a minute Walter. Surely you have some '*private buyers*' that would want it for their collection. This is no different than that Rolex with the man's name on the back. You moved that and you could move this. Ain't nobody going to say anything, not when they would have as much to lose as you would," Bobby said.

Walter rubbed his chin thinking. "Well maybe. How deep is that discount you referred to?" he asked.

"Make me an offer Walter. You've always treated me right," Bobby said.

Walter turned his desk light on and looked at the ring through a jewelers' glass. He leaned back in his chair and said, "I will give you five hundred dollars cash right now."

"Make it eight hundred Walter. I need to get back to Dallas. This cold weather is killing me," Bobby said.

Walter opened his desk and pulled out a handful of money. He counted out six hundred dollar bills and reached into his pocket for a fifty. He stacked them up and pushed them toward Bobby. "Six hundred and fifty dollars. Take it or leave it," he said.

Bobby scooped the money up and headed for the front door. "See you next summer Walter," he said as he slipped into the darkness.

Walter locked the door and pulled the shade down. He walked back to his office and rummaged around until he found the flyer. He sat down and turned the desk lamp to focus the light on the flyer. "*Reward. Five thousand dollar reward for information leading to the arrest and indictment of the person or persons responsible for the burglary of a private residence in which the below pictured World Series Ring was taken. Call The Greater St. Louis Crime Stoppers. You may remain anonymous.*"

Walter picked up the phone and dialed the number listed on the flyer.

CHAPTER 3
THE BEAST GETS LOOSE

"Hey give me a smile Tyree. The eagle flies today," Benny McBay said as he poked his friend on the arm.

"Eagle? Take a good look at that check when Jaylee gives it to you and then tell me if it looks more like an eagle or a hummingbird," Tyree turned away from Benny.

Benny knew not to push his friend. '*That rage is building in him again, what did the counselor over at the church call it, explosive anger syndrome. It is explosive but it ain't no syndrome, it is a beast. I need to get him calmed down before that beast gets loose,*' Benny thought watching the emotions playing across Tyree's face.

"Wow, Tyree. Man, you sure know how to put a damper on my payday happiness. Let's take a break and go outside for a smoke," Benny was already headed for the back door.

Tyree followed Benny reaching into his shirt pocket for the crush proof pack of Winston's. He realized he was squeezing the cigarettes and thought, '*wish I could crawl into a crush proof box.*'

"Hey, were you two going?" Jaylee shouted.

"We are going on break," Jaylee's tone made him angry, and he yelled back at her.

"No, you're not! It is already ten thirty, and we are not ready for the lunch hour rush. Tyree, you hook up to that wet mop and get these floors cleaned.

Benny, you get all the tables and booths wiped down and clean. Then both of you start filling those bins with packets of salt, pepper, and sugar.

Sara, you fill the mustard, mayonnaise and ketchup cans and make sure the pumps are clean. Come on now and let's get this done," Jaylee was spitting out orders.

"Hell no. I said I am going on break," Tyree turned and started toward the door.

"Boy, what did you say?" Jaylee asked.

"I ain't no boy, and I said I am going on break," Tyree answered without looking back.

"Tyree, you walk out that door, and you can just keep walking. You too Benny," Jaylee was standing with hands on her hips, and there was no doubt that she meant what she had just said.

Tyree spun on his heel and sprinted toward Jaylee. He saw her lift her hands and take a step back, but then he was on her. His focus was on her mouth, those bright red lips that kept spitting out orders, and that is where his fist landed.

It had started from just below his right hip, swung up in a roundhouse arc over his shoulder and came crashing down in a hammering blow exactly in the middle of those taunting lips.

The momentum of his sprint coupled with the unleashed fury of *the beast* rushed through his quivering muscles. He felt the sharp pain as his fist pushed past shredded lips and spurting blood to collide with the sharp enamel of breaking teeth.

Tyree saw Jaylee's eyes roll back. Her body was falling. He winced as her head hit the concrete floor, bounced once and then rolled to the left.

Thick, dark blood flooded from the crushed skull. He watched as it saturated her hair and then began to pool under her head. '*That is blood from her brain, thick, dark and musty smelling. Just like the blood that came out of momma's head,*' he thought remembering the day his father had shattered his mother's skull in with a hammer.

The mist was clearing, and he could hear Sara screaming. He was shamed by the look on her face as she backed away from him.

Tyree felt the pressure in his right hand and looked to see that it was still balled into a fist, the fist that he had just used to batter Jaylee.

He looked again and saw that she had stopped breathing.

He stepped out of the front door and then broke into a trot. He was running at full speed as he crossed the parking lot, down Lakeland Drive, across Garland Road and into the dense foliage of the Dallas Arboretum. As soon as he was inside the tree line, he stopped and tossed the Burger King cap and shirt into the brush.

He looked back toward the restaurant and saw Benny running along the same route he had taken in his escape. *'Damned, Benny you shouldn't be following me,'* he thought. He eased back into a bed of lush ferns and waited. Benny came puffing up and dropped beside Tyree in the dense growth.

"Are you stupid Benny? I just killed that woman! The police are going to be after me. You don't want any part of that. Go on back before it is too late," Tyree said.

Benny reached into his pant's pocket and pulled out two handfuls of cash. "Already too late. I cleaned out both registers before I followed you. We have all the money Jaylee put in the registers to open with. There should be two hundred and sixty dollars here," Benny said.

Tyree looked at the red hair and freckled face of his best friend and then asked, "How did a black kid like me and a red headed, freckled white boy like you ever hook up?"

The smile disappeared from Benny's face as he leaned back against a giant oak, "The only difference in me and you is the color of our skin. Neither one of us has anyone or anything. Folks look at me with the same sneer as they have when they look at you.

Remember what that fat dude said the other day when we carried his order out to his table? *'Did it take both of you to bring one order out? You two are just minimum wage loafers. Sorry good for nothings, wasting good air.'* That's what he said, and that's what most folks think when they see us.

I'm through licking their boots, Tyree. I say we take this money and go as far as it will take us and then see if we can join the military. My mom said that's what my dad did, he joined the army, and they sent him to Germany. No one ever heard of him again. Maybe we can do that, start over, have a life Tyree," Benny had tears in his eyes.

"You can't join the military Benny. You are just sixteen years old," Tyree laughed.

The sound of sirens filled the air, and both boys inched deeper into the brush. From where they sat they could see across Garland Road and into the north end of the parking lot at the Burger King. Two police cars raced into the lot, and the officers ran inside the café. "Why do they have their guns out?" Benny asked.

"Because I just killed Jaylee. Or maybe it was *the beast*. I just don't know anymore Benny," Tyree. They fell silent as Sara came out of the Burger King and pointed toward the park. It appeared that she was pointing to the exact spot where Tyree and Benny were hiding. One of the officers walked back to his car and drove slowly toward them.

"Here they come," Benny whispered.

"Get that red shirt and hat off and let's move down deeper into the trees and brush," Tyree said.

"What are we going to do Tyree?" Benny asked as he tossed the shirt and cap alongside Tyree's in the brush.

"We have to move. Those police will flood this area soon with dogs and officers walking the trails looking for us. They are going to be looking for a white boy and a black boy. So we are going to split up.

First, let's make our way over to the swim club and see if we can find a change of clothes in an unlocked car. Maybe even a car with the keys in it. Can you drive Benny?" Tyree was moving along the water's edge toward the swimming beach.

"No, can you?" Benny answered.

"Hell no. So what we do is get some clothes, or maybe a bathing suit, that will fit and then split up.

You go north around the lake, and I will go south. We got all day so just take your time and stay out of sight," Tyree paused at the edge of the beach and looked up the slope toward the parking lot.

"Where we going to meet and what do we do then Tyree?" Benny asked.

"Do you remember that little creek where we went fishing and saw that couple naked on the blanket?" Tyree asked.

Benny nodded, "Yep, that is almost straight across the lake from where we are now. Rush Creek, it's called. We stole her purse, and all their dope and they never knew we were there."

"That's it, that's the place. There are always couples making out there, especially after dark. The only way out of this for us is to jump a couple and make them drive us out of here. Are you up for that?" Tyree looked at his friend.

"It is what it is. Let's get those clothes and get moving. Do you go first, or do I?" Benny asked looking up toward the police helicopter that was buzzing the area they had just left.

"Me first," Tyree said as he hustled toward the parking lot.

CHAPTER 4
THE DATE

She knew that he was looking at her from across the room. Despite her best effort a smile lifted the corners of her mouth and she shot a sly glance his way. He was waiting, *'almost like he knew I was going to look,'* Mary Lynn thought.

She blushed as he winked and blew her a soft kiss. The bell rang, and the room emptied with a rush as the hungry kids hurried to the cafeteria.

Mary Lynn lingered, gathering her books and waiting for him to come across the room. She knew he would, but still, a thrill ran through her when he said, "Hey sweet thing, aren't you hungry?"

She slid out of the seat and stood looking up at him. "Why Perry Ray Gholson, what on earth does it matter to you if I am hungry or not?" she asked.

"It matters to me because I want to sit with you and make every boy in the school jealous," he said with that same trademark wink.

"Oh, you aren't eating with Amie Shaw today?" she asked moving toward the door.

"Come on now Mary Lynn; you know that Amie is my first cousin. She is a freshman and with those braces and all those freckles, well she ends up sitting by herself every day. I just couldn't let that happen one more day," Perry Ray said.

Mary Lynn stopped and turned to examine his face. "I didn't know that she was your cousin. But I do know what it is like to be a freshman and all alone. Thank you for being so tender with her. Let's go, and both sit with her today," Mary Lynn said handing her books to Perry Ray to carry.

They sauntered into the cafeteria and just as they entered Mary Lynn draped her hand through the crook of Perry's arm. She knew that all the girls would be watching him and she wanted them to know that he had chosen her.

"Well look at that Perry Ray. It seems as if the ugly duckling has found a beau," she said nodding toward a corner table where Amie focused on the beaming face of Deak Williamson.

The crowd followed her glance, and there was a lull in the buzz of conversation. Amie and Deak tore themselves away from each other and saw that every kid in the cafeteria was looking at them.

A deep crimson flush started at her throat and crept up to Amie's face. Deak reached slowly across the table and took her hand in his. She looked at him, and he smiled raising their joined hands above their heads for all to see. The crowd erupted with shouts and applause.

"That settles that," Perry Ray said.

"For now," Mary Lynn laughed.

Mary Lynn sat down, and Perry Ray walked to the serving line and brought back two trays. He sat one down in front of Mary Lynn and then straddled the stool across from her. "Hey, it's Friday, and there is a Spring Break dance at the White Rock Methodist Church tonight. Do you want to go and then maybe grab a burger afterward," Perry Ray asked?

Mary Lynn choked as she swallowed a chuckle, "Are they serving burgers at Rush Creek now?" she teased.

"Who said anything about Rush Creek?" Perry Ray looked shocked.

Mary Lynn laid her fork alongside her tray and said, "Perry Ray Gholson, let's not play games with each other. Yes, I want to go to the dance with you, and yes I want to go to Rush Creek with you after the dance.

I am in love with you, and I know that you are in love with me. Our parents know it, and all of our friends know it. So what you need to do is get down on your knee, ask me to marry you and let's set a date.

Graduation is May 16th, and I would like for our wedding to be the first Saturday in June, which is June 4th. So cowboy up Perry Ray, and we won't have to go sneaking around at Rush Creek anymore."

Perry Ray sat looking at her. Thoughts were racing through his head, *she is right of course. I have loved her since seventh grade. I do want to marry her, who wouldn't.'*

"I do want to marry you and the sooner the better, Mary Lynn. But how am I going to support you?" he asked.

"Didn't you tell me that your father offered to bring into the shop and teach you the business from the ground up? You love working with him in the summer, and you are a natural at mechanical design. Pour yourself into what you love to do Perry Ray.

That shop will be yours someday. In the meantime, I will get a job until the first baby is born. We will make it, together," she touched his hand.

Perry Ray slid off of the stool and onto his knee in front of her. A hush fell over the cafeteria, and he allowed it to build.

Then he looked into her smiling eyes and said loud enough that all could hear, "Mary Lynn Threet, I have loved you since the Sadie Hawkins Dance in the seventh grade. I will always love you and want more than anything to be your husband. Will you marry me, Mary Lynn?"

Mary Lynn felt the hot tears begin to roll down her cheeks. She had dreamed about this for so long; she had rehearsed what she would say and had determined that she would be calm, cool and in total control. Now she was dissolving in front of the whole school. She joined Perry Ray on the floor, wrapped her arms around him and sobbed, "Yes I will."

The crowd erupted. Kids were jumping up and down, climbing on tables and clapping. Then someone started to sing, and it became a roar, "Mary Lynn and Perry Ray sitting in a tree. K-I-S-S-I-N-G, first came love, then came marriage and next will come a baby carriage."

Perry Ray stood and lifted Mary Lynn to her feet. They waved to the crowd and walked out of the cafeteria hand in hand.

"I don't have a ring to give you. I will talk with dad tonight, and maybe he will loan me enough to buy the engagement ring," Perry Ray said.

"No, don't do that. A ring is not important right now, and we are not going to start out in debt.

My parents are serving as chaperons at the dance tonight. Can you bring your mom and dad by our house before we go? We will tell them together," Mary Lynn said.

"That's a good idea. I will have mom and dad at your house by seven. We will tell them, and I know they will support our decision. But Mary Lynn, I still want to go to Rush Creek after the dance," Perry Ray said with that wink.

"It's a date cowboy," she winked back.

CHAPTER 5
AT WATER'S EDGE

Tyree sat in the bush watching Benny pick his way across the opening to slide in beside him. "Are you as beat as I am?" he asked.

Benny slapped a mosquito and leaned back on one elbow and said, "You know it. I am tired of dodging cops, hiding from that damned helicopter and I could eat about a dozen of those Cheese Whoppers we used to sling out all day long."

"Duck," Tyree said as headlights swung into the lane alongside Rush Creek.

Both boys lay in the long grass and watched as the sleek Chevy Impala parked facing the lake. "Man look at that car. What kind is it Tyree?" Bennie asked.

"That my friend is a 1959 Chevrolet Impala. But it is not the car that has my interest. Check out that blonde sitting next to that big dude driving," Tyree said.

Perry Ray opened the door and stepped out of the car. The interior light remained on, and it illuminated the red leather seats and the ash blond hair of the girl laughing as she slid out to stand beside her date.

"Let's walk down to the water's edge," they heard the boy say.

"Okay, I want to sit on that big rock and let you sing to me. I love it when you sing to me Perry Ray," the blonde giggled.

Perry reached into the back seat and pulled out a guitar and a red blanket. They joined hands and walked down the slope to the big rock.

Mary Lynn sat on the rock, and Perry Ray spread the blanket beside it. He sat on the blanket and started to strum the guitar softly. Then he began to sing in a deep bass voice, *"I miss you darling more and more every day, as heaven would miss the stars above. With every heartbeat, I still think of you and remember our faded love."*

"Wait, Perry Ray," Mary Lynn interrupted.

"Our love is never going to fade. So sing it over and change *miss you* to *love you* and then change *faded* to *living* love," Mary Lynn said.

"Okay, so here we go. *I love you, darling, more and more every day, as heaven loves the stars above. With every heartbeat I still think of you and celebrate our living love,"* he finished with a shout.

Mary Lynn laughed and clapped her hands, "Celebrate? Oh, that is so good Perry Ray. We will celebrate our love every day for the rest of our lives."

Perry Ray stretched a hand toward her and said, "Then come down off of that rock and sit beside me here on the blanket. We are engaged now so why not celebrate our love right here, right now?"

Mary Lynn shook her head and laughed, "Perry Ray I am going to come down there beside you on that blanket. But I have waited eighteen years, and I am not going to spoil our wedding night here at the water's edge. I will be a virgin bride. Now, kiss your wife to be."

Perry Ray wrapped her in his arms and sighed, "You have the sweetest lips, the bluest eyes and more determination than any girl I ever met."

Tyree and Benny looked at each other and shrugged. "All they are going to do is kiss and stuff so why are we waiting? Let's take them now and make them drive us out of here," Benny said.

"You hear what she said?" Tyree asked.

"Which part? About being a virgin or about remaining a virgin until their wedding night," Benny giggled.

"Yeah, well we might have something to say about that," Tyree said.

"Whoa, Tyree. I'm all in for taking their money, stealing their car or making them drive us out of here. But I'm not into rape. If that's what your thinking just count me out," Benny said.

Tyree rolled over to his right and grabbed a dead tree limb he had seen earlier. He broke some of the little branches off and hefted it. *That is solid and heavy enough to take that big ole boy out. Probably best to let him get a little more distracted,'* he thought as he crouched and moved to the back of the Chevy and waited.

Perry Ray tugged gently on Mary Lynn, and they lay back on the blanket. He leaned over her resting on one elbow and kissed her deeply.

'Now,' Tyree thought as he streaked forward.

The loose gravel crunched under Tyree's foot, and Perry Ray heard him. He rolled to one knee and made it halfway up off of the blanket before Tyree hit him in the face with the tree limb. Perry Ray saw an explosion of lights and then darkness.

Mary Lynn screamed, and Tyree dropped beside her and clamped a hand over her mouth. He leaned in close and said, "Be still and be quiet. I am going to take what I came for, and then you and your boyfriend are going to drive us out of here in that shiny white Chevy."

Perry Ray groaned and tried to sit up. Tyree quickly placed a knee in the middle of his back and pulled both arms back to rest beside his knee. He unbuckled his web belt and yanked it from around his waist.

He grabbed both of Perry Ray's hands, brought them together and tied them with the belt. He glanced back at Mary Lynn and saw that she was frozen in fear.

He swiveled on his knee to face her. He unzipped his jeans and started pushing them down. Mary Lynn realized what he was doing and shrank back from him.

"I'm going to do this. Don't give me any trouble and you and the cowboy will live to celebrate that love he was singing about. I'm sure he would have you alive even if he won't be the first. So just lay back and accept it," Tyree said as he put his hand on the neckline of her dress and ripped down.

Perry Ray heard Mary Lynn scream, and the terror in her voice pushed him up onto his knees. Tyree heard him but had his pants down below his knees, and they prevented him from reacting in time to prevent Perry Ray from lunging into him with a beefy right shoulder.

The impact knocked Tyree over backward, and his head slammed into the big rock. The pain opened the door, and *the beast* burst forth in a rage.

Tyree struggled to his feet and yanked his pants up. Perry Ray was wrenching his hands back and forth trying to break the hold the belt had on him. In two quick steps, Tyree was on him.

The beast grabbed Perry Ray by the hair and dragged him to the big rock. In a raging fury *the beast* slammed Perry Ray's head against the rock; again and again, until blood covered his hands and the caved in skull slipped from his grasp.

The beast heard a voice calling Tyree from far away and released him. Tyree turned to face the voice and saw Benny holding his hands up and saying, "Tyree! For God's sake Tyree, stop."

Tyree was panting, and now as *the beast* retreated, fatigue pulled him down onto the blanket. The roar gradually faded from his head, and he was able to control his breathing. He saw that Mary Lynn had Perry Ray in her arms, rocking back and forth and crying, "No, No. God No."

He watched as Benny kneeled in front of her. "Hey, I'm so sorry about your boyfriend. Let me help you get him into the car, and you take him to a hospital," Benny was saying.

"No Benny. She goes with us. He is dead or dying. Leave him and let's get out of here," Tyree pushed up off of the blanket.

Benny remained on his knee beside the girl. He shook his head and said, "I'm not going anywhere with you Tyree. I don't want to see *that beast* come out again. You go, but she stays. I'm not going to let you hurt her."

Tyree could feel the heat beginning to build. He walked down to the water and then back. He stood still and took several deep breaths. Once he was sure the door was closed and *the beast* secure he said, "Think about what you are saying, Benny. We have killed two people today. Every cop in Dallas is going to be looking for us. We have to get out of town and to do that we have to have a car."

"I haven't killed anyone Tyree. Your *beast* has. I'm done. I will do my time for stealing the money, but man I had nothing to do with these killings. Go, just go," Benny said.

Tyree looked at his friend and said, "That's cool. You go your way, and I'll go mine. Give me the money Benny."

Benny dug the crumpled bills out of his jeans and handed them over, "Sure, take it and go."

Tyree stuffed the money into his pockets and then said, "She is going with me. I can't drive, and she is going to get me out of town, and then I will let her go."

Benny stepped in front of Mary Lynn and faced Tyree. "Nope. I know better than that. You will rape, maybe murder this girl and I'm not going to let that happen."

Tyree launched his right hand from belt high. It landed right on target, just above Benny's left temple.

The blow dropped Benny onto the blanket in an unconscious heap. Tyree stood over him a minute and found himself thinking, '*that was from Tyree, not the beast. But then I didn't need the beast for your skinny white ass.*'

He grabbed Mary Lynn and broke her grasp on Perry Ray. He pushed her to the car and said, "Get in. You are driving me out of here."

Tyree grabbed the keys from the car and trotted back to where Benny lay. He rolled him in the blanket and dragged him into the tree line just off the parking area.

He then went back to where Perry Ray lay and placed one hand beneath each arm. He pulled the body around the big rock and propped his back against it. He lay Perry Ray's head against the rock and then pulled his legs around so they could not be seen by anyone driving past. He took the wallet from Perry Ray's back pocket and left him there, at the water's edge.

He slid into the car and ran his hands across the red leather seats. He tapped Mary Lynn on the leg and said, "Get me out of here."

Benny woke in total darkness. He tried to sit up and couldn't. He began to push and struggle against the bonds holding him. He relaxed and then recognized the smell and feel of a blanket. He began to rock himself back and forth and felt the grip being loosened. Then he was rolling.

Sharp pain punched his knee as he bounced off of a tree truck and then he felt dampness begin to soak through the blanket. *'I'm in the water. I rolled down the slope into the water. I have to get out of here, or I will drown,'* he was fighting the panic again.

He rolled onto his stomach and then pushed up onto his knees. He rocked slowly, first to the left and then to the right. The blanket came loose, and he bolted free, out of the water and onto the bank.

Headlights swept across the parking area, and Benny dropped into the deep brush. He watched as the yellow Volks Wagon Beetle circled the parking area and then stopped just before exiting.

Benny waited for any indication that they had seen Perry Ray's body. The passenger's door opened, and a skinny kid stepped from the car and hurried across the parking lot to deposit an armful of empty beer cans in the trash barrel.

He then moved into the shadows provided by the trees and Benny could tell that he was urinating on a tree. The boy ambled toward the car zipping his pants and settled back inside. The driver hit the gas, and the tires spun in the gravel until they found traction on the asphalt and shot away into the darkness.

Benny stood and looked around. He could not see Perry Ray where he rested at the water's edge. He knew it would be awhile before the body was discovered. *'I need to use that time to put distance between me and this place,'* he thought as he jogged up and over the little rise then down to run alongside the creek.

•   •   •

Trudy winced as her husband's snoring filled the room. She pulled a pillow over her head, but it did no good. She reached over and shook him gently. "Honey, roll over. You are snoring again," she said.

K.W. heard her from deep within his warm cocoon. He rolled onto his right side and immediately fell back into the blissful darkness. He had just tipped over the edge of consciousness when the phone rang.

His eyes opened and focused on the digital dial of the clock. Two twenty-five it read. He pushed the covers aside and sat on the edge of the bed. He grabbed the receiver and spoke, "Yes?"

"K.W. this is John Long from the office. Are you awake?" the voice was tense, and K.W. knew his sleep was finished.

"Yes John, I'm awake. What do you have?" he asked.

"You caught the robbery, murder at the Burger King on Garland Road early yesterday?" it was a question.

"Yes, that's my case," K.W. said.

"Well, patrol units have picked up one of your suspects out by White Rock Lake about forty-five minutes ago. A boy named Benny McBay.

Bobby Little and I went out there to talk to him, and he started telling us that he and the other suspect, Tyree Dobbs, jumped on a couple they found parking out by the lake. He says that Tyree killed the boy and made the girl drive him away in their car. We put the description of the car on the air.

Then we had the suspect lead us over to where he said the body would be. It was there just like the boy said. They had bashed his head in and left him propped up against a big rock, sitting just at the water's edge.

Bobby called the lieutenant, and he said to call you in. You got both cases now," John said.

"Okay, John. I will be on my way. Where is the body?" K.W. asked.

"A lovers' hideaway off of Rush Creek. The patrol units have the suspect there, and the medical examiner is on the way," Long said.

"Got it. What patrol unit is out there John?" K.W. was making notes on the pad he kept beside the bed.

"Two Twenty One and his sergeant Two Twenty," John answered.

"Okay, would you ask them to hold the suspect there and would you also ask the medical examiner not to approach the body until I have an opportunity to look at it?" K.W. asked.

"You got it. K.W., there are a couple more thing you should know. This suspect in custody says that his partner has some *'beast'* living in him. Sounds crazy I know but this boy says that when that *beast* gets out, it completely controls Tyree. He said that we would have to kill the *beast* before we can take Tyree.

He also said Tyree wanted to rape the girl. He tried to stop the rape and Tyree knocked him out, rolled him up in a blanket and left him in the woods. He says that he believes Tyree will rape this girl and then the *beast* will kill her," John said.

"Thanks, John. I'm on my way," K.W. said as he slid into his trousers and reached for his shirt.

"Are you going in this time of the morning?" Trudy asked.

"I have to baby. You go back to sleep, and I will call you as soon as I can. Hey, look at it this way. You now can sleep without my snoring," K.W. said bending over and kissing his sleepy wife.

He turned from the alley onto Jupiter Road and picked up his microphone, "Eleven Forty-Eight," he said.

"Go ahead Eleven Forty-Eight," the dispatcher said.

"I am clear my residence and in route to meet Two Twenty One at Rush Creek Park. I am requesting a code two assignment," K.W. said.

"Eleven Forty-Eight is on the air and in route to White Rock Lake, code two, at Two Twenty-eight a.m., KKB-Three Sixty Four Police Department Dallas," the dispatcher repeated.

K.W. hung the microphone up and turned the Plymouth Fury onto Central Southbound. He reached down and flipped the toggle switch to illuminate the red lights mounted in the grill of the vehicle. He pushed the speed up to seventy-five and was quickly passing the Texas Instruments Plant at the Dallas, Richardson city limits line.

"Eleven Forty-Eight," the radio speaker opened.

"Go ahead," K.W. answered.

"Be advised that the vehicle in which the suspect required the abduction victim to drive him away in has been found abandoned behind the Swim Club off Garland Road, just down from the Dallas Arboretum. Two Twenty-five found it and has the scene protected. Please advise if you will go there first," the dispatcher asked.

"Yes, I will go there first. Is there a body in the car?" he asked.

"Negative. The keys were in the ignition, so the officers on scene opened the trunk. It is empty," the dispatcher answered.

"Forty Roger. I am approaching Northwest Highway now," K.W. replied and pushed the car to eighty miles an hour.

K.W. turned into the parking lot of the swim club and saw the flashing red light bouncing off of the surrounding foliage. He parked the car and walked around the corner of the building. The scene was calm and organized, but the feeling of despair hung heavy in the air.

"Hey K.W." Cody Whitaker was the first uniformed officer to see him.

"Hey, Cody. Are you working this?" K.W. asked shaking his friend's hand.

"Yep. I was doing my routine check, walked behind the building and found the car. I don't know how they managed to get it back here, but they did.

You can see that it scraped the corner of the building as they came around and the right front tire is partially in the water. It is amazing that the whole car hasn't slid into the lake," Cody said.

K.W. looked at the left side of the Chevy and saw the long crease where it had made contact with the building. He shined his flashlight inside the car and saw a pair of panties on the right rear floorboard and streaks of dried blood on the window of the right rear door.

The smell of the blood permeated the car, and he directed the flashlight beam down and across the side panel of the door. Blood with hair clotted in it was clearly visible on the armrest. He could see that the blood had run down the door panel and pooled in the carpet just where the floorboard joined the doorframe.

His heart sank. He knew in that instant that the victim was dead, 'but where is she?' he asked himself as he stood and played the flashlight beam across the water line and into the thick foliage.

"We walked the water's edge as far as possible K.W. Our best bet of finding her is going to be when the Park Police get out here with their boats. They will be here as soon as the sun comes up.

The same goes with searching these woods. The vines and

undergrowth are so thick that it would be possible to step over her and not see her in this darkness," Cody said.

"I know. Have you run the registration on this Chevy yet?" K.W. asked.

Cody nodded and reached into his front shirt pocket for his whup out book. He shined his flashlight beam on the page and read; "This Chevrolet Impala is registered to Wayne Gholson at Ninety two zero four Hermosa Drive. According to what Two Twenty-One has told me, the male victim is probably going to be Wayne's son, Perry Ray Gholson.

The suspect in custody said he heard the girl call the boy Perry Ray. He called her Mary Lynn. That's all we have for now," Cody said folding his book and stuffing it back in his shirt pocket.

"Does the body in Rush Creek Park have any identification on it?" K.W. asked.

"No, not really. But he is wearing cowboy boots with the initials stitched inside. He is also wearing a western belt with the name Perry Ray hand tooled on it," Cody shook his head.

"All right. Go ahead and get a wrecker out here and tell the driver to attach a cable onto the Chevy, so it does not slide into the lake. Tell crime scene I want a full forensic search, with video, of the car.

I am going to drive over to Rush Creek and talk with the suspect Two Twenty-One has in custody, and then I will go by on Hermosa and tell the Gholson family what we have. Maybe they can give me more information on the girl," K.W. said.

•   •   •

K.W. parked on the street in front of the house on Hermosa Drive. He could see that the lights were on in the house. He opened the door of the unmarked squad car and heard the front door of the house open.

"Who are you? Are you the police?" the man was coming down the steps and across the yard to meet K.W.

"Yes sir, I am. Are you Mr. Wayne Gholson?" K.W. asked around the lump in his throat.

"What happened? Where are our kids? We have been worried sick," he said as another man stepped onto the porch from the house and started down the steps.

"Mr. Gholson I have to ask you some questions, and unfortunately the answers may lead to some bad news. Maybe it would be better if we go inside and you can sit down," K.W. said.

"No. Our wives are inside, and we better hear this first. Just say it, give to me straight. Where is my boy?" he had tears in his eyes, and his voice was shaking.

"What is it Wayne," the second man asked as he joined them.

"Sir I am K.W. Bangs with the Dallas Police Department. May I ask your name?" K.W. said.

"I am Bill Threet. My daughter Mary Lynn was with Perry Ray tonight. What's happened to them?" he asked.

"We have found the body of a young white male in a spot that the kids refer to as Rush Creek Park. There is no wallet or identification on the body, but he is wearing a pair of boots with the initials PRG stitched inside. He is also wearing a western belt with the name Perry Ray hand tooled on the back.

We have one suspect in custody in connection with the death of this young man. He has told us that he and his accomplice were lying in wait for someone to rob and this young man and a young woman parked at Rush Creek. The suspect states that he and his partner heard the young woman refer to the male as Perry Ray and he called her Mary Lynn.

Mr. Gholson, I am fairly sure this young man is going to be your son. But we will need you to look at the body to make a positive identification.

Mr. Threet, we know that the second suspect abducted the young girl. We have found the car that he forced her to drive away.

Mr. Gholson, it is a Chevrolet Impala registered to you at this address. Mary Lynn is not in the car and at this point we do not know where she is Mr. Threet.

I do want you to know that we found some articles of her clothing and a large amount of blood in the car.

We will have boats on the water at first light searching the shoreline, and we will put men on foot searching the brush. If she is in there, we will find her.

That's all I can tell you at this point. Except that we will do everything possible to find Mary Lynn and to bring those responsible for this to justice.

"What is it, Wayne?" K.W. turned to the see a woman running across the lawn toward them.

Wayne Gholson stumbled back toward the porch and sat down. His wife sat beside him. She sobbed quietly, and he stared into the morning sky.

K.W. stepped away to allow the grieving parents some privacy. He settled into his car and drove to the Swimming Club.

The sun was just painting the Eastern sky a brilliant pink when he stepped into the boat and began the search for Mary Lynn.

He saw her body twenty yards away from the launch point. Her dress was hung on an exposed tree root and held her in place. She rocked back and forth in the gentle waves.

K.W. jumped from the boat and landed three feet behind her. He slid back down the bank into the shallow water. The shock of the night chill in the water pulled him out of his sorrow pit and pushed him to kneel beside Mary Lynn.

She lay on her stomach but her neck had been broken, and her face was turned up to stare at K.W. Her blue eyes were open and seemed to be pleading for help.

He could see that she had been beaten brutally. Her nose was pushed over under her left eye, the orbital bones of both eye sockets were crushed, and there were deep bruises reaching completely around her neck.

He eased her dress away from the root and turned her onto her back. Her face was now in the mud, and K.W. turned it gently back to face him. He winced as he felt the broken bones grating against each other as he turned her neck. "So sorry Mary Lynn," he said softly.

The front of the dress was open. Her bra and panties had been removed. Her breasts were bruised, and blood was clotted in her pubic hair and across her thighs.

K.W. felt his rage building, and he was struggling to hold back tears. He knew he was looking at the work of the *beast*.

He closed Mary Lynn's eyes, pulled the dress together to cover her nakedness and then leaned forward to whisper in her ear, '*I know what he did to you, but I cannot imagine the terror of your last minutes. This I do promise you. We will find this beast, and you will have justice. Rest In Peace Mary Lynn.*'

CHAPTER 6
TAKEN

Trudy walked into the bedroom and saw the gun belt lying on the bed. The holster was empty, but the handcuffs and two extra magazines were in place. Beside it was a dark blue sports coat. She glanced at the clock on the bedside table and saw that it was not yet eight o'clock.

She turned to the master bath and saw her husband standing before the mirror making the final adjustments to the knot in his tie. She looked to the counter and saw the Colt Forty-Five on the counter, next to the sink. *'He always has a pistol within reach,'* she thought.

She leaned against the door and asked, "You are working evenings, why are you going in so early?"

K.W. turned to look at her and was struck by the thrill shooting through his heart. They had met at sixteen, married when he was twenty-one and she twenty. Now, after five years of marriage, he was still captivated by her.

He thought her the most beautiful in the early morning like this, no makeup, and her face still soft from the night's sleep. *'How in the world did I ever get so lucky,'* he thought.

He smiled, turned back to the mirror to be sure his collar was wrinkle free and then said, "You forgot. Today is the sergeant's exam, and I am setting for it. It starts at ten o'clock and everyone who is testing must be checked in and in place by nine forty-five. No one will be admitted after that."

"How long will it take, can we meet for lunch before your shift starts at three?" she asked with a slight frown.

"They give you two hours to finish the test. I don't think it will take that long but then who knows? I want to have time to go over my answers and then I want to stay until they post the results. That won't happen until one o'clock at the earliest, then I will grab a quick bite to eat and it will be time to report for duty," he said.

He could tell she was disappointed. He stepped forward, wrapped his arms around her and said, "Hey now, take that frown off of your pretty face. Frowns cause wrinkles, and we just can't have wrinkles on the face of Miss Plano."

"Oh stop it. That was so long ago, and besides, I don't like you to tell people that I was Miss Plano. They always look surprised and then they examine me so critically, especially the women. It makes me uncomfortable, and I want you to stop saying it, " she said.

"Okay baby, I will. But now listen, I have signed up for vacation the first two weeks in June, and we are headed to Florida. Two whole weeks with no midnight calls, no court appearances, nothing but you, Kristen and me. I won't talk about anything having to do with the job, promise," he said.

Trudy smiled and said, "Right Ken Bangs, the day that passes without you talking about being police is the day that I believe the moon is made of green cheese. But I am looking forward to our vacation. We will be just another family, like normal people. I will have a husband, and I am telling you now, you are not getting away from me. Besides, I will need help with Kristen. I'm still not sure about our driving to Florida with her just three weeks old."

"It will all work out sugar," K.W. said as he strapped the gun belt on and settled the Forty-Five in the holster. He picked up the sports coat and leaned forward to kiss his wife on her cheek.

"I have to go now, baby. I will call you soon as I have my score and where I rank on the list. I love you," he said as he turned to the door.

"I love you too. Be safe tonight, I will be waiting for you," Trudy said as he walked away.

She sighed and sat on the side of the bed. *"Please Lord, protect my*

Ken and all of those who you have called as guardians. I pray Lord that every one of them will go home to their loved ones," Trudy said and moved to the nursery where Kristen had just awakened with a cry.

•   •   •

The buzzing was persistent. She opened one eye, and it was filled with the image of big red numbers. 'Five o'clock already,' she moaned.

She kicked the sheet off and swung her legs out and over the side of the bed. Leaning forward, she pushed the alarm button down, and the buzzing stopped.

She stood, stretched and headed for the bathroom. Flipping a light on, she stared at the face that popped out of the darkness and onto the mirror in front of her. 'Wow, look how white I am, all these freckles, and this reddish orange hair. No wonder I don't have a man. This face would scare any man away,' she thought.

She turned the water on and let it run while she turned to the commode. 'I will soon be thirty and not even dating. Probably shouldn't have wasted all those years in the Army, I should have been out there after my 'Mrs. Degree'.

But hey I'm trim, nice shape really, a little makeup to take the glare off of the milky white complexion that comes with being a redhead, spend some time with my updo, a cute dress and I'm not all that bad. There is still time,' she thought as she stepped back to the sink and reached for a clean washcloth.

Soaking it in the warm water, she began the morning routine. The warmth of the cloth was soothing as she ran it over her face. She patted her skin dry and then applied a light coat of makeup, some liner around her green eyes, some gloss over her full lips, and she moved into the closet for her uniform of the day.

She stepped into the dark gray shorts and then sat on her footstool and pulled on the cotton socks. She pushed her small feet into the heavy black steel-toed shoes and tied them. They were cumbersome, clunky really, but they did protect her feet from injury while working around the heavy pallets of mail being sorted and readied for loading on the trucks.

Standing once again, she chose a light blue shirt with the U.S. Postal Service logo over the left chest. She shrugged into it and let it settle on her hips outside of her shorts. Stepping in front of the mirror, she checked to be sure the squared hem of the shirt was not hanging too low. Satisfied she walked into the bedroom.

She turned to the dresser and picked up the laminated identification card. 'Linda Sweet, Mail Carrier' stared back at her. She looked at the picture, winked and said, "Hello Sweetness." She smiled at her humor and clipped the badge to her collar. One more look in the mirror and she was out the door.

She had been able to rent a small house on Hudson, just off Ross and two blocks away from the mail collection center at Lewis and Greenville. The trip from her driveway to the first stop of the day went quickly.

She swung her Ford Pinto into the parking lot of the DayLight Donuts shop just across the street from work and joined several other postal workers in line waiting for fresh coffee, warm donuts, and Sausage Kolaches.

"Hey, girl how's your morning?" Denise Jones asked with a smile.

"Lonely, but good Denise. Let me have two of the Kolaches, one of those glazed sinkers and a tall cup of black coffee," Linda replied.

"Coming up, and when are you going to stop calling me Denise. Everybody in here calls me Cinnamon. Now, about that lonely business, I told you I could fix you up.

Just say the word, or is it that you don't like anything Black except your coffee?" Cinnamon cocked an eyebrow while reaching for the donut.

"It's not like that Denise, er, Cinnamon. It's just that I don't want to be 'fixed up.' I want it to happen the old fashioned way, you know, for prince charming to come along and sweep me off my feet. So, thanks but I'm holding onto my dream," Linda said gently.

"Hey, no problem sweetie. Just remember this, you're not getting any younger and time waits for no one," Cinnamon said and moved to the next customer.

Linda knew Cinnamon was peeved. She kept pushing the issue because her younger brother was recently divorced and she had taken it as her mission in life to 'hook him up' and make him happy again. *'Don't do charity dating,'* Linda thought to herself.

Linda usually sat at one of the small tables and ate her breakfast, but this morning she just wanted to escape the tension between her and Denise. She walked to the front door with her hands full and turned to push through it with her hip.

As she turned to lean back into the door, she noticed a tall, thin, very dark skinned Black man sitting at a table watching her. She realized that he had heard the conversation with Denise. Linda smiled at him and backed through the door. She walked quickly to her car, sat her coffee on the roof and reached down to open the door. A hand slid in between her hand and the door handle. She gasped and stepped back.

The face of the man from the table came into view as he leaned forward and pulled the door open for her. "Hey, I heard the conversation in there. I saw that your hands were full and just wanted to help you into the car. And, as it turns out, I have no one either, and I understand about those lonely nights. Maybe we could help each other."

"Look, I know how that must have sounded, and I wish to God that I had not said it. But, I'm not that type of girl. I appreciate your courtesy, but I'm just not interested. I have to get to work now," Linda grabbed her coffee and settled into the seat of her little Ford."

"That's fine. But, I hope to change your mind. Folks call me King and I will be seeing you again," he smiled and pushed her door closed.

'Right,' Linda thought as she started the car and backed out of the parking spot, turning onto Ross and quickly into the parking lot of the sorting facility.

She parked and sat in the car a minute thinking, *'I've seen that guy in the DayLight before. He is always hitting on Cinnamon, trying to get her to go out with him. She shoots him down every time; now he comes on to me. He's an old man, and he smells. He gives me the creeps, wonder what he meant when he said he would be seeing me again and hoped to change my mind.'*

She exited the car and started to walk away. Then she stopped, turned and walked back to the car and locked it. Hurrying to the dock, she climbed the stairs and weaved her way through the pallets of mail waiting to be loaded on trucks.

Then she was through the door and into the bedlam that was always present at the sorting center. She stepped aside and glanced around seeking an out-of-the-way to eat her breakfast. She saw an empty desk and quickly slid in behind it and took the first long draw on the now tepid coffee. She grimaced, sat the cup down and quickly consumed the donut and Kolaches. Choking down the last of the coffee, she clocked in and reported to her supervisor.

"Hey, Linda, good to see you here early. I need you on collection route number one today. Grab a truck and hit the street. We need the mail in here for sorting as quickly as you can get it back. The first truck out to the main center runs no later than nine-thirty."

Linda nodded her understanding and grabbed the keys to a truck. Three minutes more and she was pulling out of the lot and headed to the far end of the route so she could work her way back, making the last collection just down the street from the center. She would repeat the routine four times during the shift.

●　　　　●　　　　●

"K.W. Bangs, badge number twenty four twenty five and I am assigned to CAPERS," he said as he flipped open the case to show his badge and identification card.

The uniformed sergeant smiled and said, "That's fine. Just sign in and go find you a seat K.W."

K.W. signed his name and moved forward into the carnivorous room. He paused to look around and saw that there were no more than fifty others in the room. *'Wow, I'm early,'* he thought.

"There is an empty desk right here. Best seat in the house, right in the middle of the first row," one of the proctors called to him.

"Why not?" K.W. answered and sat down. "Is it okay to look at my study notes while we wait," he asked the proctor.

"Yes sir, you can look over your notes right up until nine forty-five. Once we close the doors you can have nothing on your desk except the test booklet, the answer sheet and the pencil we supply," the Proctor said with a tight smile.

K.W. nodded and pulled his notes out. He was instantly absorbed.

"Okay. Put all your notes away and give me your attention," the sergeant said.

An hour later K.W. stood; stepped to the front desk and handed in his test booklet and answer sheet.

"Do you want to stay while we grade it?" the clerk asked.

"Sure do," K.W. smiled.

He watched as she settled the grid over his answer sheet and began to mark with the red pen. *'Whoa now,'* he thought. Finally, it was over, and she counted the red marks and wrote eighty-five on the answer sheet. "Congratulations. Most years a score of eighty-five will get you promoted. I bet it does this year too," she smiled up at him.

K.W. walked from the room and stopped at a knot of officers talking excitedly about the test. "What did you score K.W.?" R.W. Haskell asked?

"Eighty-five, how about you all? What's the highest score so far?" he asked.

"I got a ninety," D.D. Sword said.

The rest had received less, and K.W. left feeling good about his chances.

•　　　•　　　•

It was hot for May. Linda was soaked in sweat. It had been a long, hard day. Running the collection route was a never ending series of stop, unload the stuffed mailboxes into the stiff canvas bags, drag the heavy bag back to the truck and hoist it up and into the truck. Then you had to crawl up into the back, which was by now an oven, and push the bag into an open spot so you would have a place for the next one.

She jumped down from the back of the truck, closed and locked the doors and limped around to the driver's seat. She looked at her wristwatch and saw that it was two thirty. She had one more box, four blocks down at Greenville and Lewis, and that was it. Her day would be over.

She allowed the van to idle forward, looking in the mirror for an opening in the traffic, then accelerated and eased into the flow. Sweat ran down into her eyes, and she wiped it away whispering, '*Last one,*' as the big box came into view.

She turned on the flashing lights, pulled to the curb and stepped from the van. She got an empty bag from the floor of the van and then moved toward the mailbox. She noticed the man sitting on the bench at the bus stop. It was the man from the *DayLight Donut Shop.* He smiled at her, and she looked away. '*Maybe he will get the hint if I just ignore him,*' she thought.

She pushed her key into the lock on the collection box, turned it, eased the door open and bent to grab a handful of mail that spilled out onto the sidewalk.

"Hey, let me help you with that," it was King.

"No, don't. This is U.S. Mail, and only postal employees are authorized to handle it. Please, step back and let me do my job," Linda assumed the most authoritative posture she could manage.

The smile vanished, and she saw pain fill his eyes. "Hey now, hold on a minute. I'm just trying to be nice and help you. There's no need for you to be so rude to me," he said.

"I don't mean to be rude. But let's be frank here. You are not here to help. You are here to get a date. It is not going to happen. I told you this morning that I am not interested in going out with you. Now, please leave me alone," Linda looked up at him as she pushed the last of the mail into the canvas bag.

Her words and the tone of her voice sent waves of heat pulsing throughout his body. He could feel his muscles tense, and his first impulse was to strike out, to smash that look right off of her face. But then revelation hit him, '*It's because I am Black, that's it. She thinks she is too good to date a Black man.'*

He smiled and said through clenched teeth, "Ah, I see it all now. You aren't interested because I am Black. Isn't that right?"

Linda sighed and looked around at the small group of passerby's who had heard the exchange and stopped to watch it play out. She felt a need to justify herself before the accusing eyes. "No, that's not it at all. In fact, I have dated many Black men. But, I dated them because I found them attractive. I do not find you attractive. So, stop before we both say things that we shouldn't. Just leave me alone," she said.

"I say tell him what you are thinking, embarrass him! Or better yet, let me say it for you.

Dude! Why don't you take a good look in the mirror? You are way out of your league. You are at least fifteen years older than her, dressed in last year's clothes and I can smell you from here.

Now, look at her. She is young, trim and pretty. She can date anyone she wants to. Ain't that right honey?" the voice came from a young Black woman standing in the crowd of on-lookers.

There was a smattering of snickering, and many of the women were outright laughing at the man.

Linda saw the anger building and knew she needed to leave. She leaned forward, looked away from the man and reached for the mailbag. She sensed rather than saw the blow coming.

Bright lights exploded behind her eyes, and she was falling. The back of her head slammed into the concrete and darkness rushed forward. She found herself spinning in a roaring swirl, as she struggled to remain conscious.

She rolled to her right and tried to stand. He kicked her bottom sending her sprawling face first onto the sidewalk. The pain shooting through her bottom caused her to loose control of her bladder and hot urine flooded down her bare legs.

Linda could hear the screams of the now scattering onlookers. She knew that no one was going to help her.

She rolled onto her side and tried to stand, but the pain from her tailbone shot through her like an electric charge, and she sank back down. The air rushed from her lungs as he kicked her in the ribs. She felt herself being sucked deeper into the darkness and relaxed in surrender to it.

Her attacker grabbed a handful of her hair with his left hand and jerked her up onto her feet. Linda felt him lock his arms around her and lifted her off of the sidewalk.

He shuffled to the van and Linda knew he was going to take her. She could hear herself screaming and kicked backward into his shins with her heavy shoes. He yelped, and she could feel his grip loosen.

She reached back to claw at his face and found his right eye. She sank her nails deep into the flesh and heard him scream. He released her and she fell to her knees.

He grabbed her hair again and pulled her up and around to face him. She saw his fist coming and then the pain split her face. He kept pounding, sending her over the edge of consciousness. She was free falling into the pit.

•   •   •

He was still thinking about the test as he walked through the door of Crimes Against Persons. "How did you do," Susie asked.

K.W. paused at her desk and said, "I scored eighty-five. I decided not to wait to see the posting, but I'm guessing I will be in the top ten."

"Well, I guess we will have to start calling you Sergeant Bangs," Rona said as she walked into the room. "But for now, Sergeant Senkle told me to send the first *Investigator* to arrive straight to his office. You are the first," she smiled.

K.W. glanced up at clock over the squad room door. *'Three o'clock, he whispered to himself, and already in Senkel's office. This may not be a good start'.*

He stepped up to the Sergeant's door and saw that Senkle was speaking into the telephone. Senkle waved him in and pointed to the chair in front of his desk.

K.W. sat down and heard Senkle ask, "When was she taken? Around two thirty, you say? Okay, are the uniformed units still there?

Good, tell them to standby. I will have a team on the way in just a couple of minutes."

K.W. felt a flash of panic. "Hey Sarge, don't give it to me. I am due out on vacation in three days, and my wife will kill me if I get hung up and can't leave," he heard himself saying.

Senkle turned to the active case board and wrote in, 'Kidnapping, Mail Carrier -Bangs.'

Then he looked at K.W. with a tight smile and said, "Needs of the department come before your vacation. You are assigned to the Robbery, Kidnapping, and Extortion team. This one is yours.

Here is what I know so far, a female mail carrier stepped out of her truck to collect the mail from the box at Greenville and Lewis. Witnesses say a black male sitting on the bench at the bus stop next to the mailbox grabbed her and started dragging her toward the mail truck.

She struggled, and he beat her with his fist, striking her several times in the face. Finally, she went limp either from being knocked unconscious or just to stop the beating. He stuffed her into the truck and drove away with her.

All of the witnesses say it was brutal and bloody. I don't want you working this alone, so get a partner, any partner and find her. The field units are standing by at Greenville and Lewis."

"Sergeant, why is this ours? Why isn't this the Postal Inspectors or the FBI?" K.W. asked.

"Because K.W. it happened on the streets of Dallas and we *are* the police in Dallas. Now, stop arguing with me and get out there," Senkle was glaring at his investigator.

"Okay, okay. I don't have a car yet, so I will have to go over to the garage, sign one out and then I'm on my way," K.W. said as he turned toward the door.

Sergeant Bill Parker stepped into the office and said, "Beg your pardon Sergeant Senkle. I don't mean to get into your business, but I couldn't help but overhear. I already have a car and will be happy to ride with K.W. until someone else checks in."

"Thanks, Bill. K.W. it is your case but remember you are riding with a sergeant. Follow his lead, got it?" Senkle asked.

K.W. nodded and headed for the door. Parker flipped him the keys and said, "You're driving. I'm just along for the ride."

K.W. could see the flashing lights of the patrol vehicles parked behind the mail truck. He pulled around in front of the crowd of officers gathered on the street and parked next to the curb. He picked the mike up and spoke into it, "Eleven Forty-Eight show me and Eleven Thirty code six on the incident at Greenville and Lewis."

"Ten four Eleven Forty-Eight. You are both out at Fifteen Thirty hours. KKB Three Sixty Four police department Dallas."

K.W. switched the engine off and reached for the door handle. He looked back at Sergeant Parker and asked, "How do you want to handle this?"

"It is your case. I'm just here in case something comes up and you need backup," Parker replied.

"Okay, but how about we work this as partners. From the looks of all that blood on the sidewalk, this woman is in some real trouble. Let's find her and bring her home," K.W. said.

"Let's make it happen. I will interview the witnesses while you talk to the police," Parker said, and they stepped from the car.

CHAPTER 7
THE KING

Janice Beatty had just finished hanging out her freshly washed sheets and was standing on her back steps when the van came rumbling past. The van bounced down the unpaved alley lifting a wall of dust that floated across the fenceless backyards of the projects. She watched helplessly as the dust settle over her morning's work.

She saw that the van had U.S. Postal Service markings on the side and the back door of the van. The van slowed and turned into a backyard four houses down and across the alley from her unit. Ester's son, Le Roi, or *King*, as he liked to call himself stepped from the van and looked up and down the alley.

'That man is up to no good,' Janice said to herself. Ester Renau was a godly woman. She never missed church and hosted a prayer meeting in her house every Tuesday morning. Janice loved to go to the prayer meeting, but she did get tired of Ester always insisting that they pray for Le Roi.

When he had been in prison, they would pray for his safety and for him to be delivered from the deception of his prison religion, *Islam*. Ester would go on and on, praying for his release so he could come home.

Janice would squirm in her seat. She could not bring herself to join Ester in her prayers. She had on occasion peeped at the other women while Ester prayed for

Le Roi's quick release and saw that not one of them was praying. *'No one wants that no account bully to come back in our neighborhood,'* she thought.

But Ester just continued to pray and believe that a miracle was coming and that her son would soon be restored to her. She believed that each person was born with a destiny and Le Roi was born to be a leader of the church.

She also believed that names were important, and could shape a person's self image and the way others saw them. That is why she named her son Le Roi, or *The King* in French.

Ester swore that her family all migrated to America as free men and women from France before the Revolutionary War. Le Roi disagreed with his mother.

He was always ranting about how the white man had enslaved his people and that justice demanded reparation. Le Roi's hatred for white folks ran so deep that Janice and most of the other residents of the projects avoided him.

Janice was afraid of Le Roi and she did not like the way he looked at her. But Janice was also angry, and that anger overrode her normal reluctance to have any contact with Le Roi.

She jumped from the top step and trotted across the yard and down the alley intending to catch Le Roi before he got inside the house and give him a piece of her mind. *'King or no King, he has no right speeding down the alley in that mail truck strewing dust all over my laundry,'* she mumbled to herself.

Then she slowed, *'mail truck. What was he doing in a mail truck? Le Roi didn't work for the post office, in fact, the king refused to work. Something is wrong here, and I best stay out of it,'* Janice thought.

She turned back to her house. Climbing the steps, she looked again toward the van. Le Roi was hurrying into the house. *'What is he up to, why is he running like that,'* Janice thought.

She watched until he came back out of the house. He was carrying a blue wrap, *'is that the bedspread Ester made for him'* over his right shoulder. He walked around to the back of the van and stopped to look around.

'He is going to see me watching him,' Janice realized. She opened her screen door and stepped inside her kitchen just as Le Roi turned to

survey her end of the alley.

She peeped through the window and watched as he opened the back doors of the van, leaned inside for several minutes and then pulled something from the van, something he had wrapped in the bedspread.

She watched as he squatted, pulled the rolled up object over his shoulder and stood up. She gasped as long strands of red hair spilled from the rolled up blanket as he hurried toward his house, up the steps and inside.

Janice stood there thinking. *'Le Roi had a body rolled up in that spread, and the hair I saw was the hair of a white person, probably a woman. I bet that fool has kidnapped the driver of that mail truck, but why?'*

Janice did not have a telephone. She stood at the kitchen window staring at the back door Le Roi had carried the woman in through. She glanced up at the clock, *'It is Twenty minutes past three. I told Jimmy to be home by four o'clock. Do I wait and leave him on lookout while I go to the store and call the police, or do I just go now? I best stay and watch in case Le Roi leaves,'* she decided. Janice pulled a chair up and sat down by the window to wait.

As she sat in the hot kitchen, the adrenaline began to wear off and her pulse rate slowed. She dozed off. She dreamed and in that dream, a white face floated up before her begging, *'help me.'*

The sound of a car door being slammed woke her. She bolted forward in the chair and rammed her head into the window casing. The violence of the blow caused her ears to ring. She sat back down and rested her head against the kitchen wall.

Through the mist, she heard the front door of her house open and close. "Mom, I'm home. Mom?" Jimmy called.

"In here Jimmy, come help me, son," she responded.

She heard him running, down the hall, across the living room and into the kitchen, "Mom, what happened? Are you okay Mom?" the little boy was frantic for his mother's welfare.

"I'm fine son, just bumped my head. Help me stand up and then stay beside me so I don't fall," she said.

Jimmy was just 12 years old, but he was a tall, strong kid. He bent, put both arms around his mother and gently lifted her to a standing position. She leaned against him and said, "Move me to the window so I can look out son."

"Mom, what's going on?" Jimmy asked as he scooted his mother over closer to the window.

"See that mail van and the red Ford parked next to it in Miss Ester's yard?" she asked.

Jimmy leaned around his mother and peered through the dust-stained window toward the Renau house. "Yes, so what mom?"

"Le Roi drove the van up there. He rolled a woman up in a bedspread and carried her into the house. He can't keep her there long because Ester will be home from her Bridge game soon.

I figure he called someone to help him move the van and get the woman out of the house before Ester gets home. I dozed off and didn't see who drove that car into the yard.

I am going to walk down to the store and call the police. I want you to stand right here by the window and watch that house. You see who comes out with Le Roi and watch which direction they go when they leave. Write down the license plate number of that red car and make a note of what time they leave. Can you do that for me, son?" she asked without taking her eyes off of the mail van.

"Mom, are you sure we want to get involved in this? Maybe we should just let someone else call the police. I bet lots of people saw the same thing you did, and it doesn't look like anyone has called the police. Maybe this isn't our business," Jimmy said with a shrug.

Janice rested her hand on his shoulder, "You look just like your daddy when you shrug like that. But I tell you something Jimmy Beatty, if your father was here and saw what I saw this morning, he would be right in the middle of this. He never turned his back on evil. He never failed to help another who was in need. You think about that for a minute," Janice said.

Jimmy turned his head to look up at his mother. "Dad was a hero wasn't he Mom."

"No son, your father *is* a hero. He died before you were born but he lives on in you. What he did on that day in Vietnam was in the finest tradition of the United States Army. That's what they put on that Silver Star certificate hanging in your room. Remember? You have greatness in you, Jimmy. Just like your daddy," she said gently.

Jimmy nodded his head saying, "Go call the police mom. I will watch and make a note of anything happening over there."

Janice patted the boy's shoulder and hurried down the hall and out the front door. She hustled down Silkwood to the JBC Market on Bexar. She moved through the crowd of men sitting in the shade of the awning and stepped inside.

The rush of refrigerated air blew the hem of her dress up, cooling her sweat soaked skin and causing her to gasp. She pushed her dress down and moved toward the counter where Mr. Evans stood with his toothless smile.

"Sorry about that Janice. I keep the fan on high to help move the cooled air all around the store. Didn't mean for it to blow your dress up like that," he said with lowered eyes.

"That's okay Mr. Evans. I have sort of an emergency and need to call the police. But, I don't want to use that pay phone outside because all those men will hear every word I say. Would you let me use the phone in your office, I will be glad to pay you," she asked.

"No, no child. You go right ahead and you don't owe me anything. Pull that door closed if you want to," the old man said.

Janice stepped into the office, closed the door and picked up the phone. She dialed the operator and waited. "Operator, how can I help you?" came the response.

"Operator, I need to talk to the South Dallas Police," Janice said.

"Is this an emergency?" the operator asked.

"I don't know, but I saw something that makes me think a woman might be in trouble with some men," Janice said.

"Oh, honey! Wait just a minute and I will dial the main number for you. I will stay on the line to be sure you get connected," the operator said.

"Not the main number. That will be for the police downtown. I want the South Dallas Police; their station is on Bexar Street," Janice said.

"I don't have a listing for the South Dallas Police. Let me see what I have on Bexar. Yes, here is a listing for the Southeast Division at 6500 Bexar. Let me connect you to them," she said.

Janice heard a series of clicking noises and then, "Southeast Patrol, Sergeant Warren speaking."

The operator said, "Sergeant Warren, this is the Southwestern Bell operator. I have a caller on the line for you. Please stand by while I make the connection."

"Go ahead Miss, I have the South Dallas Police on the line for you," the operator said.

"Hello, Sergeant?" Janice said.

"Yes mam, this is Sergeant Warren. How can I help you?"

"Well, I don't know really. I went to our crime watch meeting last week and the officer said, *'if you see something say something.'* And, I saw a man that lives down the alley from me drive a U.S. Mail truck into his back yard this morning. I know he doesn't work for the post office.

I watched him take a woman, rolled up in a blue bedspread, out of the back of that van and carry her inside his mother's house. There is another car there now and I think they are going to carry her off somewhere. I think she is in trouble," Janice blurted out.

"Okay, you are doing just fine and I want you to remain on the line with me as I get some information from you," the sergeant said.

"First of all, what is your name and where are you right now?"

"My name is Janice Beatty and I am at the JBC Market just down Bexar from you, between Samoa and Carlton Garrett Street."

"Okay, now hold on a minute as I get a car in route down to where you are."

"No, I don't want all these people seeing me talking to the police," Janice said.

"What if that woman is hurt, you have already said you believe she is in trouble? She needs help and right now you are the one who can help her most," Sergeant Warren coaxed gently.

"Okay, but have them come inside the store. I am in Mr. Evans' office," Janice sighed.

Janice heard the Sergeant lay the phone down and then she heard him say, "Six Eighty Six."

"Go ahead Six Eight Six."

"Send a unit to the JBC Market at Sixty four eleven Bexar. Put them on a mark out to see a complainant."

"Three Thirty-Four did you copy?"

"We copied and will be in route."

"Janice, this is Sergeant Warren. I am going to stay on the line with you until our unit arrives. While we are waiting, tell me what you saw."

CHAPTER 8
THE RING MAN

"Have you lost your mind Le Roi? You kidnapped this woman? You took her right off the street in the middle of the day? And, stole a United States Government vehicle to boot. Did you realize that if there is any mail in that truck, that makes this a federal offense? I bet the FBI and those Postal Inspectors are looking for you right now.

And look at her, Le Roi! You have beaten this woman half to death. She needs a doctor, or to be in the hospital. Then you call me over here to help you move her?

Hell no! I don't want anything to do with this Le Roi," Bobby Joe Ring was shouting.

"Hold up, hold up now B.J. Hear me out, Bobby Joe. I went to see that girl Cinnamon, the sister that works at the donut shop down on Greenville, this morning. This one came in and was talking with Cinnamon about how lonely her night was. Cinnamon told her that she could fix her up.

But this bitch turns up her nose and walks out. I followed her outside and helped her open her car door, being nice. I thought I might make some small talk, and you know, maybe we could hook up. But she tells me she's not interested.

I told her that was okay, but that I hoped to change her mind. She rolled her eyes as if to say, '*I don't think so,*' and drove off.

I watched her drive across the street into the mail center lot and park. She sat in the car a few minutes, and I figured she was eating her breakfast.

I decided to walk over and chat her up some more. But then she jumped out of the car and hustled toward the office. She glanced back and saw me walking toward her and turned back to lock the car. Pissed me off, you know, like she was *'locking me out of her life.'*

I figured that if her shift started at seven then it would end at three. I made up my mind to be right there at her car when she came in. Thought I would give it one more try you know, see if she wanted to drink a cold one after a hot day in that mail truck. So we could get to know each other and see where it might lead.

I rode the bus over to Lewis and Greenville and waited. I never figured on her stopping to get the mail out of the box right there at the corner. But she did, and I stepped up and started talking.

But once again, she told me to get lost. I asked her if it was a Black thing and she said no that she had dated Black men before but didn't find me attractive. *'Leave me alone,'* she said.

And then, some young Black woman, walking by, jumped in and started taking this one's side. The sister started saying, I needed to look in the mirror, that I was too old and that I smelled.

Man, I lost it. I knocked this uppity bitch down, right out there on the sidewalk. Then, I realized what I had done. I knew that I was going to take a fall behind hitting this bitch and that made me even madder. I started kicking her and then I thought that as long as I'm going to do time behind this, I might as well make it worthwhile.

I grabbed her, thinking I would haul her off in the mail truck, drive to some isolated place and take my time with her. I picked her up and the bitch kicked me, damned near broke my shin. That did it. I beat her down, threw her in the truck and here we are.

The truth is I wish I could undo all of it, but I can't. Please Bobby Joe, you got to help me get out of this mess," Le Roi pleaded.

"I have to help you? Let me tell you something Le Roi. Ever since you got out of the joint you have been acting stupid. Coming in here wearing that crescent around your neck, talking about how you are through with the white man's Jesus and how Islam is going to lead our people out of oppression into a new Black Promise Land.

Then you hook up with the Black Panthers. You stand on the

corner down on Oakland and Pine shouting at people about the revolution is coming to bring liberty for the Black Man.

You are walking around in those dingy old 'fly suits' calling yourself *The King*! Man, you are forty years old and still living with your momma. Does that sound *Kingly* to you?

Le Roi, don't you understand what you have done? This is not one of your petty thefts. This is a major crime.

What are you going to do with her? Besides beating her half to death, have you done anything else to her? Le Roi tell me that you haven't raped this woman," B.J. said.

"No, I haven't raped her. But that won't make any difference if they catch me. I will be right back inside doing some hard time.

You got to help me, Bobby Joe. You know I would help you. I have helped you. How many times Bobby, how many times have you called and *The King* has always been there for you? This is a blood thing, a *Black* blood thing Bobby Joe," Le Roi said.

Bobby Joe walked around in a tight little circle, rubbing his head. He stopped his pacing and looked at Le Roi. "You are right. I do owe you, and I am going to help you. But then after this, we are through Le Roi. Don't ever call again, cause I will not answer.

Now, I want two things. First, I want your word as a Brother that you aren't going to kill this woman and that you are going to let her go as soon as you can. Second, I want to hear a clear statement of what your plan is," Bobby Joe demanded.

"I am not going to kill her; you have my word as a Brother on that. But, I have to get her out of here before my mother comes home. She will call the police as soon as she walks in. I need time to think this through, and I can't just put this white woman out on the street here in South Dallas, especially not in her condition. If she were to die, and the police put this on me, I will be headed for a seat in Ole Sparky and we both know it," Le Roi said with a shake of his head.

"And where, with the police looking for you, are you going to do all of the thinking," B.J. asked.

"I was figuring that the WaySide Inn on Central would be a good place. Folks in there are minding their own business, nobody going to be looking at anyone else. I can hold up there, let her heal some and figure how to get out of town until all of this cools down," Le Roi mused.

"The WaySide Inn? Le Roi, I swear! Is that your plan? How are you going to get there, how are you going to get a room without leaving a record, how are you going to get this woman, who you have beaten half to death, into a room without people seeing her?

Do you want my advice? Put her back in that van, drive right up to the emergency room entrance over at Baylor Hospital, get out and run like hell. The staff there will find her and get her the medical help she needs to survive," B.J. said.

"Come on Bobby Joe. You know that there is a police officer stationed at those emergency room doors. He would be on me before my feet hit the ground. I might as well just step out and surrender.

I need you to drive that mail truck out of here, through the back streets and alleys until we can get it close to the police impound on Choice Street. I will put her in your car and follow. That way, if you get stopped, all they will have on you is driving that stolen van. You can always say that you found it on the street with the keys in it, knew something was wrong and was taking it to the police car lot over there.

I will pick you up and drive to the WaySide. You walk in and get me a room, then help me get her inside. That's it, Brother. You won't hear from me again, and I will never say your name," Le Roi said.

"That's it? You say that like it is all so simple. My answer is that you are a fool. No way am I going to do that. Let me make this clear, I am not getting in the same vehicle with you and her together. *No way, not now, not ever.*

What I will do is this. I will drive that van out of here and dump it over on Choice Street. I will walk out of there and make my way home.

You put her in my car and take her to the WaySide. How you do it, is up to you *King*. Just leave the keys to my car on top of the left front tire. I will come by after dark and get my car.

That's it, Brother. That's all B.J. is going to do. Take it or leave it, but make up your mind because the Ring Man is out of here," Bobby Joe said.

"But Bobby Joe, how am I going…." Le Roi started to say.

"*KING!* Listen to me, man! This is your mess. You clean it up. I'm gone," B.J. started for the door.

"Wait, Bobby Joe. Okay, brother. Just hold on a minute. Give me the keys to your car. I left the keys to the van in the ignition. Be sure to wipe it down before you get out," Le Roi said.

Bobby Joe tossed his keys to Le Roi and ran for the back door. He paused, looked up and down the alley and sprinted to the van. Jumping inside he pumped the gas pedal, turned the key and the engine started. He backed the van out and thundered off down the alley.

Le Roi stood watching him go. As soon as B.J. was out of sight, he walked to the red Ford, opened the back door and hurried back to the house.

He ran to his bedroom and pushed the bedspread over the conscious, but unmoving woman. He slid his arms under her shoulders and hips and lifted her from the bed.

He hurried through the kitchen and out the back door without pausing or looking for witnesses. '*It is what it is,*' he thought as he laid the woman on the back seat and slammed the door.

Le Roi slid into the front seat, started the Ford and drove off down the alley toward Bexar.

•   •   •

Jimmy Beatty crouched by the kitchen window watching it all. He saw B.J. run to the mail truck and drive away in it. '*That's the dude they call The Ring Man,*' he said silently.

Soon as the van was moved, he could see the license plate of the red Ford. He had his pencil ready, but he had forgotten to get paper to write on. Looking around he saw that there was none close by, so he wrote the plate number on the kitchen wall, TXR-661.

Soon as he finished writing the plate number on the wall, he saw

Le Roi come out of the back door at Ms. Esters. He was carrying something all wrapped up in that blue bedspread his momma had made him.

Jimmy remembering his momma saying that Ms. Ester had made it blue to represent the Spirit of God, she embroidered white doves on it to represent the Peace of God, and she stitched a giant red cross on it to represent the Hope of Man. Several of the women had helped her so that it would be ready for Le Roi by the time he got home. She was sure it would help bring him back to Jesus and break that prison religion off of him.

Jimmy didn't know much about religion, but he did know that his momma and all the ladies at church said that there wasn't but One King and that was Jesus. That made Jimmy fairly certain that Jesus would not be happy with Le Roi running around wearing that crescent declaring himself to be *The King*.

'*If praying works, then Le Roi has wasted all that praying his momma has been doing for him,*' Jimmy thought.

Jimmy couldn't see very well from his vantage point, so he left the window and stepped outside. Now, standing on the top step, he could see clearly. He watched as Le Roi bent down to ease his burden into the car. As he did, a white arm fell free of the cover.

Le Roi pushed the door closed and jumped in the front seat of the car. Jimmy watched as he drove off down the alley toward Bexar. He ran back inside and looked at the clock. It was now three fifty-six and Jimmy wrote it on the wall, right under the license plate number. And then, he wrote next to the time, '*The Ring Man.*'

Jimmy turned away from the wall and moved across the kitchen to the 'junk' drawer where his mom kept odds and ends. He pulled it open and rummaged around until he found a scrap of paper. He slammed the drawer and moved back to his notes on the wall. He carefully copied what he had written on the wall onto the slip of paper. Then he ran from the house and turned toward the market where his mom had gone to call the police. '*She will need this information to give the police,*' he thought and increased his pace.

CHAPTER 9
WORKING THE SCENE

K.W. tugged his sunglasses into place and walked to where his partner was talking with a man and woman. As he drew even with them, he saw his partner hand a card to the man and say, "Thank you for talking with me. This is my card. My name is Bill Parker, and I am a Sergeant in the Crimes Against Persons Section. If you think of anything else, just call the number on the card. If I'm not in, the secretaries will take your number, and I will get right back to you. Thanks again."

The couple walked away, and Bill turned to K.W. "Get anything?" he asked.

Yes, quite a bit. The patrol officers did an excellent job. There are a lot of witnesses, and they took statements from ten of them.

Senkle was right when he said it was brutal and bloody. All of the witnesses said the suspect beat her unconscious, stuffed her in the van and took off, driving south on Greenville and then turning onto Munger. They watched the van until it was out of site and said he stayed southbound on Munger. What did you get?" K.W. asked.

"A couple of her co-workers were coming in, off their shifts, when this started. They saw it all, but not one of them went to her aid.

They identify the victim as Linda Sweet, a white female about thirty years of age. She works in the sorting center and reports to Jim Elemdorff, the second shift foreman. What say we hurry over there and catch him before he leaves for the day?" Parker suggested.

"Let's go. Her co-workers say she came here after being released from the Army about a year ago. Seems to be well liked, keeps to herself and is single," K.W. said as they walked across the parking lot and climbed the steps onto the loading dock.

"Pardon me fellows, but all visitors have to check in with the front office, this is a work area and for employees only," a tall, thin man said as he approached them.

K.W. extended his badge and said, "I'm K.W. Bangs and this is Sergeant Bill Parker. We are Dallas Police Officers investigating the assault and abduction of your mail carrier. We would like to speak with her supervisor, Jim Elemdorff."

The man glanced at the badge and then from K.W. to Parker. "I'm Elemdorff, but I'm not sure I'm supposed to talk with you," he said.

"Why not," K.W. asked.

"Well, ah, our policy says that we are not to speak with anyone, other than Postal Inspectors or our superiors, concerning any criminal event related to the Postal Service," Elemdorff said.

"I appreciate that Mr. Elemdorff, but this happened on a public street, not a postal facility. And, beyond that, this woman was beaten badly, and there is every reason to believe that her life is in peril. We need to find her as quickly as possible, and we need your full cooperation to accomplish that," K.W. smiled at the man.

Elemdorff looked at the small crowd of people who had gathered behind him. "Okay, I'm sure it will be alright but give me a minute and let me call my boss," he said.

"I don't have to call anyone. I will tell you all I know, just ask your questions," a short, stocky man with graying hair stepped forward from the group.

"Me too," another said as the others nodded their heads.

Elemdorff turned back and said, "Yeah, me too."

K.W. turned to Parker and said, "Sergeant if you want to talk with these folks, Mr. Elemdorff and I will step into his office."

"Good idea," Parker said as Bangs and Elemdorff walked toward the office.

"Thank you, Mr. Elemdorff. Let's start with the first time you saw Ms. Sweet this morning. About what time was that?" Bangs asked.

"She was early, so it was before seven, probably about six forty-five," Elemdorff said.

"She was early, you said. So, I take it her shift begins at seven. Is that right?" Bangs asked.

"Yes, she works from seven to three. Her normal routine is to stop across the street at the donut shop and eat her breakfast. Then she comes over here and clocks in by at seven or just before. But this morning, she brought her breakfast in and ate it in the vacant office next door," Elemdorff replied.

"Do you know if she got the breakfast from the donut shop?" Bangs asked.

"Yes, she had some Kolaches, a doughnut and a cup of coffee. She was carrying it in a bag from the shop," Elemdorff said.

"Did you notice anything else different about the way she came in?" Bangs asked.

"Yes, she seemed upset. Agitated I guess would be the best way to describe it," Elemdorff said.

"Did you ask her if she was okay, say anything about what you observed," Bangs asked.

"No, no I didn't. You have to be so careful about what you say or ask these days," Elemdorff said. "Wish I had now," he added quietly.

"I understand. I need to see her personnel file, get her date of birth, full name, address and next of kin information," K.W. said.

"Sure, I'll get all that for you. Just give me a minute," Elemdorff turned away.

"By the way, is she dating or close to anyone in particular here in the shop? Has she been in a relationship that ended badly; any arguments, having problems with anyone in particular?" Bangs asked.

Elemdorff stopped, looked puzzled and walked back to where Bangs was standing, "You know, I had forgotten, but I heard a couple of the folks talking about some incident, argument or something she had with the waitress in the doughnut shop this morning. Something about a date or fixing her up with a date," he said looking past Bangs to the group talking with Parker.

Bangs turned to follow his glance, "Do you see those folks talking with your friend? The man is Sam Waterson, and the woman is Betty Jean Cooper," Elemdorff answered.

"Fine, I will talk with them while you get that information for me," Bangs said moving toward the group with Parker.

As he approached, he heard the woman, Betty Jean Cooper, saying, "It all started when Linda came in. Cinnamon greeted her and asked how she was doing.

Linda replied and said she was okay except for the lonely nights. That's when Cinnamon said something to the effect that if she was lonely, it was her own fault because she had offered to hook her up.

Then Linda told her that she didn't want to be hooked up, that she wanted it to happen the old fashioned way, naturally. Said, she wanted her prince charming to sweep her off of her feet and carry her away.

That 'naturally' comment made Cinnamon mad; you could see it on her face. Things got tense. Cinnamon said something about Linda not getting any younger and that time waits for no one.

Linda got her food and rather than sitting down and eating her breakfast like she usually does, she walked out."

"And King followed her," Waterson interrupted.

"King who?" Bangs asked.

"King is all I know. I figure that is a street name? He hangs out in the *DayLight,* always messing with Cinnamon," Waterson replied.

"Cinnamon, I take it is the waitress. Do you know her full name?" Parker asked.

"All I know is her first name, Denise. King is the one who started calling her Cinnamon. Said she is sweet and lightly toasted, just like a Cinnamon Roll," Betty Jean snickered.

"You said that King followed Linda outside. Did anything happen between them?" Parker asked.

"Yes, he opened her car door for her. They were talking, but of course, we couldn't hear what they were saying," Sam said.

"But, we know they had words you might say," Betty Jean said.

"How's that?" Bangs asked.

"Because of the expression on their faces. He looked angry, and she looked like she just wanted to escape; you know to get away from him," Betty Jean answered.

"Was there any physical contact between the two?" Parker asked.

"No, but he stood and watched her drive across the street, park her car and walk into the building. Then he went across the street and over to her car. I thought that strange, so I stood by the window to see what he was going to do," Sam said.

"What did he do?" Bangs asked.

"Nothing, just looked around and walked off," Sam answered.

"Here you go, officer. I sure hope you find her," Elemdorff said while handing over the information Bangs had requested.

"We will Mr. Elemdorff. We might have some more questions for your crew," Bangs said.

"Anytime," Elemdorff said as he walked away.

Parker and Bangs compared their notes and Bangs said, "The donut shop is closed. Let's see if we can get dispatch to crisscross the address and get us an after hour's number for the owner. Maybe he can tell us where to find this Cinnamon. Maybe she can put us on King. When we find King, we will find Linda Sweet. I just hope she is still alive."

CHAPTER 10
THE WAYSIDE INN

Le Roi turned into the parking lot of the WaySide Inn. He drove slowly past the office and parked halfway down the line of rooms strung out beside the arched overhang. He switched the engine off and looked into the back seat where Linda Sweet was laying. Her eyes were open, but vacant.

Fear flashed through Le Roi. He reached over the seat back and checked her pulse. It was faint, but it was there. *'Don't you die on me girl,'* he mumbled to himself.

'But, what if she does? A dead woman in the room I rent, might as well just call the police and say come get me. I will give them a false name, and that shouldn't be a problem here at this short stay hotel. I mean they will not be asking for any identification,' Le Roi sat thinking it through. He took a deep breath, opened the door and walked toward the office.

Le Roi forced a smile and stepped through the doors into the lobby. The slim woman standing behind the counter asked, "Why did you drive all the way down there to park your car? That makes me think that you have someone or something in that car that you don't want me to see."

Le Roi paused at the directness of the question. Then he chuckled and said, "Well let's just say my partner in this little tryst does not want to be seen."

"She, or he, must really be paranoid. You drove past so slowly that I got a good look at the car. You were the only one visible," the woman lifted her head and stared at Le Roi.

Le Roi saw her eyes drop to the gold crescent hanging around his neck. It took all his self-control to keep from reaching down to tuck it inside his shirt. He held his gaze on the woman's face, trying to gauge her reaction to him. He saw years of experience in dealing with the lies and subterfuge of the WaySide's customers. *'Nothing to be gained by continuing this,'* he thought.

"I need a room. That's all we need to discuss. Do you have one or not?" the King asked.

"Easy now, big boy. Don't go getting Froggy with me. How long do you want the room for?" she asked.

Le Roi glanced at the nameplate fastened to her dress and said, "Okay Charlene, how about we start all over and try to be civil to each other. I need a room for a couple of days. Do you have one that you can rent me for that long and if so what is the rate please," he said with a bright smile.

Charlene looked at him for a few seconds and then said, "Yes, I have one that I can let you have for two days. It is $50.00 a day, payable in advance. We accept cash or credit cards but not checks."

"One hundred dollars is a lot of money, my Sister. Is there anything cheaper that you could let a brother have?" Le Roi asked.

"I am not your sister, and you are not my brother. Are you going to be paying with cash or a credit card? If it is cash, how much do you have?" Charlene asked.

"I have seventy five in cash, and that taps me out. If I spend all that on the room, I could not eat for the next two days," Le Roi said.

"That is not my problem. I do have one room that is due to be renovated. It is a mess, but I will let you have it for twenty-five dollars a day. That totals to fifty dollars for the two days. That leaves you some to eat on, big spender. Take it or leave it," she turned back to her ledger.

"Take it," Le Roi said as he handed over the cash.

Charlene took the money, counted it and turned to the board where the room keys were hanging. She chose the key to room number sixteen.

"This room is all the way at the end of the row and around the corner. The door faces the railroad track. The train comes through three times a day and it will be loud. The room will shake a little. But what do you expect for $25.00 a day? Enjoy your stay," Charlene smiled.

Le Roi accepted the key and asked, "Is that it, you don't need my name or for me to sign a register or anything?"

Charlene laughed, "Mister, as far as I'm concerned you don't exist, this didn't happen, and if there is no record then there are no taxes to be paid."

Le Roi smiled, winked at Charlene and breathed a sigh of relief. He left the office, turned to his left and walked past the row of green doors. At the end of the row, he turned the corner and there it was.

The number sixteen was painted in white on the door. The door itself was covered in peeling green paint. He pushed the door open and was greeted by a rush of stale, hot air.

Wrinkling his nose, Le Roi waded through the stink and flipped on the air conditioner. It hummed to life, and he moved the blower selector to high. The old unit was soon whistling as it pushed the air in the room into a swirling mass of musty humidity.

Shaking his head, Le Roi opened the door and allowed the foulness to escape the room. He pulled the shades down and then closed the drapes to block anyone's ability to see into or out of the room.

Satisfied, he walked to the car, drove it around the corner, and parked it parallel with the edge of the sidewalk in front of the room. He made sure that the back left door was as close to the room door as he could get it.

He stepped from the car, leaned around the corner to be sure no one was approaching or watching him. He opened the back door. He reached in, slipped both arms under Linda and lifted her limp body from the seat. He took two steps back from the car, pivoted and carried her into the room. Pausing, he kicked the door closed and laid Linda on the bed.

Le Roi stood looking down at the semi-conscious woman for a few seconds. Then he turned and headed out to move the car. He backed around the corner and then pulled forward into a parking slot. He stepped from the car and placed the keys on top of the left front tire.

Straightening up, Le Roi looked up and down the empty parking lot and then stepped around the corner and into the room.

CHAPTER 11
BURNING THE KING

K.W. and Parker settled into the unmarked vehicle. "What next?" Parker asked.

"Waterson is going to be right. *The King* is a street name. Let's run that name on channel seven. If there are any intelligence or gang units on the air, I bet they will jump right in," Bangs answered.

Parker watched as he started the car to power the radio up. Bangs lifted the microphone and said, "Eleven Forty-Eight will be on channel seven."

"Ten four Eleven Forty-Eight. You are on channel seven at four forty-seven; KKB-Three Sixty Four, police department Dallas.

K.W. flipped the channel selector to seven and said, "Eleven Forty-Eight."

The dispatcher answered, "Go ahead."

"I'm looking for information on a Black Male using the street name 'The King.' Will you check the log and see if you have anything on that name?"

"Standby one, Eleven Forty-Eight," the dispatcher said.

"Fifteen Forty-One to Eleven Forty-Eight," was the next transmission.

Bangs looked at Parker and smiled as he lifted the mike to respond "Go ahead to Eleven Forty-Eight."

"I have that individual on my watch list. Are you working an abduction where The King is a suspect?" the officer asked.

"We are, but how did you know that," Bangs answered.

"Where are you?" the unit asked.

"Greenville and Lewis," Bangs responded.

"We have a call from a woman who witnessed this individual drive a mail truck into his mother's back yard and carry what she believes is the body of a woman into the house.

A second man came to the house a few minutes later. He drove the van away while your man left with the woman in the accomplice's car. The witness copied the license plate number, and we have him identified also.

I have a complete file on both suspects. Stand by your location while I run to the office, get the files, and I will be at your location in twenty minutes," the intelligence officer responded.

"Ten-four. We will be in the parking lot of the postal facility at that location," Bangs said and hung up the microphone.

●   ●   ●

Linda was swimming upward, reaching for the rim of light just above her. There was a roaring in her head and pain pulsed through her as rough hands pushed her over onto her left side. The exposed nerves screamed in agony as the ends of her broken ribs grated against each other.

She sensed more than felt that her clothing was being removed. Her subconscious mind was saying fight, resist this violation, but her muscles were not responding. She lay helplessly, but fully aware of the pillaging of her womanhood, staring through sightless eyes as her abductor touched, probed and finally penetrated her.

Spasms of pain raced through her as her mind recorded every detail of the ravaging of her physical body. The circle of light grew smaller and dimmer; then she fell once again into the quiet darkness.

Le Roi rolled off of the quite body and stood beside the bed. Shame flushed the last vestiges of lustful passion from his body.

He lifted his hands to cover his face. Her scent stuck to them and struck him a smothering blow. He staggered back and gasped, turned his head to one side and gagged as his stomach churned.

Dropping his hands to his side, he forced himself to look at her.

'*My word, what have I become? Why did I do that, why did I feel the desire to rape an unconscious woman?*' he asked himself.

He stepped toward the bathroom and his foot tangled in her shirt that he had thrown on the floor. Bending down, he picked it up and saw the badge clipped to the collar. Her face stared at him from the picture. He shifted his eyes away from hers and looked at her name, Linda Sweet.

A moan from her pushed through the fog of his shame, and he looked toward the bed. '*She is regaining consciousness,*' he thought.

He watched as her muscles began to jerk in spasms. Her head thrashed back and forth, and her breathing was getting faster and faster. She twisted more and more and rolled toward the edge of the bed.

Le Roi bent and put his hands on her to push her back toward the middle. She was feverish and had started to retch. '*I have to get that fever down,*' he thought.

He bent and slipped his hands under her shoulders and hips. Lifting carefully, he carried her to the bathtub and settled her into it.

He stood and turned the shower on, testing the water to ensure that it was cold. He adjusted the showerhead so that the water was being sprayed over her as evenly as possible. He dropped to one knee and reaching under her put the stopper in the drain ensuring the tub would fill with the cooling water.

Le Roi stood and grabbed a washcloth from the stand next to the tub. He held it under the stream of cold water and then kneeled and leaned forward so he could pass the soaked cloth over her face, throat, and chest.

As he lifted her breast to bath her, he felt himself becoming aroused. '*No, stop that,*' he said. His voice bounced off of the walls, but Le Roi no longer was hearing. The demons of lust had overtaken him once again.

He stood outside of and above his body. He watched, with no control, as he violated the helpless woman again. He knew when the pain took her and was relieved that she was not aware of the debauchery being visited on her unconscious body.

• • •

The pain awakened her. Nausea was like a burning knot in the center of her stomach. It was growing, pushing up and spewing out if a great eruption. The falling vomit splashed across the face and chest of Le Roi, where he lay sleeping, on the floor next to the tub.

The hot contents of her stomach woke him and he instinctively ran his tongue out over his befouled lips.

The stench was sour, and the taste was acidic. He looked down and saw that he was covered in the chunky mess. He bolted to his feet, struggling not to empty his own stomach. That struggle became harder as he realized that his befouling of her mouth had been returned to him as her stomach had rejected the deposit.

Le Roi stepped into the cold water causing it to flood over the brim full tub. He bent and removed the stopper and then stood and turned the shower on full force. He stood with one leg on either side of Linda's still body as he washed the vomit from his body onto hers.

He finally stepped from the tub but left the shower splashing across her. Slowly the mess was washed off and swirled away down the drain.

Le Roi stood thinking while he toweled himself dry. *'If she doesn't die soon I am going to have to kill her. If I leave her alive, she will tell it all. I will be tagged a freak. And, the Brothers in the joint will execute me when they hear it.'*

She coughed, and Le Roi turned to the tub. She was awake. She looked at him, moving her eyes along his naked body. Then she looked at her own nakedness and realization flooded her face.

Her eyes held no fear, just a loathing indictment that struck him so violently that he took a step backward. He bent to turn the water off and then straightened up and stood silently looking down at her. He decided to move her from the tub to the bed and bent once again to lift her from the tub.

As he slipped his hands beneath her, she pulled back and said, "No, please. The pain is too great. Just leave me here. Fill the tub with cool water again please. It helps me control the nausea."

Le Roi replaced the stopper and turned the shower on. He adjusted the cooling spray and stood watching her as the tub filled. He turned the shower off and kneeled beside the tub. He stuck his hand into the water and watched how high it came up his arm as he touched the bottom of the tub.

"You are going to kill me, aren't you?" she asked.

He nodded his head slowly and said, "I have no choice."

"When, how?" Linda asked.

"I don't know yet. I have to figure some things out," he said.

Le Roi pulled a wet towel from the floor and held it so she could see it. "I am going to leave the room for a while. I have to gag you, so you don't start screaming or yelling. Sorry, but it has to be done."

He bent over, rolled her to her left side and pulled the towel around her face, forcing it into her mouth. He tied it securely behind her head. He then moved quickly to the bedroom and took the laces out of her shoes. He used one to tie her hands behind her back and the other to wrap around and tie her legs together at the ankles.

He rolled her onto her back, moved her so that she was stretched out along the bottom of the tub. He then walked to the front door of the room and looked back toward the tub. *'Perfect, you can't see her unless you walk right up to the tub,'* he sighed.

Le Roi dressed and stepped from the room. He pulled the door closed and checked to be sure it was locked. He peeked around the corner of the building and across the now dark parking lot. B.J.'s car was no longer where he had left it.

He stood staring at the parking lot as he thought about his next move. *'Mom will be asleep this time of night. If I can get into the house without waking her, I can rob her stash of rainy day money. Must be four, maybe five hundred dollars in that coffee can. That will get me to Chicago, and I can figure it out from there.'* His mind was made up. He turned and climbed the embankment and trotted off down the railroad tracks toward the projects.

•   •   •

The headlights flashed across the windshield striking Bangs and Parker in the face. The gray Ford had pulled off of Greenville into the postal service parking lot and stopped. Bangs reached down and flicked the headlight of his car on and off. The Ford turned left and pulled up alongside the detectives.

Bangs leaned forward so he could see into the car through the thickening darkness. He didn't recognize the driver or his passenger.

"Don't guess we have met. I am K.W. Bangs and this is Sergeant Bill Parker. We are assigned to CAPERS and are working the abduction of a postal worker off of the street, right out in front here.

The information we have points to a suspect who goes by the street name of *The King*. We are hoping you can help us put him down and tell us how you knew what we wanted him for."

"Hey, K.W., Sergeant. I am R.L. Kennedy, and this is B.R. Thomas. We work intelligence out of the Southeast Division. Your suspect, *The King*, is Le Roi Renau.

First, let me tell you how we know Le Roi. He is an ex-con whose last stretch was for an armed robbery of the Henderson's Chicken on South Oakland.

He had worked there for a while. He wore a mask, but they recognized his voice and the way he handled himself. The police were waiting he got home that night. He coped a plea for twenty-five, did just under eight and is on parole. Here is his picture," Kennedy said as he stretched his arm toward Bangs with the picture in hand.

Bangs turned the dome light on and held the picture so Parker could see it also. "The witnesses say that he beat this woman severely. And, judging from the amount of blood on the sidewalk, she is going to be low sick. Our gut tells us that she won't have much time," Bangs said.

Kennedy nodded his head and said, "Le Roi lives with his mother at 6400 Samoa, in the projects just down from the JBC Market on Bexar Street. Our desk sergeant got a call this afternoon from a woman who lives across the alley from King and his mom. She was hanging out wash this afternoon when he came barreling down the alley in a U.S. Mail van.

She knows he doesn't work, so she watched him. She saw him pull a woman from the back of the van and carry her into the house. Then she saw a red Ford pull up next to the van and figured that Le Roi and his friend were going to move the woman.

She left her son to watch and ran down to the market to call us. We sent a unit to the house, but by the time we got there they were gone, in fact, the house was empty."

"So then, no one knows the police was there?" Parker asked.

"Well, it is probable that some of the neighbors saw the black and white, but in that neighborhood, the odds are that no one will want to get involved. Chances are good that Le Roi and his mother will not know, at least for a while," Kennedy answered.

"Okay, so we know where he lives. But we also know that the woman has been moved. Do we run on the place on the chance he is there, and we can squeeze the information out of him?" Bangs asked.

"There is no way he will be there this early in the evening. His usual routine is to come dragging in just after sunup. He sleeps most of the day and prowls at night. If we hit the house and miss him, he will be in the wind and hard to find. But then it is your call. What do you want to do?" Kennedy asked.

"How about the red car? Do you have any information that might help us there?" Parker leaned forward and asked.

"Yes. The caller's son saw the second man who drove the mail van away. He knows the man as the 'Ring Man.' We have handled him also. His real name is Bobby Joe (B.J.) Ring.

We have him in a squeeze. Patrol caught him in a stolen shoat a while back. The trunk was full of reds and blues all packaged for a commercial deal.

He claimed he was repossessing the car for the Goss Car Lot over on Ross Avenue and didn't know the dope was in the trunk. Goss wouldn't stand behind him on it. The long and short of it was that the Ring Man was looking at riding the bitch on both charges until we stepped in. We offered him a deal, and he flipped. We have been working him like a rented mule ever since.

The caller's son saw Le Roi put your victim into B.J.'s car and drive away with her. It just stands to reason Bobby Joe will know where Le Roi was taking her," Kennedy said.

K.W., do you know where Sonny Circle is behind D.G. Clark's at Spring and Lagow?" Thomas asked.

"Yep, it runs from Lagow to Spring behind the Rosie Cliff Supper Club," Bangs replied.

"Right. B.J. is still selling a little dope here and there. Business is good at D.G.'s this time of night. He will be sitting on the bench just outside so he can catch the customers coming and going.

Let us troll through. B.J. will see us. He knows to slip off and meet us on Sonny, around behind the Club. There are no streetlights back there. There are a couple of abandoned houses that we can pull in behind and talk without being seen. If he knows where *The King* is, he will tell us." Thomas looked at his partner who was nodding in agreement.

"Okay, what do you want us to do in the meantime?" K.W. asked.

"Come south on Spring. Turn onto Swanson and cut over to Copeland. Black out and wait. When we are sure B.J. has seen us, we will pull in behind the vacant house at Four thousand and six Sonny. Give us a few minutes to be sure B.J. has the right attitude and then we will call you to join us," Kennedy said as he reached for the ignition.

"Sounds like a plan. We will be waiting," K.W. said and pulled from the parking lot and turned south on Greenville.

•   •   •

Linda heard the door close and the lock turn. She knew that her captor was gone, but she didn't know for how long. She was having trouble breathing because the towel he had used to gag her with forced her to breathe through her broken nose.

She lay still a minute thinking, '*I can't just lay here and wait for him to kill me. I have to get out of here, or make enough noise that someone will hear me and come to investigate. First, I must get my hands free,'* she thought. She tried working her hands back and forth, but every time she pulled against the restraints, her broken ribs and the crushed tailbone pulsated in pain.

She pulled and twisted trying to push through the pain until the waves of nausea told her that she was about to vomit again. She feared she would aspirate the vomit into her lungs and asphyxiate.

She stopped struggling against the bonds and lay still. She rested her swollen face against the cool porcelain of the tub and let the nausea subside. She lay still, catching her breath and to let her strength build. Soon, she drifted into a shallow sleep.

Noise at the door pulled her out of the slumber. Startled, she at first thought it was her tormentor returning. But then she heard it again, a knocking and then, "Housekeeping, may we come in."

Linda struggled to sit up. She was able only to raise her head off of the tub before the pain forced her to lie back down. She tried to yell, but the towel was forced so deeply inside her mouth that all she could do was grunt weakly. She heard voices but could not understand what was being said. They faded away, and she was alone.

Louise Johnson and Millie Beets stood together on the sidewalk just outside the room. They were silent for a minute and then the older one, Louise, said, "I tell you, Millie, something is not right."

"I know, did you see those panties on the bed?" Millie replied.

"Yes, and that uniform laying on the floor between the bed and wall," Louise said.

"Uniform, what kind of uniform?" Millie asked.

"Like postal workers wear. I smelled vomit and blood in that room. Let's go to the office. Charlene needs to call the police," Louise said.

"Let's go back in there and look around," Millie said.

"No. Evil is in that room, and we need the police to deal with it," Louise said as she hurried toward the office.

• • •

K.W. turned the cruiser off of Spring Avenue onto Swanson and let it coast slowly down to Copeland. He parked in the deep shadows provided by an ancient Oak. He switched the engine off and then turned the key to auxiliary so the radio would remain powered up. He glanced at his wristwatch and saw that it was now just past midnight.

"What are you thinking Bill, is this '*Ring Man*' going to give the *King* up?" he asked Parker.

"If they play him right. I would rather be the one squeezing him, but he's their flip, so they get the first shot at him," Parker said with a shrug.

The squelch broke on the Motorola and both officers looked at the radio, "Come on around Eleven Forty-Eight."

Parker clicked the microphone in response as K.W. started the car and drove from the shadows down Copeland and onto Sonny. Parker pointed toward a dilapidated house with peeling white paint and sagging green shudders. "There it is, Four Thousand and Six."

K.W. switched his headlights off and swung the Ford into the driveway. At the end of the drive sat a detached garage. A lone figure stepped out of the darkness to the side of the building and waved them forward.

K.W. drove off of the driveway and behind the house, parking next to the other Ford and completely out of sight from the street.

He switched the engine off as Parker stepped from the car. K.W. exited on the far side and saw Kennedy sitting on the back steps of the old house talking with a second man. Parker came around the back of the car and stood beside K.W.

"Let's give him a minute," Parker said.

K.W. nodded watching the men sitting on the back steps. He could hear the voices, but they were talking so quietly that he couldn't understand what they were saying.

Kennedy stood and approached K.W. and Bill. "He cops to seeing Le Roi and the woman. She was alive but in bad shape when he last saw her. He thinks Le Roi is going to off her. He knows where he is. But, he says Le Roi has been hanging out with the Black Panthers and to cut to the chase, he is afraid that if he gives Le Roi up and the Panthers find out, they will waste him. He wants a deal for protection before he talks."

Parker stepped forward and stood in front of B.J. "Look at me," Parker spit out.

B.J. winced as the harshness of the words hit him. He looked up as Parker leaned forward, "I am Sergeant Bill Parker of the Dallas homicide division. Listen carefully to what I have to say because I am going to say it only one time. You know about King having this woman. You know that he has injured her. You have just admitted to four police officers that you believe her life is in danger. I want you to understand that if he kills her, I will personally file on you, just as I will on him, for her murder.

Now hear this, the murder of a kidnapping victim is a capital offense. You will fry. I promise you, you will fry. Now, nod your head if you understood all that I have said."

B.J. looked toward Kennedy but slowly nodded his head. "Okay Sergeant, but how are you going to protect me from the Panthers?" B.J. Asked.

"To hell with your protection, you pitiful Scrote. I could not care less about your protection. You should have called us as soon as you got away from Le Roi this afternoon. As far as I'm concerned, you are not worth protecting. Now, where are they?"

B.J. sat back, sighed and said, "Le Roi took her to the WaySide Inn off of South Central. I went over there early tonight and found my car in the parking lot. He had left the keys on top of the left front tire, just like he said he would. I took my car and got out of there. That's all I know."

Parker turned to Kennedy and said, "Take him to our office and tell them I said to hold him as a material witness. Both of you stay with him until you hear from me. I will call your watch commander to let him know what's happening."

Bangs had started the Ford and backed it out from behind the house. Parker stepped inside and asked, "Do you know where the WaySide Inn is?"

Bangs flipped the headlights on and pushed the squad down the driveway and onto Sonny before answering, "Yes, I worked that beat in harness for a while. I'm going to light it up while you call this in. We are going to need blue suits, at least two units."

Parker picked up the microphone and turned the channel selector to three. He pressed the transmit button and spoke, "Eleven Thirty."

"Eleven Thirty," the dispatcher responded.

"Eleven Forty-Eight and I will be in route to the WaySide Inn on South Central from the Four Thousand block of Sonny. Have a patrol unit, and a sergeant meet us there on a mark out," Parker said.

"Three Sixteen meet Eleven Thirty at the WaySide Inn, Twenty Six Hundred South Central. Three Ten you will be the supervisor."

Parker keyed the mike and said, "Eleven Thirty to Three Sixteen."

"Go ahead to Three Sixteen," came the response.

"How close are you?"

"I am just turning onto Forest Avenue from South Harwood. I will be there in under five minutes."

"Roger that. We are a ways off. Go to seven for me," Parker said.

Looking at K.W., he said, "I'm going to risk putting this on the air."

Bangs said, "I agree."

Parker keyed the mike and said, "Three Sixteen."

"Go ahead Eleven Thirty," the patrol officer responded.

"We have reason to believe that the victim of an abduction we are working is being held in a room at the WaySide. The suspect is Le Roi Renau A.K.A. *The King*.

The victim was beaten severely during the abduction, and her life may be in danger. As soon as you get there, go into the office and ask if Renau has checked in or in the alternative if they have seen anything suspicious. Renau is dangerous and may be armed. Do not approach him alone if you have a choice."

"Copy that. I am three blocks away. I will get back to you," the officer responded.

*   •   •

Le Roi stepped gingerly onto the back porch. He pushed the key into the lock and turned it. The click of the old lock opening seemed to ring in his ears. Sighing, he pushed the heavy door inward and winced again as the hinges squeaked in protest.

He stepped through the doorway and into the dark kitchen. He stopped, leaned against the counter and listened. He could hear his mother's faint snoring from her bedroom just off the kitchen. She slept with her door open so that she could '*hear*' what was going on in the house at night.

Le Roi smiled to himself and removed his shoes. The floors were hardwood, and he wanted to move about as quietly as he could so as not to awaken his mom. He bent, picked the loafers up and sat them on the counter so he could grab them on the way out.

He moved to the old metal breadbox his mom kept on the counter next to the fridge. He knew the old hinges would squeak, so he lifted the lid slowly. The noise bounced off of the walls and seemed to fill the quite house. '*Dang it*' Le Roi thought.

He stood still waiting. '*Had the noise awakened his mother?*'

Her breathing changed. The snoring had stopped. Le Roi waited. She turned over in her bed and was soon snoring again.

Le Roi gingerly removed the Folgers Coffee can from the box. He lifted the plastic lid and pulled the money from the can. He smiled as he saw that his mom had rolled the cash tightly and had it held in place by a rubber band. The roll was thick, and he smiled again. '*At least five hundred,*' he thought.

Stuffing the money into his pocket, he moved from the kitchen, down the hallway and stopped by his mother's room. He pulled her door closed softly and then moved a few feet more and opened the door to his bedroom.

He stepped quietly inside and closed the door behind him. He flipped the bedside lamp on and kneeled. He reached under the bed and removed the old pasteboard suitcase. He laid it on his bed and opened it gently.

'Think. You have to travel light. Take enough to get you through a week without laundry. That will be enough. You can buy clothes once you get established in Chicago,' he mused.

He quickly filled the bag with underwear, socks, three pairs of pants and three pull over shirts. Looking around, he said softly, "That's it."

Le Roi opened the door and tiptoed down the hall to the bathroom. He gathered his razor, some shaving foam, his toothbrush, a tube of Crest and his hairbrush. It was a handful, and he considered making two trips but decided that he needed to make the best of his time.

He turned to leave the bathroom, and the throw rug slipped from under him. He stumbled, and the can of shaving foam fell, clattering down the hall.

Light spilled from under his mother's door, and he heard her getting up from the bed. "It's me, mom. I just dropped something. Sorry, go back to bed," he said hoping she would not come out of the room.

The door swung open, and there she stood, "What are you doing Le Roi?" She stepped from the room and moved toward him. "Why did you close my door and why are you sneaking around in your bare feet?" she asked.

She glanced in his room as she passed the open door and stopped. She turned back and looked at the open bag on his bed. "Le Roi. What's going on? Where are you going in the middle of the night?" she asked.

"Chicago. I'm going to Chicago mother," he said while looking at the floor.

"Are you in trouble son? What have you done to make it necessary for you to run off like this?" she asked.

"Yes, I'm in trouble. I had a squabble with a lady and hit her a couple of times. Once my parole officer finds out, I will be right back inside.

I don't want to go back to prison mom. I figure my best chance is just to run and try to start all over. Chicago first and then who knows, maybe San Francisco or L.A. I will let you know where I am when I get settled," he said.

"Running is not the answer Le Roi. You just go in there tomorrow and tell your officer what happened. He might lock you up for a day or two, but he won't send you back to prison, surely he won't. You can't run from your problems, soon as you set down, they will catch up, and there you have it. Don't run," she said.

"I don't have time to argue with you mom," Le Roi said as he hustled to his room, dumped his shaving items into the suitcase and closed it tightly.

He turned to his mother and took her in his arms. "I know I have been a disappointment to you mom. But I want to change. The police are sure to come here looking for me. Please don't tell them where I have gone, mom. Just give me this chance to start over," he asked.

He felt a sob run through her frail body. Then, she stiffened and pushed him away. "No, I will not be a party to you running from the law. I am going to call them now. Best you face up to what you have done. That is how you start over. That is the only chance you have," Ester said.

She walked out of his room and turned to hurry down the hall to the kitchen. Le Roi grabbed his suitcase and hustled after her. He stepped into the kitchen just in time to hear her say, "Operator, get me the police."

Le Roi grabbed the phone, but Ester refused to let it go. "No Le Roi," she screamed.

Rage filled him. He grabbed her by both shoulders, picked her up and slammed her back against the wall. Her head bounced off of the corner of the cabinet, and her eyes rolled back. He eased the limp body to the floor and kneeled beside her. "Mother, Mom!" he called.

Her gown had come open, and he could see that her chest was still. He leaned forward to check for a pulse and saw the blood. Le Roi stood and stepped back. "Hello, hello." He heard the operator speaking on the open line.

Grabbing the phone, he ripped it from the wall and slammed it across the room. He picked up his suitcase and stepped toward the back door. His foot slipped, and he felt the warm wetness of his mother's blood soaking through his socks.

Le Roi grimaced, grabbed his shoes and stuffed his bloodied feet into them. He glanced at the still body of his mother and ran from the door, through the back yard toward the tracks.

•　　　•　　　•

"Three sixteen to Eleven Thirty."

"Go ahead Three Sixteen."

"I am out at the WaySide. There were two women from housekeeping talking with the front office clerk when I walked in. The clerk says that she rented a room to a man that was acting strange and the housekeeping personnel state they just opened the room for service and that it is in disarray and smells of blood and vomit. They were frightened and came to the office to report what they had found. Advise what you want me to do."

"We are half a block away. Get a pass key and stand by for us."

"Ten-four, Eleven Thirty."

•　　　•　　　•

The night was quiet, and Le Roi made the trip quickly. He stood on the far side of the tracks, surveying the WaySide parking lot. There was no movement, no sound. He moved quickly across the tracks, down the embankment and to room sixteen. The door was slightly ajar. Le Roi stepped back and listened. Total silence.

'Did I not close that door all the way, or did someone open it while I was gone? Maybe I should walk down to the office and check things out,' he reasoned.

Then he realized that if Linda had been discovered, the place would be crawling with cops and emergency personnel. He stepped forward and pushed the door open. Glancing around he saw the room appeared to be exactly as he left it. He went inside and closed the door behind him.

He moved to the bathroom and saw Linda sleeping in the tub. He stepped back into the bedroom and sat his suitcase down. He sat on the bed and removed his shoes. He pulled the soggy socks off of his feet, grabbed the bedspread he had wrapped Linda in and cleaned the blood from his feet.

Linda moved, and he heard the water slosh from the tub onto the bathroom floor. He sighed deeply and thought, *'Got to do it so might as well get it done.'*

He stood and stepped across the room and into the bathroom. Linda was awake and had turned onto her back. Her eyes locked onto his. He could see that she knew it was time.

"I'm sorry. I wish there were another way. But, I just have too much to lose by leaving you alive," Le Roi said.

Le Roi kneeled beside the tub and placed both hands on her shoulders. He began to exert a gentle pressure, intending to push her head under the water and hold her there until she drowned. Rather than surrender to her death, Linda placed both feet against the end of the tub and pushed with all her might against his effort to submerge her. She flounced from side to side, splashing water from the tub, soaking the front of Le Roi's shirt and pants.

He stood and backed away. "Okay, I was trying to make it easy for you. But, you are still acting like a bitch. So, you are going to die like a bitch," he said.

He bent over at the waist and placed both of his hands on top of her head.

K.W. swung the big Ford across the median, just squeezing in front of the oncoming traffic. Horns blared as he slid to a stop next to the marked vehicle. The uniformed officer waved the key and trotted toward the end of the complex. K.W. and Parker ran along behind him.

"This is it, room sixteen," the officer said turning to the detectives. He inserted the key and turned the knob. He pushed the door open, and it bounced back as the safety chain caught.

K.W. slammed his right shoulder into the door, and the frame splintered. The door swung in, and K.W. stumbled, falling against the bed.

Parker raced past K.W. into the bathroom.

Le Roi had just pushed Linda's head under the water when the door crashed open. Instinctively, he turned toward the door. As he did, Parker hit him in the chest with both hands propelling him backward. The back of his legs struck the commode, and he fell onto it.

Linda now had her head above water and was staring at the detective sergeant with fear-laden eyes. He turned, grabbed Le Roi by the shirt and slung him from the bathroom onto the bed.

K.W. pushed his pistol into Le Roi's gaping mouth. His eyes turned to K.W. and he saw the hate pulsing from them. K.W. pulled the hammer back on the big Colt and leaned into Le Roi and whispered, "Tell me one reason I should not pull this trigger. You worthless piece of filth."

Le Roi rolled his eyes down to the pistol and that back up to K.W.'s face and sobbed a garbled plea, "Please Officer, don't hurt me."

Spittle sprayed across K.W.'s gun hand and pistol. K.W. stepped back, repulsed by the befouling. He saw a pair of socks lying on the bed and reached for one to use in wiping the slobber off of his pistol. The sock was soggy, and he dropped it back onto the bed and noticed that his hand was smeared with blood. Looking at both socks, he realized that they were soaked in blood.

"Cuff him and put him in the back of your car. Read him his rights and sit with him until we get this worked out. Call an ambulance for her," he said to the officer.

Parker turned to Linda and removed the gag from her mouth. "We are police officers. You are safe with us. Are you Linda Sweet?" he asked.

Linda nodded her head and started to speak, and then she began crying. Parker reached behind her, untied her hands and opened the drain. The water started to empty form the tub and Linda watched it go.

"We will have an ambulance here in just a minute. I am going to wait for them to move you. They will cover you, once they can assess your injuries. But for now, we will stay right here with you. You are safe," Parker said as he patted her on the shoulder.

K.W. pointed to the socks and asked Parker, "Sounds strange I know, but these look to be his socks, and they are soaked in blood. Is she bleeding?"

"No, it looks like all her bleeding has stopped," Parker said.

K.W. stepped past Parker into the bathroom, "Linda, do you know how his socks come to be soaked in blood?"

Linda lifted her head and shook it slowly side to side, "No, but he left the room for a while and had just returned. He sat on down on the bed and removed his socks, then came into the bathroom. I figured he didn't want to get them wet in all the water sloshing out on the floor. He told me he was going to kill me…" her voice dissolved into a cry.

"Okay, you are safe now. We will stay with you. No one is going to hurt you, Linda," K.W. said.

"K.W., look at this," Parker called from the bedroom.

K.W. stepped into the bedroom to see Parker lifting a suitcase from where it had been resting between the bed and wall. He placed it on the bed and opened it.

The detectives looked at each other. "He is packed and ready to run. Crazy, but it looks like whatever his reasoning, he left her here and went home to pack. Why didn't he kill her and then go home to pack?" Parker asked.

"Detectives, I wanted you to know that the S.W. Bell operator just reported a call for police with an open line. She could hear the sounds of a struggle and someone screamed, "No, Le Roi." She figured someone could be hurt. So, she called us.

The address came up as Sixty Four Hundred Samoa. The same place our units checked on earlier this evening.

The name on the phone number is Ester Renau. Le Roi's last name is Renau. We sent a unit to the house on a welfare check. They found the owner, Ester Renau dead on the floor in the kitchen. The back of her head had been smashed against a cabinet.

Also, when I shook him down, I found a roll of money in his pants pocket. There is a little over five hundred dollars. Just thought you would want to know," it was the uniformed officer.

K.W. glanced at Parker and then turned to the officer. Glancing at his nameplate, he saw, R.G. Ellis.

"Thank you, R.G. Is your sergeant here yet?" K.W. asked.

"Yes sir, he is watching Le Roi while I came to give this information to you," Ellis replied.

"Hey, don't call me sir. I work for a living, just like you," K.W. winked at the officer.

"Would you ask your sergeant if he will allow you to transport to central and book him for the abduction and Investigation of Murder related to his mother's death? We will swing by the house and then come to central to close this out," K.W. asked.

"Sure thing," Ellis said.

The officers turned to the noise of the ambulance arriving. They stepped back as the paramedics gently eased Linda out of the tub and onto a stretcher. The three of them stood silently for a minute. Each one was thinking of what could have been.

K.W. turned to Parker and said, "Feels good when it works out like this. I wish we could save them all. But, the best we can do is keep answering the call. We are their *guardians.*

CHAPTER 12
THE SUMMER MARRIAGE

Joram was hungry. He had slept late this morning, and the July sun was high in the Eastern sky by the time he was up. It was Ramadan, and he considered himself a devout Muslim. Still, he had hurried into the kitchen and grabbed a quick meal for the daily suhoar.

He hurried from the house intent on being on time for his day shift. The first hunger pains hit him at noon, and by three o'clock, the thirst was maddening.

He glanced at the clock on the wall opposite the counter and saw that it was now five o'clock. He had checked, and the sun was not due to set until seven fifteen today. It was still more than two hours until he could eat the evening iftar.

His head was aching, and he needed a cigarette badly. He opened the desk drawer and removed a bottle of aspirin and his pack of cigarettes. He pulled a Lucky Strike from the pack and laid it on the desk. Then he opened the aspirin and shook out three of the tablets. He popped them into his mouth and tried to swallow them whole. His mouth was too dry, and they hung in his throat. He gagged, and they popped out onto the desk.

Joram sighed and rose from the desk. He walked across the office to the water cooler in the corner. He ran cool water over his hands and then rubbed his face and the back of his neck. '*Ah, that feels so good,*' Joram thought.

He opened the spigot and held both cupped hands under it, filling them with the refrigerated water. Stooping, he splashed it onto his face and ran his cold hands through his thinning hair. The relief was amazing, but the dull headache was still there.

Joram stood erect and looked at his image in the mirror on the wall just above the water cooler. Rivulets of the cool liquid were streaming down from his head onto his shirt collar, and several beads of it had collected on his mustache. He moved both hands up and pushed his hair back, then brought them down the back of his head, to his neck and around to his throat using them as to squeegee the excess water away.

He looked again at his mustache and the water trapped there. The temptation was too great for a thirsty man to resist; his tongue darted out and lapped it up. Shame and guilt hit him immediately, 'Allah forgive me,' he whispered.

The ringing of the phone pulled him out of the guilt, and he hurried to answer it. "Lamp Lighter Inn," he said.

"Happy birthday my friend," was the response.

Joram smiled. Moonif was his best friend in America. They had grown up together in Aleppo and had served in the Syrian army together. They had immigrated to the U.S. together to escape the poverty and constant sectarian fighting.

"My birthday is not until tomorrow. Don't be in such a hurry to see me grow old," Joram laughed.

"Ah, but my friend. We were boys together, and now we are maturing together," Moonif said.

"Maturing, is that what you call it? Moonif, we need to face the truth, I will be forty six tomorrow and you my friend are not far behind me," Joram said.

"Forget it Joram. Being forty-six in America is not the same as being forty-six in Syria. Here, life is not so hard. We are well nourished; we have access to the best healthcare in the world and one does not have not have to worry about being shot because they are Shia or Sunni.

We will live long, and we will live well my friend. But enough of such talk, Hanin and Fatima have arranged a party for you at tonight's iftar. It is supposed to be a surprise, so don't let on that I told you. There is another surprise I have for you," Joram could hear the smile in his friend's voice.

"Really, what is it," Joram asked.

"Bassel and Duha are going to bring their daughter Fadilah. She is fourteen, about to turn fifteen and the word is that they want to marry her off," Moonif said.

"You aren't suggesting that I might be interested in this fourteen-year-old are you Moonif?" Joram laughed.

"Yes, I am. We both like them young, why not admit it. Bassel is desperate. He has nine children, all female, and is struggling to provide for them here in America. And besides that, this girl has taken up with a Hispanic boy; he is eighteen and a Christian.

This boy has a job with a pool cleaning service. He picks her up after school each day in the company van and drives her home. Duha saw them kissing yesterday, in the van, right in front of the house. You can imagine how desperate they are to break this relationship up.

You can negotiate him to a good price; he might even be open to a summer marriage," Moonif said.

"A summer marriage? The Americans do not allow that. What will they say about a man my age taking a fourteen-year-old girl?" Joram asked.

"It is our tradition. Such things need to remain in our community. The American's do not have to know," Moonif replied.

"That is so easy for you to say Moonif, but it is me that the Americans will come after if they find out. I am starving, so I will be there waiting for sunset. That will give me time to look her over and chat a little with Bassel before we eat. Then, we will see," Joram said.

"Good. I will see you there my friend," Moonif said and broke the connection.

As soon as he heard the dial tone, Moonif called Bassel. Bassel was expecting the call and answered on the second ring.

"Hello."

"I just talked with Joram, Bassel. He is leery of her being so young and what the Americans will say if they find out," Moonif said.

"And, what does that mean? Is there no chance? " Bassel asked.

"It does not mean that at all. What it does mean is that you must have a cover story ready for him, something that will allay his fears of the American police," Bassel replied.

"What cover story, I don't understand?" Bassel said.

"Tell Joram that you appreciate the delicacy of this arrangement. Say that you will tell those who ask that he is doing you a favor by employing Fadilah to work as his "house girl" and to help him with the books at work.

You will tell Joram that you will let it be known how appreciative you are that he is doing this to help you through this time of economic distress. He will like that and will see that it is a "haven" for him to park this relationship in," Moonif smiled at his ingenuity.

"And you think this will work?" Bassel asked.

"Yes I do, chiefly because Joram wants it to work. Joram has always preferred the youngest of girls. Also, let's be frank. Joram is not physically attractive. This is a win for you and him. You make sure that Fadilah is under control. Her Western ideas could kill it quickly," Moonif frowned at the thought.

"I will see to it. Thank you, my friend," Bassel said.

"Your thanks is appreciated, but remember our agreement. I am brokering this deal for you, albeit behind the scenes. You will pay me five percent of the dowry," Moonif said stiffly.

"As agreed, once I have the money you get your fee," Bassel said and hung up the phone.

●　　　●　　　●

The sun worked its' way through the partially opened drapes, bounced off of the mirror attached to the dresser and rested on his closed eyes. He was not quite asleep but had not yet surrendered to wakefulness. Fitfully, he swatted at the annoying beam of light with a meaty hand. But the probing light continued to pry and finally forced him to open his gummy eyelids.

'Damned sunlight, how many times do I have to tell Fadilah to close

those drapes completely,' was Joram's first conscious thought of the day.

He sat up on the side of the bed and lit a Lucky Strike. He inhaled, drawing the smoke deep into his lungs. The nicotine raced into his blood, and the dull ache in his head began to fade.

He stood and made his way into the bathroom. He laid the smoldering cigarette on the counter and twisted the knob as far to the left and as it would go. He wanted the water for his shave to be as hot as his flesh could tolerate.

He let the water run and placed both hands on the counter. He leaned in close to the big mirror. His hair was beginning to thin, the bags under his eyes were puffy, and the bulge around his waist was dropping into his lap when he sat. *'I am forty-six years old and look sixty,'* he sighed.

He glanced through the open door, into the bedroom and ran his eyes over the sleeping Fadilah. She was beautiful and young. He had always preferred young women, *'It is tradition,'* he shrugged.

'Only one thing I enjoy more than a hot shave in the morning, but for that, I need a willing or at least a submissive woman,' Joram was faintly conscious that he had started talking to himself.

'Talking with myself, eating by myself, doing everything with myself,' he said with a sigh. He looked again at the bed where Fadilah lay sleeping.

She was so young, so beautiful but she resisted him in subtle ways that denied him the pleasures he so desired. *'I have made a bad deal. I spent my money unwisely. She does not adhere to the agreement. She does not cook; she does not clean the house, and she has no concept of how to manage the office books.*

She and her father have played me for a fool. Bassel will have her back at the end of the summer, and I will be out seven hundred dollars. It could have ended so much better; she could have been my real wife, my only wife,' he said.

At first, after speaking with Moonif, he had been wary. But as soon as he saw Fadilah, he began to think about the possibilities. She was young, and she looked her age. Not like an older woman. Then when Bassel had shared his idea of the *'cover story'* he was hooked.

Bassel had asked for a dowry of one thousand American dollars. Joram had declined saying, "Look, let's not haggle like two old women. I will give you four hundred, and that is all. Take it or leave it Bassel."

"She is fourteen and a virgin. She will be submissive, obedient to your every wish and she will keep your house and help you with the books at work. You are getting three in one. Surely that is worth more than a mere four hundred dollars my friend," Bassel had countered.

Joram looked across the room where Fadilah stood behind her mother and the other women. He could not see her well. "Call her here to us and let us step inside the next room. I want to see her without the veil and to be better able to look at her figure," Joram had said.

"But, you will not touch her," Bassel chided.

"Of course not. But I want to see her face, and I want your assurance that she is in good health," Joram said.

Bassel had turned and beckoned Fadilah to join them. The buzz of conversation died immediately as the others recognized that an arrangement was in the making.

Fadilah walked across the room and stood before her father with her head down and her eyes directed to the floor. He took her firmly by the arm and led her into the next room. Joram followed at a respectful distance.

"Remove your veil and lift your head. Look at Joram and respond to his questions and do what he asks of you," Bassel instructed his daughter.

Fadilah lifted the veil, letting it rest on top of her head. She turned to face Joram, lifting her head and meeting his eyes. Her heart sank. Standing before her was a man who was overweight, had bags under his eyes and who was going bald. Her flesh crawled at the thought of him touching her. *'Why didn't I listen to Javier, we could be together in his father's house in Mexico,'* she whispered to herself.

Joram looked at her hair, at her face and then let his eyes rest on her breasts and then on down. "Turn around slowly," his voice was thick with lust.

She closed her eyes and turned as he said. She could hear his rapid breathing and knew that he was undressing her in his mind. She completed the turn and lowered her head once more to look at the floor.

"Are you a virgin?" he rasped.

Fadilah gasped and looked sideways at her father. She saw his shoulder twitch and turned away just in time to avoid the open handed slap striking her in the mouth. Instead, it landed a glancing blow on her cheek sending her reeling backward a step.

"Answer him you insolent girl," he barked.

She looked at Joram and nodded saying, "Yes. I am a virgin."

"But you have kissed this boy that brings you home from school. Have you kissed others also?" Joram asked.

"No, only him."

"Did you allow him to touch you inappropriately?"

"No, just the kiss," she said in what she hoped was a convincing tone.

"Hmmm. And you know that this arrangement will include the housekeeping and the office work as well as you meeting my masculine needs?" Joram wanted to be sure he was not going to have trouble getting what he was paying for.

"Yes. My father has told me, and I will obey his wishes, and yours," Fadilah knew that she had no choice.

Joram turned to Bassel and said, "You asked a thousand, and I offered four hundred. We are six hundred apart. I will come up three, and you come down three. We agree at seven hundred from now until the end of the year, and then I have the option of ending the 'summer marriage' or taking her permanently."

"Do you want to settle on what the fee will be if you choose to keep her?" Bassel asked.

"No, not now. For now, my offer is seven hundred until the end of the summer. That is all I will do," Joram said with finality.

"Agreed," Bassel offered his hand.

Joram shook his hand and said, "Bring her to my house tonight after the iftar. I will pay you then."

The steam rising from the sink caught his eye, and he turned the knob to slow the flow. He ran the cloth through the water for a few seconds and then placed it over his face and allowed the steaming heat to soften his bristly beard.

Holding his shaving mug under the tap, he captured just enough water to form a rich lather. A smile tugged at his lips as he remembered his father saying to him, "Joram, a man should leave some beard, in deference to the Prophet, but the rest should be removed by sharp steel running through hot lather."

He moved the brush carefully over his face, leaving the beard over his top lip and on his chin, free of lather. He rinsed the brush carefully, shook it over the sink to lessen the saturation and laid it on the counter to drain. Then he opened the razor and held it under the steaming water, heating the blade as evenly as possible. Shaking the excess water from the blade, he pulled it through the lather. He could hear the steel harvesting the beard, but the blade was so sharp that there was no resistance, no notice of its' passage through the coarse stubble.

Lifting his chin, he pulled the sagging skin to make it taught and then ran the razor down and across the soft skin of his throat. *'My life's blood is just beneath this blade. One slip and it would splash against the mirror, and Joram Amine would be no more. Ah, but as my family name means trustworthy, so I find this aged steel. It served my father, and now it serves me,'* he mused.

He rinsed the lather from the blade, wiped it dry and folded it carefully for storage until its' next call to duty.

Fadilah had been awakened by the sound of the gushing water. She lay on her back, listening to Joram mumbling. She wondered if he was aware that he talked to himself.

She knew he had fallen in love with her. She used this to get anything she wanted. But she shuddered at the thought of another day with him. *'Was the money worth living with such a disgusting man?'*

He had been amorous last night, as he was most nights, and she had to push him away. His pawing made her nauseous. She could barely tolerate a perfunctory peck on the cheek. She always found herself thinking of the times in the back of the van with Javier.

She flushed as her blood surged at the thought of Javier. She had called him the first day of her *'summer arrangement'* with Joram. He serviced a pool, three streets over on Wednesdays. He would call to be sure it was safe and then come to the house. Theirs was what the soap operas termed a *'torrid affair.'*

She knew that like Joram, Javier was in love with her. He was growing more and more possessive, more demanding. He was again pleading with her to run away to Mexico and live with him. But, to her, he was just her *'man toy.'* He had no money, no education, and no prospects. Besides, Fadilah intended to stay in the U.S.

Joram had started coming home for lunch on Wednesdays. She suspected a nosy neighbor had told him that there had been a pool service van parked in front of his house on Wednesdays. He had asked her about it, and she had lied, telling him she had no idea and suggesting that he call the service and ask.

She could tell that he was still suspicious. *'Maybe I should show him some attention this morning, that would keep him happy for a while, and give me time to figure out how to handle this growing storm'*. She turned onto her side to look at Joram and consider if she could tolerate him.

A rustling of the bed caused him to turn for another glance at Fadilah. She had turned onto her side and now lay facing him. Her eyes were open, and he could see that she was studying him, his physical appearance. She frowned and said, "You have to lose some weight Joram. You have become a fat, old man."

The blood rushed to his face, and he whirled to face her. "Why do you speak to me in such a manner. It is bad enough here, in the privacy of our bedchamber, but you insulted me with your critical slurs last night in front of our friends. Let me think, yes, you said, *'Joram is showing his age more every day, the bags under his eyes look like pus filled pockets, his belly is bulging so that his shirt will not button properly and he smells like a nursing home patient.'*

At home, in Syria, such actions would require that I beat you. You need to think, Fadilah. It would be wise for you to walk more circumspectly. Even in America, I am still Muslim man, a follower of the Prophet and there are limits to how much latitude I can give you, as a concubine and as a woman," Joram said.

She laid still, her breathing slowed and her eyes filled with anger. Joram watched and said to himself, *'I have spoiled her. She is in full rebellion. I must quell this now.'*

Reaching down, he loosed the string around his waist and let his pajama bottoms fall to the floor. They pooled around his feet, and he kicked them aside.

"Arise and disrobe. I will take my pleasures this morning. It has been too long, and I will no longer tolerate your *'right to say no'*. You do not have the right to deny me," Joram was determined.

"I am impure," she said.

"No, you're not. For me to believe that I would have to believe that you menstruate daily. Now disrobe, or I will take you by force," he said as he stepped from the bathroom into the bedroom.

Fadilah was frightened by his approach. She did not want him to touch her. But, she knew that she could not hold him off. She had to escape. She leaped from the bed and turned toward the open bedroom door.

Joram saw her eyes dart toward the door. He had anticipated her trying to escape him. *'No, you will not escape me. I will have you,'* the blood was pounding in his head.

Fadilah saw that he had cut off her escape and knew that she was trapped. She remembered the pistol he had given her for protection when he worked late hours. It was a Berretta Thirty-Two Caliber Tom Cat, and she kept it in the drawer beside the bed.

As Joram flipped the lock on the door, he heard the drawer of the bedside table being pulled open, *'The pistol, that damned pistol,'* he thought.

Two quick steps brought him behind her. He raised his right hand, clenched it into a fist and leaned in, using the momentum of his forward motion to add force as he clubbed her above and just behind her right ear. She slumped to her left and half turned toward him. He saw the pistol in her right hand.

Fadilah tried to raise the hand holding the pistol, but her arm was too heavy, and the darkness was closing in. *'He is going to rape me,'* she heard in her head and then he was wrenching the pistol from her hand.

She was conscious of him picking her up and dropping her in the middle of the bed. He ripped her pajamas, and she felt the rush of cold air as it bathed her exposed flesh.

She tried to concentrate on the cold air, as he raped her. Tears ran from the corner of her eyes, but they were not tears of pain or pity. They were tears of anger and hatred. *'You have had your way with me Joram, but it will be a costly victory. I swear by the prophet, you will forfeit your life for this,'* she whispered.

Joram stood over her, "Today is a new beginning. Now you understand that I am a man. You are a woman, nothing else. You will submit to me. You will serve me. You will cover your flesh when you go out, and you will no longer speak with Javier. Now, rise from the bed and clean yourself."

Fadilah heard his voice. She knew that she was still at risk, so she nodded her head and turned to bury her head in the pillow. A sob escaped.

'She dares turn her back to me,' Joram was enraged. He reached forward and grabbed her hair with his left hand. He yanked her head up off of the pillow. Holding the pistol in his right hand, he slapped Fadilah hard across the face with it. "Do not turn your back on me you whore," he shouted.

Pain rolled over Fadilah as the flesh of her right eyebrow parted beneath the cold steel of the pistol. She felt the warm blood flowing down her face and fought the nausea building in the pit of her stomach.

"Answer me, say yes husband I understand and I wish to please you," Joram shouted.

'I must survive,' she thought. Fadilah rolled onto her back facing Joram and said, "Yes my husband. I wish to please you, and I will do as you say."

Joram stood looking down at the bleeding woman and felt the rush of power, *'Today she knows I am a man. I will use her until she pleases me no more. Then I will find me another.'*

"I will be home at the regular time tonight for dinner. Then I will sleep. The late night clerk is on vacation this week. I will work the desk from eleven tonight until eight, tomorrow morning. That will be my schedule all week. Make your plans accordingly. Do you understand?" he said in a soft voice.

Fadilah sat up on the side of the bed, looked at him and said, "Yes my husband. I understand and will make plans to meet your schedule and to please you."

Joram walked from the room once again talking to himself, "*I have set my house in order today.*"

He realized he still had the pistol in his hand and thought, *'I will keep this with me while I work the late shift this week. Better have it and not need it than to need it and not have it.'* He walked from the house whistling.

Fadilah sat still listening to the garage door close. Once she was sure Joram had left the house, she moved to the bathroom and looked at her broken face in the mirror. The gash was ugly, but not as deep as she had feared. No stitches, just a band-aid and some makeup to cover the bruising. But first, she needed to be cleansed of his presence.

She stepped to the shower and turned it on full force. She waited until the steam wafted out over the glass door, then stepped in under the soothing stream. She wanted to cry but could not.

Fadilah turned this way and that, lifting and probing with the soap to remove as much of him as she could. Then she stepped from the shower and turned the water on in the jetted tub.

Easing herself into the steaming water, she stretched full length and pushed the buttons activating the pumps. The pulsing jets of water soothed her violated flesh, and she felt the tension leaving.

She lay there thinking, *'He will take me again tonight and every night until I can find a way to be free of him. I want him dead. But how do I accomplish this without being held accountable? Javier? Yes, Javier will do whatever I ask. This will take some time. I have to think.'*

Stepping from the tub, Fadilah wrapped a towel around her and moved to the mirror. She flipped on the recessed lighting and leaned in to see better the wound left by Joram's conquest.

The swelling was not as bad as she had feared; still, it needed ice. She moved to the kitchen and rummaged around in the pantry until she found a plastic zip bag large enough to cover the wound from brow to cheek. She filled it with crushed ice and walked to the office where Lawrence kept all the important records, both personal and business. She held the bag of ice to her cheek and sat in the big swivel chair.

She pulled on the middle drawer and found it to be locked. '*Figures*,' she thought. Quickly, she rose from the chair and hurried into her closet.

She slipped the towel off and pulled on a running suit. She then found a scarf and carried it to the mirrors. She held the ice bag in place and wrapped the scarf around her head and over her right eye. With the bag secured over the wound, she returned to the office and sat at the desk again.

On top of the desk was a circular pencil holder. Sticking from it was a letter opener. '*I can use that to jimmy the lock and open this desk,*' she thought. She was so short that she could not reach across the desk for the holder.

She stood and placed one hand on the desk to support her as she leaned forward. The desk protector slid across the polished oak surface and there laid the key. Smiling, she picked it up and unlocked the desk.

She pulled the big drawer open and saw all the folders she needed. They were arranged neatly in alphabetical order. She smiled and whispered, '*thank you Joram, for making this so easy for me.*'

She chose the folder marked banking, the one for the house, the one for the business and then one marked life insurance. Spreading them out on the desk, she thumbed through collecting the information she wanted.

An hour later, she sat back and looked at her notes, '*The business is debt free; the house is paid off, and his life insurance is paid up. There are some advantages to being with an old man,*' she smiled to herself. '*But, I am not legally married to him. So what, if any claims do I have on his estate.*'

The insurance policy she found listed Ahmad Amine as beneficiary. He was also listed in the *'pay on proof of death'* section of the checking account, and the savings accounts. Ahmad had an address in Aleppo Syria.

'Ahmad is his brother. Hmmm, all of these are dated before the 'summer marriage' arrangement between my father and Joram. I might be able to contest this and exert a claim, but that will be risky and attract attention. The best thing to do is grab some cash using the American Express advance, take some money from the accounts just before Javier kills him and then run by the bank again as soon as it opens the next morning,' she jotted down her thoughts, realizing she had already made the decision to have Javier kill Joram. The best time would be while he was working the deep night shift this week.

She turned to the credenza and picked up the yellow pages. She flipped to the Attorney's section and found the listing, "The Baraka Firm." Joram had selected this law firm because the owners were Syrian immigrants. They represented him in all of his personal and business affairs.

Joram had taken her with him once when he went in to tell them that she would be working with the business finances and should be granted access to all of the information she needed for such purposes.

She smiled when remembering Azark, the owner's son. He was twenty-four, just out of Law School and working to assume control of the firm one day.

He was tall and had sharply defined features. His interest in her was obvious. That is until he found out that she had just turned fifteen. *'I will call him and ask him to come by the house for a 'business consultation. He may not be so concerned about my age if he can be assured no one will know. If he agrees to come, he just might be pliable enough to help me through this,'* she thought with a smile.

But first, I have to call Javier.

Fadilah picked up the phone and dialed the number she had for Javier. She wanted him to see her before she put makeup on.

•   •   •

Javier drove slowly past the motel. He leaned forward, looking toward the front window to see if Joram was in the office. But it sat back from the street and the angle made it impossible to see in.

Javier made a U-turn and pulled up next to the curb facing the oncoming traffic. There was not much traffic this time of the morning, and he was able to sit long enough to see movement inside the office and then to identify Joram.

He pulled away from the curb, drove down a block, and made another U-Turn. '*I need a place to park the van. Some place where I will not be seen leaving,*' he thought.

The car in front of him slowed, and the right turn signal came on. '*They are going into the parking lot of those apartments. I will follow them in and park the van,*' he thought.

He sat in the van looking around. The spot he had selected was dark and close to the gate. '*I will have to wait for a resident with a pass card to get into and out of the lot. That will slow me down. But, if I work this right, it won't matter.*'

He pulled the pistol from his waistband and opened the cylinder. He ran his fingertips over the six brass loads. He closed the pistol, pulled the hammer back and then eased it forward. The weapon was heavy, and its' weight gave him comfort. '*Six rounds from this Three Fifty-Seven Magnum will take him out. Two rounds in the face, one in each eye,*' Fadilah had said.

Javier looked back at the suitcase behind the passenger's seat. He was going to ditch the van, pick up his uncle's car and drive straight through to El Paso.

Fadilah had given him cash for expenses. She would join him in El Paso as soon as she could, and they would start their life together. The money she would take from the bank would be a good nest egg for them, and if she were able to get the money from Joram's life insurance, they would be wealthy.

Javier picked up the pistol and stepped from the van. He walked to the gate and stood in the shadows waiting for the next car to come through. His wait was short. He let the car get through and then stepped from the darkness and through the gate just before it closed.

He covered the distance to the motel quickly. He hesitated a moment at the entrance to the parking lot and seeing no one outside the rooms, stepped toward the office. The door was propped open, but a buzzer sounded as he stepped through and into the office. "Be right with you," a man's voice came from the back room.

Javier stepped up close to the chest high counter and removed the pistol from his pants. He cocked it and held it beside his right leg.

Joram came around the corner, wiping his hands on a towel. "Yes, how can I help you?" he said.

Javier said nothing, just stood and looked at this man who he was about to kill. "Sir?" Joram said again and began to back away from the counter.

Javier knew that Joram was suspicious, but somehow he could not stop staring at him. He looked at his face, concentrating on his eyes. '*Shoot him in the face, once in each eye,*' Fadilah's words echoed in his mind.

"You raped Fadilah, and I am going to kill you for it," he said lifting the pistol. "But first I want you to know that after I kill you, we are going to be married and we are going to use your money to establish our life together."

Joram listened to Javier, and then he laughed, "So you are Javier, her pool cleaner. You fool. Do you think that she loves you? She is a whore, one who uses men. I didn't rape her, how would it be possible to rape her when I have bought and paid for her services?"

"You forced yourself on her! That is rape. You raped her, and now I will kill you for it," Javier yelled. He heard a woman laugh and looked to his left. Out of the corner of his eye, he saw Joram move to the desk behind him.

Javier turned back and saw Joram raising a small automatic pistol, bringing it to bear on him.

Javier had the revolver centered on Joram and pulled the trigger. The explosion filled the room, bouncing off the walls and filling Javier's head with a roar.

The shock of the recoil of the magnum was more than Javier had expected. The pistol bounced up, causing the barrel to point at the ceiling. Javier watched as the impact of his bullet rocked Joram back.

He saw the surprise and pain race across Joram's face. Then he saw the flame leap out of the little pistol Joram was holding. It reached for him, and Javier heard the passage of the bullet.

Then, the little pistol winked again, and he was falling backward. A hot rod pushed into and through his chest. His knees buckled, and he dropped behind the counter.

'*Breathe, I have to breathe,*' Javier gasped. He rolled onto his all fours and crawled along behind the protective cover of the counter.

He reached the end and peeked around. Joram was on his knees. The pistol lay on the floor in front of him. His belly was open, and Joram was desperately trying to push a wad of gray tissue back inside his body. Blood was pouring from him, washing through his fingers and pooling on the concrete.

Javier no longer hated this man, but he had come to kill. He stood and stepped around the counter. Joram lifted his head and looked at his killer.

Javier stood over Joram. He raised the pistol, placed the barrel just inches from Joram's left eye. Javier pulled the trigger and Joram's blood, bone and flesh bounced off of the concrete block wall. Javier saw life leave and pointed the pistol at the right eye. He pulled the trigger, and the angle of the shot took the right side of Joram's face and skull off.

Joram's body bounced off of the wall and then fell forward with his forehead on the floor. He aimed the pistol at the middle of Joram's back and fired the final three shots. The last round severed Joram's spine causing the body to collapse in the middle.

His chest was burning. Javier looked down and saw that his shirt was covered in blood. He watched as big drops of blood fell from his now soaked shirt, across his shoe top, and onto the floor. He turned and ran from the office, stumbling as the loss of blood weakened him.

He stopped and leaned against a light pole. He thought he heard voices, '*did someone see me?*' he wondered.

Javier was weak from the loss of blood, and the pain was causing him to retch. *'Have to get to the van, find a doctor.'*

He stumbled on and finally made it to the gate. A car was just driving through, and he was able to stagger in before the gate closed. He stood leaning against the van, collecting his strength to climb up, and in.

Settled in the seat, he checked the wound again. The blood was still flowing freely. He reached into the glove box and found a shop towel. It was muddy, but he pressed against the hole in his chest. *'Here comes a car, have to get out before the gate closes.'*

He started the van and raced through the gate as soon as the car entering had cleared. The quick exit and his lack of strength caused him to lose control of the van.

He swerved across the centerline and jerked the wheel back. The over correction was too much, and he bounced off the curb. He regained control and drove North on Greenville to Mockingbird. He turned left on Mockingbird and then South onto U.S. Seventy-Five.

'Where did I leave Uncle Julio's car? Can't remember, have to get to his house,' Javier mumbled.

CHAPTER 13
LAMPLIGHTER INN

K.W. grimaced as the squelch broke on the Motorola. The speaker opened, and he heard, "Eleven Forty-Eight".

He glanced at his wristwatch, ' *I would have been off in another ten minutes,*' he sighed as he reached for the microphone.

"Eleven-Forty Eight," he answered.

"Eleven Forty-Eight, take the signal Twenty-Seven at the Lamp Lighter Motel, Nineteen-Nineteen Greenville Avenue. Uniformed officers on the scene have ordered crime scene and the medical examiner. Early reports indicate the victim has multiple gunshot wounds."

"Eleven Forty-Eight, I'm working robberies, kidnappings, and extortions. This sounds like a homicide," K.W. knew it was hopeless but said it anyway.

"Stand by one Eleven Forty-Eight," the dispatcher responded.

"Eleven Forty-Eight, call Sgt. Little on extension five fifty-one from the scene."

"Ten-Four," K.W. said knowing he was about to get his tail feathers trimmed.

He replaced the mike and took the Mockingbird exit, crossed over Central Expressway and turned south onto Greenville. It was a Tuesday night, so the traffic was no problem. The garish neon of lower Greenville was visible just ahead as he moved along the avenue. He could see the Lamp Lighter Motel just ahead.

As he drove into the parking lot, he glanced down the row of dingy rooms. *'Looks like any of the other short stay, no-tell motels on the avenue,'* he thought.

He switched off the engine and stepped from the Ford. A uniformed officer was standing outside the office door, and he could see the crime scene crew had beaten him there.

As he approached the office door, he noticed that the young officer was fidgeting and unsure what he was supposed to do. *'A rookie,'* K.W. smiled and showed the youngster his badge and identification card.

The smell of blood and burned gunpowder greeted him as he stepped through the door. He glanced to his left and saw the body of a man. He was on his knees and had slumped forward until his forehead rested on the floor in front of his knees.

K.W. stopped and stood still, soaking up the smells and allowing the lingering violence to settle around him.

He had found that becoming a part of the scene, being one with the environment, aided him in understanding what had happened, how it had gone down and where to start tracking those who had survived to leave the violence. They always left a trail, both in physical evidence and in the metaphysical. To connect with the metaphysics of the scene was paramount and the connection could not be made until he was one with the event.

K.W. looked at the floor before him and saw dark splotches, smears really, on the concrete just in front of the counter. He played the light from his flashlight over the area and saw that the smears were right against the bottom edge of the counter. He squatted next to the area and leaned as close as he could without contaminating any evidence. *'Brown, those splotches look to be dark brown,'* he thought.

Moving the beam of his flashlight along the bottom edge of the counter K.W. saw what appeared to be handprints on the polished concrete. *'Look at that; someone was on their knees here. Those brown marks back there are shoe polish off of the toes of this person's shoes. These smudges here are their handprints. It looks like they were leaning against the counter, almost like they were using it for shelter,'* he mused.

He ran the light along the counter, working his way from the floor all the way to that point where the top surface overhung the front panel. He saw dark red specks and then just under the lip of the overhang was something else. *'Blood splatters here and that is a piece of flesh that was torn from a body and flung against the counter where it stuck,'* he reasoned.

K.W. rocked back on his heels and rested a minute. He could see and feel what had happened here. *'A shooter stood here. He was in a gun battle with another. He was struck and dropped below the counter for cover. But there is more. I can feel it.'*

He heard a sound behind him and turned to see a crime scene tech staring at him. K.W. smiled and said, "Hi, I'm K.W. Bangs. I caught this one. What do you have so far?"

The tech nodded a hello and said, "I'm Steve Overn. I don't have anything yet. I'm by myself and a scene this big is going to take a while to process."

"I understand. Tell me what you have cleared so I can know where it is safe to move around," K.W. said.

Overn shrugged and said, "I haven't cleared anything. I have taken pictures of the whole scene, but that's it."

K.W. nodded and said, "Dispatch told me the uniforms were still here. Have you seen anyone besides the rookie at the front door?"

"Yes, the senior officer is talking with a couple who saw the shooter. There they are, standing beside the green Caddy," he said with a nod of his head.

K.W. followed the nod and saw a uniformed officer talking with a man and woman sitting inside a Green Cadillac. "I'm going to join them but first, notice here in front of the counter there is what appears to be smudges of shoe polish, and here it looks like there are two palm prints on the floor. Now look, these appear to be specs of blood, and here, this looks like a piece of flesh.

Bet you the shooter stood here firing at the dead man. His target returned fire, and this man was hit. The impact blew the blood and flesh onto the paneling, and he dropped to the floor for cover. I want you to photograph all of this, scrape that shoe polish and preserve it. Then lift that flesh and blood for lab analysis.

Also, it stands to reason that if shots were being fired from behind the counter, there might well be some in the wall across from us here. Look it over closely," K.W. said as he ran the beam of his light up and along the top of that wall.

"See, there is a hole, right there at the top of the wall. That is a bullet hole. The bullet is probably from the victim's firearm, but I want it," he said as he strode from the office toward the green Caddy.

He had taken about three steps from the office when he heard the phone ring. He turned back and saw Overn moving toward the switchboard. "No, don't answer it," K.W. said as he raced back inside and around the counter.

He smiled at the startled Crime Scene technician and said, "Let me get it."

He picked up the handset and flipped the toggle switch under the flashing light marked incoming. "Lamp Lighter Motel, how may I help you?" he said.

"Who is this? Where is Joram? Why didn't he answer, is he okay?" a female voice asked.

"This is K.W. Bangs. I am a police officer for the City of Dallas. Whom am I speaking with?" he asked.

"Police Officer? What's wrong, why are you answering the phone?" the caller was insistent but strangely calm.

"Whom am I speaking with?" K.W. asked again.

"My name is Fadilah. I live with Joram. He owns the Lamp Lighter. Now tell me what is going on," the tone of voice was becoming more demanding.

"Ms. Fadilah, we are at the Lamp Lighter to investigate a shooting. There is a deceased man here, but we have not identified him yet. There is no one here that we have been able to contact who identifies himself as the owner or as Joram. It would probably be helpful if you would come to the motel," K.W. said.

"No, I'm not coming down there. Did he shoot Joram in the face? Never mind, call me at 214-959-0011 once you establish if the dead man is Joram," she said and broke the connection.

K. W. laid the handset down and opened his notebook to record the time of the call and as near as possible the exact words of the wife. *'Received a call from a woman identifying herself as Fadilah. She said she lives with the owner of the motel, a man she called Joram. When I told her we were there to investigate a shooting, she asked 'did he shoot Joram in the face.' She refused to come to the scene. Seemed very calm.'*

"Hey, K.W." a voice interrupted his thoughts.

K.W. turned to the voice and saw Robert Bridges. "Hey Robert, man it has been a long time," he said as he stood and extended his hand.

"Guess you caught this one and my dispatcher just told me to have you call Sergeant Little on five fifty-one," Bridges said.

"Ugh, that's not going to be good but guess I might as well get it over with," K.W. said as he picked up the phone and dialed his office.

"Crimes Against Persons, Sergeant Little," came the voice over the phone.

"Sergeant, this is K.W.," he said.

"What the hell was that on the radio? I work robberies and not homicides. Look at that badge and tell me if it says Dallas Police. Then if it does, tell me what part of being police don't you understand. Listen to me K.W., you take calls just like anyone else. You understand me?" Little was furious.

"I got it, sergeant. I'm on the scene and working it. Put it on the log as mine, and I will work it to the end," he said.

"Damned right, you will. Don't ever let me hear you say anything like that, especially on the air. Richard McKenzie from the Dallas Times Herald has already been in here wanting to know why we don't have a deep night homicide crew on the street. Do we understand each other or should I leave a note for Bill Senkel?" Little asked.

"No, no. Please don't leave a note for my sergeant. I will get this done," K.W. said.

The line went silent, for a minute and then Little said, "Okay, and I just took a call from the St. Louis Missouri Police Department. They have a lead on that skull case you caught a while back.

Seems a pawnshop owner called their crime stoppers and turned in a guy who brought him a World Series Ring that he had taken in a burglary. When they got to talking with him, he gave the guy up on a Rolex that he had pawned earlier. That Rolex was the one you had put on the NCIC. It belongs to a guy named Spurgeon. It was his skull the dog drug up out of the woods.

I left you a note with all the information. You can pick it up when you come in. Call them tomorrow. Got it?"

"Yes sir. I got it sergeant," K.W. said and hung up.

K.W. looked at Bridges and said, "Whew, finest chewing out I've had in a while. But the good news is that we just got a call that may clear another murder case I have.

Strange the way these things work out. A rich man's skull, his Rolex watch but the break came on a World Series Ring. Go figure."

Bridges nodded and said, "Funny, but on this one, I have two witnesses who may have something for you. They had met here for a little *no tell motel time*. They were reluctant to give their names, but I made them give me their driver's license and have all their identifying information written down.

Here's what they say. They had just left their room and were walking to their car when they heard loud voices coming from the office. They saw a young Hispanic male standing at the counter shouting at the clerk, who was behind the counter. They both say the man's voice was heavily accented, but they believe he said to the clerk, '*You raped her, and I am going to kill you for it.*'

They said that the clerk behind the counter said something in reply, they could hear him, but they could not distinguish what he was saying. They said that the men started shooting at each other.

The Hispanic man fired the first shot, and they saw the clerk fall backward and then lurch forward. As he came forward, they saw that he lifted a pistol and started firing at the Hispanic male.

The woman witness ducked down behind their car, but the man said he could still see what was happening. He said the Hispanic male was hit, but leaned over the counter and fired several more shots at the clerk who appeared to be on the floor.

Then he saw flashes from behind the counter and saw the

Hispanic male stagger back, grasp his lower chest and fall to the floor. He watched as the wounded man crawled on his knees along the counter, then around behind it. He saw him stand over what he assumes was the clerk on the floor and fire several more shots. He says the man then ran from the office and down Greenville towards Oram.

He and the woman used the pay phone there at the front of the property to call us. They say that while they were on the phone with our operator, they saw a van swerve across the center lane into oncoming traffic and then bounce off of the curb as the driver overcorrected, attempting to regain control. They both say the driver of that van was the Hispanic male. The van was marked '*Aztec Pools.*'" Bridges closed his pad and looked at K.W.

"Great job Robert. The motive seems clear, but you can bet that we are seeing only the tip of this iceberg. Now, let's look for a blood trail. We know he was hit and we have a direction of travel for him," K.W. said as he flipped his flashlight on and moved the beam around the area in front of the office.

Bridges had moved to the entrance of the parking lot as K.W. worked the area around the office. "Here it is K.W.," he called.

K.W. moved toward Bridges, keeping his light on the pavement in front of him. He did not see any blood. "Where is it Robert?" he called.

"Not on the ground, look here on this light pole. See the blood smear. Bet he was holding his hand over that chest wound. Running along here he either slipped or staggered, either way, he reached out with his bloody hand to steady himself and left this smear," Bridges was shining his flashlight at the light pole.

There in the middle of the beam, K.W. saw it. He could tell the wounded man was bleeding heavily. There was a glob of blood and then smears wrapping around the pole. '*Looks like his palm was filled with blood and that it had run down onto his fingers. He leaned against this post with enough force to cause the blood to be pressed into a full pattern, almost like he was being printed. This man is hurt badly. He was staggering and trying to keep himself from going down,*' K.W. mumbled to himself.

"He's bleeding out Robert," K.W. said.

"I think you are right. Here is more blood just off the sidewalk in the grass. K.W. these aren't drops, this man is streaming blood," Bridges was squatted beside a ribbon of blood still wet on the grass.

The officers moved on down the sidewalk, found where the man had left the walk, and entered the parking lot of the Vue Greenville Apartments. The apartments were gated, and the closed gate stopped their progress.

K.W. shined his light through the gate and saw what was now a trail of blood. "Look at that R.W. He is bleeding heavier now. See, it leads right in beside that red Volkswagen convertible. That's where he was parked.

He must have tailgated someone into the parking lot. And look right over there. That's a code box on that little post there. You have to swipe a card or enter a code to get the gate to open. That means he had to wait for someone to exit so he could get out.

Think about that now. We have at least two more witnesses, the one he tailgated in and the one he followed out. We just have to find them.

Here's another thing, he was still bleeding while he sat waiting. A man bleeding that heavily may well have bled out by now.

I will stay here while you go back to your car and put out what we have on the Aztec Pool Van and his description including the wounds. Have the patrol officers in this area start circling looking for the van.

Next, ask the dispatcher to check the call lists to see if we have any hospitals, clinics, and the like reporting gunshot victims.

And finally, I think this is going to be too big a scene for our man Overn. Would you ask the dispatcher to call the Southwestern Institute of Forensic Sciences and have them send a full crime scene crew out here? Tell them to put on it on this service number with my name for authorization," K.W. said.

Bridges was already moving back toward the Lamp Lighter. "Got it K.W. I'm also going to see if we have an officer working security here at these apartments for rent deal. If we do, I will have the dispatcher call him and send him to meet you at the gate."

'Why didn't I think of that,' K.W. asked himself.

K.W. was pacing back and forth processing all he had learned when the gate began to open. He stood aside as a car turned from off of Greenville into the parking lot.

He saw a young woman in the car and could tell that his presence startled her. She quickly rolled up her window and sped past him to the back of the lot.

K.W. stepped through the gate and moved toward the Beetle Convertible. As he stepped around into the vacant parking space, he saw a pool of dark, blackish red, blood that was just beginning to congeal.

He squatted beside the blood and shined his flashlight in ever-larger sweeps around the pool and across the parking slot. *'No way this man is still alive unless he got to a hospital within five minutes of leaving this lot,'* he thought to himself.'

"Hey, you. What are you doing? Stand up and keep your hands where I can see them," a voice came out of the dark.

K.W. stood, taking his time and moving slowly. Looking for the voice, he could just make out a darker form in the darkness at the corner of the first building. "I am a Dallas Police Officer, working a crime scene," he called in the direction of the dark spot.

"Okay, I too am a Dallas Police Officer. I am in uniform and will step from the corner of the building toward you. I have my weapon in my hand. Do not make any sudden moves until I am closer to you and then I will need to see some identification," the voice said.

K.W. stood still and silent. The form approached and then there he was. The dark blue uniform had help conceal the officer, but now K.W. could see the silver badge on his chest and the patch on his left shoulder.

"I'm K.W. Bangs out of CAPERS. There has been a killing down the street at the Lamp Lighter. Witnesses say the shooter was hit in an exchange of gunfire with his victim. I have followed the blood trail to here," K.W. said pointing his flashlight down and illuminating the pool of blood.

"I'm T.C. Danby. I work this beat and live here at the apartments. I work security for a break on my rent. One of the residents just called me saying there was a man acting strangely at the front gate. So here I am. No offense, but I do need to see that badge and identification card," Danby said.

K.W. nodded and said, "It is in the pocket on the left side of my coat. I'm going to reach inside my jacket to get it, but it sure would make me feel more comfortable if you would lower that pistol just a bit."

Danby lowered his pistol, so it was no longer centered on K.W. and accepted the badge and identification card with his left hand. He merely glanced at the badge but paid close attention to the card and the picture on it. "Shine your light on your face," he said to K.W.

K.W. lifted the light so his features were clearly visible and Danby compared them with those on the card. "Thanks, K.W. Sorry for the hassle," he said holstering his pistol.

"Not at all. Like the fact that you didn't concentrate on the badge, they are a dime a dozen. It is the card that makes the case," K.W. said.

Bridges stepped through the still open gate and called out, "Are you, Danby?"

"Yep. I just met K.W. I guess you are working the shooting at the Lamp Lighter," Danby replied.

"Yes, I'm R.W. Bridges. Dispatch just gave me your name. I asked them to have you meet us here at the gate. They are probably calling your number right now," Bridges said.

"The machine will catch it. Tell me how I can help you guys," Danby said.

"The suspect in this killing was driving a van with Aztec Pools on the side. Have you seen a van like that in here before, could he possibly be a resident?" K.W. asked.

"No. I would know if there was a resident driving that van," Danby said.

"Does the apartments have a camera covering the gate or parking lots?" K.W. asked.

"No they don't," Danby replied.

"Okay, so here's what I'm thinking. This guy is not a resident, does not have a code for entry or exit, which means he had to tailgate in and out. Will you put the word out among the residents that we need information on the van and see if anyone comes forward?" K.W. asked.

"Yes, I will have the office make up a flyer and put one in each resident's mailbox. I will call you with any information that comes out of it," Danby said.

"Thanks, Danby. I will need to get the forensic team in here later to collect samples of that blood and to photograph the tire tracks left by the van. Will you be around to let them in?" K.W. asked.

Danby pulled a card from his shirt pocket, extended it to K.W. and said, "This is my gate card. They can use it to get in and then have them walk to the after hours bell beside the office door. It will ring in my apartment, and I will come down to get the card back from them and let them out."

"Perfect. Thanks again," K.W. said and turned to the gate.

•   •   •

K.W. saw the black station wagon pull into the parking lot. As the driver turned, he saw the white lettering on the door, "Southwestern Institute of Forensic Sciences."

'Good, the team arrived just as I am ready to work the office,' he thought and increased his pace. He raced into the parking lot and called out, "Hey, hold up a minute and let me brief you before you go inside."

The crew consisted of two men and one woman. The woman balanced a camera on her shoulder. She had a power pack around her waist, and K.W. saw that she had a microphone clipped to the front of her shirt.

The younger looking man was holding a metal frame with spotlights attached. He too was wearing a power pack, and the wiring from the lights was connected to it. 'Perfect. This crew will make a video and audio record of every facet of this crime scene,' K.W. thought.

"I'm K.W. Bangs from Crimes Against Persons. I am the detective assigned this case, and I asked for your presence here," he said.

The older man stepped forward offering his hand and said, "I'm Clifford Watkins, this fellow here is Blake Edwards, and our camera pro is Tiffany Smithson."

K.W. shook their hands and said, "This is a bad one. We have not moved the body yet but here's what we believe happened. It looks like a lone shooter came into the office and engaged in some verbal altercation with our victim. We have two witnesses who say that shooter fired the first shot and then was hit by the victim's return fire.

The first shooter fell to the floor, and from blood smears and what appears to be shoe polish, it looks like he crawled along the floor, around the counter and then stood over the victim and emptied his weapon into the body.

Two other things I want you to know before we go inside. First, there is blood and flesh stuck to the counter, and it makes sense to suspect that it was blown from the first shooter as he was struck by the victim's return fire. There is another round at the top of the wall opposite the position of the victim's body.

Secondly, a woman who has identified herself as the victim's significant other called the office shortly after I got here. She asked a question that I find odd. She asked if '*he shot Joram in the face.*'

I want to put that on tape as we are turning the body over. If he has been shot in the face, I want the camera to zoom in for a close-up on the wounds. Can you do that for me?"

"Absolutely, we can," Clifford said as he looked up from taking notes.

Tiffany led the way. K.W. noticed the red light on the front of the camera and knew she was ready to film. Blake was to her side and just one step behind. As they entered, the door of the office Blake switched the lights on. The whole area was bathed in white light.

Tiffany swept the camera from side to side and spoken into the microphone, "Today is Tuesday, October 25, 1973. I am Tiffany Smithson with the Southwestern Institute of Forensic Sciences. I am entering the office area of the Lamp Lighter Motel located at

Nineteen-Nineteen Greenville Avenue in Dallas, Dallas County, Texas. It is now Twelve-Fifty a.m. As I enter the doorway of the office, there is a counter on my left, a passageway approximately five feet wide and then a sheetrock wall that is approximately eight feet tall.

At the approximate mid-point of the aforesaid counter is what appears to be a deposit of human flesh. The deposit is small and has attached to it what appears to be human hair. Blood is present on the flesh.

Along the floor next to the counter are deposits of blood, which has been smeared across the floor. There is also an unknown brown substance, which may have been deposited by something being dragged along the floor.

Moving to the wall and then up to its' juncture with the ceiling, there is a hole that appears to have been made by an unknown object which is still present in the wall.

I am now moving around the end of the counter and see the body of a male human being on the floor. The body is resting on the knees with the face and forehead on the floor as if the subject were to be kneeling.

There are numerous deposits of bone, flesh, and blood on the wall, behind the body, and large quantities of blood and other body fluids, to include what appears to be urine and fecal matter, on the floor surrounding the body.

There are obvious wounds on the back. It appears that the spine has been severed causing the body to lose support. The mid-section of the abdominal area is resting flat on the floor. It is impossible to tell how many wounds there are or from what source those wounds originated.

It does not appear that the body has been moved since the instance of death.

The lead member of our crew, Clifford Watkins, is now going to turn the body, rolling it onto the back so we can see the face and frontal portion of the victim.

As the body is turned, we will note that the detective on the scene reports receiving a call from one purporting to be the significant other of the motel owner. She asked '*did he shoot Joram in the face.*'

There is significant trauma to the face and side of the head. Both eyes are gone, and it appears that they each have suffered violent events. The right frontal portion of the skull is gone. The lower abdominal area is open, and the intestines are visible.

As the body was rolled over, there became visible a small pistol. I am now focusing the camera on that firearm. Lettering is visible on the barrel or frame. As I zoom in it is possible to see that the lettering describes the pistol as a Thirty-Two caliber Berretta Tom Cat. This concludes the filming of the scene."

Tiffany switched the camera off, and Blake killed the lights. Watkins looked at K.W. and said, "We will now process the scene. Is there one area where you would like us to start?"

"Yes, there is. First, I want to remove the magazine from the victim's pistol and count the rounds. I know that the magazine holds seven rounds. With one in the chamber, the effective capacity is eight. Next, I would like to see that bullet at the top of the wall, and then I want to watch you take the flesh off of the counter," K.W. replied.

Tiffany kneeled beside the pistol and looked at Clifford who had taken out a notepad and pencil. He nodded at Tiffany, and she said, "The pistol is a blue steel thirty-two caliber semi-automatic. The hammer is back or in the cocked position. I have dropped the hammer. This pistol has a 'pop-up' barrel, and I have engaged that feature. I have removed the magazine and count six unfired rounds."

K.W. nodded and said, "So, he got off two shots. The blood trail we found and the flesh on the counter suggests that he hit his killer with one shot and the other is probably in the wall behind the counter."

Blake had moved to the station wagon and now returned with a folding ladder, a small metal probe, and a plastic bag. He set the ladder up and climbed to the point on the wall where the hole was visible. K.W. watched as he probed gently, prying the projectile up enough to enable him to remove it from the wall.

He held it up for K.W. to see and said, "It is not damaged at all. We will be able to make a good comparison with rounds fired from the victim's pistol. But from my experience, this is a thirty-two caliber round."

K.W. stood and looked around the lobby. He stepped through the open door and into the manager's office. He turned and stepped back into the lobby and said, "I am going to go through his papers while you process the scene."

Tiffany looked up and said, "I have just removed his wallet and found his identification. He has a green card. He is a Syrian national named Joram Amine. He is 46 years old."

K.W. nodded remembering the phone call. *'So he is the owner, and his significant other asked if he had been shot in the face.'*

He sat at the dead man's desk and looked through the window into the lobby. As he sat there, he began to *'feel'* the event. Slowly it unfolded before him.

He saw the shooter walk into the lobby. He felt the hostility. The killer had wanted to make sure that Joram knew who was killing him and why. Their voices were raised, and the departing lovers heard them.

The shooter must have been distracted, maybe by the appearance of the witnesses, and that gave Joram a chance to go for his little pistol. The shooter fired first, and Joram fired back.

'I am going to say that the belly shot was the first one fired. Then Joram's return fire hit the shooter. The killer crawled around the counter, saw Joram on the floor and moved in for the kill.

The next two shots took Joram's eyes and the side of his head. Joram was slumped forward when the last three shots were fired. Not as a coup de grâce because Joram was dead at that point. Those last three shots were the period at the end of a statement, a personal statement.'

K.W. opened the desk drawers and found little to help. *'There are no papers related to the business. That means he had a home office. Bet the 'significant other' refuses me permission to go through them. Wonder if I can get a search warrant.'*

K.W. stood, took one last look around Joram's office and walked back into the lobby. The medical examiner had arrived and was about to lift Joram onto the stretcher.

"Wait one," K.W. said.

He moved to the stretcher, and the medical examiners agents stepped back. K.W. kneeled beside Joram and leaned forward. He looked at what was left of the man's face. Reaching forward, he laid his right hand over the stilled heart and said, "I will find those who did this to you and bring them to justice."

He stood and moved away without looking back.

CHAPTER 14
THE SERGEANT

K.W. pushed through the door and walked into Crimes Against Persons. He had just finished his two days off and was ready and eager to get back to work. He had made little progress on the killing of Joram Amine at the Lamp Lighter Motel.

K.W. had been sure that the killer would be found dead or at a hospital seeking treatment for a gunshot wound. But, there was no sign of him or the Aztec Pool Service van.

The live-in girlfriend, Fadilah, had hired a lawyer and refused to be interviewed. K.W. had been surprised to learn that she was only 15 years old.

During the investigation, he had learned that some of the Syrian immigrants still held to the 'old country' traditions and one of those was the practice of 'summer marriages.' These were temporary arrangements and usually involved financially strapped parents placing their young daughters with older men in return for money.

The courts refused to grant a search warrant that would have allowed an examination of Joram's house. They had refused in large part because K.W. had not been able to articulate any specific evidence, which might be present that would be relevant to the murder. The judge correctly assumed that K.W. wanted to go on a 'fishing expedition' hoping to find something to link Fadilah to the crime.

The Syrian community had closed ranks and would not give any information about Fadilah, her parents or Joram. There was nothing, other than her call to the motel on the night of the killing, to cast suspicion on her.

Three weeks after the killing, he received a call from a Hartford Insurance investigator. The investigator told K.W. that they held a one million dollar life insurance policy on Joram. The beneficiary was listed as his brother.

Ten days after Joram's death Hartford had been served with a lawsuit challenging the payment of benefits to the brother. The lawsuit contended that Fadilah and Joram had lived in a state of common law marriage and that she, as the wife, took legal precedence over the brother. Accompanying the service of the lawsuit was a temporary restraining order preventing the release of funds until the matter had been resolved at trial.

The investigator had one other piece of information that K.W. found interesting. The investigator had followed Fadilah as she boarded a flight for Cancun; then, shadowed her for two days. On the third day, a man joined her. He was identified as Azark Baraka.

Mr. Baraka was with the law firm that had represented Joram. He now represented Fadilah in her efforts to gain control of the deceased's assets. The investigator reported that Fadilah and Azark shared a room while in Cancun.

This was suspicious or not, depending on one's point of view. The courts held that it did not rise to the level of probable cause and once again refused search warrants for the home or business records.

K.W. had asked Sergeant Bill Parker to review the file. They had returned to the scene, walked the area around the Lamp Lighter, re-interviewed bartenders and regulars of the Motel and came away with nothing new. They were at a dead end with no new leads to work.

He had been assigned other cases, and the investigation was soon suspended.

Then the nightmares started. He would be asleep when Joram's head would float up beside his bed. Joram always looked at him through those hollow eye sockets and said the same thing, "*You promised.*"

147

K.W. was pulled from his thoughts by becoming aware that someone was staring at him. He looked up to see Susie and Rona, the administrative aids smiling at him from across the room.

"Sergeant Bangs, it is good to see you back," Susie said with a huge smile.

"Hey now, don't jump the gun. I haven't been promoted yet," K.W. said.

Rona held up a clipboard and thumbed through a sheaf of papers. "That's not what these orders say," she said with a wink at Susie.

K.W. felt the rush of excitement as he realized they were serious. Reaching for the clipboard, he looked at where Rona was pointing. "The following officers are promoted to Sergeant," he read aloud.

"And?" Susie giggled.

"Sergeant K.W. Bangs, 2425 is transferred from CAPERS to Southeast Patrol," he read.

He stood staring at the order. He turned as a hand was laid on his shoulder. Sergeant Bill Senkel stood smiling around his cigar at K.W.

"Congratulations Sergeant Bangs. Clean out your locker and report to the Chief's office at four o'clock for the ceremonial action. You better step on it and come back later for the goodbyes," Senkel said looking at the clock.

K.W. saw that it was already three-thirty. He shook Senkel's hand and hurried toward the door.

"Wait one. I almost forgot. You have a call from Special Agent Frank Cantoni with the U.S. Army Garrison at the Caserma Ederle Military Police in Vicenza, Italy.

They are holding a soldier named Perry Ray Gholson on a rape charge. During their investigation, they ran a search warrant on his room and found a Texas Driver's License in the name of Perry Ray Gholson, but that license showed Gholson to be a white male. The soldier they are holding is a black male. So they ran the name of Perry Ray Gholson through NCIC and got a hit on our case.

This Sergeant wants you to call him. Why don't you do that before you leave, get the information from him and then do a supplement for me? I will assign the follow-up to someone else, but you know more about the case, so it is best for you to talk with the Military Police.

K.W. grabbed the note and sat down at a desk. He contacted the city hall operator, and she made the connection for him.

"Military Police, Caserma Ederle. Specialist Talley speaking," was the answering response.

"Specialist, this is Sergeant K.W. Bangs with the Dallas Texas Police Department. I am returning the call of Special Agent Frank Cantoni," K.W. smiled at the use of his new rank, Sergeant.

There was a series of clicks and then, "Special Agent Cantoni."

"K.W. Bangs with the Dallas Police Department returning your call," K.W. said.

"Yes, thank you. We have in custody a soldier that we know as Terry Ray Gholson. He is a black male and shows his permanent home address to be in Dallas.

During our investigation, we found a Texas Driver's License with the name we know him by, but the information on the license identifies Perry Ray Gholson as a white male.

When I ran the name, Perry Ray Gholson, through NCIC I got a hit on him as deceased, the victim in a murder case filed by you. The suspect, in that case, is listed as Tyree Dobbs a black male.

I believe we might have your man, but I sure would appreciate an explanation," Cantoni said.

K.W. sighed deeply. He took a few seconds and said to himself, *'we have him, Mary Lynn. Now you will have justice.'*

"Cantoni, you have no idea how much this phone call means to me. Tyree Dobbs murdered three people here in one day. He raped and brutally beat his last victim to death. I found her body and the image has been in my mind ever since. I promised her that we would find him and that she would have justice. You have made it possible for that promise to be fulfilled. Let me tell you the story on him," K.W. said.

Forty minutes later K.W. glanced at the clock and knew that he had missed the promotion ceremony, but Mary Lynn would have her justice. He shoved back from his desk and walked to Senkel's office. He handed over the supplement and turned to the front door.

"Hey, you big dummy. You have time to hug our necks, or is it that you still consider us just unsworn clerks?" Susie and Rona were walking toward him.

K.W. grabbed them both in a bear hug and squeezed them. "Thank you for overlooking my arrogance and making me feel welcome. Thank you for all you have done for me," he whispered and slipped out the door.

●　　　●　　　●

K.W. swung the blue Dodge in a loop and pulled away from the gas pumps.

"Three-Ten is clear Southeast Station," K.W. spoke into the microphone.

"Three-Ten is clear at fifteen-thirty hours. KKB-Three Sixty Four, Police Department Dallas," the dispatcher acknowledged.

Exiting the service area, he turned right onto Bexar and settled in for a Friday night in South Dallas. He drove slowly along Bexar, examining with a practiced eye, the crowds of folks roaming the sidewalks outside the bars and clubs that lined Bexar.

He knew that most of these folks lived in the projects surrounding the Southeast Patrol headquarters. The absence of air-conditioning and the August heat combined to chase them from their homes.

The beer drinking that came with the effort to forget the projects and overcome the heat would, as the night progressed, lead to arguments. Some of those arguments would end in violence.

If patrol units could see the conflict starting, they could intervene and prevent injury or death. *'Sometimes the Guardian has to protect the flock from itself,'* K.W. mused.

He turned from Bexar onto Second and then south on Oakland. As he approached Pine, he heard gunshots.

People were rushing from The Green Parrot Club, spilling into the street and bringing traffic to a standstill.

K.W. yelled at a man as he ran past the car, "Hey, what is going on?"

The man turned back to K.W. and dropped down on one knee beside the car, "A woman came into the Parrot looking for her man. She found him sitting at a table with another woman. The Dude was kissing on this gal and had one hand halfway up her dress.

I could tell from the look on that woman's face that something bad was about to go down. I pushed my chair back and eased up and away from the table.

Sure enough, I saw her pull a big ole silver pistol out of her purse. She yelled, *'Slim, you cheating son of a bitch.'*

Slim jumped like he had been stuck. He got up and started backing away saying, *'Now Agnes, put that pistol down and let's talk about this.'*

Agnes was crying and blubbering. She turned toward the woman Slim had been kissing on and started yelling *'You Jezebel.'* Then she shot that gal right between the eyes.

Slim took off running for the back door. Agnes lifted that pistol and fired. The bullet hit Slim in the back of the head, slammed him to the floor and rolled him up under one of those pool tables lined up on the back wall. That's all I saw before I was able to get out of the club Sergeant," the man said.

K.W. picked up the microphone and said, "Three-Ten I am out on a Forty-One Nineteen at the Green Parrott. Start me some cover."

He stepped from the Dodge, lifting his pistol from the holster. He moved toward the door of the Green Parrott. Peeking around the frame of the door, he could see people lying under the tables, trying to hide in the corners of the room and crawling behind the bar.

K.W. dropped to one knee and scooted around the door and into the club. He had his pistol raised and was ready to engage, but no one was moving, and the room was quiet except for the muffled crying of a few frightened patrons.

K.W. waited, resting with his back against the wall, allowing his eyes to adjust to the dimness of the club's lighting. Then he saw movement in the shadows by one of the pool tables in the back of the room. He leaned forward focusing, willing his eyes to see through the murkiness.

Then he saw her, *'There she is, the woman with the silver pistol kneeling beside a man.'*

K.W. watched the woman as she sat crying, rocking back and forth on her knees. The man moved, trying to get away from the woman. Then with a shout of pain and anger, she placed the pistol behind the man's left ear and pulled the trigger.

The flash of burning powder filled the room as the explosion bounced around the walls. K.W. stood, leveled his pistol at the woman and shouted, "Police, put the gun down."

In a surreal reaction, the woman dropped from her kneeling position and lay stretched out full length on the floor. K.W. stood transfixed as she rolled behind a second pool table and then lifted herself to a crouch and waddled across the floor and into the women's restroom.

He could see her face and knew that her sanity was stretched to the breaking point. He moved slowly to the door of the women's restroom and peeked in. He could see her feet under the panels of a stall.

He quickly stepped across the room so that he could fire directly into the stall without presenting a target for return fire. "Lady, this is Sergeant K.W. Bangs of the Dallas Police Department. I need you to place your pistol on the floor and then slide it out from under the stall door."

"Are you going to shoot me Sergeant?" came the plaintiff cry from inside the stall.

"No, I will not shoot you. Just do as I say, and we will get this over with," K.W. said.

He watched in some surprise as the woman placed the big silver pistol on the floor and then shoved it firmly out from under the stall panels. The pistol was sliding right toward him. K.W. watched as it slowed, turned one circle and rested.

"Okay, now I need you to turn your back to the stall door, place your hands on top of your head and back out of the stall. Do not look at me and do not make any sudden moves," K.W. said.

The woman came backing out of the stall with her hands on her head. As she did, a voice called from outside the restroom door. "Sergeant Bangs, this is Linda Patterson. I'm coming in."

She stepped into the restroom, saw the situation and holstered her weapon. Linda stepped up behind the woman, took her hands off of her head and handcuffed her.

K.W. holstered his pistol and slumped against the wall. Linda looked at him with a raised eyebrow. She mouthed a silent, "Wait for cover next time."

K.W. smiled at her and winked. She was one of his best officers, and he knew she could handle it from here.

"Looks like two signal twenty-sevens. Take the prisoner to Southeast and call for CAPERS. This is a quick and easy killing, and they will come down here to work it out. I will hang here until we can get another unit to standby for Crime Scene and the Medical Examiner," K.W. said.

Linda walked out with the prisoner, and K.W. picked up the murder weapon. He turned it over, opened the cylinder and removed the live rounds. He shook his head as he realized this woman was shooting a Forty-Four Long Colt. *'Glad we didn't go to war,'* he thought as he hefted the weight of the big slug.

CHAPTER 15
TO BE OR NOT TO BE

The sergeant pushed through the double doors, made his way through the press of blue uniforms, and stepped onto the dais. "Okay, let's get started," he said.

The sergeant sat and let his eyes roam over the officers as his boss read the chief's letter. It had been thirty-four months since he and the team had pulled the all-nighter, arresting the Jones brothers, the band-aid bandits and the killers of the guard during the Big World Liquor robbery. Thirty-four months since he and Bill Parker had kicked the door on Le Roi Renau as he was pushing Linda Sweet under the water for the last time.

The caseload had continued to grow but working as a team had enabled the detectives to clear the cases. '*Predators, lots of predators were locked up. There are more still out there...always will be. But, bless the Lord we make a difference,*' he thought to himself. He squirmed in his seat thinking about one that he had not been able to bring to justice. Joram still visited him at night.

"You can call roll now Sergeant Bangs," the Lieutenant said.

K.W. shifted into his new role as a patrol sergeant and called roll, making beat assignments and giving the watch special instructions on the area around Fair Park where the State Fair of Texas was underway.

"Any questions. Let's go to work then and be safe out there," K.W. dismissed the detail and walked into his office to check the citations and reports from this crew's last watch.

He worked his way through the stack of citations and pushed them aside. As he reached for the sheaf of reports, he felt a heavy dread pushing its way to the top of his emotions. He hated this. '*I am a guardian, not a paper pusher,*' he groused.

K.W. leaned back in his chair and stared out of the window, watching the officers checking their equipment and settling into their black and whites. He felt envy as they pulled from the drive, each one clearing for service.

"Got a minute Sergeant Bangs?"

K.W. turned toward the voice and saw his watch commander, R.B. Bengay, standing in the doorway.

"Sure LT. You want me to come to your office?" K.W. asked

The lieutenant shook his head no, stepped into the office, and closed the door. He settled into an empty chair and stretched his legs out in front of him.

K.W. waited quietly as the watch commander stared at the floor gathering his thoughts. Then, he shifted in the chair and sat up pulling his legs back so he could rest his arms on his knees.

"I want to talk with you about the number of arrests you are making K.W. I know that the shift to first line supervision from working the street is hard. But, you are now a Sergeant, a patrol Sergeant. I need you to be a supervisor, not a street cop.

Monday night I heard you check out on a shooting at the Green Parrot. A few minutes later, you were on the air with a code four saying that you have the shooter in custody.

Hell, K.W. you didn't wait for cover, you walked into the club and made the arrest. That violates policy and sends a message to the officers that if Sergeant Bangs can do it, we can too. That kind of policing will get someone killed.

That is not what we are paying you to do. I do not want you responding to calls, working cases and making arrests. Do you understand?" the lieutenant spoke gently but firmly.

K.W. looked away, thinking over what his commander had just said. He lifted his right hand and caressed the gold badge resting on his left chest. He ran his fingers over it, tracing out the letters *POLICE*.

Finally, he dropped his hand and looked at his lieutenant.

"Boss, I rolled up on a forty-one nineteen. I didn't jump a call. The street was full of people running, trying to get away from the gunshots. There were lives at risk. My job is to protect those lives. I checked out on it and went in to suppress the gunfire. I did what I have been trained to do. And, I will do it again.

I am police. It is what I was born to be, and it is what I am going to be. I will do my best to be the supervisor that you need me to be, but I am never going to stop working the streets, clearing cases and making arrests. Now, how are we going to resolve this?" K.W. asked.

The commander looked at K.W. and said, "The question is not how we are going to resolve this. The question is, are you going to be a supervisor or do you want to turn those stripes in and go back to working the street?

I'm going to give you some time to think this over, but let me be clear. One or the other is going to happen."

He turned and left the room.

K.W. sighed deeply, looked at the waiting paperwork and thought, *The real question is how does a man advance through the ranks and still be police?'*

He picked up his hat, looked at the gold badge on it and walked from the office. He grabbed the keys to a supervisor's unit and walked out. The best place to think this through was on the street.

CHAPTER 16
PILLOW TALK

Pai-han woke with a start. The room was still dark, but something had changed. He had felt it, as if something had touched him.

He heard the sounds of rapid breathing and realized it was his. He tried to swallow. There was no moisture. He closed his mouth and ran his tongue over his parched lips. *'I was sleeping with my mouth open again. Did my snoring wake me up?'* he wondered.

He lay still, allowing his senses to test the darkness. His heart was pounding, and there was that familiar knot in the pit of his stomach.

He rolled from the mat to a kneeling position. He waited on one knee. He could just make out the soft, slow breathing of his woman; Hui-ting. There was no other sound, but he could feel another presence in the room.

"You sleep too deeply. I entered through the back window. I have been all through your house. I could hear you sleeping, the loud breathing.

The sound led me down the hall and right into your sleeping room. I have been through your closet, I have looked in all the usual hiding places and finding nothing of interest, I sat down here in the corner to watch and listen.

You continued to sleep. Never knowing, until I touched your mat. Your life and the life of your wife were mine to take," he recognized the voice speaking out of the darkness.

Pai-han felt his face flush, as shame rushed in. He was relieved that Chih-hao could not see his countenance, or could he?

"Why have you done this, Chih-hao? Why enter my home like a thief, why disrespect my woman's modesty by entering our sleeping quarters while she is asleep on her mat?" Pai-han asked.

"Whom are you talking to?" Hui-ting had rolled onto her side and lay staring at him.

"We are safe but keep yourself covered. There is another in the room. Just lay still until we both have left," Pai-han said.

He had heard the gasp and felt her fear. He reached over to place his hand on her, "It is okay. Don't worry."

He stood and heard Chih-hao stand also. He stepped from the room, and the other man followed. Pai-han closed the door and walked down the hall toward the living quarters. As he did, he heard the floorboards squeak, 'How did he come this way without me hearing that,' he asked himself.

Pai-han lit the lamp and turned to face Chih-hao. "You have not answered my questions. Why have you entered my home in such a manner?"

"We are engaged in a high-risk enterprise, in which failure is measured in the cost of life. It is necessary to know all you can about those who you associate with in such an undertaking.

My experience has shown me that the best information comes from the unsuspecting. Most are less guarded in the deep hours of the night, on his mat. So, it has proven to be with you Pai-han," Chih-hao spoke from the shadows of the room.

Pai-han lifted the lamp and said, "Come into the light. Sit at the table while I brew us some tea. I have many questions. The first is, how did you see all of this without turning any lights on?"

Chih-hao stepped from the shadows and said, "I live in the darkness. I learned long ago that the ability to see in the environment in which I live is a necessity."

Pai-han nodded and turned to fill the teapot with fresh water. He opened the firebox of the stove and bent to ignite the kindling. With the fire going he turned back to Chih-hao and asked, "And, what did you see in the darkness of my home?"

"I saw a man who lives without alarms, traps or weapons. That tells me that he has nothing to hide. I saw a man who leads a simple lifestyle; one that is supported by what I know he earns.

That tells me that he is not engaged in secondary endeavors. I saw nothing to indicate that he is untrustworthy. I saw nothing to indicate that you Pai-han are anything other than that which you purport to be, an import-export specialist for your American employer. And seeing all of that tells me that you can be a trusted participant in our enterprise.

But, there is one question for which I do not have the answer. Why are you so aggressively seeking to join our organization?" Chih-hao was looking at Pai-han carefully.

Pai-han knew that he had to control his emotions. *'Keep your breathing slow and steady. This man reads people like others read books,'* he mused.

"I want more than the salary the Americans pay me will provide. More than our present arrangement allows me to earn. I want to sleep in a bed, not on a mat spread on a hard floor. I want electricity and gas in my house. I want a car and a television. I want all of these things, and that takes money," Pai-han replied.

Chih-hao watched the young man as he spoke. He saw the effort to remain calm, the forced rhythmic breathing. He did well, but he could not control the tightening of the skin around his eyes, nor the narrowing of the pupils. He also closed his hands, almost in a clench. *'That is caused by his effort to convince me. What he doesn't know is that I was in the house long before he went to sleep and heard their pillow talk. No, it is not him that wants all these things. It is his young woman. She controls him. We will use that to our advantage,'* he thought.

"And your woman, we know she is not your wife? Does she know how you intend to provide all of these things?" Chih-hao was baiting Pai-han.

"She is a woman. She does as I say," Pai-han snorted.

"She is young. You are not. It has been my observation that a young woman has more influence with an older man. Do you find this true?" Chih-hao pushed the goad in further.

Pai-han blushed. Then he laughed, "You are wise. You have seen much. This woman is for my pleasure, and she serves me. But enough of this talk. Let's get down to the business of today. Have there been any changes?" he asked as the teapot whistled.

Chih-hao sat thinking. He stared into the steam rising from the tea, *'Show me the secrets here. I feel a check, but why?'* he was sorting through his thoughts.

Finally, he sighed. "I find no reason for any change. Yes, I will tell those who sent me that it is safe to go," he tested the tea and then drank deeply of the dark sweetness.

CHAPTER 17
LEMONADE AND OMELETS

K.W. sat at his desk reviewing the weekend reports. He had resigned his commission with the Dallas Police Department two months back and was now the Director of Physical Security and Investigations for Texas Instruments Dallas. He supervised a uniformed security force of one hundred and twenty-five armed officers and was responsible for the investigation of all crimes against persons occurring on TI Property.

Jolene tapped on the door and pushed it open, "Mr. Purvis and Mr. Moody want to talk with you."

K.W. leaned back in his chair and rubbed his head. "Okay, tell them I need to stop by the men's room and then will be right with them," he said as he stood behind his desk.

"No, sir. They wanted me to see if it is okay for them to come here. To your office," she smiled.

"Are you kidding? My bosses want to know if they can drop in on me?" K.W. asked.

"Do you have a few minutes for them?" Jolene was giggling.

"Sure thing. Tell them to come on," K.W. said.

"Do you want to go to the men's room first?" she asked.

"No, I'm too curious. Tell them to come now. Oh, never mind here they come," he sat back down.

"Come in boss or should I make it plural. To what does your faithful servant owe this visit?" K.W. smiled.

Purvis sat down as Ken Moody closed the door. "K.W. what do

you know about our operations in Taipei?" Purvis asked.

"I know we opened the plant in the late seventies to manufacture the plastic housings for our consumer products division. I know that all the plastic is flown by air to Hawaii, where we have received great favor from U.S. Customs, who are not offloading or running the dogs through the planes.

In fact, those planes are on the ground just long enough to refuel and then they are airborne inbound to DFW. I find it interesting how we have so much favor. I thought maybe it could be that an old FBI man had a friend in Customs. But then I digress.

After being cleared by Customs, the shipment lands at DFW. The plane is refueled and flies into Lubbock International Airport. The product is then loaded onto our trucks and driven into Lubbock where all our consumer products are warehoused," K.W. responded.

"Right. Now, what do you think our greatest risk is during that shipping operation you just described?" Moody asked.

"Well, I know the plastic is of little value until and after the consumer product is assembled. Then, of course, it is at risk of loss through theft. In fact, I just presented four cases to the Lubbock County Grand Jury last week. Two on calculators and two on those blasted watches that everybody and their cousins are wearing. But, that's not your point. So tell me, what's up"" K.W. said.

Moody shifted in the chair and looked at the door. He then looked at Purvis who was busy studying his fingernails. Moody dropped his head to look at the floor and remained silent.

"Oh, wait a minute," K.W. said.

"Let me guess. Given that possible Customs connection mentioned earlier, how about smuggling? Could that be that someone has discovered our sweetheart arrangement with the Customs station in Hawaii and are taking advantage of it by smuggling contraband into the country on our flights?

And, if that were to be the case, then our friends in customs stand to lose a major portion of their hindmost quarters. Am I getting warm gentlemen?" K.W. was looking at the top of each man's bowed head.

Purvis cleared his throat and looked up, "We are in a real bind here. An agent in Hawaii decided to use one of our shipments to train his dog. He hid a lure in the cargo, thinking that the odors of the plastic would be a real challenge to the dog.

Well, the dog found the lure but then he alerted on another container. The agent tried to pull him off, but the dog kept going back. Curiosity got the better of the agent, and he had the container set off and opened.

Inside he found a kilo of cocaine. Fortunately, this agent had enough experience to know that someone had arranged for our favored status. He called a 'trusted' supervisor, and they had the container re-loaded on the plane and then had the plane towed inside one of their quarantine hangars.

The agents rounded up some help and went through the entire shipment. They found a kilo of cocaine hidden in each of four containers.

They ended up with four kilos of dope with a street value of about two hundred and fifty thousand dollars. Now count the number of flights we have each week, and you can see that this could be a major drug smuggling operation.

The fat is in the fire so to speak. Our choice was to fess up or to make lemonade out of lemons. We chose the latter.

All of this is top secret of course. It is especially critical that you protect the next bit of information I am about to give you.

It is obvious that the dope had to be placed inside the shipment before it left our plant in Taipei. We have to know how and by whom. About the only way to get that information is by having a spy inside the plant.

Our contact in Customs combed their agency and found a young female agent who is of Taiwanese extraction. We put her inside the plant as a shipping specialist.

She is young and very attractive. It didn't take long for the smugglers' inside man to hit on her. She did not hesitate to use her 'charms' to work her way into his confidence. In fact, she is now living with him as husband and wife.

She is feeding us information that will allow us to make the bust without exposing the Hawaiian 'lemons.' We need you to help us make it happen," Purvis leaned forward with a pleading look on his face.

K.W. looked from Purvis to Moody and then said, "I like lemonade. But let's be clear. When the dust clears on this, somebody is going to jail."

"Agreed," Purvis said.

K.W. looked at Moody and said, "Ken?"

"Agreed," Moody said.

"Good. Now I have several questions. What happened to the four kilos of dope? Who is the smugglers' inside man in Taipei and what is his role? Who is the contact in Lubbock and how do they know which shipment is carrying dope? When is the next shipment due and how do we plan to take it down?" K.W. asked.

"Let's take your questions one at a time. The inside man is an import-export specialists. His name is Tai-Pan. We don't know whom they have on the ground in Lubbock and we suspect that every flight has dope on it.

Tai-Pan lets the smugglers know the flight schedules and provides them access to the shipment so they can stash the dope and then signs off on the paperwork to get it past the Taiwanese Customs.

You already know that the shipment clears Customs in Hawaii and then flies on one of our Seven Forty Seven Heavies to DFW. The plane is refueled and flies on to Lubbock.

The smugglers have enlisted members of the ground crew there to meet each flight that has dope. They take it off of the plane before it is put on our trucks for the drive into the city.

The smugglers on the ground carry the dope off property and give it to a man named Yarnell. From there it is cut and shipped all across the nation.

The next shipment arrives in Lubbock this Thursday. It is scheduled to land at fifteen hundred hours. We have contact with a U.S. Customs Special Agent. He will be in charge of the operation and you are to assist him," Moody said.

"You didn't answer my question about the four kilos. Where is it?" K.W. asked.

"Well, remember now K.W. you have to break eggs to make an omelet," Purvis said.

"We are talking about lemonade, not omelets. But just to be clear, I'm not letting either eggs or lemons go. I want you to answer my question. Where is that dope?" K.W. insisted.

"All we can say is that Customs has it. We don't know where it is or what they are doing with it. But, rest assured that an agency of the Federal Government took possession of the dope and removed from our property," Purvis shrugged.

K.W. twisted in his chair, turned to look out the window and considered what Purvis was saying, '*It makes sense that Customs would not let that much coke out of their custody. It also makes sense that they intend to use it to hang a charge on those responsible. But how? Unless they plan to add it to the total seizure when they fall on this bunch. Bet that's it, and by golly, I'm okay with that,*' he thought.

"Okay then. I take it that you want me to go to Lubbock, hook up with this Special Agent and fall on these bad guys when they go for the dope. He will make the arrest, and the newspapers will get an engineered story of how our security personnel worked with U.S. Customs to uncover and bring to justice a major Asian smuggling ring. Is that about the way this will go down?" K.W. asked.

Purvis nodded and looked at Moody.

"We have you scheduled on the Lear out of Love Field at five o'clock this afternoon. The agent will contact you at the Rio Vista Hotel, just off the airport grounds in Lubbock.

You two are in charge of the operation from there. Make it work K.W. We need this cleaned up," Moody said.

K.W. smiled at Moody, "The Rio Vista, is it? Okay, I like their steaks. Let's break this up, so I can run home and grab a clean shirt. I will be on that Lear when it lifts off."

"Let us know as soon as it's over," Purvis said.

He and Moody moved to the office door. Moody pulled it open and then hesitated before stepping through it and said, "Take your pistol, K.W. These folks are serious."

Moody and Purvis left, and Jolene stood up from behind her desk. She looked at K.W. and said, "Pistol?"

"Forget it, Jolene. You didn't hear that. Clear my calendar and keep it clear until you hear from me," he said as he hustled out the door.

CHAPTER 18
LUBBOCK INTERNATIONAL

The hum of the air conditioner was mocking the men. Sweat had soaked through their clothes, and the sting of the heat rash was a testament to the ineffectual efforts of the machine.

Charlie Tulling stood from the stool where he had been sitting for the last two hours. He stepped away from the camera and lifted his hands over his head, stretching his cramping muscles.

"So, tell me K.W., what made you leave Dallas P.D. for a security gig with Texas Instruments? I mean, we checked you out after you called us on this deal and by all accounts, you were doing well. You had made sergeant and looked to have a bright future, so why?" Charlie asked.

"The best job I ever had was working robberies in CAPERS. But, hey you know, we started having kids, and I needed the money. So, I took the sergeant's exam. Ended up passing the test and the next thing I know I'm a patrol sergeant assigned to the Southeast Patrol Division.

I was the junior sergeant, so I had to work relief for a while, but then I got my own sector. Things were rocking right along. I had eighteen of the best officers a man could want, and we were fighting crime and locking up bad guys.

I was working the street, making some arrests, enjoying myself. That is until the Watch Commander walked in one day and corrected my understanding of what it meant to be a patrol sergeant.

He reminded me that I was being paid to supervise, not work the street. I begged to differ and that kind of forced his hand. He was patient but made it clear to me that I had a choice to make, give up the stripes and go back to working the street or concentrate on supervision.

At first, I was ticked off. But as I thought about it for a while, I realized that the lieutenant was exactly right. It had been my choice to take the promotion, and it was incumbent on me to fulfill the duties of that position. Or, I could step back.

I called an old friend, W.A. Huddleston, a retired sergeant who was working in the security department at Texas Instruments. I told him what I was struggling with and asked for his advice.

We met for coffee. Huddleston heard me out and then told me to grow up. I had the stripes. The officers needed the benefit of my experience, and I should give it to them.

I went back to work, apologized to my boss and knuckled down to being a first line supervisor. But I lived for the times when the officers needed me on a scene, those times when I was in middle of the action.

I called my old friend and told him I had given it a shot but was going to give up the stripes. I called the Captain in CAPERS to see if I could come back. He told me yes, as soon as he had an opening. I told my buddy that as soon as that call came, I was stepping back.

I was doing my best to be Sergeant Bangs but every day was a challenge. Then the phone rang, and it was Huddleston. He told me that Floyd Purvis, the corporate director of security for Texas Instruments, was looking for an investigator experienced in public law enforcement. He needed someone who can work cases worldwide.

Huddleston told me that Purvis would like to talk with me about the position. I went out for coffee, and it turned into an interview. I liked Floyd, and he liked me.

Two days later a lady from Texas Instruments human resources called and said Floyd wanted to hire me. She told me what the starting salary would be and it was more money than I had ever expected to make. Seemed to be the right thing at the right time. So I resigned my commission and signed on with T.I. Corporate Security.

Now here I am sweating like a hog in beautiful Lubbock, Texas, working a dope case with Special Agent Charlie Tulling of the U.S. Customs," K.W. said.

Charlie nodded and said, "Well, like the bumper sticker says, Lucky Me I Live In Lubbock. Now, tell me. Are you happy or not?"

K.W. looked at him and asked, "Want me to take the camera for a while?"

"Yeah, I need to take a leak and wash my face. I'll be right back, and then you can answer, or not," Charlie said with a grin.

K.W. moved over behind the camera, pulled the stool up close and sat down. He leaned forward and looked through the viewfinder with a sigh. *'Hope this information is reliable. If it is, the grabbers should be coming to take the dope off of the plane anytime now. '*

Slowly he moved the camera to sweep the lens over the plane and then back across the space between the secure area and the hangars fifty feet away.

Movement caught his eye. He watched as three men slipped from the space behind the parking area and slid along beside the hangar. They paused, pressed against the building and kneeled.

'There they are,' he smiled.

Quickly he adjusted the focus and flipped the record switch.

•   •   •

Cisneros leaned against the hangar wall and stared at the big plane. It was sitting on the apron just outside of the U.S. Customs office.

Sweat ran down from his forehead and dropped into his eyes. He wiped the stinging salt away and sat back on his haunches.

'Man, it is hot on the High Plains today! Where are all those cap rock breezes the chamber of commerce is always spouting off about,' he thought.

He leaned around the corner enough to see the number printed on the side of the plane, just in front of the wing. "TI 1241, that's our plane, and the ramp is already down," he whispered to Pete who was kneeling behind him.

"Well, hell boss, why are we waiting? It's hot and the longer we sit here, the better the odds that one of those customs agents over there will see us. It is not going to be easy to explain why the three of us are all gathered up as if we are at a prayer meeting," Pete said.

"I know Pete. But like the song says leaping before you look always leads to a fall, or in this case, gets you ten to fifteen in the federal joint," Cisneros said.

"Man, stop all that talk about doing time. Let's get the blow or let's get the hell out of here," Willis whined from the back.

"Yeah, right. Are you ready to tell Yarnell that we decided to exercise our options and leave the snort on the plane?" Pete asked as he looked back at Willis.

"How many times do I have to tell you guys? Quit using names," Cisneros said.

"Okay, but let's do this boss. I don't see anything different from any other time," Pete said.

Cisneros nodded and said, "You're right Pete. Let's do it."

•   •   •

K.W. heard Charlie leave the restroom and turned, "We got action, Charlie."

Tulling trotted up, and K.W. moved to let him have the stool. The agent leaned in and grunted as he watched the three men strolling casually toward the plane.

Cisneros slowed as they approached the back of the jet. He spoke slowly without looking at either of the other two men, "No one stands good eye on this job. There is just too much chance someone will start asking questions. We all walk up that ramp like we are supposed to be here, grab the coke and walk away."

"Just like that?" Willis gasped.

"Just like that. Yarnell said the stuff is stashed in the first container on the right as we enter the plane," Cisneros said.

"Isn't that the first place the dogs would search? Why not put it in one of the containers in the middle of the load?" Pete asked.

"Because that is too obvious. The agents always look in the middle. Pete, you and Willis shield me. I will pull the dope, and we are out of here," Cisneros said.

K.W. and Charlie watched until the three walked up the ramp. Then Charlie pulled the door open and stepped out onto the tarmac. K.W. noticed that the agent had a pistol in his hand. He reached back and removed his Walther from the holster and flipped the safety off. They rounded the rear of the plane and heard one of the men shout, "Cops."

"You are too late. I am a Federal Agent. Lift your hands and turn your backs to me. Do not look at me and do not move," Charlie shouted.

K.W. holstered his pistol and moved up alongside Charlie. "Do you have any cuffs?" he asked.

Tulling kept his focus on the three men at the top of the ramp but replied, "No. Do you?"

"I grabbed some flexcuffs before we left the office this morning. Here is how I am going to do this. First, I will step up, cuff them all and then bring them down the ramp one at a time.

Once I have them down the ramp, I will search them and sit them down on the tarmac here at the foot of the ramp.

You cover me, and if they jump me, you shoot them. Don't come up the ramp, kill them from here," K.W. said.

Charlie nodded his head and said, "Be careful. You can tell they are itching to run. Get those flexcuffs on them as quickly as possible."

K.W. moved up the ramp and said, "I know you heard our conversation. Make no mistake, he will kill you where you stand. Just do what I say and we will get this over quickly."

He put the flexcuffs on and walked them down the ramp. Once down the ramp, he searched each man. He then turned to Charlie and said, "No weapons, no dope on any of them."

"That's right! We don't have anything on us. We are just doing our job. What the hell are you two doing? That's the question," Cisneros was twisting around to look at Charlie and K.W.

Willis laughed and said, "You boys were too quick on the trigger.

You jumped us too soon."

"Shut up Willis. You fool didn't you hear the man say he was a federal agent. They don't have to have a written statement. They can use anything you say, so just kept your mouth shut," Cisneros said.

K.W. looked at Charlie and said, "How long before the press crew gets here? Should we just leave them on the tarmac or take them inside to set it up?"

"Set what up?" Cisneros asked.

K.W. turned to look at the three who were now still and quite, "Well you see boys, how it is looks now will not be how it looks once the press is here. We cannot afford to go along with your assumption that we picked you green.

So, when the press crew gets here, you will be standing behind a table with the coke laid out to make the best possible impression. The caption will read something to the effect that we captured you in the process of removing smuggled dope from the shipment of plastic product on this plane," K.W. smiled down at them.

"What dope?" Willis sneered.

"Shut up Willis. Shut up or face the consequences," Cisneros snapped.

"Ah, I think he means for you to be quite, or he will tell Yarnell that you messed the deal up by running your mouth," Charlie said.

The shock of Charlie using Yarnell's name hit them hard. They looked at each other, and then all of them leaned back against the ramp and looked at the tarmac.

Anxious to maximize the shock Charlie said, "We already have a plan to put the story of the bust in the paper. That's the political part of the plan.

But there is another part. We take the pictures, run the story, and lock you three up. Then after a few days, we let you go. Of course, your release would be just after we arrest Yarnell."

"Yarnell will never believe that we snitched him off. We've worked together too long," Willis said.

"That's a big gamble. Are you sure you want to take it?" Charlie asked.

"Look cop; I am not interested in your deals. Do whatever you are going to do. Charge me with whatever. I will do my time, but I will not be a rat," Cisneros said.

"Better think that over. This is federal time, which means no good time, no parole. You will do day for day, every day for ten to fifteen years," Charlie said.

"Not interested," Cisneros said.

"I am," Pete said.

"You shut up too, Pete," Cisneros said.

"I might be interested too," Willis said.

"What kind of deal are you talking about?" Pete asked.

"You give us the names of everyone involved in this, the route and the destination for the dope. Then you testify. We will put you in witness protection, give you a new identity and a new life. You get to start all over. Not many get the chance for a do-over like we are offering you. And it will all be on the government's dime," Charlie said.

"Don't fall for that. A Customs agent can't make that deal. Only the U.S. Attorney can make that deal," Cisneros said.

"We cleared it all before we came out here. We knew that you were the grabbers. We want the bosses and the information needed to take the organization down. It is a good offer," Charlie said.

"I'm in," Pete said.

"Me too," Willis said.

"How about you Cisneros? Once I take this off the table, it will be too late. Take it now or take the fall," Charlie said.

"Don't be a fool. Take it and get the hell out of this desert," Pete said

"Think of yourself man. I guarantee you that no one else is going to give a damn about you sitting in the joint for the next fifteen years. How old are you, about thirty aren't you. That means you will be fifty or close to it when you get out of the joint. Man, that's old. Take the deal and live your life," Willis said.

Cisneros sighed and looked at Cobb, "There are four kilos of coke in the first container. Four is about all they put on a plane. They used to do only one or two flights a week, but lately, they are putting dope on every flight. So they are moving twenty keys a week. And that is just through this operation. Get us up and out of sight, and we will answer all your questions."

K.W. looked at Charlie and smiled, "Deal partner?"

"Deal," the agent said.

CHAPTER 19
BACK TO THE BADGE

"Mr. Bangs, the Director wants you in his office," Jolene said.

K.W. heard the voice, but his mind was focused on the weekend log report. *'We are having too many possessions of marijuana within the plant. There has to be a patch of it inside the gates. We will check every atrium in all the buildings today. I bet we find that some innovative mind has seeded one of those beds and we are watering and fertilizing it for them,'* he was thinking.

"Sir, Director Purvis wants you in his office now," Jolene repeated while tapping on the office door.

Her voice punched through the fog, and he lifted his head to look at her, "The Director is in Attleboro this week."

"No sir. He is in his office and he is asking for you. There has been a payroll robbery in France, and he wants you on a plane as soon as possible. I have already scheduled you out tomorrow morning, at four o'clock, on the Lear," she smiled nervously.

K.W. looked at her a few seconds and asked, "A robbery you say. Well, that's a relief. I was afraid that he was going to start in on me about taking the Director's job in Attleboro. I was hired to work cases, not be tied to an administrative job. I am not going to Attleboro, and that's final."

Jolene looked at him and shrugged, "Okay," she said.

"What do you know about the robbery?" he asked.

Jolene stepped inside his office and closed the door. "I took a peek at the Director's link. It was the payroll for the plant in Villeneuve-

Loubet. We have to pay the French nationals in cash. We pulled the money from the bank in Paris as soon as it opened at nine o'clock. It was transported by armored car to the airport.

One of our jets then flew it to the municipal airfield at Villeneuve-Loubet where our security personnel took custody of it. They usually convoy it to the plant, and that was the operation plan this time.

They had just left the airport when they were ambushed, and the money was taken. There were no shots fired, and there is no evidence of resistance by our officers.

The site manager reports that they shrugged when asked why they handed the money over without a fight. The Director says he smells a rat and that he is sending you to ferret it out," Jolene whispered.

"Are the National Police investigating," K.W. asked.

"No. Villeneuve-Loubet is considered rural with a population of less than twenty thousand. That means the Gendarmerie has jurisdiction," Jolene answered.

"The Gendarmerie are military police; they deal mostly with National security issues. Why are they involved in a criminal investigation?" K.W. asked.

"That is one of the reasons the Director wants you in France. I read his response to the site manager. He said, and I quote, '*K.W. has both civilian and military police experience. He will be able to relate to them. I will get him over there as soon as possible,*' Jolene said with a faint smile on her face.

"Do you see some humor in this?" K.W. asked her.

"Oh, I know how you hate to fly, and I was just thinking about that old saying the French have," she said.

"What old French saying is that Jolene," he asked.

"C'est la vie," she snickered and hurried back to her desk.

•   •   •

"Good morning Shirley. Jolene said the boss wanted to see me," K.W. said to the receptionist.

"Does he ever? He is in the conference room, and he is not happy you have kept him waiting. Go straight on back, and then I need to talk with you about your move to Attleboro," Shirley whispered.

"What move to Attleboro?" K.W. stopped and returned to her desk.

Shirley looked up with the realization that he had not been told about being transferred to Attleboro. "Ah, maybe I shouldn't say anything else," she said.

"Too late, the cat is out of the bag. Tell me, and I promise not to burn you with the boss," K.W. stood in front of her.

Shirley looked around him toward the conference room. "Don't 'burn me' as you say. He will fire me for sure," she said.

"He would be a fool to fire you and Floyd Purvis is no fool. Tell me quickly so I can get into the meeting," K.W. urged.

"He has appointed you the site security manager for Attleboro. He signed the papers yesterday. I have notified HR, and they are setting your household move up now. I just need to know when you and Trudy will be available to fly up there to look for a house," Shirley said.

"I'm not going. I will tell Floyd after this meeting," K.W. said.

"Well, remember your promise. I need this job K.W.," Shirley said.

"Don't worry. I have your covered," K.W. said and turned away.

K.W. stepped around the counter and down the hall to the Directors' conference room. Purvis looked up and said, "Come in K.W. I have John Dunlap, the site manager in Villeneuve-Loubet, on the speaker. He is just about to brief us on the payroll robbery. I want you to hear this because it is your case and I want you able to walk out of here informed, and ready to sort through all this smoke the French are blowing at us."

K.W. nodded to the other security managers present and sat without saying anything. There was a buzz, then a click and John Dunlap came on the line, "Floyd, are you there?"

"Yes, John and I have my management team with me. That includes K.W. Bangs who is the new site manager at Attleboro. He is going to be the lead investigator on this case before he moves up there. Go slow and work your way all the way through the robbery. We will hold our questions until you finish," Purvis said.

"Well, what I have is pretty sketchy. Our security team, comprised of all French nationals, met the payroll shipment at the Aeoport de Nice-Cote d'Azur and followed procedure in securing the cash and getting it locked in the van. We have reviewed the video from the hangars' security cameras and can see that everything was done right.

Once the money was secured, the officers got inside and locked the vehicles before the hangar door was raised, as the SOP requires. They drove out and met the two other escort vehicles, each manned by two of our armed personnel.

The convoy proceeded without incident to the industrial gate of the airport and exited onto the Boulevard Maryse Bastie'. They drove to the roundabout and entered Rene' Cassin driving West toward Villeneuve-Loubet.

Once again, all was well until they left the city of Nice. Two miles outside of the city they had to cross over the River Or.

As the lead vehicle drove onto the bridge, two men dressed in military uniforms, stepped into the roadway and leveled automatic weapons at the car. Rather than take evasive action or try to escape, our employee stopped the vehicle.

That left the armored van, with the money in it, trapped in the middle of the bridge with one car blocking it from the front and the trail vehicle blocking it from the rear.

Two more men came up from under the bridge and ordered our employees to open the van. They had military type weapons and our security team, armed with handguns only, complied.

The armed men demanded the payroll and our crew handed it over. All four of the armed bandits then climbed over the bridge railing and rappelled down to the water. They used oiled ropes tied to the main support beams of the bridge. They left in a powerboat operated by a fifth individual.

All the bandits wore ski masks, gloves, military type uniforms, and boots. They all were armed with long guns that our personnel describe as SIG Five Fifty assault rifles.

When I questioned our security personnel as to why they didn't try to resist, their reply was that they were *'boxed in and outgunned.'*

Also, our team said that the bandits all had earpieces that they believe to be a link to someone that was directing the operation from another location. Each bandit knew and executed their role so well that there was no need for talking back and forth between them.

They also noted that in addition to the long gun, each man wore a sidearm. They describe it as an HK USP 9mm compact and somewhat hesitantly said that both the long guns and the pistols are the models issued to the French Naval Forces and the maritime branch of the Gendarmerie.

Reading between the lines and from the body language of this security team, I would say that they believe the bandits were rogue Gendarmerie, which of course makes this a rather delicate issue. I am now ready for your questions," Dunlap finished up.

"A couple of questions right off the bat John. First, why did we not have police involvement in the escort? Or in the alternative why did you not include off-duty police officers in the security team?

Secondly, your team seems to be observant and to know a lot about the weapons these bandits carried. Are any of them former Gendarmerie?

And finally, was the payroll in dollars or francs, how much was taken and do you have a manifest with the serial numbers of the bills recorded?" K.W. asked.

"I will answer each question in the order asked. Because the population of Villeneuve-Loubet is less than twenty thousand the only police agency present is the Gendarmerie.

We tried to employ off-duty Gendarmerie officers for security purposes both on the property and off. But the local security unions raised all kind of hell about it depriving their members of employment. We appealed it up the chain but the socialist government now in power sided with the unions.

Next, yes all of our security personnel are former military and most served in the Gendarmerie including the maritime branch.

About your question on the loss, we pay in francs. We do so every two weeks, and the payroll is almost the same each time. This time it was F 1,050,000 or one hundred and ninety-three thousand dollars. And, yes we do have the shipping manifest which does include the serial number of each bill," Dunlap said.

"Great, now tell me about the boat that was waiting to take the bandits away. What I want to know is if it was a civilian craft or if it was one assigned to the maritime forces of the Gendarmerie," K.W. asked.

"What? Why would you ask that?" Dunlap asked.

"Because of the organization, the uniforms, and the weapons," K.W. answered.

"Hold one K.W," Dunlap said.

"Ah, you have hit on something K.W. I have the security team waiting down the hall in another office. I stepped down there and asked your question, they nearly fainted. To make it short, yes. It was a maritime craft with the numbers covered by burlap bags hanging over the side," Dunlap said.

"Did you ask them why they didn't volunteer that information in the initial report?" K.W. asked.

"Yes I did, but they only shrugged and looked at the floor. I think we need an experienced investigator to get to the bottom of this. Are you coming over here?" Dunlap asked.

"No, there is no need. I will handle this from here on the phone. But now listen. I know the press is going to be all over you wanting the details. I want you to tell them that this matter will be handled at the highest levels of the French government and that you have agreed to make no comments. Say nothing else. We will be in touch as soon as we have something else for you," K.W. said.

"Okay, if that's what you say. I will have our communications folks put out the statement and then wait to hear from you," Dunlap said.

"Great. Just relax. Talk with you soon," K.W. said and broke the connection.

He looked at the others and then at the Director.

Purvis sat open mouthed for a moment and then asked, "What the hell are you thinking K.W."

"Boss, this is so obviously an inside job. One of our team set this up with his pals in the maritime branch.

All we have to do is have you call the FBI SAC in Paris, get him to call his French law enforcement liaison and tell him that we have the serial numbers, on all the notes, and have already released them to the national banking system.

Tell him that we will be working with the National Police and expect an arrest soon. Tell them that we are prepared to hold a press conference once the rogue Gendarmeries are in custody.

Then offer him an alternative. Say that we are willing to allow the French to handle this whole matter, as discreetly as they wish, with our guarantee that we will say nothing to the press.

Be sure to have him stress that we find ourselves in this predicament because the Gendarmeries feel disenfranchised by the governments' ruling on our requests to hire off-duty officers for security.

Suggest that a case could be made that an American company is being extorted by the military police on the one hand and the government unions insisting on employment of their private security professionals on the other," K.W. sat back with a smile.

"Everybody out, except for K.W," Purvis shouted.

After the last man had scooted through the door, the Director said, "I hired you as my Crimes Against Persons expert. Not as a foreign-service officer. Damn it K.W. you are playing with fire here. If this blows up, we will be hung out to dry. Don't you understand that?"

"Boss, I don't know what you hired me to be or to do. But, the truth is I think like a police officer and that thinking tells me that the way to handle this is obvious.

Call your FBI buddies and put this puppy to bed. You will have your money back in short order.

Then you can go over to the Executive Building and give them the news. You will be a hero, again.

But regardless of your decision, I'm not going to France. And, while I'm at it, I might as well tell you that I'm not going to Attleboro either."

Purvis leaned back in his chair and said, "K.W. you will go where I say when I say. That is as long as you are working for me."

"Well shoot boss, that's easy to solve. I will have my resignation on your desk in an hour. I'm going back to the badge," K.W. said.

K.W. stood and reached across the table to shake the hand Floyd was offering. With a smile on his face, Purvis said, "You know what K.W.? That's where you belong, behind that badge.

Thanks for giving it a shot. I was hoping it would work, that you could shift from public safety to industrial security, but hell boy, I knew in my heart that you wouldn't stay. Go on, get back to being that guardian you were meant to be.

CHAPTER 20
TOO LATE FOR VIRTUE

She scowled at the blinding stream of light sliding in between the slats of the window blinds. Looking up she was mesmerized by the collection of dust particles and debris floating freely in the air just above her desk. The late August sun stripped away the illusion of a *'clean and green work environment'* boasted of by her employer, ACE Legal Services.

The buzzing of her phone drew her attention back to the desktop. She punched in the blinking button and said, "This is Shirlene Minkus."

"Shirlene, where are you in the examination of the Capital Wire case?" her boss asked.

"I am just finishing it up, Mr. Howard. Give me five minutes, and I will have my report on your desk," she said glancing at the clock.

"No, I don't need the full report. Just tell me what your findings are. What kind of exposure does Capital have?" he asked.

"Yes sir. Well, the police report charges the Capital Wire driver with failure to obey a traffic control device. In other words, the driver ran a red light and T-Boned, if you will, the other driver in the exact middle of the intersection.

The officer, a DPS Trooper named Wiley, stated in his report that the driver insisted he applied the brakes to stop for the red light, but they failed.

Trooper Wiley investigated the driver's claim and found that the brakes master cylinder had a hairline crack in the wall. Every time the brakes were applied the air pressure within the cylinder pushed the fluid out through the crack.

The Trooper interviewed the driver who admitted that he knew about the defective cylinder and had reported it to the Capital Wire mechanics several times. According to the driver, the mechanics just kept adding fluid and never took the truck out of service to make the repairs," Shirlene reported.

"So you are telling me that our client knew about the defective equipment and continued to operate with it?" Howard asked.

"Yes sir, that is what my investigation shows. But as of now, the only claim filed against Capital is for the replacement of the car. The insurance company has totaled it.

The Blue Book values the car at twenty-nine thousand and five hundred dollars. The NADA value is thirty-one thousand dollars. My thought is that we send them a check with the stipulation that endorsement constitutes a total release of any future claims and get this over with," Shirlene said.

"I see. Your thoughts are that once the other party sees that we admit liability; they will add bodily injury to the claim. Is that what you're thinking," Howard asked.

"Yes, sir. That's it exactly," Shirlene said.

"Okay, here's what I want you to do. I want you to call this Trooper Wiley and ask him if his investigation is closed. If it is, then call finance and tell them to settle this.

Now remember Shirlene, in cases like this, the Troopers will often continue their investigation. If they find a pattern of conduct that poses a hazard to the public, they file those charges against the company.

Ask Wiley if he intends to do so. If he says yes, try to get him to tell you what the supplement will include. You let me know if he is going to recommend filing charges of negligent conduct against Capital Wire so we can alert corporate legal," Howard said.

"I will call him Mr. Howard, but I doubt that he will share his investigation with me. The usual practice is for the Trooper to submit his report to the chain of command and the decision to file these sort of charges against a corporation is made by the State Attorney General's Office," Shirlene didn't like being put on a spot like this.

"Oh, you have always been able to get this sort of information before. I expect you to do it again. Just keep your receipts and turn them in with your final report. I will see that you are reimbursed. Get back to me first thing Monday morning," Howard said and broke the connection.

Shirlene sat back and sighed, 'Really? Just like that Mr. Howard?' She looked at the clock again and saw that it was now five minutes to three.

She picked up the phone and called the Collin County Sheriff's dispatcher. "Sheriff's Office, Miss Perkins speaking. How may I help you?"

"My name is Shirlene Minkus. I am a paralegal for ACE Legal Services. I am working on an accident investigated by Trooper Wiley. Can you have him call me please?" Shirlene said in her most positive tone.

"Did you call the DPS office?" Miss Perkins asked.

"No, I didn't. In the past, I have found that they put a note in the Trooper's mail slot and it is sometimes a couple of days before they call me back. My boss is kicking me to get this claims examination finished, and I sure would appreciate it if you would ask the Trooper to call me," Shirlene had her fingers crossed.

"Okay, I will give him the message as soon as he checks into service. Are you in the Plano office?" Miss Perkins asked.

"Yes, that's right and thank you so much, Miss Perkins," Shirlene jotted her name down with a note to send a thank-you card and a box of chocolates to her.

She hung up the phone and saw Donna Fullbright walking toward her desk. Shirlene smiled despite the pressure Howard had put on her. "Hey, girlfriend! What's up?" she asked as Donna stood in front of her desk.

"It is Friday, and I am ready to party! That's what's up. Are you going home after work?" Donna asked.

"Yep. I have to get my kids some dinner and be sure the sitter shows up. Then I will join you. Where are you going to be?" Shirlene felt the excitement growing.

"Well, I would rather go to Rowdy's and dance with some cowboys. But I know you like the police, so I guess we are going to the *Code Three*. Is that right?" Donna asked.

Shirlene giggled, "I do like those police, and yes I do have to go to the Code Three for a while. I need to buy some drinks, lose a little money on the pool table and you know, press the flesh. I need to keep my connections current and strong so that I don't get the run around when I call for some information on an accident report.

Then we can leave and still have time to dance with those cowboys over at Rowdy's. How does that sound?"

"What a deal! Tell me, Shirlene, do you think that strawberry blond Adonis we met the last time we were there will show up tonight? If he does, forget about leaving. I will just *get rowdy* with him," Donna snickered.

"What do you mean, *we met*? That was all about you and him. I was nothing more than a third wheel that night.

Just a word of warning; his name is Clint Abshire, and he has been married three times. He is currently divorced and running wild. You be careful with him. Don't go falling into those deep green eyes of his. His philosophy is to tell you what you want to hear, take what he can get and move on," Shirlene cautioned her friend.

"Woo, sounds like Mama Shirlene! I'm a big girl. If he's there, I want to stay. How about you?" Donna asked.

"I will meet you at the Code Three about seven-thirty. Let's just do that and see where it leads," Shirlene said as the phone rang again.

She picked up the receiver and punched the blinking button as Donna walked away with a giggle and wave. "This is Shirlene Minkus," she answered.

"Ms. Minkus or Mrs. Minkus, this is Trooper Wiley with the Texas Department of Public Safety returning your call," he said.

Shirlene pulled the file over in front of her and said, "Thank you, Trooper Wiley, for returning my call, and it is Miss Minkus. I am a paralegal with ACE Legal Services. I have been assigned to do an evaluation of our client's exposure in a traffic accident involving a Capital Wire truck and a privately owned vehicle. The report shows you as the investigating officer. Do you recall the accident I am referring to?"

"Yes, I do. How can I help you?" Wiley asked.

"We, that is ACE Legal Services, are ready to issue a check to the driver of the privately owned vehicle. But before we do, my boss has instructed me to ask you if the investigation is complete and closed or if you intend to file any supplementary reports. Do you?" she asked holding her breath.

There was a pause, and then Wiley said, "Don't I know you, Miss Minkus? I think we met at the Code Three Club some time back. Yes, I remember now because you were passing out your business card and 'politicking' the police.

I asked the officers there about you, and they told me that you come in and buy drinks, play a little pool and do you best to establish and or maintain a working relationship with the police.

If I remember the right lady, you are a honey blond with bright blue eyes and like to wear dangling earrings. Am I right or wrong?"

"You have me pegged. I just don't remember you. What is your first name?" Shirlene asked.

"Justin, my first name is Justin. I called you out on purposely losing the pool games so the police could pick up the money," he said.

"Ah, I remember you now Justin," she said seeing in her mind a short, pudgy young Trooper with thinning hair and a rough complexion.

"Yeah, and do you remember that you were not all that friendly to me? I asked you to dance, and you said no. But I saw you dancing with a Plano officer named Stew. Now you are asking me for something. How interesting," Shirlene could hear him breathing.

Shirlene rolled her eyes and swallowed her pride and said, "Well hey Justin, I'm sorry about that. If I remember that night, I was there on a date, sort of a working social engagement.

I would be happy to dance with you anytime I'm not with a date, but I just don't think it is right to dance with others and leave my date at the table. You do understand that, don't you?"

"Oh, were you on a date with Stew that night? I wondered about that. Okay, so maybe I will see you there again. In fact, I'm going to be there tonight, are you?" he asked.

"Yes, I am. I look forward to seeing you. Maybe you will let me buy you a beer," Shirlene said.

"Well, sure. That'll be great. Now, back to your question, yes the investigation is complete. I ran the cracked cylinder thing past my sergeant.

We ran a check on the driver and turned out he is a convicted felon. He has no credibility as a witness, and since it is his word against the mechanics, we are going to leave it there," Wiley said.

"Wow, thanks, Justin. I owe you one," Shirlene regretted it as soon as the words had left her mouth.

"Okay, well I look forward to us settling up. See you at the Code Three," he said with a chuckle.

Shirlene hung up the phone and sat thinking. A knot began to form in her stomach. She knew that Wiley was expecting more than she was ever going to deliver and she also knew that he would not take her *"just saying no"* kindly.

'This is going to be nasty. I might as well make my position clear and get it over with. Tonight I will draw a line in the sand and he had better not cross over it,' she said to herself.

•　　　•　　　•

"Mommy, are you going out tonight?" Jeannie asked from the doorway.

Shirlene looked at her little daughter and held her arms out to her. Jeannie ran into her mom's embrace and whispered, "Please mommy. Stay home with Stevie and me tonight. Please!"

Shirlene pulled back and looked at her daughter, "Jeannie, are you okay? You know mommy has to go out for a while. It is part of my job, the way I support you and Stevie," she said.

"I know mommy, but not tonight. I have this feeling that you won't come home if you go tonight. Please stay home mom," Jeannie whined.

Shirlene found herself considering what her daughter said. *'What is this? Does she have the same gift of premonition that I do? Should I stay home? But I'm not getting anything'* she sat thinking.

The doorbell broke through her reverie, and she heard Julie say, "Miss S. It's me, Julie, I'm here early."

Shirlene stood, smoothed her mini skirt and admired her legs. They were her best feature, and she often wore short dresses to show them off. Now she wondered if this dress was too short, *'should I put pants on tonight?"*

She shook off the doubt and stepped into the kitchen. "Dinner is in the oven, Julie. Don't worry about the dishes, I am going to be home early, and I will take care of them. Just spend time with the kids, get them to bed early, and then you can watch television. But no boys Julie! Agreed?" she asked.

"Agreed Miss S. I might talk with Richie after I get the kids to bed. Is that okay?" she asked.

"By telephone you mean?" Shirlene didn't want the kids to see Julie and Ritchie making out on the couch.

"Yes, on the phone," Julie grinned.

"That's fine," Shirlene said as she kissed her kids and started to the door. She stopped and turned back to the table. Leaning over she kissed each child and said, "Always remember that your mommy loves you."

She hurried out of the house and sat in the car a minute wiping her eyes and making sure her makeup was not smeared. Then she backed from the driveway and turned toward the Code Three.

Shirlene took the Arapaho exit and turned back East, crossing under Central Expressway and driving toward Greenville Avenue. The traffic was heavy this time of night, and Shirlene took her time.

Turning off of Arapaho into the parking lot of the club she drove slowly up and down the lanes looking for a parking spot. Seeing none, she exited the parking lot and drove her car into the dark driveway of the now-closed gas station sitting adjacent to the club property. She saw the sign that read, 'No Club Parking. Towing Enforced At All Times,' but then she had parked here before and never had any problems.

Shirlene stepped from her car and started to walk toward the club. "Hey lady, can't you read? We do not allow club patrons to park here. If you leave that car I am going to have it towed," a voice came from behind her.

Shirlene turned to see a man wiping his hands on a red shop towel and nodding toward the sign. "Yes, I saw it, but I have parked here before and never had any trouble. I figured that was just to keep your driveway open for customers while you were open," she said.

"Nope. The problem is the trash all these folks coming out of the club leave behind for me to clean up. Sorry but you are going to have to move your car," the man said.

Shirlene could tell that arguing or pleading would get her nowhere. "Okay, I'll move it," she said as she walked back to her car.

She drove back to the club lot and parked in a handicapped space near the front door. She hustled inside and found the bartender. "Roscoe, I had to park in the handicapped spot outside. Will you loan me your card, so I don't get a ticket?" she asked with a smile.

Roscoe reached under the counter and pulled a handicapped placard out. He handed it to Shirlene and said, "You know I made this one up. It is not legit, so if you get busted, it is all yours."

"I know Roscoe. Thanks," Shirlene said as she hurried outside to hang the placard on her rearview mirror.

"Handicapped? How are you handicapped," Shirlene recognized the high, thin voice of Justin Wiley?

She turned with a slight blush and said, "Busted! I'm not handicapped but there are no parking spots, and I borrowed this so I wouldn't get a ticket."

"Really? I found one," Wiley said with a smirk.

Shirlene followed his nod and saw a black and white patrol vehicle parked in the fire lane next to the club. "Well, I guess so. But hey, are you allowed to drive a duty vehicle to a club and then drive it home after drinking?" she asked.

"What they don't know won't hurt them. I am on call for injury accidents tonight. I have a uniform shirt and my gun belt in the trunk. I watch my drinking; mostly I am just looking for some female company. If they page me, I suit up and work the wreck. Forget about that and let's get that beer you owe me," he said reaching for her arm.

Shirlene allowed him to escort her inside realizing that anyone seeing them come in would assume they were a couple. Just as Wiley opened the door to the club, Shirlene turned away saying, "Oh, I forgot to lock my car. You go ahead and order us a beer. I will meet you at the bar."

She scurried back to the car as he said, "Just click it."

"Can't. The battery in my clicker is out," she answered as she inserted the key and fumbled around waiting for him to go inside. Seeing that he had entered the club, she leaned against the car and waited a minute or so to allow him time to make it to the bar. Then she took her time walking inside.

As she entered the dark club, she stepped aside out of the doorway to allow her eyes to adjust. She saw Wiley sitting at the bar talking with Roscoe. He was drinking a beer, and another one sat on the counter next to him.

Shirlene put a smile on her face and crossed the room, greeting friends along the way, and settled in on the stool next to Wiley. "So, how's the beer?" she asked.

"Frosty man, frosty," he said with a silly smirk.

She took a long pull on hers and swiveled on the stool to look at the dance floor. Hank Williams Junior came on the jukebox singing, 'You Wrote My life.'

'Might as well get this over with,' she mused.

"Hey, that's one of my favorite songs. Let's dance," she said jumping from the stool and grabbing Wiley's arm.

He followed her to the dance floor and wrapped his arm around her. He pulled her in tightly and began to steer her around the floor. She decided to put up with the vise grip and just get through the song. Then he dropped his hand down to the small of her back, and then on down to her hips.

"Whoa, now cowboy. Keep those hands above the waist," she giggled as she moved his hand back to the small of her back.

She felt him tense up. The song was winding down, and she pushed away from him, held onto his left hand and twirled around in a finishing flourish. "That was great," she gushed leading him back to the bar.

As soon as she sat down, Bob Wills and the Texas Playboys came on singing *Big Ball's In Cowtown*. She felt a tap on her shoulder and turned to see the smiling face of Will Turner. He was holding out his hand and said, "I do believe this is my dance, Shirlene."

Her heart skipped a beat as she slid off of the stool and into his arms. At that moment no one else existed except her and Will. She knew she was in love with him and she also knew he was married. But she couldn't resist his smile.

He led her to the dance floor, and as she slid in close and rested her head on his chest he said, "Hey what's up with the fat boy at the bar? Are you two together tonight or what?"

Shirlene looked toward the bar and saw that Wiley was watching them with a scowl on his face. "No, we are not together. He is a Trooper that I had to call on a case I'm working. He had seen me here once before and asked me to dance. I said no, and he got huffy about it. I bought him a beer, danced once with him and that's going to be it. Just don't leave me alone with him, please," she settled back into his arms.

"I have an idea. Let's leave now. I will buy your dinner and then maybe we can catch a movie or something," he whispered.

"I have to stay a while. Buy some beers, dance a couple of dances, and lose a few bucks on the pool tables. But we have had this conversation. You are married, with kids," she was saying when he interrupted her.

"Don't go there, Shirlene. Let's just take what we have and let the chips fall where they will," he said with a frown.

She stepped back from him and said, "Really Will? What do we have? Stolen hours in the Como Motel, sneaking around afraid we're going to be seen? That's not me, I will not be responsible for breaking up your family."

Will walked away and glanced over at Wiley as he left the club. Shirlene followed his glance and saw that Wiley was still watching her every move. She took a deep breath and moved toward the bar. "Hey, Shirlene. I saw you dancing with Will, and I saw him leave. Are you two hooking up already?" it was Donna asking.

Shirlene was struggling to hold the tears in check, "No. I told him that I wasn't going to be the other woman and he walked out."

"What do you mean the other woman? Is he married Shirlene?" the shock was showing on Donna's face.

Shirlene sobbed, caught her breath and said, "Yes. He lied to me at first but things didn't make since. I confronted him and he admitted that he is married and has two kids. Listen Donna; I'm a wreck. I have to get out of here but that guy at the bar, the one that is staring at us, is a DPS Trooper that is coming on to me. I can't deal with him right now. Will you please go dance with him, distract him for a few minutes so I can grab my purse and leave? I will owe you one," Shirlene pleaded.

"Ugh. Okay, Shirlene but just one dance. Clint is coming, and we have plans," Donna said.

"I know Donna. Thanks for doing this," Shirlene said heading for the ladies room. She stepped inside and then peeked out to see Donna dragging Wiley to the dance floor. She waited a minute more and then dashed out, grabbed her purse at the bar and was out the door.

She saw the note on her windshield and pulled it from under the wiper blade, "*I know I should have been upfront with you Shirlene. I'm sorry. I will accept your decision and move on. My wife, Cindy, is suspicious. She went through my wallet and found your name and number. I told her you were a confidential informant. I think she bought it, but if she calls please don't give me up.*

By the way, there was a guy looking at your car when I came out of the club. I thought at first he was looking at the Roscoe's fake handicap placard but then I noticed that he was leaning over peering into your car. I badged him and asked him what he was doing and said he was trying to figure out if it was your car. I asked him why and he said he had been checking you out and wanted to hit you up for a cup of coffee after the club closes tonight. Turns out he is a Crime Scene Tech out of the Plano P.D. Weird guy, Bill something or other. Just thought you would want to know. Thanks for the memories. Will.'

Shirlene folded the note and looked around the parking lot. She knew the tech Will was talking about in the note. He had asked her out a couple of times and she finally told him straight out that she was not attracted to him and would not be going out with him. He gave her the creeps, and she had seen him following her a couple of times. At least she had seen him in traffic behind her. He always turned off but still, the thought of him looking into her car alarmed her. *'Hope that creep is not out there in the dark looking to follow me again,'* she fretted as she got into her car and drove away.

•   •   •

Wiley stood in the shadows of the club's doorway watching Shirlene drive away. He waited until she was clear of the parking lot and then sprinted to his patrol vehicle and turned to follow her car.

It took him a few blocks, but then he saw her stopped at the signal light waiting to turn left onto the Central Expressway service road. The light changed and Shirlene moved away from the signal and merged into the traffic heading south toward Dallas.

He followed, keeping a couple of cars between her car and his until she exited at North West Highway. She drove east on Northwest to Abrams Road and pulled into the Kips Big Boy Restaurant.

He passed the entrance, went down to the first street and turned right. He drove past the restaurant and saw Shirlene sitting alone in a booth talking to the waitress.

'I know that guy she was dancing with. He is a Richardson officer. I met him and his wife at the Collin County Law Enforcement picnic last summer. I wonder if she is meeting him here. I bet she is. That is why she drove all the way down here, so they wouldn't be seen in Richardson.

She dropped me as soon as he came in. But that's not the end of it Miss Shirlene. If the candy store is open, then by golly Justin is going to get his,' he mumbled out his frustration.

He felt a vibration at his belt and realized the pager had been going off for some time, "Damn it to hell. If I leave now I will miss my chance to follow her," he moaned.

He heard the squelch on his radio break as the receiver opened, "Sixteen twenty-four."

Wiley grimaced and reached for the microphone, "sixteen twenty-four," he answered.

"Sixteen twenty-four, take the injury accident involving an Allen Police vehicle at Highway five and Main Street. The Allen officer driving the patrol vehicle has ordered an ambulance and two wreckers. Make your assignment code three," the dispatcher said.

"Ten-four, I will be traveling to the location from Abrams Road and Northwest Highway. My ETA will be approximately twenty-five minutes," Wiley said and hung up the microphone.

He stepped from the vehicle, grabbed his uniform shirt from the trunk and shrugged into it. He tucked the shirts into his jeans, strapped his gun belt on and got back into the patrol vehicle. He drove through the parking lot and stopped in front of the entrance to the restaurant. He could see Shirlene's car parked near the front and noticed a guy sitting three slots down. He had backed his car into a parking slot and appeared to be watching Shirlene's car.

'That's interesting, but I don't have time to check it out,' Wiley said. He pulled away, flipped on his overhead red lights and merged into the traffic on Central Expressway.

Shirlene had just given her order to the waitress and they both were surprised to see a DPS cruiser light up and speed away with siren sounding. "That is a DPS car. I wonder what he was doing here," the waitress said.

Shirlene felt that knot return to the pit of her stomach. "Oh no," she said.

"What?" the waitress asked.

"There has been a Trooper following me around. He thinks I owe him some personal 'favors' in exchange for giving me some information on a case I have been working. That is not going to happen, but he is not taking no for an answer. It bothers me to think he followed me here," Shirlene said.

"You can't tell me anything about cops. I was married to one for eleven years. Write your name and this Trooper's name down just in case something happens. If I hear about you being found on the side of the road, I will call the Rangers," the waitress said.

"What are you saying? Do you really think a police officer would go that far just over being told no?" Shirlene asked.

"Honey, you wouldn't believe some of the stories I could tell you. Just write your name and his name down on a napkin and leave on the table for me," she said and hurried to the next table.

Shirlene felt silly but pulled a pen from her purse and jotted *Shirlene Minkus and Justice Wiley (DPS)* on a napkin and folded it over. She handed it to the waitress when she brought the order to the table. Shirlene watched as the waitress unfolded the napkin and read it, and she stuck in her pocket.

Shirlene walked out of the Kip's and strolled to her car. She felt guilty about splurging on the hot fudge sundae, '*that's okay, I will work it off doing the lawn tomorrow,*' she said as she settled into her car.

Shirlene started her car and backed from the parking slot. She noticed a man slumped over in a car a few slots down for her. '*That's odd,*' she thought.

She drove from the parking lot and turned left onto Northwest Highway. She stopped at the first signal and a car pulled up beside her. She glanced over and saw the driver was the Crime Scene Tech from Plano. He waved at her and she looked straight ahead without acknowledging him. "*What am I, a magnet for weirdo's? Lord, just let me get home and away from all of this,*" she prayed as she sped away from the light and moved to the right so she could exit onto Central Expressway.

She merged into the traffic and looked into her rear view mirror. There was no sign of the Plano tech and she relaxed, '*Next stop Allen, Texas,*' she breathed a sigh of relief. She looked again in the rear view mirror and thought she saw his car. '*I'm so skittish that I'm seeing things. I think I will speed up, get ahead and jump off of the expressway and run down old highway five into Allen. He would never expect that,'* she reasoned.

•   •   •

"Sixteen twenty-four is clear the major seven," Wiley spoke into the microphone.

"Sixteen twenty-four is clear at twenty-three thirty hours. Your number is Seventy-Six –Forty-One Eight One A," the dispatcher replied.

"Seventy-six –Forty-One Eighty-One A," Wiley reported and hung up the microphone.

He wanted to get away from the scene so he could complete the paperwork on the accident. He drove north on Highway Five intending to stop at the State Materials station just inside the Plano City Limit sign.

He approached the site and drove around behind the pile of gravel the Department of Transportation kept stored there. Out of habit, he drove the vehicle forward just enough that his radar unit would be able to monitor oncoming traffic.

Shirlene saw the DPS unit pull off of the roadway and behind the pile of gravel. She zipped past just as he drove behind the materials. *'Whew, I don't think he saw me and it's a good thing cause I am doing twenty over,'* she smiled. Maybe her luck was changing.

She glanced into the rear view mirror and saw a car gaining on her quickly. Then she saw a red light come on.

She started to brake and then thought, *'Who is that? That red light is on the dash of that car. Maybe I should drive on into Allen and stop in a lighted area.'*

Shirlene took her foot off of the brake and pressed the gas pedal. The car behind her now flashed its' headlights. She heard a siren and looked into the rearview mirror again.

"What the hell. I can handle this guy. If he writes me, he writes me," she said as she slowed and pulled to the side of the road.

She opened her purse and removed her driver's license. She then rolled down her window and watched in the side mirror as a man stepped from the vehicle and approached her car. *'This doesn't feel right,'* she thought.

Then he was at her window and said, "We meet again Miss Minkus."

He grasped the door handle and pulled the door open. Shirlene put both hands on the window frame and leaned back resisting him with all of strength and body weight.

"What are you doing?" she said closing the door.

"You know exactly what I am doing. You lay down for all those others, now you are going to lie down for me. Get out of that car," he demanded jerking the door open again.

Shirlene shrank back pleading, "No, please. Why are you saying that? You don't know me. I am not like that."

"The hell you aren't. Get out of that car. It is too late for virtue now," he leaned all the way into the car and placed one hand around her throat and slapped her with the other.

As slapped her across the mouth she heard her daughter say, *'Mommy I'm afraid you won't come back home.'*

The premonition had now become a prophecy, as the enraged man at her door pulled her from the car and into the night.

CHAPTER 21
COMING HOME

"Plano Police Department. How may I help you?"

"Hello, my name is K.W. Bangs. May I speak with Sergeant Tommy Ashley?"

"Yes, hold one please," came the response

"Sergeant Ashley," he heard the speaker say.

"Tommy, this is K.W. Bangs. We met in the police supervision school at UTD. Do you remember me?" K.W. asked.

"K.W. Bangs with the Dallas Police Department?" Ashley asked.

"I was a sergeant with Dallas when we met, but I'm no longer with Dallas. In fact, I'm no longer in law enforcement. That's what I want to discuss.

I saw in the paper that you are giving the test for police officers. I would like to run by and talk with you," K.W. said.

"Sure thing K.W. Let me ask you this. Are you eligible for rehiring in Dallas?" Ashley asked.

"Yes, I am. But Plano is my home, and I would like to check out the possibilities here first," K.W. said.

"Okay, where are you, how long will it take for you to get here?" Tommy said.

"I'm here at my house on Jupiter. I can be there in ten minutes if that is okay," K.W. said.

"Come on. I'll be waiting," Tommy said.

K.W. hung the phone up and turned to Trudy, "Tommy said he would talk with me. Are you sure about this? You know what it means. Starting over, working rotating shifts, being away from you and the kids. And, it means less money for the family."

"I know. But, I want you to be happy. I believe the Lord will honor your obedience to His plan for your life and I believe He will provide for our needs, I believe He will make it possible for our family to be together. I know He will," Trudy said.

K.W. reached for her and said, "Thanks, baby. Pray for me as I meet with Tommy. Pray for guidance."

K.W. approached the steps leading up and into the building and stopped. He looked at the dark lettering on the side of the building, 'Plano Police Department,' he whispered.

As he stood there, the thoughts came flooding back. The little house on Avenue K, the long nights spent in fear of the dark shadows, and those guardians who came by night after night to bring light to the darkness, to push the shadows aside and to teach him how to face his fears.

Then faces from out of the past floated up before him. The face of Dick Sheridan, George Apple, Nathan White, Billy Joe Hicks and all of those town fathers who had given so much to him, who had lifted him up and helped him believe that he could achieve his dreams.

'I owe you all so much. You have given so much to me, and now I want to stand where you stood. I am coming home,' K.W. nodded and stepped forward, and climbed the steps into the next phase of his life.

"Hello, Tommy. Thanks for seeing me on such short notice," K.W. said.

"Hey, first of all, it is good to see you, but it is also my job as the supervisor for our recruiting effort. I want to be open with you. I called Dallas personnel as soon as I hung up from talking with you.

I asked two questions. First, I asked if you were eligible for rehire, and secondly, I asked if there were any investigations, personnel actions or accusations pending or unresolved relative to your service. They were as direct with their answers as I was with my questions.

You are eligible for rehire, and you have a clean record. They added one other thing; you are eligible for reappointment to your civil service rank of sergeant.

So now, I want to know why you would want to come to us where you will start at the bottom rather than returning to Dallas where you can pick up where you left off?" Tommy leaned back and waited for K.W. to respond.

"Well, to be frank, I had not thought about the possibility of having my rank reinstated. But, that doesn't change my desire to work here, in Plano where I grew up," K.W. said.

"Fair enough but let me ask you this. If working in your hometown means so much, why didn't you come to us in the first place, rather than going to Dallas?" Tommy asked.

"I did, or at least I tried. J.B. Toler was chief when I tried to apply. He told me that I had to be 21 to be a police officer. He did offer me a job as a jailer or dispatcher. But I wanted to be police, and Dallas was willing to hire me as a police officer at age nineteen. That made the decision easy for me," K.W. said.

"So, you were nineteen years old and Dallas commissioned you as a police officer," Tommy asked.

"Let me explain it. In 1967 Dallas, Houston, and the Texas DPS begin recruiting candidates who were at least nineteen years and six months old.

I applied to DPS and Dallas. Dallas called first. I was tested, went through the background investigation and was hired June 14th, 1967. I was 19 years and ten months old. My warrant of appointment was issued on that date. It conferred on me the right to bear arms in the performance of my duties as an apprentice police officer for the City of Dallas. That was my commission.

I was assigned to the Academy, class ninety-five, and upon graduation to the patrol division. So, yes, I was a commissioned police officer at age nineteen in June, turned twenty in August while still in the academy," K.W. said.

"Wow. I didn't know that. What do you know about our department?" Tommy asked.

"I know you are State Civil Service, which means that I get five points on my test as a military veteran. I know the city is about to experience explosive growth which means the opportunities for promotion will be great within the department. And I know that the department has always had a great reputation," K.W. said.

Tommy nodded with a frown on his face, "Something I don't understand here K.W. You said you are a veteran, but the timeline doesn't seem to work.

I know you are a local boy, I know about your being on the State Championship team in sixty-five. Then you went off to play ball in college, you came back and went to work for Dallas in sixty-seven. So when were you in the military?"

"I was walking a beat downtown when I received my notice of induction in December of sixty-seven. I reported for duty on the second day of January sixty-eight. I served twenty-one months, got a ninety-day early out to return to Dallas as a police officer.

I was released from the military October first nineteen sixty-nine and was sitting in a patrol car October fifth.

I resigned my commission in June seventy-six after being recruited as a Crimes Against Persons Specialist to work for Texas Instruments Corporate Security. I have just now resigned that job.

The next question will be why did you leave TI. The answer is two-fold. First, I want to return to public law enforcement. It is my calling.

Secondly, TI had just promoted me and ordered me to Attleboro, Massachusetts. I didn't want to go to Massachusetts, so I resigned. And, here I am without a job. What do you think? Can I take this next test?" K.W. asked.

"Sure. We will need you to fill out the application, and then we will start your background. That will not take long. Then you take the written test and immediately report to our training facility for the physical endurance, agility test.

If you pass both of those, we will schedule you for your polygraph. If everything works out, we should be able to have you on board within a month," Tommy said.

K.W. reached across the desk and offered his hand to the Sergeant. Tommy stood, shook K.W.'s hand and said, "Come with me and let's get you started."

CHAPTER 22
PASSING THE TEST

K.W. parked the car downtown. He and Trudy looked at each other, and she said, "You know you passed that test. Stop looking so worried. Come on let's go see your score."

They stepped from the car and walked toward City Hall. As they approached the front doors, they could see the results posted on the glass. Trudy reached over and took her husband's hand.

The setting sun cast a glare across the glass, and K.W. had to raise his hand to block it. Then he saw his name was first on the list with a score of 104. *'That means I missed one question, wonder which one it was?'* he mused.

He felt Trudy squeeze his hand and turned to look at her. "What did I tell you? You passed the written and then the physical tests. What is next?" she asked.

"I don't know. I would guess the polygraph exam. I will call Tommy tomorrow and ask him where we go from here," K.W. couldn't keep the grin off of his face.

●　　　●　　　●

The shadows were yielding to the probing of the morning sun. K.W. lay in bed watching the room come alive with the soft yellows of the new day.

He looked at his sleeping wife and rolled quietly out of bed. The glaring red numbers on the digital clock told him it was five-thirty.

He grabbed his robe and shuffled down the hall. The door to Kristen's room was ajar, and he could hear her soft breathing. Two steps more and he was outside the nursery.

He pushed gently on the door and winced when it creaked. *'Got to oil those hinges today'* he thought. He stepped into the room and eased over to the crib. His infant son lay sleeping on his back.

K.W. was mesmerized by his son's face. It was so peaceful, so perfectly formed. He grinned as his son's deep red lips pursed and then moved in a suckling motion. *'Kenneth Wheat Bangs The Second. What does life hold for you my son?'*

He turned and moved to the door, closed it carefully behind him and then down the hall, through the den, and into the kitchen. The automatic coffee maker had done its' duty, and the earthy aroma of Columbian Coffee filled the air.

'Thank you Juan Valdez and all your friends at Folgers for your attention to the raising of this wonderful bean,' K.W. smiled as he poured a cup of the steaming dark brew.

He sat the cup down and walked to the front door. He flipped the deadbolt and opened the door slowly. Just as expected, the hinges greeted him with a hearty protest.

Fortunately, the glass door opened smoothly and without protest. He grabbed the morning paper from the front porch and allowed the door to close quietly. He latched it and headed toward his reading chair, leaving the heavy front door standing open.

An hour later he finished the paper and glanced at the clock over the fireplace. *'It is just now Six thirty. I need to wait at least two hours before I can call Tommy,'* he mused.

"Daddy."

K.W. turned to see his daughter, Kristen, walking toward him. His heart leaped at the sight of her. Her head was a mass of blond curls, all tangled from her nights' sleep.

She was wearing a long-tailed gown that her grandmother had made for her. Her favorite little bear was held snuggly in one hand while she grasped her pink blanket with the other. She crawled up in his lap, and he tucked her blanket in around her.

She was very still, and he suspected she was not ready for the day. He sat quietly, letting her drift off to sleep. Her deep, steady breathing was hypnotic, and soon he was nodding off too.

The sound of rustling silk caused him to open his eyes. He saw Trudy leaning against the hallway entrance with her arms folded. "What a sight that is. How long have you two been sitting there asleep?" she asked.

K.W. looked again at the clock on the mantel and saw that it was now 7:25 a.m. "Wow, can't believe I sat here and slept nearly an hour," he said.

"Well, I can't believe that Kristen is still sleeping and I just peeked in on Ken, and he is sleeping soundly as well. This has to be some kind of record," Trudy smiled at her husband.

"Better come take Kristen so I can shower, shave and get dressed. I have a feeling Tommy will want me to come in first thing this morning," K.W. said shifting in the chair and easing Kristen up for her mom to take.

●   ●   ●

K.W. heard the phone ring just as he pulled the blade across the last patch of lather on his cheek. He rinsed the razor in the hot water and laid it aside. He was wiping the remnants of the lather from his face when Trudy stepped into the room.

"That was Tommy Ashley. He wants you to call him when you finish up," she said with a smile.

K.W. nodded and moved to the phone beside the bed. He dialed the number Tommy had given him and sat down as the phone began to ring.

"Sergeant Ashley," he heard.

"Good morning Tommy, this is K.W.," he said.

"You nearly aced that test K.W. You scored 99 out of 100 and then with your five-point veterans preference your total score is 104. That makes you number one on the eligibility list.

You passed the physical agility test, and we have completed your background. All that you need now is the polygraph. Are you ready for that?" Tommy asked.

"Yes, sir. All I need to know is when and where" K.W. felt his pulse racing.

"We contract with the Garland Police Department to do the polygraph on our applicants. I have you scheduled for two o'clock tomorrow afternoon. It will be at their main office, Two hundred North Fifth Street. Will that work for you?" Tommy asked.

"I will be there. Is there any special I need to know, what do I do after the test?" K.W. asked.

"No, nothing special. Well, wait one. Have you every had a polygraph exam before?" Tommy asked.

"No, Dallas wasn't using the polygraph for applicants when I was first hired, and I never had occasion to be tested after that," K.W. replied.

"Okay, so you don't know what to expect?" Tommy asked.

"Well, I have watched suspects and some witnesses being tested. So I know how the routine goes," K.W. said.

"I see. Since you are a former police officer, there will be some questions that most applicants don't get asked. But, the operator will explain all that to you. Just show up, and they will be expecting you.

Go on home after the test. They will call me with the results, and I will be in touch with you," Tommy said.

K.W. hung up the phone and looked at Trudy, "Polygraph tomorrow at the Garland Police Department," he said.

"What is a polygraph?" she asked.

"It is commonly called a lie detector. The operator hooks you up to a machine that measures your respiration, blood pressure, pulse rate and galvanic skin response. These are automatic or uncontrollable physiological functions.

The theory is that these remain unchanged from a norm, which the operator establishes before testing, when the subject gives a truthful response to a question. On the other hand, an untruthful answer or attempt to deceive produces stress which causes an increase in the indicators," K.W. replied.

"I understand the respiration, the blood pressure, and pulse rate; but what is galvanic skin response," she asked.

"The body produces electrical impulses. The skin is a conductor of those impulses. Psychological stress, like that which occurs when we want to escape detection in wrongdoing, produces physiological responses one of which is an increase in the activity of our sweat glands. The more active our sweat glands become, the better the skins' ability to conduct electrical impulses. The increase in electrical impulses then is taken as an indicator of one's attempt to deceive," K.W. explained.

"Then the whole purpose of this test is to see if you are a liar or that you have done something wrong that you are concealing," Trudy asked.

"Basically. But in pre-employment testing the polygraph is used to determine if there is a pattern of behavior that is inconsistent with the requirements or expectations of one who holds the job being applied for," K.W. said.

"How do you feel about taking the test? Does it make you think they don't trust you?" she asked with a frown.

K.W. chuckled, "No, not at all. They just want to be sure that I am fit to serve as a peace officer and that I will be a guardian of the public trust."

•   •   •

K.W. sat quietly as the operator placed the blood pressure cuff on his arm, the receptors on his fingers and then leaned forward in the chair so the band could be placed around his chest. The operator moved to his desk, which was directly behind K.W. and began the calibration of his equipment.

"Are you ready Mr. Bangs?" he asked.

"Yes," K.W. responded.

"Okay, I am now going to ask you a series of questions to establish a norm for your indicators. First, select a card from the deck on the table in front of you. Be careful to conceal the card, so I cannot see it. Now return the card to the deck.

I will now name each card in the deck and ask you if that is the card you chose. You will answer no each time I ask you. Do you understand?'" the operator asked.

"Yes I do," K.W. replied.

"Was the card you chose the Ace of Spades?" the operator began.

"No," K.W. responded.

"Was it the two of clubs," the operator asked.

"No," K.W. asked.

"Well, that didn't take long. You have just lied to me. The card you chose was indeed the two of clubs, was it not," there was a smirk in the examiners' voice.

"Yes, it was the two of clubs," K.W. admitted.

"Good. That shows you that you cannot lie to me. Now, let's get started.

Is your name Kenneth Wheat Bangs?"

"Yes," K.W. answered.

"Have you taken any substance to assist you in defeating this polygraph examination?" the examiner asked.

"No," K.W. answered.

"Have you participated in any training to assist you in defeating this polygraph examination?" he asked.

"No," K.W. said.

"Do you intend to give truthful answers to every question I ask you?" the examiner asked.

"Yes," K.W. responded.

"Is all the information you have provided during this application process true and correct to the best of your knowledge?" he asked.

"Yes," K.W. responded.

"Are you a practicing homosexual?" the examiner asked.

"No," K.W. answered.

"Have you ever participated in a homosexual act," he asked.

"No," K.W. asked.

"Are you attracted to men sexually," the examiner asked.

"No," K.W. answered.

"Have you ever participated in sexual activities with a child?" came the question.

"No," K.W. answered.

"Do you or have you ever looked at homosexual or pedophilia pornography?" he asked.

"No," K.W. answered.

"Have you ever engaged in an act of bestiality," the examiner asked.

"No," K.W. answered.

"Do you or have you ever worn women's clothing," the question came.

"No," K.W. answered.

"Do you use illicit drugs," the examiner asked.

"No," K.W. answered.

"Do you consider marijuana an illicit drug," he asked.

"Yes," K.W. answered.

"Have you ever smoked marijuana," the examiner asked.

"No," K.W. answered.

"Have you ever committed a crime that has not been discovered," the examiner asked.

"No," K.W. answered.

"Have you ever declared bankruptcy?" the examiner asked.

"No."

"Do you pay your bills?"

"Yes."

"Do you abuse animals?"

"No."

"While working as a police officer, have you ever abused a prisoner?" the question came.

"No," K.W. answered.

"While working as a police officer, have you ever concealed or participated in the concealing of a crime by another officer?" the examiner asked.

"No," K.W. asked.

"As a police officer, have you ever solicited or accepted a bribe in exchange for performing or withholding police action?" he asked.

"No," K.W. answered.

"Have you ever used your official position for personal gain, in any manner?" the examiner asked.

"No," K.W. answered.

"Have you ever planted evidence on or otherwise framed an innocent person?" was the question.

"No," K.W. answered.

"Have you ever known of a police officer committing a crime and not reported it?" the question came.

"No," K.W. answered.

"Have you given false testimony either in a court of law or any administrative hearing?" the examiner asked.

"No," K.W. answered.

"Have you ever used deadly force in the line of duty, either as a police officer or in the military?" the examiner asked.

"Yes," K.W. replied.

"Was the use of deadly force reported and was it found to be justified?" he asked.

"Yes," K.W. responded.

"Do you gamble," was the question.

"No," K.W. answered.

"Have you ever told a lie?" the examiner asked.

"Yes," K.W. answered.

"Have you told me a lie here today?" the examiner asked.

"Yes," K.W. answered.

There was a pause, and the examiner said, "Do you want to reconsider your last answer?"

"No, I lied to you about the card I chose from the deck, just as you told me to," K.W. answered.

The examiner laughed, "Right. Let's continue now."

"Other than the lie about the card, have you lied to me in answering any other questions here today?" the examiner asked.

"No," K.W. answered.

"Is your name Kenneth Wheat Bangs?" he asked.

"Yes," K.W. answered.

"Okay, that's it. You can relax," the examiner said as he moved to K.W. and started to unhook him from the machine.

"Why did you ask me my name again?" K.W. asked.

The examiner smiled and said, "Your answer shows deception. Could be a lot of reasons for that. The most common reason is that you don't like your name, probably your middle name. Don't worry about it. The fingerprints show you to be who you say you are. Or at least, who you have been known as for the past thirty years."

"Can you tell me the results of the examination?" K.W. asked.

"No, for a couple of reasons. First, I have to examine the chart and then have another licensed examiner review my findings. Secondly, the test was paid for by the Plano Police Department. The results go to them, and they can share them with you if they wish. But, I can say congratulations," he answered with a wink.

●　　　●　　　●

He stepped into the cool lobby and saw Tommy waiting for him. "Thanks for coming so quickly K.W. I called Judge Robinson, and he is waiting to swear you in."

"Judge Raymond Robinson?" K.W. asked with a smile.

"That's right. Do you know him?" Tommy asked.

"Known him for a long while. We are in lodge together," K.W. said.

"So, you are a Mason?" Tommy asked.

"Yes, I am. I am a member of the Plano Lodge, seven sixty eight," K.W. said

They walked into the courtroom, and Judge Robinson waved them to the front. "Hello K.W. I understand you are now a member of Plano's finest," he said.

"I will be as soon as you swear me in Judge," K.W. said shaking his friend's hand.

"Well then raise your right hand and repeat after me.

I, Kenneth Wheat Bangs, do solemnly swear and affirm, that I will faithfully execute the duties of the office of Police Officer of the City of Plano, State of Texas, and will to the best of my ability preserve, protect and defend the Constitution and Laws of the United States and of the State of Texas and the Charter and Ordinances of the City of Plano, Texas against all enemies both foreign and domestic;

And I furthermore solemnly swear and affirm, that I have not directly or indirectly paid, offered, or promised to pay, contributed, nor promised to contribute any money or valuable thing, or promised any public office or employment as a reward for the giving or withholding a vote to secure my appointment to the office of Police Officer for the City of Plano, Texas. So help me God."

K.W. lowered his hand and shook the Judge's hand again. "You are now officially a police officer in and for Plano, Texas. I enjoy seeing one of our young men coming home to help move Plano forward. I am here if you need me," the judge said.

"Thank you, Judge Robinson. I am glad to be here," K.W. said.

"Let's go K.W. I have to get you on a schedule. Jerry Scott will be your sergeant," Tommy said.

CHAPTER 23
BACK IN THE SADDLE

"Two twenty-two, what is your location?" the dispatcher asked.

"Eastbound on Park at Jupiter," K.W. responded.

"Take the robbery in progress at the Thunderbird Apartments, sixteen hundred East Fifteenth Street," the dispatcher said.

"Sixteen hundred East Fifteenth," K.W. acknowledged.

"Stand by one Two Twenty-Two; we have another caller on the line. Let me get more information for you."

"Ten-four, are you assigning a code on this call?"

"Your assignment is code three, two twenty-two. Copy additional information."

"Ready to copy," K.W. said.

"The suspect is a white male, with no shirt on, wearing blue jeans and tennis shoes. He is armed with a handgun.

The caller reports the suspect is kicking in the doors on individual apartment units and holding the residents at gunpoint as he takes their television or other electronics.

He is carrying the stolen merchandise downstairs and placing it in the back of a white Ford Van parked in the parking lot on the west side of the complex.

The Complainants state the individual appears to be impaired. They state he is very violent," the dispatcher said.

"Received, if the suspect is still there, you had better start me a cover squad," K.W. said.

"Two fifteen you will be the car two on this call," the dispatcher said.

"Two fifteen received. Show me in route from Jupiter and Fourteenth," Ken Powell acknowledged the call.

"Two Twenty-two is out at the scene," K.W. said.

"Two Twenty-two is out at Sixteen hundred hours. KKZ Nine Five Four, Police Department, Plano," the dispatcher said.

K.W. stepped from the black and white and started toward a crowd of people standing at the base of a staircase on the west side of the Thunderbird Apartments.

"Who called the police?" he asked.

A slender young man stepped forward and said, "I did officer."

"How can I help you," K.W. asked.

"The man sitting in that van just kicked in the door to my apartment and held my girlfriend and me at gunpoint while he stole my stereo," the young man said while pointing across the parking lot in the direction of a white Ford van.

"Do you know this man, is this the result of some disagreement between the two of you?" K.W. asked.

"No, sir. I have never seen him before in my life. The dude just kicked in the door, stole my stuff and carried it to the van. He has been sitting there ever since " the young man said.

"He kicked in our door too, and he took our portable television. He told my husband to sit down and shut up, or he would feed him some pistol," a red-haired woman said.

Her comment seemed to break the reluctance of the crowd to speak up, and different ones started shouting that the man had broken into their homes also.

"Hold on now. Let me talk with one at a time," K.W. said.

"What's your name, sir?" K.W. asked the first one to speak to him.

"Jason Steel."

"Okay, Mr. Steel. Did you say he had a firearm when he kicked in the door of your apartment?" K.W. asked glancing toward the van.

"Yes, sir. It is a big black revolver. My girlfriend and I were sitting on the couch talking when he kicked in the door.

I jumped up, and he shoved the pistol in my face and told me to sit down and keep my mouth shut, or he would blow my mother loving head off. Then he took my television and left with it," Jason said.

K.W. looked around as he heard the sound of a car and said, "Hey K.P. Thanks for the cover. These folks say there is a white male sitting in that van. They tell me that he kicked their doors and stole their property at gunpoint. Why don't you park your car just close enough that he can't back that van out and then let's go have a talk with him."

K.P. nodded and pulled the squad in behind the white van. He stepped from the vehicle and walked to the right rear of the vehicle and K.W. walked to the left rear.

"Sir, I am Officer K.W. Bangs with the Plano Police Department. I need you to step from the van so I can talk with you. Keep your hands away from your body and in the open, so I can see that you are not armed. Step from the vehicle now," K.W. said.

He could see the reflection of the suspected robber in the mirror mounted on the drivers' side of the van. The man did not move. He just stared at K.W.

"K.P., I can see him in the mirror on this side. He is wasted. Let's go ahead and move up. I will open the door and pull him out on this side.

As soon as I open that door, you step up to the window on that side and cover me. Don't you let him shoot me or I will haunt you every minute of the rest of your sorry life," K.W. winked at his partner.

K.P. drew his weapon, and they started inching up the side of the van. K.W. kept his left-hand free so he could open the door and grab the suspect quickly.

As they reached a point, just behind the edge of the door, K.W. said, "Sir, we have been told that you have a firearm in your possession. For your and our safety, I am asking you to put both hands out of the window and leave them there while I open the door and remove you from the van."

The man just stared at K.W. He neither moved nor replied.

K.W. reached across his body with his left hand and opened the door of the van.

"Gun, he has a gun in his hand," K.P. yelled.

K.W. pivoted forward and slammed his left fist into the chest of the suspect. He heard the suspect grunt and saw him slump forward over the steering wheel of the van.

K.W. holstered his weapon and stepped into the opening of the door. He grasped the subject by the shoulders and pulled him from the van. The suspect grabbed the doorframe with his left hand and raised his right hand. K.W. saw the pistol.

K.W. smashed his right fist into the suspect's face and reached for the pistol with his left hand. K.W.'s fist ruptured the man's lips, and blood splattered across the windshield and onto K.W.'s arm.

K.P raced around the rear of the van. He ripped the pistol from the man's grasp and stepped away with it.

K.W. saw the fist coming, but there was nothing he could do to avoid it. Lights exploded behind his eyes, and he felt his knees buckle as the blow landed on his left temple.

The pain in his head brought instant nausea. K.W. knew he was in trouble; he felt the darkness reaching for him and knew he had to act.

He pushed up with his knees and hammered the suspect with an elbow to the mouth. He heard the gasp of pain and felt the mutilated flesh part and teeth give way.

Turning to face the suspect, K.W. was met with a left hook to his ribs followed by a right uppercut that barely missed ending the fight. K.W. reached into his back right pocket and withdrew his slapper.

He pushed back against the open door and allowed the spring from the hinges propel him forward. He lifted the lead filled leather over his head and brought it down in a vicious arching chop that struck the suspect across the left eyebrow. The slapper opened the flesh; crushing the bone and peeling the man's eyebrow and eyelid back to rest across the bridge of his nose.

The suspect wrapped his arms around K.W.'s knees and dragged him to the ground. K.W. rolled the dazed combatant onto his stomach and quickly snapped a handcuff on his left hand.

The suspect twisted away and slammed a knee into K.W.'s ribs.

The force of the blow knocked him onto his side. K.W. rolled into the legs of a bystander and looked up to see that the crowd had surrounded him and the suspect. They moved away, but no one offered to help him.

He heard a grunt and turned back to see that the suspect had managed to stand. K.W. placed his right hand on the concrete and pushed himself up onto his knees.

The suspect stepped forward and swung his right foot toward K.W. The booted foot struck him in the abandon.

The air rushed from K.W.'s lungs, and he fell forward. As he was falling, he wrapped his arms around his assailant's legs. Hardened hands battered the back of his neck, and the one loose handcuff slammed into the side of his head.

K.W. pushed forward and felt his opponent losing his balance. He pushed again, and the suspect toppled over backward. The man's head bounced off of the feet of an onlooker.

K.W. crawled forward quickly and straddled the suspect. He looked into the man's eyes and saw raw hatred. A meaty right hand raced toward K.W.'s face.

He lifted his left arm and warded off the blow. K.W. shot home a right to the nose of his opponent. He heard and felt the cartilage give way and blood gushed out and into the mouth of the belligerent armed robber.

The blood blocked the man's throat, choking him and ending the fight. K.W. quickly rolled him onto his stomach.

K.P. had secured the suspects' firearm in the trunk of his patrol vehicle and raced back to assist K.W. He placed his left knee in the middle of the suspects' back and grabbed the right hand in both of his. Together, he and K.W. were able to exert enough force to bring the arm and hand behind the back of the suspect and handcuff him.

K.W. rocked back on his heels gasping for air. He watched as K.P. rolled the suspect onto his back and was shocked at the swollen, bloody lump of broken bone and pulpy flesh that had been a recognizable human face a moment before. "Get him an ambulance K.P.," K.W. said.

"I don't want any damned ambulance. Just take these handcuffs off of me, and I will kill your sorry ass," the man shouted as he struggled against the metal restraints.

K.P. walked back to his patrol vehicle and sat down. Lifting the microphone, he said, "Two-Fifteen, we have the suspect in custody, and the scene is secure. We do need an ambulance to examine injuries the suspect suffered during his resistance to arrest."

"Ten Four Two-Fifteen. All units code four on the robbery in progress. I will order the ambulance for you Two-Fifteen," the dispatcher replied.

•   •   •

The paramedics stood by the blood-soaked man. "Sir, you have a broken nose, your mouth is a bloody mess, you have one broken tooth that I can see, and it looks like a couple more have been knocked out. It also appears that your left cheekbone is broken. You need more help than we can give you.

We are going to transport you to the hospital so a physician can give you the medical assistance you need," the crew chief said.

"Hell no. You are not taking me to the hospital. Just get me to the jail so I can call a lawyer," the man said.

"That's up to the police. But the fact that you are obviously not feeling the pain that these injuries should produce leads me to suspect that you are under the influence of some chemical agent. If you are, that could also pose a risk to your well being. Will you tell me what drugs you have taken?" the paramedic asked.

K.P. held up a baggie containing a white substance and said; "I found this in the van. It is probably coke. That could explain his aggressive behavior and the fact that he is not feeling much if any pain."

"Is that it? Did you do some coke," the paramedic asked.

The man shook his head and said, "I don't do coke. That is PCP, and I don't care who knows it," the man said.

"If this is PCP, and you have taken as much as I suspect, you can be in real danger of a cardiac arrest. Let us transport you to the hospital," the crew chief said.

"No, leave me alone," he snapped.

"Okay, that is it for us. We are going to list you two officers as witnesses to his refusal of medical services," the paramedic said as he closed his bag and walked away.

K.W. and K.P. lifted the man from his sitting position and escorted him to K.W.'s vehicle. "Put him in the front with me," K.W. said.

K.P. opened the passenger side door and eased the man into the vehicle. He leaned over to fasten the seat belt, and the suspect head-butted him.

K.P. stood up and backed away. "That is the meanest son of a bitch I have seen in a while. Are you sure you want to transport him alone?"

"No, not after that. Let's get him out of the car, move him to the back seat and buckle him in tight. I will drive, and you can ride back there with him. I will bring you to your car after we get him booked in," K.W. said.

"No K.W. I will drive, and you ride in the back with him," K.P. grinned.

"Okay, let's get this done," K.W. said reaching for the prisoner.

•   •   •

Sergeant Jerry Scott was standing in the booking area when K.W. and K.P. brought the prisoner into the jail. He winced when he saw the man.

"Sit him down right there. You can't put this man in jail. He has to go to the hospital," the sergeant said.

"Fine with us, Sergeant. But he refused medical treatment on the scene, and I doubt he will agree to go to the hospital," K.W. said.

"What is his name?" Scott asked.

"He refuses to give us his name, and he has no identification on him," Ken Powell said.

Scott looked at the prisoner and said, "What's your name

partner?"

"One thing for damned sure. I am not your partner, and I am not saying anything else. Except, I want a lawyer," the man replied.

"Okay, that's it. Did the paramedics document the refusal of medical services?" Scott asked.

"Yep, and listed us as witnesses," K.P. answered.

"Good, who has the paper on this?" the sergeant asked.

"I do, but there are so many loose ends. I need some help," K.W. said.

"Like what," Scott asked.

"We had Mike Anderson stand by and protect the scene while we brought this guy to jail. I need crime scene to process the apartments he robbed. Then, they need to process the van and place those electronics he took into evidence.

I can get the booking finished on the suspect, I will just do a John Doe with a refusal to identify, and then get back out to the scene to interview the victims and have the van towed in," K.W. said.

"Sounds like a plan. In the meantime, I have to notify the duty chief, and he may want to come down to look at the prisoner. I would suspect that the chief will have some questions for you, given the injuries to this man," Scott said.

"I will be right here, doing the John Doe booking sheet," K.W. answered.

"No need for that. We have the returns on the VIN and the plate off of his van," K.P. said.

"Let's hear it," K.W. said.

"The van is a seventy-two Ford Econoline. The plates on it come back stolen out of Sioux City, Iowa. We checked the VIN on this van against the one the plates come back to and of course they are different.

Then we ran the VIN off of his van. It is clear and comes back registered to Wilfred Agnus Pinafore out of Lawton, Iowa. Lawton is about twelve miles East of Sioux City.

There is also an NCIC hit on the van. There are three warrants issued for Wilfred, and the notes indicate he is expected to be driving this Ford Van.

The first warrant is for the burglary of a business in Sioux City. Guess what was taken? Televisions, he took nothing but televisions. The second warrant is for the burglary of railroad boxcars out of Dakota City, Iowa. Guess what was taken, televisions again.

And the third warrant is a blue warrant for parole violation. It seems Wilfred did some time in the Iowa State Corrections Department, got paroled and is in violation of the conditions of that parole.

We have confirmed the warrants and the Woodbury County Iowa Sheriff's Office say they will extradite," K.P. said.

"How do we know this man is Pinafore?" Scott asked.

"I asked the Sheriff's office to send us his photo. It should be here in a minute, along with his fingerprint classification. We will get Bill in here to print him and compare his prints with those on the want sheet. Then we will know," K.P. said.

"You are not going to take my prints until I talk with my lawyer," the prisoner said.

"Yes we are," Scott said.

"Then by God, you can get ready for another fight," the prisoner said from behind the cell door.

The speaker spluttered above the booking desk, and the officers looked up at it. "K.P. your picture and fingerprint classification just came in," a Jerri Brookalieu said from the dispatcher's office.

K.P. was out of the booking area on the run to get the photograph. He came back with a grin and said, "No need for the fight. This is our man."

He handed the photograph to the sergeant, and K.W. leaned in to look over his shoulder.

"Yes, sir! It is without a doubt him. Confirm the identification to the Sheriff but tell them we have felony charges to be filed here. We will let the District Attorney handle the extradition issues. Book him for aggravated robbery," Scott said.

"Well, what about his resisting arrest and assaulting me," K.W. asked.

"Comes with the job. Get over it. Get him booked in and then get back in service," the sergeant said as he walked away.

K.W. stood looking at the sergeant's retreating back, and then he smiled, *'I'm back in the saddle again. And that is exactly where I want to be.'*

CHAPTER 24
THE BLUE MOON

His skin was slick with sweat. A drop trickled down his neck, found the channel of his spine and slid all the way to his belt line. He leaned forward, away from the vinyl seat covering and reached back to pull the sticky shirt free of his overheated body.

The light changed, and he moved through the intersection and took the first right onto Avenue F. The street was deserted. He slowed the car and made a U-turn, stopping in front of the McHenry house.

He glanced at his wristwatch and saw that it was already half past ten. *'This is perfect timing. Judge Ryan set his curfew at ten o'clock on weeknights. That was nearly half and hour ago. He will have no excuse for not being home,'* he smiled.

He switched the engine off and stepped from the county car. He closed the door quietly and stood for a few seconds looking at the front of the house. *'There is not a light showing. I'm going to wake some folks up, or I'm going to find no one home,'* he mused as he stepped onto the front porch.

He shifted his flashlight to his left hand and rapped on the front door with it. A light came on inside the house, and he heard movement, the sound of someone shuffling toward the front door.

"Who is it?" came the call from inside.

"Glen Stone. I'm Anthony's probation officer. I'm doing a check on him and need him to come to the door," he spoke.

The door creaked open, and a sliver of light fell across Stone's face. One eye and part of a cheek pressed against the opening. Stone lifted his badge and held it so the eye could see it. "Open the door and let me in or tell Anthony to come talk with me," he said.

The door closed and the light inside the house was turned off. Stone knocked again but there was no response.

Stone sighed and tapped his flashlight on the door again. No one responded. *'Just as I thought, he is not here. And, when I file a revocation he will just say that he was asleep and his sister didn't wake him up. I can't get into the house and will not be able to prove otherwise. Same song, different verse,'* Stone mumbled as he turned and stepped off of the front porch.

Stone walked back to the car and sat down. He pressed the button on his flashlight and moved the beam over the stack of folders lying on the front seat. Flipping through the stack he saw the one he was looking for, *'there it is, Anthony McHenry.'*

He opened the folder and scanned the probation report for McHenry's known associates and places he was known to frequent. *'The Brakes, he likes to run with the Brakes. And I see that they like to hang out at Susie Bill's and the Blue Moon. If I can testify that he is there in violation of his curfew, the Judge just might lock him up for a while,'* Stone tossed the folder aside and started the car.

He stopped just down the street from The Blue Moon. The parking lot was filled with light spilling from racks of lights hanging from wires running from the building and nailed to trees, or anything that would hold them up.

Men sat around tables, playing cards and dominoes. Beer cans and bottles sat on the ground beside each chair. Collin County was dry meaning the sale of alcoholic beverages was prohibited.

Stone knew from experience that should the police show up; the players would disavow ownership of the alcohol declaring that someone else must have left the can beside the chair. But he didn't care about the alcohol, unless he could catch Tony McHenry in possession. That too would be a violation of his probation.

Stone had no intention of walking into the Blue Moon alone. He lifted the microphone and said, "Collin Sixteen."

"Go ahead Collin Sixteen," came the reply.

"Contact Plano P.D. and ask them to have a unit, preferably a two man unit, meet me two blocks north of the Blue Moon on Avenue I," he said.

"Stand by one Collin Sixteen," the dispatcher said.

Stone sat still, watching the activity at The Blue Moon. "Collin Sixteen, a Plano unit is in route to meet you. Their ETA is three minutes," the dispatcher said.

"Received. We will be on a mark out at the Blue Moon as soon as they get here," he said.

"You are on mark at the Blue Moon," the dispatcher said, and the car was quite again.

Stone sat thinking about Anthony McHenry. He had been caught burglarizing a business here in Plano. He had no prior convictions, and his attorney had cut a deal with the district attorney for a five-year probated sentence in exchange for Tony pleading guilty. Judge Ryan had assigned him to do a pre-sentence investigation to determine if Tony was eligible and a good candidate for probation.

He remembered doing the family study. There was no father in the home, but he was present and well known in the tight-knit Douglas Community. His name was Silas. He and Tony's mother, Eva, had never married. But they remained a couple producing five boys and two girls over the years.

Silas was a burglar by trade. He was always getting caught and spent so much time in the Texas Prison System that he joked about being *'from Huntsville.'* His multiple convictions and years in prison meant that he provided no support for the family. Eva survived by cleaning the offices and sometimes the homes of the wealthy white folks in town.

Every time he got out, he would come back to Plano and Eva would take him back in. Soon, there would be another McHenry on the way.

Silas was also a drinker. He was the self-proclaimed *'moon king'* of Plano. Every Friday and Saturday night he could be found at the Blue Moon or Susie Bill's *'rattling the bones'* as he liked to say.

He had no money but would badger and threaten until someone

would '*spot*' him a game. If he lost, he would owe the winner and if he won he would demand payment in an instant.

Fearful men would buy him a beer, and as soon as he had consumed a couple, he became belligerent. A big man, he would insult and push until someone stood up to him and fought.

Silas would beat them to the ground and take their money as '*the spoils of war.*' It was robbery of course, but no one would testify against Silas McHenry.

Stone had found that Silas was as brutal at home as he was on the street. Eva had defended Tony's lawlessness by telling Stone that Silas beat him as a baby and continued the abuse into Tony's teenage years.

She said that Silas started teaching his boys to steal as soon as they were old enough to go into stores with him. He would keep the clerk busy while the boys would shoplift. Soon he was giving them lists of what to steal from each store. And then, the last time he came home from prison he had taken Tony and Zeke with him on his forays into the night.

Eva claimed that a police sergeant named Dennis Bolly had caught Silas and the boys burglarizing the feed store and made them split the goods with him. She said that was why Silas had been out of prison so long this time; the sergeant was protecting him and the boys.

Eva said that Anthony had got caught on this last burglary because he went out on his own, without the cover of his dad and the sergeant. He had broken into Wheeler's television repair shop and been caught by officers responding to a silent alarm.

Stone had pressed her on this, looking for information that would enable him to file a case on the police sergeant. When she realized what he was angling for, she had clammed up. Finally, she told Stone that she would deny ever saying anything about Silas and the sergeant.

She did say that she would testify that her son had become a burglar because he feared the beatings his dad would give him if he refused. Silas would beat her too, and she had had enough. She wanted him to go back to prison, to be filed on as a habitual offender so he would never be able to come back to Plano.

Stone had taken the information to the District Attorney. After many long hours of looking for a way to prove what Eva was saying, they realized that the proof just was not there.

They consulted with the Judge, and he had directed the District Attorney to have an unofficial visit with the Chief of Police. Not long after that visit, the sergeant resigned his position with the Plano Police and Silas was caught burglarizing the Lumber Yard. He was filed on as a habitual offender and Eva had her wish.

Anthony dropped out of school. He was soon the new bully in the Douglas Community. Anthony McHenry was the prime suspect in every business house burglary in the City. He had become his father's son.

Light splashed across the back window. Stone glanced up at the rearview mirror and saw a black and white squad car pulling up behind him. The lights switched off, and two officers stepped from the cruiser and approached Stone.

Stone stepped from his car and held his badge up, "Glen Stone with Collin County Probation. I am looking for Anthony McHenry. He is supposed to be home by ten o'clock. I just left his house, and he is not there. He is known to associate with the Brake boys and to hang out at The Blue Moon and Susie Bill's. If I find him at either, I am going to take him into custody and file for a revocation of his probation. Will you two cover me while I take a look see?"

"To answer your question, sure we will. But we know Tony. We also know Willis and Cedric Brake. Those are his main running buddies. They are all three tush-hogs. Tony will not go without a fight and if Tony fights, Willis and Cedric will too. Just so you know, there will be a fight," one officer said.

Glen looked at the officer's name badge and saw that his name was R.L. Smither. He looked at the other officer and saw that his name was A.R. Hibbs. "Thanks, guys. I figured we would be in for a fight, but Tony will not report, he does not pay his fees, he does not work or go to school and he has no regard for any of the other conditions of his probation. It is time he was held accountable.

Word will go out that we are on the street as soon as we hit the Blue Moon. Could you get another unit hit Susie Bill's at the same time we hit the Moon and hold Tony if they see him?" K.W. asked.

"Sure. Wait here for me. I will get on the radio and have a unit get over to Susie Bill's," Smither said.

Stone and the uniformed officers stayed in the shadows as they walked alongside the old building. They paused before leaving the shadows.

"As soon as we step out and they see us there will be a mass exodus out of that back door. One of you need to be stationed back there to grab Tony if he comes out," Stone whispered over his shoulder.

"I got the back door," Hibbs said as he turned and hustled toward the back of the building.

"Ready?" Stone asked.

"Let's go," Smither said.

They stepped around the corner of the building and men started running. Stone continued on, right up the steps and into the building. All conversation stopped as every black face in the building turned toward the white officers. Milo Windage came from behind the bar, "Good evening officers. What can we do for you?"

"I want Tony McHenry, Mr. Windage. Soon as I have him, we will be gone and you good folks can get back to your entertainment. Simple as that," Stone said.

"Well sir, Tony McHenry is not here. I have not seen him tonight, and I have no idea where he is. You officers are welcome to look around. Just take your time and let me know if you need anything from me. Yes, sir. Just let me know," Milo said with a smile.

Smither leaned forward and whispered in Stone's ear, "If Milo says that Tony is not here, you can believe him. Milo does not lie to us."

Stone nodded and said, "That's good enough for me. Thank you, Milo. I am sorry to interrupted your evening folks."

They stepped from the building into a now empty parking lot. Beer cans rolled where the occasional breeze took them, and dominos lay scattered across the empty tables.

A Plano Police cruiser drove into the lot, and the driver said, "Just left Susie Bill's. Neither Tony nor the Brake boys are there. I talked with a snitch on the sly, and he said they haven't been around tonight. If I were a betting man, I would bet that means they are breaking into somebody's building."

Stone nodded and said, "Yes, and now that we have missed him he will be in the wind. I will have a Blue Warrant tomorrow and get the information out to all the Police Departments in the county. I know your shift is about to end. I sure would appreciate you all passing the word to your deep night crew that we want him."

CHAPTER 25
COMING IN

Alex Brake watched the officers leave The Blue Moon from his Auntie's porch across the street. He was sitting in the swing, behind the Burford Holly that his Auntie had shaped into what she called a poodle tree. The shadows were deep enough and the foliage trimmed in such a manner that he could watch them without being seen.

He remained hidden until the officers had left and he saw the taillight of the last car turn off of Avenue F onto Fourteenth Street. Then he moved, walking slowly down the steps and across the street toward the club.

Still jumpy from the police poking around his neighborhood, Alex stood just out of the light, at the corner of the building. He heard voices and saw Jim Ray Sawyer emerge from his hiding place in the bushes across the parking lot.

He waited until Jim Ray was closer and then said, "Jim Ray, it's me Alex. Could you hear what those police officers were saying? Why were they down here?"

"I heard them all right. They are looking for Tony McHenry. The one in the suit said he wanted him on a probation violation."

"Damned! I got to find Tony and let him know. Have you seen him tonight?" Alex asked.

"I saw him earlier, as I was walking here. He and Ruben were standing on the porch over at the Simpson's house. But that was two hours ago. I haven't seen them since " Jim Ray said.

Alex waved his thanks at Jim Ray and leaned back against the building to think. *'Jim Ray saw Ruben and Tony at the Simpsons. I bet they are still there smoking some weed.'* He pushed away from the building and headed for the Simpsons' house.

Alex darted across the street and between the houses and into the alley running parallel to F Avenue. Six houses down was Pete and Ralph Simpson's house. He pushed the rusted gate open and ran quickly across the yard and up the back steps. He pounded on the door and waited.

"Who is it?" Alex recognized Ralph's voice.

"Alex, open the door," Alex whispered.

The door swung open, and waves of smoke wafted out. "Man, you dudes are smoking some strong dope. That must be Maui Wowie," Alex said inhaling deeply.

He looked past Ralph at the shadowy figures in the dark room and saw Tony McHenry. "Tony, the police are looking for you. They just left the Moon. Jim Ray heard them talking, and he said they are looking for you on a probation violation."

"I knew that was coming. I haven't reported in three months," Tony said.

"Why not dude? I mean you fall behind this, and Judge Ryan is going to lock you up," Alex said.

"I can't report, Alex. I have been smoking dope all day long every day. When I walk into that office, Stone is going to make me pee in a jar, and as soon as the results come back, I'm busted. On top of that, I dropped out of school and don't have a job. That means I don't have any money to pay my fees or fines," Tony said.

"So now what?" Ralph asked.

"I say we pull some jobs and get some money together. We can hide Tony long enough that the weed won't show up in his pee, we use the money we make to pay his fines and fees, and he will just have to take his chances on the rest of it," Ruben said.

"What jobs?" Alex asked.

"Tony and I have been looking at that line of buildings on Park, just west of Avenue K. The Adobe Village they call it.

There is a television repair shop, an auto repair place, cleaners, a donut shop and a pizza place all sharing common walls. After we get into one, we simply knock a hole in the wall and crawl through into the next one.

The pizza place, the cleaners, and the donut shop should have some cash stashed away for the morning crew to use when they open the shop. The car repair and television shop will have things that we can kipe and sell easily.

The crew at the donut shop is the first to arrive. They get there about four o'clock to start cooking. The rest of them don't open until eight or later.

It is a quarter to eleven. If we leave now, we can hit all of those shops and be back home before the donut shop crew shows up," Ruben leaned back and toked on the number.

"Works for me," Tony said.

"Whatever," Ralph nodded.

The three of them looked at Alex who was shaking his head back and forth, "Whoa, now brothers. Let's talk about this for a minute. That is a good five miles from where we are sitting. We don't have a car. How are we going to get out there, to this Adobe Village?

Then once we are there, how are we going to get inside? Do they have alarms and what about the police patrols? Then, let's say we pull this off; how are we going to get all that loot back here? Where will we stash it? And, who is going to buy it from us?

We got to think this through. We can't just be running out kicking in doors and expect to accomplish anything except getting locked up with Tony," he said.

"We will have to boost a car," Tony said around a drag on the joint.

"I got that covered. Old Miss Gladys, who lives over by Shiloh Baptist, has a clean little Chevy Bel Air. Bet that car doesn't have ten thousand miles on it. It is a stick shift, and the ignition is a piece of cake. I can have it rolling in three minutes top, and she is so deaf she won't hear a thing.

I have used it a couple of times, put it back before she woke up, and she never knew it had left the yard," Ralph said with a smile.

"Okay, so we got wheels. Now, where will we stash all the goods and who will fence it for us? And what about the alarms and the police" Alex asked again.

"Man Alex, you are too tight. Relax brother! Here, hit this and let me explain it to you," Ralph pushed the joint toward Alex.

"Those cracker box buildings don't have any alarms. They set so far out in the open that we can see the police coming from three blocks away. We just set us a good eye and get busy.

Once we have all the stuff we want, we pull the Chevy around into the back alley and load it into the trunk and back seat of the Chevy. We will drive right back to Miss Gladys' house, back the car up to that old shed at the end of her driveway and unload.

The shed has a side door. I have already jacked the lock on it. I have been taking my girl in there you dig?

Inside the shed is a pile of tarps. We set the stuff inside the door and pull a couple of tarps over them. I will put the Chevy back where she keeps it and bam we are gone.

Then, tomorrow we see Joe Stinson. He is that old white dude that owns the big red building on Avenue K just across the tracks. He has been known to buy at midnight sales.

He has that old Ford panel truck sitting out back. It runs good, but he never learned to drive, and he doesn't like to be seen out in public. He's what you might call a recluse, but he still needs things, and he hates having to leave his 'private little world.'

He calls Buddy Brannon's Supermarket and they will carry an order of groceries to his place. That works well for him.

But he also loves to drink. He will drink anything, but he prefers whiskey. That man drinks all day long.

The problem is, the Creek is the closest package store where he can legally buy anything to drink, and he doesn't drive. He could get it from bootleggers, but he doesn't trust them. He is afraid they will rob him or see all the stuff he has stashed in that old building and tell somebody.

I heard about him buying out of the back door and went by with a load. He took it all and gave me a good price. The next time I went by, he hit me up to bring him a load of whiskey. I worked a deal with Susie Bill, and we were in business.

And, then one day I went by there and he was about half drunk. He bought my stuff and then offered me a drink.

I could see that he had something on his mind, so I took a glass and set down with him. We chatted a minute, and then he opened up and shared a 'secret' with me.

He likes to look at pictures of naked boys; I mean little guys. He told me that he had been getting them through the mail. Then he said that one day he noticed the package appeared to have been opened. This made him nervous. He figured the feds were onto him. So he stopped ordering them.

After a week or so, he said Lee Mayfield and Scott Bell came by to do an inspection of his buildings. After they had been there a few minutes, Vernon Robinson drove up. He said they walked around but weren't doing an inspection.

Finally, Scott walked over and stood in the door. Joe said it looked to him like Scott was a lookout and he got scared. Then he said that Lee told him that the word was out that he had been looking at dirty pictures of little boys. Vernon asked him if that was true.

Stinson denied it all, but he said they knew he was lying to them. He said Vernon told him that the brothers over at the lodge would not take kindly to it, should they find out he was looking at naked kids. Lee nodded, agreeing with Vernon and told Joe that the fire department was worried about the hazard his building presented to the safety of the town.

Then they both explained to him that the safety of the town and the safety of the kids were their main reason for talking with him. They told him they were going to keep an eye on him and would be back if and when it became clear that some 'corrective action' needed to be taken.

That scared the hell out of him. But, after a while, that urge to see those nasty pictures got the better of him. So, he asked me to drive into Dallas and buy them for him. He said I could take the panel truck and offered to pay me fifty bucks.

'*Hell yes,*' I said. Then, I got to thinking. All this knowledge might be worth a lot more than fifty dollars to me.

One day we were having a drink, and I told him that I had been thinking about what the brothers over at the lodge might do to me, me being a Black Man, if they found out that I was getting those pictures of little white boys for him. I told him that I didn't want the lodge brothers after me and that I wasn't going to have anything more to do with those pictures.

He told me that he had been expecting me to say that and was prepared to increase the incentive to assume such a great risk. '*Tell me what you have in mind,*' I said to him.

To make a long story short, we went into business together. He lets me take the panel on some moonlight jobs and pays me top dollar on what I bring in. Sometimes, I drive a load down to a pawnshop in Red Oak.

The dude who owns the pawnshop and Joe are working together. The old man down there will give me a list of what he wants Joe to get for him. Joe pays me to fill the order for him.

Now, that '*special relationship*' we share is going to ensure that we have a market for our loot and that we get top dollar for it. The old cooter is tighter than Jakes' Hatband, but we can get enough to make our night worthwhile. Trust me, Alex; we got this."

Alex sat back staring at Ralph. He looked around at the others and saw the grins on their faces. It hit him; they had been in this with Ralph all along.

"Wow! You all knew; everyone but me knew all about this. I feel like such an idiot," Alex said.

Ruben stood and said, "Nothing personal brother. We were just watching, seeing how much we could trust you. We have been working jobs with Ralph all along. Like the man said, we got this.

If you want in, come on. But this is not a onetime deal. If you come in, you are in all the way. Dig?"

Alex stood with the others and said, "I dig, and *I'm coming in.*"

CHAPTER 26
IN THE ALLEY

He pinned the badge on the left chest of the shirt and checked the collar brass. Satisfied that all was correctly placed, he removed the shirt from the wire hanger and slipped into it.

He was running just a little late, so he worked the buttons quickly, tucked the shirt into his pants and then reached for the gun belt. He wrapped it around his waist, put the keepers in place and adjusted the placement of the holster.

Turning, he picked the pistol up off of the bench in front of his locker. He opened the cylinder and checked the rounds. '*Six, hot and ready*' he mused and slid the firearm into the holster. He fastened the safety strap and turned to the door.

The squad room was alive with the buzz of men's voices. He smiled as he walked to the back counter and signed the duty roster. He was amazed at the comfort the sound of those voices; the creaking of Sam Browne duty belts and the smell of Hoppe's gun oil brought him. '*This is a man's world*' he mumbled softly.

" K.W.? Don't be a chauvinist. I am a part of this world too, you know," a soft voice said beside him.

K.W. glanced to his right and saw a troubled face. Habit caused him to run a glance over her uniform, across the leather and down to her boots. "Well, do I pass inspection?" she asked.

He nodded and said, "Kim, you are a fine example of a police officer. And, I apologize about the man's world comment. I didn't mean any disrespect."

"Oh, I know that K.W. But, like the good book says, "Out of the fullness of the heart the tongue speaks,'" she said with a roll of the eyes.

"What does that mean?" he asked.

"That means that you are an old mossback who thinks a woman's place is at home with a husband and not on the street as a police officer. That's what you think, and it slipped out. But hey, I'm going to show you that I can do this job just as well as any man," she said as she moved to the front of the room and sat down.

K.W. watched Kim for a minute. He felt distressed, but not about her viewing him as a chauvinist. It was that parting statement, *'I am going to show you that I can do this job as well as any man.'*

He walked to the front table and sat down beside her. She glanced at him out of the corner of her eye.

K.W. looked at the young face, the determined set of her lips and thought, *'she believes that she has to prove herself.'*

He turned sideways in the chair so he could face her. He placed his left arm on the back of her chair and leaned in so she could hear his lowered voice.

"Kim, listen to me. You think you know me, but the truth is that you don't even know what you *don't know* about me. Granted, I am old school in a lot of my thinking.

But that does not extend to a prejudice against women as police officers. I don't see gender, I don't see race, and I don't see Creed. All I see is one who is willing to stand the line between right and wrong.

Every time you pin that badge on and toe the line, look to your left and your right. You will see me standing with you. And when I toe that line, I know you will be standing right beside me. That is the way it has to be if we are to survive, if we are to be there for those we have sworn to defend and serve."

Kim sighed heavily and shifted in the chair, turning away from him. K.W. pressed on, "I know you think I'm preaching. Maybe I am, but my intention is to give you the benefit of my years on the street.

That experience allows me to recognize traits in young officers that can be fatal. I see one in you.

It is this determination to prove that you can do this job as well as a man. That attitude will eventually lead you to take a chance that could be fatal."

She turned, and he could see that her eyes were glistening. "What gives you the right to lecture me, to speak to me as if I am a trainee and you are my trainer? I am not your trainee and you are not my trainer. We are peers, aren't we K.W.?" she asked.

Her words stung and he was tempted to say the hell with it and walk away. He started to stand, but then he sat back down. "I apologize if I came off as lecturing you. I know you are not a trainee and I am not assuming the role of your superior.

But I have seen this before. None of us are looking for you to prove anything. Don't go out trying to prove anything to yourself.

Follow procedure, every time. Wait for cover, do not enter a building alone, be firm in you approach to enforcement, but don't be so hard that you provoke folks.

There was only one John Wayne, and he worked from a script. If things didn't go well, he could re-shoot the scene. On the street, there are no do-overs. Overextend and someone will get hurt.

I don't want to be a pallbearer. I want you to go home at the end of the day. That's all I'm saying."

He saw her face soften. Her shoulders slumped, and she took a deep breath. She lowered her eyes and said, "Okay, I hear you. I do want to be the best police officer I can be. But I also want to go home at the end of the day. I will do what you say; and I need you to tell me when I'm pushing too hard, I want to learn," she whispered.

They sat looking at each other. Each knew that a bond had just been forged. They were linked together in the call to be guardians.

•   •   •

"Two Sixteen is clear the minor seven."

"Two Sixteen will be clear on service number seventy seven ten forty-five B. It is two forty-five a.m. KKZ Nine Five Four Police Department, Plano."

"Seventy-Seven, Ten Forty-Five B," K.W. confirmed the service number and replaced the microphone in its holder.

He folded the accident report, stuck it above the sun visor and stepped from the cruiser to stretch his cramped muscles. He walked to the back of the car and leaned against the fender.

The parking lot was empty at this time of night. He swept his eyes across the darkened storefronts looking for any movement, anything out of order. Satisfied that all was well, he pushed away from the car and moved toward the open driver's door. He placed one hand on top of the door and the other one on the steering wheel and stepped inside with his right foot. He froze, half in and half out of the car.

'What was that?' he asked himself. He stood still, waiting for the sound to come again.

'There it is again. That was the sound of something being bashed. Where did the noise come from?' his pulse was now pounding in his head.

K.W. switched the engine off and stepped from the car. His muscles were taut with the tension. Then it came again, and he knew that the noise was coming from The Adobe Village, across Avenue K from where he was standing. He moved back to the car, settled in and picked up the microphone.

"Two Sixteen."

"Go ahead Two Sixteen."

"I am going to be in the alley behind The Adobe Village at Avenue K and Parker Road. Start me a cover unit this way. Have them step it up," K.W. said as he drove through the intersection and cut the headlights on the patrol unit.

He moved slowly and quietly along Parker Road until he could turn into the alley leading to the back of the buildings. He stopped the vehicle just before he reached the back edge of the line of business buildings.

He placed the car in park, switched the engine off and opened the door carefully. He had disconnected the dome light for occasions just like this one. He sat in the dark cruiser a few seconds listening. He heard a shuffling noise, 'someone is walking in the alley. They are dragging something. It sounds like they are moving slowly and are so close to *the buildings that they are scraping against them as they move along,'* he thought.

K.W. reached across the seat and ran his hand along the stock of the Ithaca. His mind ran back through his preparing the shotgun for service. He had loaded it with five double-ought Buckshot Shells, but the chamber was empty. To pump one into the chamber now would make too much noise.

He stepped from the vehicle with the shotgun held in front of him. He walked to the edge of the building and leaned forward. As he looked down the alley, he noticed that the security light mounted above the third store down was not working. He remained in place a few seconds to allow his eyes to adjust, to be able to discern the difference from that area flooded with light and that one dark spot.

He saw something glistening on the pavement, and then it hit him, *'that's the glass dome that covered the security light. It has been broken out.'*

The back door of each store was recessed into the wall about two feet to prevent rain from splashing into the back room. Now it prevented K.W. from seeing if anyone was at the door. He moved away from the building's edge and started walking toward the door as quietly as he could.

He was within three feet of the door when he saw a sledgehammer come out of the darkness and rocket forward with a crashing sound of metal on metal. K.W. stepped out away from the buildings and took two steps forward.

Three dark shapes huddled in front of the door. They were so focused on their efforts that none of them saw him. K.W. smiled and pumped a round into the chamber of the big gun. The sound of the round being slammed home spun the three shadows toward K.W.

"Police. Stand still. I have this scattergun centered on you, and there is no way to miss with you all boxed in as you are. My cover unit will be here any second now, so just stand easy and still, and keep those hands where I can see them," K.W. said.

The shadow holding the sledgehammer took a step forward, and K.W. raised the shotgun to center on his chest, "Drop that hammer and stay where you are."

"Why should I? There are three of us, and you are all alone. I don't believe you have anyone coming. You don't even have a car, how did you call for cover?" he asked and took another step out of the alcove into the alley.

K.W. could now see the face of the man holding the hammer. "Tony you are about to make a fatal mistake. Do you think I am going to let you get any closer to me with that hammer in your hand? Take another step, move again and I am going to be in fear for my life," he pressed the butt of the gun against his shoulder leaned into it.

"Tony, don't be a fool man. If he pulls that trigger, he is going to hit us too. Just be cool man, I don't want to die in this alley," a voice from the dark spoke.

Tony looked back at his companions. Then he turned back to face K.W. Headlights flashed across his face, and he glanced to his left watching the black and white race down the alley toward them. He smiled at K.W. and said, "I'm going to kill me a pig one day. But I guess this is not that day." He dropped the hammer and raised his hands.

The driver of the approaching car turned the headlights to high beam, and the alley was now flooded with light. K.W. had his cheek pressed against the stock of the shotgun and was sighted on the group in the doorway.

As the light illuminated them, he lifted his head and looked along the blue steel barrel at the two figures huddled against the door. He recognized them. "Pete, Ruben, stand slowly and step forward with your hands over your head."

He watched warily as the two young men stood, faced him and lifted their hands over their heads. He saw total surrender on the face of Pete, but Ruben's face reflected the same hatred, as did his brother's.

The vehicle stopped, and K.W. heard the driver's door open. The officer exited the vehicle and stepped in beside him. Without turning his focus off of the three men before him, he was able to see out of the corner of his eye that the officer had drawn her pistol and leveled it at the trio in front of them.

Ruben stepped up beside his brother and glared at K.W. He shifted his gaze from K.W. to the officer standing beside him and said, "Your cover is a woman, and a rookie at that. Tell me, Officer Bangs, now that you have caught us, how are you going to keep us?

I think we just might run, everyone in a different direction. Then what are you going to do, shoot us? I don't think so. I know she ain't going to hit us shooting that pistol. Look at her man; she can barely hold that big ole gun."

"Holster that pistol Kim, and grab your shotgun," K.W. spoke out of the corner of his mouth.

He felt the void as the officer moved away to get her shotgun. He saw that Tony and Ruben were tense and was watching each move of the officers.

"Tony, she may be a rookie, but I'm not. I don't want to shoot you but I will. I will waste you on the first move either of you makes," K.W. had laid his cheek against the stock of the weapon once more and had it centered on the chest of Tony McHenry.

Kim returned to his side with the shotgun in hand and leveled at the prisoners.

"Do you have a round in the chamber?" K.W. asked the young officer.

"No," she answered.

"Point the barrel to the sky and pump one into the chamber. Keep your finger off of the trigger and level it at the prisoners," K.W. said.

"Okay, if you say so," Kim said as she pumped a round of Buckshot into the chamber and lowered the shotgun to cover the burglars.

"This is going to be dicey. So listen to me..." K.W. was interrupted by the sound of a police interceptor engine. The engine was wound tight, and K.W. could tell that it was traveling north on Avenue K, fast approaching Parker.

He heard the vehicle being downshifted and the tires squealed as the driver accelerated through the turn from K onto Parker. He heard the sound of the tires grinding through the loose gravel at the mouth of the alley and coming to a stop behind his vehicle. Then the radio in Kim's patrol vehicle broke squelch, "Two Ten put me out with Two Sixteen and Two Eighteen."

The sound of leather pounding on concrete was a sweet sound as Sergeant Jerry Scott sprinted along the alley to join his officers. The sound of a round being pumped into the chamber of a riot gun echoed across the alley and then there were three officers standing side by side facing the felons across two feet of concrete.

"Who we got here and what are they up to, K.W.?" Sergeant Scott asked.

"We have a trio of misguided young men caught red-handed in an attempt to burglarize a business house," K.W. replied.

"Man, you ain't seen us do nothing cause we ain't done nothing. All you got is us three in an alley, and there is no law against that," Tony smirked.

"Let's secure them and then we can figure this out," Sergeant Scott said.

"Right. I will put my shotgun on the front seat of Kim's cruiser and then come back and cuff them. Kim, you and Sergeant Scott will cover me but point that scatter-gun down when I step out front," K.W. said as he walked to the open door of the black and white.

"Turn your backs to me and place your hands on the top of your heads. I am going to step up behind you one at a time, place handcuffs on you and move you back to stand with the sergeant.

Do not turn on me, do not resist me, and you will not be harmed," K.W. said as he removed his handcuffs from their case on his Sam Browne and stepped up behind Tony.

He handcuffed the men one at a time and moved them back to sit on the concrete in front of Kim's patrol vehicle. Then he pointed at a spot four feet from the where the men sat and said to Kim, "Stand here and do not get any closer to them. Do not take your eyes off of them for any reason. Do not talk with them."

Kim moved to the spot he had pointed and said to him, "I thought we had this discussion before detail. I am not your rookie, and you are not my trainer. You are ordering me around like none of that matters to you."

K.W. looked at Kim and was pleased to see that although she was speaking to him, her eyes were locked on the prisoners. He smiled to himself and said to her, "We will talk about that later. Right now, let's get this done in a manner that keeps us and our prisoners safe."

He stepped back to where Sergeant Scott was standing, far enough away that the prisoners could not hear their conversation but in a position where they both could keep an eye on Kim and the prisoners.

"I looked at the door K.W. It is obvious they were bashing it with that sledgehammer. They have knocked the doorknob off, but the door is still secure. They did not get it open, so burglary will not fly," the sergeant said.

"I know, but they took steps in preparation to burglarize the building and then they acted on those preparations by actually attempting to break the door down. That is a solid attempted burglary," K.W. said.

"I think you have a better criminal mischief case, at least against Tony. And that is going to be circumstantial unless you can testify that you saw him break that knob off or saw him slamming that hammer into the door.

You have nothing, except loitering under suspicious circumstances, on the other two. That is unless you saw them with the hammer or you can testify to other circumstances that would implicate them in the damaging of the private property," Scott said.

K.W. knew the sergeant was right. "Yeah, I picked them green. We all know what they were attempting, but you're right. What we know and what we can prove are vastly different. I will book Ruben and Alex on loitering under suspicious circumstances and Tony on criminal mischief.

And, according to the bulletin from Collin County Probation, Tony has a blue warrant out on him for probation violation. This should get him a trip to Huntsville," K.W. conceded.

"Strange they are on foot with no car in sight. Wonder if they had a good eye positioned in a getaway car and they ran when they saw you?" Scott asked.

"Probably. Tony nor Ruben will say anything but I will leave a note for the detectives, and they might be able to work Alex for the names," K.W. said as he strode forward.

"Okay gents, on your feet," he said as he reached down to assist the men up off of the concrete.

"What are you charging us with?" Tony asked.

"I am booking you for criminal mischief and on the blue warrant that Collin County Probation has out on you. Alex and Ruben will go in on loitering under suspicious circumstances," K.W. said as he opened the rear door of Kim's cruiser and seated Tony inside.

"So, Alex and Ruben get a walk, and I take a ride. Is that it?" Tony asked as K.W. was closing the door.

"Yes sir, that's about the size of it, Tony. You have had your get out of jail card and wasted it. Now you will do some time," K.W. said.

"Okay, so it's like the man said. Some days you eat the bear, and some days the bear eats you," Tony said and settled back as much as the handcuffs would allow.

K.W. closed the back door of the squad and walked around to open the driver's door. "Hey, did you sign up to take the exam for detective?" Sergeant Scott asked.

"Yes, I did. It is to be given at eight o'clock and I'm not sure how well I will do after working a deep nights' shift, but I'm going to take it," K.W. replied.

"It is going to take you a couple of hours to get the paperwork on these three finished. Give me a call once you get it done. If things are quite, I will let you take some comp time and study," Scott said.

"Thanks, sergeant, but I think I will pass on that. If I know it, I know it. If not, I don't deserve the promotion. I will clear soon as I get this written up," K.W. said.

CHAPTER 27
TOGETHER FOREVER

Everett Smithson cruised the parking lot searching for the orange AMC Hornet. The car belonged to James Wilson, and Everett was hoping to talk with James before the workday started. He found it parked in its' usual spot, but James was not inside the car.

"Damned! I told him we needed to talk. If he thinks he can avoid me, he is totally wrong," Everett said slamming his hand against the steering wheel. He parked in the slot next to the Hornet and hurried into the lobby of the Star Insurance building.

"Good morning Mr. Smithson," the receptionist smiled at him.

"Good morning Elisa. Did you see James Wilson come through yet?" Everett asked glancing around the lobby.

"Yes, sir. He came through early, maybe twenty minutes ago. He went straight back to his desk," she said.

Everett nodded his thanks and turned toward the claims adjusting department. He walked to James' cubicle. James looked up as Everett walked into the cubicle and dropped into an empty chair.

"You were supposed to wait in the parking lot so we could talk this through," Everett said.

James swiveled around to face Everett and said, "There is nothing to talk about. I told you that Wilma found out about our little *'thing'* and demanded I break it off or she would expose me to the kids and file for divorce. I am not going to allow that to happen. We had our fun, but it's over. Now I want you to leave me alone."

"*Little Thing!* Is that what you think about us James? I have given myself to you totally. Whatever you wanted, I have done. I have been your slave. I have not denied you one request.

I am not going to just let you use me and kick me to the curb. I told you in the beginning that I had deep feelings for you but that I was not interested in being your whore. You assured me that you loved me. You told me that you were going to tell Wilma and that we would be together as life partners.

This is not over. I am going to fight for you," Everett's voice had become louder as he talked.

"Lower your voice, Everett. This is not the time, nor the place to have this discussion. Meet me at my car at eleven forty-five. We will leave the property for lunch, and I will give you the opportunity to have your say. Now go to work and my word man, stop crying," James said.

"I want to go to your house. If it is over, if you are going to dump me, then I want one to be with you one last time. You owe me that much, don't you think James?" Everett asked.

James sat still, staring at Everett. He felt alarms going off, warning him that this was not wise. But, he heard himself saying, "Okay Everett. I would like that too, but this is the last time. After this, it is over. Agreed?"

"Agreed, it will be over. I know that you will or maybe already have, withdraw your request for a transfer to the San Francisco office; but I am going to press forward with mine. I couldn't handle seeing you every day," Everett said and walked from the cubicle.

James heard a snicker from the cubicle next to his. 'Oh no,' he thought.

He stood and looked over the wall. Ralph Tyson was bent over, hands over his mouth. His face was red, and he was rocking back and forth in an effort to control his laughing.

He walked around the wall and stopped at the opening to Ralph's work area.

"So, you heard it all, hey Ralph?" James asked.

Ralph leaned back in his chair and gulped, trying to swallow his laughter. Unable to speak he nodded yes and reached for a Kleenex to wipe his streaming eyes.

Taking a deep breath, Ralph said, "I'm sorry James. It's just that I never suspected. Then to sit here this morning and hear you two fussing like that was just more than I could bear."

James said, "It's complicated, Ralph. Maybe we can grab a beer one day, and I will fill you in."

"No thanks James. I don't think that would be a good idea. I'm totally straight. But hey my thought is to each his own. Your secret is safe with me. You have my word," Ralph said shaking his head.

•   •   •

James glanced at the clock and saw that it was eleven forty. He sighed, stood and walked out. He saw Everett leaning against the Hornet, man purse over his shoulder. *'Dang, I wish he wouldn't be so obvious. Carrying that purse around like a woman,'* James thought.

Everett smiled as he walked up and said, "Thanks for this James."

The mood was tense, and both remained quiet as James drove to his home. He pulled into the back driveway, and Everett leaned over to kiss him.

"Not here, you idiot. I don't want the neighbors seeing us like that. Wait until we are inside," James said pushing Everett away. James reached for his door handle and looked back at Everett.

Everett was sitting still, making no move to exit the vehicle. He leaned against the door, resting his head against the window. "Start the car and switch on the air conditioner. I've changed my mind. I don't want to go inside. We will settle this here," Everett said.

James shrugged and looked to the ignition as he inserted the key. He heard Everett move and looked to see him with his hand in the man purse. James panicked. He reached for Everett but was slammed in the face with the purse.

James swatted the purse away and saw Everett pointing a pistol at him. "Everett put that gun down. This is crazy," James said.

"No, I'm not going to put the pistol down James. Like I said we are going to end this here, and now. Did you think I was going to allow you to just toss me aside and walk away? And what about Wilma?

I know you will not be able to understand this, but I identify with her. We both love the same man, we both have given ourselves to you without reservation, and we both have suffered because of your infidelity.

I am going to end the suffering for both of us. I am going to kill you James, and then I will kill myself. By doing that, I release her from you and put an end to my pain and shame.

I have left a note on my desk explaining all of this, in detail. I want people to know the truth about you, about us, and about why I did this.

It will do you no good to plead for your life because my mind is made up. But I will allow you to make any last statement. I brought a pad and pen if you want to leave a note to Wilma or the kids or if you just want to say a prayer. Do you?" Everett asked.

"Are you totally mad?" James asked.

"Mad, as angry or mad as insane?" Everett asked with a raised eyebrow.

James looked deep into Everett's eyes and saw that his decision was firm, '*he intends to kill me,*' he thought.

He looked out of the windshield for a few seconds and finally said, "Would you give me the pad and pen so I can leave a note to the kids?"

Everett reached for the purse and glanced down to find the paper and pen. As he did, James lunged at him. James was able to grasp the pistol in both hands and push it upward to point at the roof of the car.

Everett was stronger than James had anticipated. He leaned forward and yanked the pistol free of James' grasp. As he brought the barrel down, James made one last effort and pushed the barrel aside.

The pistol discharged sending a bullet through the top of the windshield. James grabbed the pistol and struggled with Everett for control of it.

Everett was too strong for James. He slowly gained control and was able to push the muzzle of the pistol against James' mouth. He smiled at James and pulled the trigger.

The bullet blew through the pallet of James' mouth and into his brain. James never heard the explosion. His dead body slumped forward into Everett's lap.

Everett sat for a few seconds, stunned by the violence. He looked at James and said, *'we will be together forever."* Then he calmly placed the pistol into his mouth and fired a round into his brain.

CHAPTER 28
"NO DADDY"

Jeanie worked through the crowded hallway hoping to get into the classroom with enough time to scan her notes one last time before the pop quiz began. One good thing about having physics the last period of the day was that there could be no surprise or pop tests. All the earlier classes talked about them, so the classes meeting later in the day were somewhat prepared. Squeezing through the door, she hurried to her seat and quickly opened her notes.

This was her second semester with Mr. Fuller, and she had made a practice of studying the manner in which he devised his tests. She felt sure that the test would have no more than three questions.

There had been a tense discussion in class recently when Bill Kilter had given a definition, other than Mr. Fuller's approved one, for the periodic table. So knew that the first question on this quiz would be to define the periodic table.

She also knew that any definition other than Mr. Fuller's, delivered verbatim, would not receive full credit. So she opened her notes to the definition and read it again, *"The periodic table is a tabular arrangement of the chemical elements, ordered by their atomic number (number of protons), electron configurations, and recurring chemical properties."*

"Got that. Next question will be to list the elements with their symbol and weight," she said in a whisper.

She flipped to the table and scanned down the list, repeating each just as he had given them, "hydrogen – H, 1.008, Lithium – Li, 6.94,

Sodium – Na, 22.989…"

"Okay class, settle down. Jeanie put your notes away," Mr. Fuller said as the bell was ringing.

The chatter of the students died away. Mr. Fuller looked out over the class and said, "Now don't tell me you don't know what's coming. Clear the books and notes off of your desks and prepare for your quiz. And, I have a treat for you. It's Friday, and as soon as you complete your quiz, you may leave, *IF,* you do so quietly without disturbing the other classes."

Jeanie sighed. It had been a horrible week both at school and at home. Frankie Mantel had been hounding her for a date, and she loathed the very sight of him. He was such a bore.

Two days before, she had been sitting with her girlfriends chatting about their summer plans when Frankie came strutting over to the table.

All the girls had stopped talking and groaned as he pushed his way onto the bench beside Jeanie. Frankie had physical education before lunch and rather than shower he drenched himself in cologne. The fumes were nauseating as they radiated from him.

"Hey Jeanie," he crooned as he leaned over, so their shoulders were touching.

Jeanie rolled her eyes and moved away to put space between them. She found herself gagging from the mixture of sweat and cologne.

"Are you okay, Jeanie? Your eyes are all red and, are you crying?" Frankie asked.

"Frankie, you idiot. When are you going to get a clue? Jeanie does not want to date you, and you smell like a combination drug store and locker room. Go take a shower and find someone else to bother," Sharon Turret said from across the table.

Frankie looked around at the girls and saw that they were all nodding their heads in agreement with Sharon. He also noticed how quiet the lunchroom had become as the other kids stopped talking and turned toward the raised voices.

Toby Wilmer sat at the next table. As usual, girls surrounded him.

He laughed out loud and said, "Hey it's Stinky Frankie. You ought to listen to Sharon and try showering. Maybe the girls will let you sit with them then."

Laughter rolled across the lunchroom as the kids pointed at Frankie. He could feel his face ablaze with embarrassment. He stood and crossed the short distance between the two tables.

Toby stood to face Frankie, and the lunchroom grew quite once more. The tension was thick as the antagonists stared each other down. Then Frankie took a step back, turned his back to Toby and expelled gas loudly saying, "Hey Toby, tell me how this smells."

The insult was too much for Toby. He charged into Frankie. The two combatants crashed into the table where Jeanie and her friends were seated. Jeanie was pushed from her stool and fell onto the floor with the boys.

When the teachers got them untangled, she was directed to the principal's office along with the boys. Mr. Runnels, the principal, had decided that she was a participant in the whole affair and assigned her to after school detention hall.

Mr. Fuller laid the test sheet on her desk, and she pulled herself together and looked at the exam. *'Yes, just as I thought. Two questions with the first being the definition and the second being to list the elements, their symbol, and weight. This is a piece of cake,'* she thought and began to write.

Jeanie handed her test to Mr. Fuller and left the classroom. She walked to her locker and opened it to gather her books for the weekend homework. As she gathered her materials, she thought about the problems at home. She hated the discord and having to live in it all weekend.

As Jeanie walked toward her home, she replayed in her mind the shouting that had come from her parent's room the night before. She couldn't hear it all, but it seemed that her mom was accusing her dad of having an affair. Jeanie had been able to make out part of one exchange, but she was confused by what she had heard.

"James you are lying to me. I found the evidence in your underwear while doing the laundry this afternoon. You promised me that it was over with him and that you would tell him so. How do you think this makes me feel? Having my husband taken from me, not by another woman but by a man," her mom had said.

"Keep your voice down, Wilma. I don't want the kids to hear you. I did talk to Everett, and I did tell him it is over between us. But, he broke down and threatened to kill himself. I can't live with that on my conscious. Just give me time. I will work through this," her dad had pleaded.

"So you care more about Everett and his feelings that you do about me and mine. And what about the kids? How are you going to explain this to your son and daughter?

And another thing, you might as well know that there will be no physical relationship between us until this thing is settled. I don't know if there will ever be. I will stay with you until the kids graduate, but I do not promise anything past that.

You end this thing now, or I am going to tell the kids and file on you for divorce," her mom had said.

Jeanie stopped to check the mailbox and then hurried toward the front door. She wanted to change into her swimsuit and lay in the pool for the hour or so before her mom and brother came home. *'Just some peace and quiet, and no worrying about mom and dad,'* she promised herself.

Jeanie changed quickly and stopped at the refrigerator for a Pepsi to drink as she floated in the pool. She pulled the tab on the cold can and moved to the sliding patio door. *'What's that noise, sounds like a car engine,'* she thought as she opened the door.

Stepping from the house, she looked toward the gate and was able to see, through the cracks, her dad's car sitting on the driveway. *'Dad's home early,'* she thought as she lifted the latch on the gate.

She pushed the gate open and walked toward the car. She saw the hole in the shattered windshield; the blood spattered across the windows and then she bent over and looked into the car. She saw the bloody bodies of two men and recognized one of them as her dad.

"*NO DADDY,*" she screamed.

Jeanie dropped her soda and sprinted into the house. She grabbed the phone in the kitchen and dialed the operator.

"Operator," came the response.

"I need the police," Jeanie was crying.

"Honey, calm down. Where are you?" the operator asked.

"Twenty Three Hundred Northcrest Drive in Plano. I think my daddy is dead," Jeanie said.

"Okay, honey you stay on the line with me. Are you okay, are you hurt or in danger?" the operator asked.

Jeanie heard the line clicking and said, "No."

"Plano Police," the male voice said.

"This is the GTE operator. I have a young woman on the line that says she is at Twenty Three Hundred Northcrest Drive and she believes her dad is dead. She needs the police," the operator said.

"Miss, this is Mike Ryan with the Plano Police. I have a unit in route to your location. Are you okay?"

CHAPTER 29
THE DETECTIVE

He pushed on the brake pedal, but the cruiser would not stop. He reached across and around the steering wheel with his left hand and slammed the gearshift lever into park. The big Ford refused to stop, sliding across the concrete. K.W. watched as the man lifted his right hand. In it was a pistol.

K.W. lifted the door handle and shoved the door open with his left foot. He had the shotgun in his right hand. He yanked the slide down and then slammed it forward, lifting the barrel of the gun against the roof of the patrol vehicle and locking a round into the firing chamber.

He stepped from the car as the pistol leaped in the hand of the man in front of him. He saw a smoke and flame spit from the barrel and winced as the wayward bullet shattered the plastic lens covers on the lights atop his car.

The shrouds of plastic peppered him as he watched the man level the pistol and adjust his aim for the second shot. A fiery lance raced from the barrel of the pistol and K.W. felt the force of the bullet as it passed by on the right side of his face.

K.W. stepped from behind the door of the black and white, leveled the shotgun at his assailant and pulled the trigger.

The double ought Buckshot lifted the man off of his feet and spun him in a half circle. He slammed into the corner of the building and slid down the brick to the pavement.

The spreading pattern of the pellets had hit him to the left of center mass. One had struck where the leg joins the hip. The fury of the blast had lifted the ball at the top of the femur out of the hip socket and pushed it through the skin. It now gleamed in the neon lights, extending from the body at a right angle.

K.W. approached the downed man carefully. He saw the pistol lying beside his opened right hand and pushed it aside with his foot. He looked down and winced.

This man lying before him had just seconds before been vibrant and full of life. Now that life was pooling around him on the litter-strewn parking lot.

K.W. looked into his eyes and saw his life's light dimming. The man knew his time was short and was struggling to speak. K.W. leaned in to hear him say, "*I am Billie Deerinwater, a Comanche Warrior, and I have died in battle.*"

Then there was silence. K.W. remained kneeling, looking at the face as it relaxed. The body convulsed, and a long gasp escaped as another soul was swallowed by the deepness of the night.

There was a noise; a ringing that would not stop. K.W. struggled, caught between the dream and the ringing. He climbed out of the dream and rolled into a sitting position on the side of the bed. He glanced at the clock and saw that the time was One Fifteen p.m. He had been asleep for a little over four hours.

He looked around the room and listened for sounds other than the ringing. The house was silent. '*Trudy must have gone somewhere,*' he thought.

He picked the phone up and said, "Hello."

"K.W. this is Sergeant Scott. I know you are working deep nights and I apologize for waking you up. But, as you know, you finished number one on the detective's test, and we now have that list certified. Chief Kinsey wants you in his office at three this afternoon so he can promote you. Get yourself together and be here by three."

K.W. listened and the fog cleared with the excitement of the news. "Okay, sure. I will be there. Do you know what my assignment will be?" he asked.

"Yes, the chief is assigning you to Juvenile. You will be working for Sergeant Terry Box," Scott said.

"Juvenile?" K.W. said.

"Yes, that's right. Is that going to be a problem?" Scott asked.

"No, not at all. I will be there at three o'clock sharp," K.W. said and hung the phone up.

K.W. lay back on the bed. He was wide-awake, and his mind was running. *'Juvenile? Okay,'* he said out loud.

He laid still thinking back over his latest face-to-face contact with the Chief. He and several other officers had been sitting in the lounge before detail.

None of them had dressed for duty yet, and he had been wearing an old blue uniform shirt from his Dallas P.D. days. He had removed the shoulder patch, but the shirt was easily identifiable as a uniform shirt. The chief had walked through and glanced at the officers.

He stopped and stared at K.W. for a few seconds. Then he walked over to the table and said, "K.W. is that a Dallas P.D. shirt you are wearing?"

"Yes sir," he had replied.

"Well take it off. I don't want to see it again. I'm beginning to think that it may be best for you to go back to Dallas. But if you stay here, I don't want to see or hear anything else about your Dallas experiences. Do you understand?" the chief's voice was thick with emotion.

K.W. nodded and said, "Okay Chief Kinsey."

Now, he lay on the bed wondering. *'Why did the Chief choose to censor me in front of my peers, why did he say that about Dallas? Does he want me here? Whatever, I am going to salute and take orders.'*

K.W. rolled from the bed and headed to the shower.

•   •   •

He heard steps and turned to see a young woman detective walking toward him holding a stack of reports. "Hey Z, what you got there?" he asked.

"I have just been across the street picking up our cases. Let me see, this one is assigned to K.W. Bangs, as are the next three. You have four new ones, and I got none," she dropped them on his desk.

K.W. picked the paperwork up and flipped through them. "Here's an interesting one, a criminal mischief. Someone got into one of those new homes that Coy Gathwright is building out west, off of Custer Road. The vandals stopped up all the sinks, turned the water on and flooded the house.

They ripped fixtures from the walls, knocked holes in the sheetrock, broke all the windows and defecated on the counters in the kitchen. All the appliances are in the house, but none were taken. And, none of the copper from the plumbing or the HVAC equipment was taken. So we know this is just pure vandalism.

The estimate of damage is listed at one hundred and twenty five thousand dollars. The house is a two hundred thousand dollar project, so the insurance company is going to declare this a total loss."

"Is Gathwright the injured party or is it the insurance company?" Z asked.

"If the insurance company is making Gathwright whole, then they suffered the loss, and we will have to work this with them as the complainant. I will make that change with a supplement, but first I want to ride out to the house and talk with the neighbors and some of the workmen in that area. This happened sometime between Friday evening and Monday morning. The contractor found it at six, when they came to work.

I bet it happened on Saturday, which means there would have been a lot of people out and around. Someone had to see something. Want to ride out there with me and check this out?" K.W. asked.

"Yep. Got nothing else to do," she said.

K.W. stopped the unmarked Plymouth in front of twenty four fifty-one Baffin Bay Drive. He stepped from the car and said to his partner, "Z, let's talk with these construction workers first. Maybe they haven't repaired the damage yet. That will help us get an idea of how this went down."

The detectives walked into the house, and three painters dropped their tools and ran out the opening where the sliding doors had been. An older man turned to look at the detectives and said, "I wish you had let me know you were coming. These Hispanic workers see the police, and the first thing they think is that INS is after them. It will take me all afternoon to get them back on the job."

K.W. said, "Sorry. I never thought about that. We are here to investigate the vandalism and are not the least bit interested in hassling those hard working men."

"How did they know we are police," Z asked.

The foreman laughed and said, "Are you kidding me? Both of you are walking examples of the heat. What can I do for you?"

"Tell me what you know, what you suspect and what you have heard," K.W. said.

"I know that whoever did this came in on a bicycle because they left their tire tracks all over the floors. I suspect this was a kid because the tire tracks look like small bikes.

I heard, from the folks living right across the street, that a boy who goes to school with their son came by and asked if he wanted to go riding Saturday morning. They told me that they would not let their son go because of this boy's reputation as a dope-smoking delinquent who is always looking for trouble."

"Wow! Are you serious? You have all that information and haven't called us with it? Why not?" K.W. asked.

"Because I don't want to get on the witness stand and testify. I am an ex-con and want to stay away from the bulls and the courtroom. So, why don't you two go across the street and talk with those folks? Their name is Walter and Jean Jameson. She teaches, and he sells pharmaceuticals," the man said with a chuckle.

"What's funny?" K.W. asked while writing the names down.

"Life, life is funny. Ole Walter sells drugs all day long, and he is getting rich, living in a big house with a beautiful woman. Me, I sell a few drugs and end up doing ten of a twenty-five year gig at Ferguson," the foreman said.

"You did time at Ferguson? I went down there to talk with some hi-jackers one time. I met a Corrections Officer that everyone called Bear Tracks. Is he still around?" K.W. asked.

"Bear Tracks is still there. He is the meanest C.O. in all of TDC.

An inmate got a shiv stuck in him one day, and Bear Tracks knew that I saw the whole thing go down. He called me into his office and wanted me to rat the con out.

I knew that I would be a dead man if I snitched; so I just stood there and kept my mouth shut.

Bear Tracks told me to go outside. Then he told me to climb up on top of an ice chest he had sitting there. He turned to walk away, and I asked him how long I had to stay on that box. Without even looking back he said, '*Until you give me that name.*'

Shoot, he knew I couldn't give him that name. But he still made me stay there all day long in the one hundred and five degree heat. By the time the sun went down, my legs and feet were shaking so bad I could not walk. So, yes sir. I know Bear Tracks," the Con said.

K.W. turned to Z and said, "I want you to do a Field Interrogation Report on this man. Be sure you have his current address and the name of his parole officer. While you are doing that, I am going across the street and talk with the Jameson family."

K.W. walked across the street and reached for the doorbell. Before he could ring it, the door swung open. K.W. stepped back and said to the woman standing before him, "Are you, Mrs. Jameson?"

"Yes, I am. Are you with the police department?" she asked.

K.W. held his identification card and badge up for her to inspect and said, "Yes I am. My name is K.W. Bangs and I am assigned to investigate the vandalism of the home across the street. May I come in and talk with you about what you saw?"

"Come in," she said as she turned and walked to the foot of the stairway.

"Ronny, come down here now," she called out.

K.W. stepped inside and looked up the stairs. He saw a small framed, redheaded boy covered in freckles trudging down the stairs. His head was down, and he was crying.

"Stop crying, Ronny. Dad and I told you that a day like this was coming if you continued to keep company with that boy. This man is a police officer, and he is going to ask you some questions about Tommy Daurman," Mrs. Jameson said.

She led K.W. and her son into the den and sat down. "Sit down officer Bangs and ask your questions," she said.

K.W. looked from mother to son and then asked, "Well first, is Mr. Jameson home?"

"No, he is at work, but I called him as soon as I saw you stop in front of the house across the street. He said to tell you everything and that he would be happy to speak with you if you want to call him," she replied.

"Fine, I will work that out. But for now, the foreman across the street said you folks know who is responsible for vandalizing Mr. Gathwright's house. If so, I need you to tell me what you know, and I need your permission to record your statement," K.W. said as he showed her the portable tape recorder.

"You have my permission to record my statement, and any statement my son makes. This is what we know for sure. Tommy Daurman is a troubled kid who goes to Haggard Middle School with our son. I teach there, so I am well acquainted with his antics in school. He has a reputation as a bully, a liar, and a thief. He is also into dope.

He came to our door Saturday morning around ten o'clock. He wanted Ronny to go bike riding with him. My husband told him no and closed the door.

We both watched as he rode circles in the street staring at our house. We saw him ride up to the front door of the house across the street. He got off of his bike and tried to open the front door but couldn't. We watched as he got on his bike and rode away.

We thought that was the end of it. But then Sunday morning, just before we left for church, Ronny came into the den and told us that water was running out from under the door of the house across the street. We looked out the window and saw that it was running onto the porch and down the sidewalk.

Walt walked across the street for a better look and saw the vandalism. He came back and called the police department. Some of your officers came out and took the report. They called Mr. Gathwright, and he came out with a crew to shut off the water and close up the house.

Then Monday, at school, Tommy sat down with Ronny at lunch. He asked Ronny if we had seen the damage in the house. Ronny was frightened of Tommy and lied to him. He told Tommy no that all we saw was the police over there with Mr. Gathwright.

Tommy then told Ronny in detail what the damage was in the house. He never said he had done it, but what he told Ronny matched exactly with what Mr. Gathwright told us about the damage," Mrs. Jameson finished her statement and sat back.

K.W. turned to the boy and said, "Ronny, you know that I am recording what I ask and what you answer. Do I have your permission do to so?"

Ronny nodded his head, and K.W. said, "I need you to speak so the recorder can get your answer on tape. Now once more, do I have your permission to record you?"

"Yes, my mom said you do, and I don't care," Ronny said.

"Did you hear everything your mom just told me about what happened last Saturday?" K.W. asked.

"Yes, I heard, and she told the truth. It all happened just like she said," Ronny answered.

"Did Tommy approach you at school on Monday and ask you if you had seen the damage in the house?"

"Yes, he sat down at the table during lunch and asked me," Ronnie said.

"Did you lie to him and say no, that you had not seen the damage and did not know what how the house had been damaged?" K.W. asked.

"I lied to him because he has beaten me up before and I am afraid of him," Ronny said with a glance at his mom.

"Why did you just look at your mother, Ronny? Are you telling me the truth or is there something you don't want me to know? Why did Tommy beat you up?" K.W. asked.

Ronny looked at his mother again, and she said, "Tell him, Ronny."

"Tommy brings marijuana to school and sells it. He makes me

keep it in my locker so that he won't get caught with it. He takes the money and sends the kids to me, and I have to give them the marijuana.

I told him that I was not going to do it anymore and he waited for me after school. He beat me until I said I would do it," Ronny said with a whimper.

"Okay, did he tell you that he vandalized Mr. Gathwright's house?" K.W. asked.

"No, but he told me everything that had been done, and it was the same as what Mr. Gathwright had told my dad. So, I knew it was him," Ronny said.

"Why would he tell you all this Ronny? Why would he take the chance that you might tell someone?" K.W. asked.

"Because he wanted my parents to know that he was mad at them for not letting me ride with him. He wanted them to be afraid that he would do something to our house. Then he told me, '*Your old man and old lady better not mess with me or they will get some of the same,*'" Ronny said.

"He said that, when did he say that?" K.W. asked.

"He didn't say '*not to mess with him,*' he used the f-word. You know, '*they better not f... with me*'," Ronny said.

"When did he say that?" K.W. asked.

"Monday, at the lunch table. Right after he told me everything that happened in the house," Ronny said.

K.W. looked at the boy and felt his fear. "Ronny, I think this goes deeper than you being afraid Tommy will beat you up. Tell me why you are so afraid of Tommy."

Ronny said, "I don't want to say it in front of my mom."

"Mrs. Jameson, would you step out and let Ronny and me talk privately?" K.W. asked.

She stood, laid a hand on her son's shoulder and left the room.

"Now tell me Ronny, and I am going to be recording," K.W. said.

"After he beat me up that time, before he let me go he told me that I was his bitch and that I was always going to be his bitch. He said that if I ever messed him over again that he would take me into the bathroom, bend me over the sink and show me exactly what it meant to be his bitch. He said that he would put eye shadow on me and make me wear it all day at school," Ronny was crying.

"Okay, look at me, Tommy. I am going to take care of this bully. That is what police officers are for, to be your guardian against such people. You just put it out of your mind; he will never harm you again. Now go get your mom for me," K.W. said.

"Yes officer," Mrs. Jameson said as she came back into the room with her arm around her son's shoulders.

"I have enough here Mrs. Jameson. I will take this information back to my sergeant and let him review it. If he agrees, I will take the case to the District Attorney tomorrow morning and see if he can get us an order of immediate custody for Tommy Daurman. If the judge issues it, I will go to Haggard and take him into custody," K.W. said.

"Should I keep Ronny home tomorrow?" Mrs. Jameson asked.

"No, let him go to school. Ronny, just act like everything is normal. If Tommy asks you any questions about the vandalism or what your parents are saying, just tell him they don't want to be involved," K.W. told the boy.

•   •   •

The hallways were jammed with kids hustling to their next class. Keith Sockwell stood with a watchful eye until the last kid had darted into their room. Then he turned and walked into the front office. He smiled and reached out a hand saying, "Kenneth Bangs. What brings the long arm of the law to Haggard Middle School?"

K.W. grasped the strong hand and smiled back, "Hello Coach. It is good to see you. How is Carolyn?"

"Carolyn is doing great. She works at the administration building now. How is Trudy, is she still teaching English for Doyle at the senior high school?" Sockwell asked as he led K.W. to his office.

"Still teaching seniors. I'm afraid I'm not here for a social visit. I have an order of immediate custody for one of your students. A youngster named Tommy Daurman," K.W. extended the order to

Sockwell for his review.

Sockwell looked the instrument over and said, "Daurman is trouble. He may fight you and if he does, I would rather it be here in the office rather than the classroom or out in the hallway. Let me call him to my office, and you arrest him in here. I think it might be a good idea to get one of my staff in here too, is that okay?"

"Sure, but just so you know Coach, this order is for a felony offense. If he starts to fight I will end it quickly," K.W. said.

"That's fine. You are the police," Sockwell said as he opened the door and told his secretary to call Daurman to his office.

K.W. stood beside the door as Tommy walked into the front office. He looked at K.W. and stopped. K.W. saw the recognition on his face and then saw him swell up in defiance.

"You a cop?" Tommy Daurman asked.

"Yes, my name is K.W. Bangs. I am a detective with the Plano Police Department. I have an order of immediate custody, issued by State District Judge Tom Ryan, commanding me to take you into custody for the vandalism of the home under construction at twenty four fifty-one Baffin Bay Drive, here in Plano, Collin County Texas.

You are now in my custody. Turn your back to me and place both hands behind you," K.W. said as he withdrew his handcuffs from the case where they rested on his gun belt.

Daurman said, "What if I say no? What if I kick your ass for you? What are you going to do then, shoot me?"

K.W. stepped forward quickly, reached down and snapped a handcuff on Tommy's right wrist and leaned into him pressing him back against the wall.

"None of that is going to happen young man. You are fourteen years old, and you think you can take me? Don't embarrass yourself in front of all these folks and all those who will hear this story. Turn around now and let's make this as painless as possible."

Daurman looked at K.W. with lips pursed so tight that they were white. He turned and allowed K.W. to put the other cuff on him. As soon as the cuff clicked locked, he relaxed and allowed K.W. to lead him from the building and set him inside the police car.

K.W. walked around to the driver's side and sat down. As soon as the car was in motion, Daurman said, "You took quite a chance coming for me by yourself. I could take you, no doubt."

"You are delusional Tommy. Two things I am going to tell you. First, if your attitude does not change you are going to end up in prison.

Second, if you grow up to be as big a man as it looks like you will, police officers will not fight with you. It is not our job to fight toughs like you. You will break bad on the wrong officer, at the wrong time and he will waste you.

Believe it or not, but I've seen hundreds just like you. They each had a different name, a different face, but the same destiny. I hope you listen," K.W. said.

K.W. parked the car and walked into the detention area with Daurman. The jailer stood in the hallway waiting to process the prisoner.

"Colonel Throng, this young man is a juvenile. Which cell is certified to hold him until I can get the paperwork completed and take him to McKinney?" K.W. asked.

"I will place him in the proper cell. You just hurry the paperwork and get him out of my jail," the Colonel said.

K.W. hustled across the street to his office and sat down to start the paperwork on Daurman. The phone rang, and he picked it up with a sigh.

"This is K.W." he spoke into the phone.

"K.W. this is Jerri in dispatch. You are assigned as the detective for a call at

Twenty Three Hundred Northcrest Drive. Patrol is there now. A girl called in and said she came home from school and thinks her father is dead," Jerri said.

"I can't take it right now Jerri. I just arrested a kid, and the Colonel wants him out of his jail ASAP. Besides, I work juvenile, not homicide, if it is a homicide," K.W. said.

"All I know is that Chief Kinsey called over here, when he heard patrol ask for a detective, and said to send you. Do you want me to tell him that you are tied up and can't go?" Jerri had a smile in her voice.

"No, but get someone to do the arrest report on the kid. I will leave the order of immediate custody on my desk with the offense report attached. I will do the supplement later. Mark me out to Twenty-Three Hundred Northcrest Drive," K.W. said as he stood and reached for his jacket.

CHAPTER 30
SEAN'S ISSUE ~ JAMES' DAUGHTER

The scene was like any other that K.W. had worked in his eleven years as a police officer. The presence of the black and white patrol cars had attracted a crowd. The officers were kept busy constantly moving the curious off of the lawn and away from the house.

"Are you the detective working this scene? What has happened, we heard on the scanner that there are two dead men here. I'm with the press and want to get some pictures. Will you come back out and talk with me before you leave?" a young woman holding a camera called out as K.W. passed through the crowd.

Her announcement that there were two dead men at the house caused a ripple of excitement to run through the onlookers. K.W. looked back and saw that the curious were pressing forward in earnest now.

"Pat, you had better call for a sergeant and another unit for crowd control before this gets out of hand," K.W. said to the tall, thin officer struggling to maintain order.

"You just take care of your job, and I will take care of mine," came the tart response.

K.W. shrugged and walked through the open front door and into the house. He removed his sunglasses and stood for a few seconds to allow his eyes to adjust to the dimness. He heard voices and followed the sound into the kitchen. An officer stood there, watching a young girl and a woman holding each other and crying. The officer heard K.W. approaching and turned to look at him.

K.W. could see the darkness that held him captive. The officer's eyes were red, and tears had left a salty trail down his cheeks.

K.W. laid a hand on the officers' shoulder and said, " Roy Jackson, didn't I train you better than this? Eife has his hands full trying to control the crowd out front, and there is a reporter out there just itching to get inside to take pictures.

You have left the front door standing open and unprotected. You need to be there, preserving this crime scene. Didn't I teach you to steel yourself against allowing your emotions to drag you away from your duty and into the misery of these scenes? Come on now, get it together and do your job."

Jackson gulped, shook his head and said, "I know K.W., but that little girl came home and found her daddy dead. No kid should have to go through that. She won't ever be able to forget what she saw out there in that driveway."

K.W. patted his shoulder and gently nudged him toward the front door. He cleared his throat and said, "Ladies, I am detective K.W. Bangs with the Plano Police. I have been assigned to find out what has happened here today. Are you able to speak with me at this time?"

The woman wiped her eyes with a cloth and looked at K.W. "Yes officer, we can talk with you. I am Wilma Wilson, and this is my daughter Jeanie Frederickson. My husband, James, is one of the dead men in the car. The other dead man is Everett Smithson. He is, or was, my husbands' lover."

"Don't say that," Jeanie wailed.

"Well, it's true Jeanie. I have done my best to keep it from you kids, but now, all the world will know, and we might as well get used to it," Wilma said lifting her chin and looking at K.W.

"How do you know that they were lovers?" K.W. asked Wilma.

"I had suspected it for a long while. Right after we married, I began to see behaviors in James that led me to believe that James was gay or at least bi-sexual.

Then I began to find evidence. A card from a club called the *Bayou Landing*, in Dallas. Numerous phone calls with the caller hanging up when I answered. Unexplained bruises and then I found stains in his underwear that I knew were from sperm.

I confronted him, and he admitted that he was indeed bi-sexual and that he had known it since his earliest days in scouting. He blamed it all on his scout master who he said molested him during summer camp before his sixth-grade year.

I made James tell me all about it. As he did, I could tell that he had made the first advances to his scoutmaster. I confronted him, and he admitted that too.

I made him tell me whom he was seeing, and he said it was Everett Smithson, from work. As soon as he said the name, I knew it was true. I had been suspicious of Everett and his interest in James since the office Christmas party two years ago.

I told James that he had to stop seeing Everett. I threatened to tell the kids and to file for divorce if he did not. James told me he would tell Everett and promised that he would not be unfaithful to me again.

I didn't believe him, but I agreed to give the marriage one more chance. And, of course, he cheated again.

We had a huge fight last night. I told him our marriage was over, but that I would stay with him until the kids graduated high school and then I was going to file for divorce.

He begged me not to tell the kids or otherwise expose him, and I agreed, contingent on him breaking off the affair with Everett. He promised he would, and I heard him call Everett after I had gone to bed. I asked about it at breakfast, and he said that he had told Everett that it was over. I believed him, and now we come home to find this."

K.W. looked up from taking notes and asked, "Mrs. Wilson, I take it that Jeanie is not James' biological daughter. Is that right?"

"Yes, that's right. Jeanie and my son, Sean, Jr., are the children of my first husband, Sean Frederickson. He was a lineman for Texas Power and Light. He was killed, electrocuted while working on a transformer. Sean, Jr. was two and Jeanie was three and a half.

I met James shortly after Sean's death. He is, was, a claims manager for Sun Insurance and worked the death claim on Sean.

Sun withheld payment of benefits because the examiner assigned to the case wrote a report saying that Sean had not followed T.P.& L. safety practices. He said that Sean's failure to do so caused or at least contributed to his death.

I appealed the decision, but in the meantime, I had no income. Our monthly bills ate up what little savings we had. I could not make the mortgage payment, and the bank was threatening to foreclose on the house.

James was assigned as the claims manager to review my appeal. He ruled that we were due partial payment because Sean's actions only contributed to and were not the sole cause of his death.

He was so nice, so caring and I was vulnerable. My parents helped all they could, and so did Sean's. But, I knew they couldn't continue to give. James asked me out, and I said yes.

We were soon together every day. The kids loved him, and I know he adored them. It wasn't long before he was staying all night.

We were intimate, but I knew something was not right. I had to initiate all our physical contact. James would never look at my body. He never wanted to see me naked. Sean had been my one and only sexual partner, so my experience was limited, but that experience was vastly different than with James.

Then Sean, Jr. got sick at school one day. The school nurse called the house, but I was not here. We had listed James as a secondary contact. So, she called him at work. He went to the school to get Sean Jr., and the office staff questioned him as to who he was and why he wanted to pick Sean up. He explained that the nurse had called, but she had left for the day, and they would not let him have Sean.

James came home that night and insisted that we had to ensure that never happened again. As we talked through it, he just out of the blue said, '*we need to get married.*'

I knew better. All of my alarms were going off, but again here I was with no job, no education to speak of and two kids. So, I said yes, and we went to the courthouse, and the Justice of The Peace married us. That's about all there is to tell."

K.W. moved the tape recorder closer to Jeanie and asked, "Jeanie, do you want to add anything to what your mother has said?"

"All I want to say is that we may have different names, but James is my dad, and I love him," she replied.

"Okay, Jeanie. Tell me how you came to find your dad and Everett this afternoon," K.W. said.

"I came home from school and wanted to float in the pool for a while. I walked out of the back door and heard dad's car running.

I opened the gate and saw all the broken glass, the blood on the windows of the car and then when I looked into the car I saw dad slumped over in Everett's lap.

I looked at Everett, and I saw the gun in his hand. I knew they were dead and I ran into the house to call the police. That's all," Jeanie said.

"Jeanie, did you say that you saw a gun in Everett's hand?" K.W. asked.

Jeanie nodded, and K.W. said, "Jeanie I need you to answer orally so the recorder can make a record of your answer."

"Yes, I saw a black pistol in Everett's right hand. His hand was lying on his right leg, and his fingers were curled around the handle of the gun," Jeanie said.

"Good. That's all of the questions I have for now. I may want to talk with Sean, Jr. later and I may have some more questions for both of you as the investigation goes along. Do either of you have any questions to ask me before I go out to the examine the car and the bodies?" K.W. asked.

"What happens now? I heard you say that a reporter was in the front yard. Do we have to talk with them? When can we make arrangements for James' funeral?" Wilma asked.

"No, you do not have to talk with anyone from the press. That is your decision.

Our public information officer will give the press a short statement saying two men were found dead and that an investigation is underway to determine the circumstances. That's all they will get until we file our final report.

The Justice of The Peace will send the bodies to the Institute of Forensic Sciences in Dallas for an autopsy. The medical examiner will give me the cause of death and rule on the manner of death for each man. That will take about three days. After that you can have James for burial," K.W. said as he stood and prepared to leave the kitchen.

Jeanie collapsed on the table, sobbing as K.W. was speaking. He walked around the table and stepped through the sliding glass door, retracing Jeanie's route in approaching the car. Just before he stepped from the house, he heard Jeanie sob out, '*No Daddy.*'

He stood for a second looking at her and thought, '*she may be Sean's issue, but she is James' daughter.*'

●　　●　　●

The building was old. It appeared to be made of granite, but as K.W. approached the front doors, he saw that it was constructed of concrete blocks that had, over the years, gained a dingy gray patina. He looked closer and saw black specks of mold and realized that they followed an arched pattern left by the spray of the lawn sprinklers.

The automatic doors swept open allowing a draft of stale air to rush out and over him. He instantly felt slimy and in need of a hot shower. '*Great and my day has just begun,*' he groused as he approached a curious receptionist.

K.W. stood before the desk and watched as the eyes of the receptionist swept past the buckle on his gun belt to the bulge under his jacket. She lifted her eyes and looked at him with a smile, "I know that look. You are police. What can I do for the law today?" she asked.

"I am a police officer, but how do you know?" he asked.

"Honey, I been married to a police officer for thirty-five years. You all have that same swagger. That gun belt and the bulge under your coat gives it away to anyone who takes the time to look," she said.

K.W. smiled back at her and said, "Well that's okay because I'm not trying to hide it. Have you heard about James and Everett?" he asked.

"It is the talk of the building. I guess you are here to see what information you can pick up on them. Let me hook you up with

Scotty Friday. Scotty is our director of security, and he can get you where you need to be," she said as she punched a number into the switchboard.

"Scotty, there is a police officer here at my desk looking for information on James and Everett. Can you come and talk with him?"

She clicked out of the call and said, "Scotty has been expecting you. He will be right here."

K.W. looked at her employee badge and said, "Thank Margie. Where does you husband work?"

"Carrollton. He is a patrol sergeant. He needs two more years to put him at forty years service, and then he is going to retire. I am going to retire at the same time. We are going to sell our house, buy a motor home and become full-time R.V. dwellers. We love to travel, and that by golly is what we are going to do," she winked at K.W.

"Good for you. Is this Scotty coming across the lobby?" he asked.

"That's him," Margie said.

K.W. stepped toward the man with an outstretched hand and said, "K.W. Bangs with the Plano Police."

"Scotty Friday, Director of Security for Sun Insurance, Companies. Mind showing me your credentials?" Scotty asked.

"Not at all, K.W. said and extended his badge and identification card.

Scotty nodded and said, "Come with me to my office. Where do you want to start?"

"Can we talk first, just let you share what you have learned. And then, we can go from there," K.W. asked as they walked into Scotty's office.

"I thought as much. I have a note that we found on Everett's desk. I called into your department and left a message that I had it. Never got a return call so I just held onto it," Scotty said.

"They probably left a note on my desk. I worked the scene and went to the medical examiner's office last night. It was late when I finished there, so I went straight home. I haven't been to the office yet today.

Is this the note?" K.W. picked up a folder with *Everett Smithson* written in the margin. He opened the folder and saw an unfolded note, neatly written on lined paper. He glanced at the signature on the bottom of the page and saw

Everett Smithson.

K.W. sat back in the chair and began to read:

August 10th, 1978

My name is Everett Smithson. I have written this note to explain my actions that will have, by the time this note is read, resulted in the death of James Wilson and myself.

Let me say from the outset, I killed James and then myself. I did so after long and careful deliberation. I guess the police will consider this a premeditated murder and suicide. They are correct on both counts.

The question is why? The answer is simple and as old as love, lust, and rejection. I love James Wilson. I have from the first time I saw him. We met first here at work and then ran into each other one Saturday night at the Bayou Landing on Lemmon Avenue in Dallas. The Landing, as we call it, is for men who love other men, like James and me.

We were soul mates from the first. He told me that he was married to a wonderful woman. He told me all about her. Wilma is her name, and I met her at the office Christmas party a couple of years back. I could tell that she was suspicious of James and me, love like ours just cannot be hidden.

James was a lustful man, but he did love me. I told him that he had to choose, that I was not willing to continue to be his whore. He agreed to tell Wilma, and we both put in requests to be transferred to Sun's San Francisco office. We could live there, openly, as a happily married couple.

But James backed out. He just could not bring himself to 'step out of the closet' and face the reaction and or rejection of his parents, especially his dad, and the loss of Wilma's kids.

He called me at home late last night, August the 9th, and told me it was over and that he did not want to talk with me again. 'Just leave me alone' he said.

How silly! Did he think that he could just use me and throw me away?

I tried to talk with him this morning, the 10th. He refused, insisting that we were finished and that I should not bother him again.

Like I said before, James is a lustful man. I convinced him to meet at lunch for one last 'liaison' just for old time sakes. I knew that there would be no loving. I knew that I was going to kill him and then myself. The adage

about hell having no wrath like a woman spurned can also be said for one such as me.

So there it is. By the time you read this, I will have killed us both. We are together forever.

Everett Smithson

K.W. laid the note aside and picked up a second sheet in the folder. He saw that it was marked 'Affidavit In Any Fact.' He glanced at the bottom and saw that the Affidavit had been sworn to and notarized. The signature of the Affiant read, Ralph Tyson.

K.W. scanned the affidavit and saw that it detailed a conversation between James and Everett, that he had overhead on the day of the killing. Tyson repeated almost verbatim what Everett had said and added that James had confronted him about eavesdropping on their conversation.

K.W. looked at Scotty and asked, "Who is Tyson?"

He is another claims manager and works in a cubicle next to James. He was present when Everett confronted James and heard the entire conversation. He is solid, has an unblemished work record with us. He will make an excellent and unimpeachable witness for you.

K.W. sat a minute and asked, "Scotty did you or anyone else know or suspect this relationship between Everett and James?"

"Not that I am aware of K.W.," Scotty answered with a shake of his head.

"Have you looked at each man's file to see if either had any mention of the other, beneficiaries on insurance or to be notified of an emergency," K.W. asked.

"I did, and no, there is no mention of each other in their personnel jackets. James listed Wilma as the beneficiary on his life insurance and Everett listed his parents," Scotty said.

"I think that does it for me, Scotty. The medical examiner tells me that James was killed with a gunshot wound through the mouth and into his brain. He has ruled that Everett died from a self-inflicted gunshot wound to the head. His tests show that Everett fired the weapon. With this information validating what the family has given me, it is a wrap," K.W. said.

CHAPTER 31
THE COLD CASE

It was late September, but the Texas sun was still bringing temperatures in the mid-nineties. The coat and tie seemed to trap the heat and he felt the sweat running down his back.

He tossed his keys and sunglasses on the desk, laid the jacket across a chair and walked to the coffee bar. The steaming sludge sloughed from the glass pot, leaving clumps of a dark, thick substance behind.

"When was this coffee made?" he asked.

"Probably sometime this morning," came the answer.

He took a sip and grimaced. *'It's hot, and it's coffee,'* he thought as he carried it to his desk. He sat down in the creaking chair and took another drink of the brewed bean.

He put the cup down and saw a folder pushing out from under the desk blotter. He pulled it out and opened it. It was the initial report and investigative notes on a murder case that had gone cold. A yellow sticky note read, *"K.W. take a look at this and brief me on what you see. T.A."*

'Why does the LT. want me to look at this old case,' he mumbled. He grabbed his coffee, and as he picked it up, he noticed that there was a dark, wet ring on the desk where the Styrofoam cup had rested. *'Dang, this coffee is eating its' way through the cup,'* he chuckled. Tossing the acidic brew into the trash, he leaned back and began to read the case report.

The victim was a white female in her early twenties, identified as

Shirlene Minkus. She had been found after a highway patrolman spotted her abandoned car sitting on the side of Highway Five, near Spring Creek. The officer found the victim's purse and car keys in the vehicle and became suspicious.

He called for backup, and then began a search of the area. Her partially clad body had been found along the creek.

Her dress was bunched around her waist, her panties were around her knees, and her pantyhose were wrapped around her neck. Her blouse had been torn open, and her bra had been pulled awry. One shoe was partially on her left foot, and the other one was missing.

The autopsy determined the cause of death as asphyxiation by strangulation. The hyoid bone was broken.

There was bruising of both wrists, and the neck. There was no sperm found in her vagina or on her body. There was no evidence of violent sexual contact.

The scene where the body was found was strangely void of the usual activity related to such cases. There were no footprints, drag marks, broken or trampled vegetation. All the first responders found was her body, lying there on the side of the creek.

The DPS Trooper had checked out on her car at Three Twenty-Eight that morning. Her body was found at Four-Eighteen or some fifty minutes later. The medical examiner determined that she had been dead for less than twelve hours when brought into their offices at Five Forty-Five.

The investigation revealed that the victim lived in Allen, which was north of Plano. The front of her car was pointed north, and the investigators had surmised that she had been headed home.

The investigators had noted that the victim had a reputation for frequenting *The Code Three*, a bar where police officers hung out. The witnesses interviewed were split on whether her actions were promiscuous, flirtatious or if she was just working the cops to curry favor for business reasons.

It was also noted that the DPS Trooper had observed tire marks on the highway forty-six feet south of where the victims' car was parked.

He believed those tire marks indicated a vehicle that had been traveling in a southerly direction executed a U-Turn, crossed the centerline and continued onto the graveled shoulder and then back onto the payment traveling in a northerly direction. He believed that the car had circled the victim's car and left the scene. There were no pictures nor was there a diagram of those marks.

There were no clues or evidence to follow, and the case was suspended at the end of three months. In the suspension summary, the investigators had noted that their working position was that the most likely scenario was that the victim had been traveling home and had been stopped by a police unit or that she had stopped to talk with someone she knew or trusted. An altercation followed, and she was murdered, and her body dumped along the creek.

The investigators concluded that *the evidence suggested that it was possible* someone who was familiar with police crime scene search procedures had cleaned the scene.

K.W. picked up his phone and punched in the number for his Lieutenant. The phone rang several times, and K.W. was about to hang up when he heard the connection completed.

"Captain Daniels," came the greeting.

"Oh, hey Cap. This is K.W., I thought I had dialed the lieutenant."

"You did. I was walking past his office and heard the phone ringing, so I answered it. Can I help you?" he asked.

"Well, the Lt. left a file on my desk and asked that I review it and get back with him on what I thought. I can just call him later," K.W. said.

"What file was that?" the Captain asked.

"The Shirlene Minkus murder case," K.W. replied.

"I thought that case was suspended," the Captain said.

"It is," K.W. said.

"Wait a minute, let me get something to take notes with. Okay, now give me your thoughts and go slow enough that I can take it all down. I will leave them for the lieutenant, and he can take it from there," the Captain said.

"Well, let me start by saying that there were a lot of officers, including a Texas Ranger, on the scene. I don't see on the offense report or in the supplements that there was ever a specific detective in charge at the scene, and no supervisor is identified as taking charge of the scene.

A DPS Trooper found her car sitting along the highway and stopped to investigate. But there is no statement, just investigative notes, from him related to what he found and in what order he found it.

If I were working the case, I would start with that Trooper and ask him why he initiated a search of the area without calling for backup.

Did he check her purse and find her driver's license? Did he have his dispatcher crisscross the address, get a phone number and call that number to see if she was there or if anyone had heard from her or in the alternative when was the last time she was seen?

And then, I would like to know who decided to expand the search to the creek area. Who was the first to spot the body? Did anyone touch or move the body? Who took the pictures? Did they move or stage the body to allow the pictures to illustrate any point of interest?

The supplement includes a statement about a red vehicle, unknown make and model, driving slowly down the dirt road adjacent to where the body was found. What time was that vehicle seen? Who saw it? Did anyone interview the driver? Why was he driving slowly, could it be because he was curious about all the activity in the area?

Next, we need to build a timeline of her activities for the night of her death. There is not one in the file. There is some indication that she had gone to a club in Richardson, *The Code Three*, earlier in the evening, but there is no indication that anyone from that club has given a formal statement.

Who was she with at the club? Did she have trouble with anyone while there? What time did she leave, and did she leave alone or with someone?

The medical examiner found a partially digested hamburger in her stomach. That matches with a note in the file that an anonymous caller identifying herself as a waitress said the victim ate at her restaurant and that she was concerned about being followed by a DPS Trooper. The note itself is not present and as far as I can tell no effort has been made to follow up on this lead.

I would start with our taped calls and try to trace this one down. When did it come in? Can the telephone company records tell us its' origin? Who was this waitress? Where does she work? What does she know about this DPS Trooper following the victim? What moved her to call us?

We also need to work the victim's family and friends, especially her female friends, to ensure that we have the names of every man, boy, woman or girl that she has dated, been friendly with, had problems with or even mentioned relative to any sort of interaction or relationships.

We are nearly three years behind but we need to determine what has happened to her clothing, her papers, and her personal possession. We need to look through everything that is still available, go through the pockets of every article of clothing she owned, look through her correspondence, pictures, a diary or any other evidence of relationship.

I would also get a warrant for her phone records, both her home phone and work phone. We need to know whom she talked with and about what during the last hours of her life.

Now, let me address the scene a minute. The supplements indicate that the "*working premise*" is that she was stopped on the side of the road by a police officer or someone that she thought was a police officer and something went wrong. What drives that supposition?

I agree that the way the car is parked and the fact that her billfold is out of her purse, and that her driver's license is lying on the seat suggests that an officer may have stopped her. So, let's follow that train of thought for a minute.

Have we checked with the communication logs for all area law enforcement to see if any of their officers checked out on her vehicle or made a stop in that area at that time?

Next, let's ask why she left her vehicle. Did she do so voluntarily or was she forced from the vehicle?

All of this is possible. But there are so many problems with this theory. Her car was not found in a secluded area. It is sitting beside the highway.

A patrol vehicle, with lights flashing would certainly been noticeable. If it was an officer and he killed her and then deposited her body in the creek, did he just drag her out of the car, across the highway and down the creek while leaving his vehicle unattended along the highway? I find that a bit of a stretch but then, all things are possible.

The autopsy shows that the hyoid bone was broken. This a very small bone located in the throat near the Adams Apple. I know from previous experience that it is broken in fifty percent of strangulations.

But of that fifty percent fewer than five percent are broken by ligature strangulation, in this case the panty hose found around her neck. The other ninety five percent are broken by manual strangulations.

That means the odds are the killer put his hands around her neck and strangled her. That would be consistent with the bruising both on the neck and on the wrists. I include the wrist because if he were strangling her with his hands she would have been fighting him. Scratching, clawing and hitting.

There are no bruises on her hands or knuckles commonly seen with fist or closed hand strikes. No skin or blood found under her nails. So, it is possible that she was restrained at the wrists at the time she was killed.

The report suggests that the Ranger on the scene said that he was not sure the victim was murdered. Really? Why would he say that? We need to interview him.

What about motive? There are so many possibilities. Some have to be eliminated so others can receive the time and attention they deserve.

That's a quick look at how I would start if this cold case where assigned to me. Is there anything you want to ask me, Cap?

"I don't think so. I will leave these notes on his desk.

That's all you need to do on this for now. Just go back to working your cases," the Captain said and hung up the phone.

CHAPTER 32
HEADS UP ~
THE CALL

"K.W. line two is for you."

"Bangs," he spoke into the phone.

"Ken this is Pete Barnes. Do you know who I am?" the caller asked.

"Sure I do. You are a retired Dallas Police Sergeant working in juvenile probation for Collin County," K.W. said.

"Yes, well that's right. Judge Ryan appointed me to work with the juvenile offenders coming through his court, but since most of my cases come out of Plano and the Plano Schools, I have more or less been working out of their offices," Barnes said.

"I have heard some talk about that. I don't know how you're set up, who you work for, but that's not my business. How can I help you?" K.W. asked.

"Are you still assigned to the juvenile section over there?" Barnes asked.

"Yes, that's right. I am working juvenile and anything else that comes my way," Bangs said.

"How are Mac and Maridell? I haven't seen them in a while?" Barnes asked.

"Do you know my mother and father in law?" K.W. was now becoming curious about the call.

"We grew up together. Maridell and I dated in high school, and I've known Mac for 50 years or more," Barnes said.

"Okay, well they are doing fine," Bangs had determined that he was going to wait until Barnes got to the point.

"I called downtown and checked you out. You have a good reputation with Dallas. You were a sergeant when you left. Mind telling me why you left and why you didn't go back there rather than applying at Plano," Barnes asked.

"Pete, I remember more about you as we talk. You worked a three-wheel motorcycle around the downtown area. I saw you working traffic around the El Fenix on McKinney every time my crew would meet there for lunch. I remember now that Elmer Boyd, Millie Sims, and H.O. Wilkerson liked you a lot.

So, based on my memories I am going to say that you are a stand-up guy, but I'm wondering why you would ask me such a question," Bangs said.

Barnes laughed and said, "I like a man that comes to the point. I am about to resign my job with the county and go to work full time for the School District.

Ray Hopper is the Assistant Superintendent for Business over there. One of the departments that report to him is the transportation department. He has asked me to take that department over and run it for him. I am going to take the job and will start with the district on October 1st.

That means they are going to need someone to do what I have been doing for them. Wayne Hendrick asked me about you. I have done my due diligence and told him that you would be a good man for the job.

You can expect a call anytime now. He will ask you to go to lunch and talk about the job. I wanted to give you this heads up so you can think about it some before he calls," Barnes said.

K.W. sat thinking for a few seconds and then said, "Well thanks for the call but I have a ton of questions, Pete."

"I've got time, so go ahead," Barnes said.

"Let me start my questions with an answer. I came to Plano rather going back to Dallas because this is my home. I grew up here and want to work here.

Now, the questions; how in the world did my name come to Dr. Hendrick's mind? Obviously, I remember him because he was the Superintendent when I was in school, but he doesn't know me.

Next, what are you doing for Plano ISD? I thought you were a probation officer and just had an office at the high school available to you when you were checking on your probationers.

What do they want me to do for them? Would I be working for the district or Plano PD?

I don't want to leave the police department, Pete. I like being a police officer," K.W. said.

"I did have an office at the high school, and I did use it when seeing my kids, but I also talked with kids who were headed in the wrong direction. I used my position to get their attention, but my purpose was to help kids get back on the right track and not end up on my list of juvenile offenders.

I was not, am not being paid by the district. My salary comes from Collin County. And I like what I am doing. But, Judge Ryan wants me to limit my time in Plano and concentrate on building the juvenile department for the County.

Plano is my home too K.W. I was born in Murphy, went to school in Plano and I want to finish my working years here. So, the timing of this offer is perfect for me.

As for what they want you to do, they want you to be a police officer. Keith Sockwell talked with Dr. Henderick about you coming out to Haggard recently and arresting a kid for vandalizing a home under construction. He liked the way you handled the situation, and Dr. Henderick remembered that when this deal came up.

Dr. Henderick also likes your wife, Trudy. He told me that she is one of 'his teachers' at the High School. He talked about both of you as kids, and he remembers that she was Miss Plano and that you were Captain of the first state championship football team in Plano. He wants you, Ken. He has already called David Griffin," Barnes said.

"He called the city manager? Why?" K.W. asked.

"I was sitting at his desk when he called. I heard his side of the conversation only. But what I heard him say to David was that he needed a law enforcement presence in the district and that he wanted that to come from you.

I heard enough to know that David said he would what the city could do to help the district. Dr. Henderick told David that the District would be happy to reimburse the city for your salary and expenses," Barnes said.

"I would keep my commission and work all of the cases coming out of PISD. I wonder if that would include adult offenders as well as kids. That might be too much for one man," K.W. said.

"I don't know more that what I've told you. Except, I do know that Dr. Henderick told David that no one in the District would supervise you, that your line of supervision would still be through the department and that your contact in the district would be him personally," Barnes finished.

"Well, thanks for the heads up Pete. This gives me a lot to think about, and I am grateful that I won't be caught flat-footed by the call," Bangs said.

•   •   •

He heard the phone ringing but this was his day off, and he was determined not to answer it. He shifted his position on the couch and turned the page. Trudy was at work, and he had the house all to himself.

He had slept late, ate a leisurely breakfast and settled in for a second reading of *The Onion Field*. *'I love reading Wambaugh, and I am not going to let anything interrupt me,'* he mumbled.

The phone stopped ringing, and he smiled to himself. Then it started again. *'Frustrating,'* he said as he laid the novel aside and sat up on the couch. He looked at the phone and hoped it would stop, but it just kept ringing.

He gave up, walked to the phone and picked it up, "Yes."

"Ken, this is Pete Barnes," a familiar voice said.

"Hello, Pete. What's up?" Bangs asked.

"I am following up on the previous conversation we had. Dr. Henderick is ready to talk with you about taking my place with the District. We would like to take you to lunch and discuss the details," Barnes said.

"Pete, you know I am employed by the Plano Police Department. I feel uncomfortable about meeting with the Superintendent of Schools about a job, a transfer or whatever this should be called, without the Department being informed," Bangs said.

"Chief Kinsey called Dr. Henderick this morning to talk about how all this would work. The bottom line is that the Chief does not want to assign you full time to work with the District.

The most he will agree to is to make it a priority for all cases coming out of the District to be assigned to you, as long as that will not interfere with your availability to the meet the needs of the Department.

Dr. Henderick knows the Chief is not on board, but he still wants to meet with you. Can you come by for lunch with him today about noon?" Barnes asked.

"Why Pete? For what purpose? It seems to me the issue is settled with the Chief's answer," Bangs said.

"Ken, you should not blow this off. The man wants you, and this might be good for you and your family in the long run," Barnes said.

Bangs was quiet a minute and then said, "Shoot Pete. I feel like I'm in a box here. I like Dr. Henderick, and I like being a police officer."

"Go to lunch with us. Here the man out. I have told him that you want to remain a commissioned officer and that I don't believe you will come to the District if it means resigning your commission. It might work out that you can be a police officer and work for the District," Barnes said.

"How is that Pete?" Bangs asked.

"The only thing I know for certain is that Dr. Henderick has a plan for a law enforcement presence in the District. He wants you in that role. Knowing the man as I do, my bet is that he is going to make it happen. How, I don't know.

But remember this, the City of Plano and The Plano ISD are committed to a cooperative growth strategy. They are linked in everything from the joint purchase of land for schools, parks and playgrounds to traffic and fire safety commissions. The man is a visionary. He knows Plano is about to experience an exponential growth surge and he intends to have District personnel in places of influence," Barnes said.

"I had not thought of that Pete. Okay, I will be there at noon and listen to what the man has to say," K.W. said.

CHAPTER 33
COOKING THE SPECS

Jean Steeps turned left in front of the oncoming traffic and was greeted with blaring horns and the sound of screeching tires. *'Tough luck sister, I need to get to work,'* she smirked as she parked the new Metallic Rose Cadillac.

She stepped from the car and hurried toward the building. "Hey Jean, is that a new car?" Jean turned to see that it was Joe Sims asking the question.

"Yes. Phil got it for me yesterday," Jean answered with a smile and pushed through the doors and up the stairway. *'Damned nosy auditor,'* she mumbled as she climbed to the third floor and her suite of offices.

"Good morning Jean. Your husband called and said that he needs to speak with you as soon as you come in," Robbie, her assistant said as Jean entered the office.

"Okay, I will call him after I meet with the campus managers," Jean said.

"Jean, he said it is important and asked that you call him the minute you walk in. He needs to talk with you about the request for bids that went out yesterday," Robbie whispered.

"Don't say that out here. I've told you before that you should come into my office if you have anything like that to say," Jean looked around to see who might have heard the conversation.

She walked into her office and sat down. She dialed her husband's number and waited as the call clicked through the switchboards. She heard the line open and then, "Good Morning, North Star Foods. Mallory speaking, how may I direct your call?"

"Mal, this is Jean. I am returning Phil's call," she said in a clipped tone that said '*Get my husband on the phone, I don't have time for chit chat.*'

Mallory pushed in the numbers for Phil Steeps office and disconnected her line. "You snooty bitch," she snapped.

"What is that all about?" the other switchboard operator asked.

"I'm sorry Sharon, but that was Jean Steeps. I just can't stand her better than thou attitude and the way she struts around here flashing all her diamonds and that big Rolex watch. Yesterday Susan heard Phil call Crest Cars in Plano and tell them to deliver a new Cadillac to her. She and Phil will get found out someday, and then we'll see how uppity she is," she whispered.

"Thanks for returning my call so quickly," her husband said.

"Okay, but make it quick. I have all my kitchen managers waiting for me," Jean was being a little rude, but she didn't care.

"I just read the specifications on the new request for bids to supply meat, poultry, and fish to the District for next school year. It is the most general list of specifications I have ever seen. Every Tom, Dick, and Harry in the food service industry will be able to bid on these. Why didn't you use the specifications I gave you?" Phil questioned his wife.

"Because people are beginning to notice that the company where my husband serves as Vice President of Institutional Sales is getting the lion's share of our business. We don't want to kill the goose that is laying those golden eggs.

Let this be a truly competitive bid. It would be smart to let someone else have this bid. We can make it up this summer when not so many are watching," Jean glanced at the clock.

"There are a lot of payments to be made on that new Cadillac between now and summer. I don't mind letting some other companies have the fish, but we need that meat and poultry contract, Jean. I have promised the boss that I would deliver on that. Now you have to re-write those specs," Phil urged.

"I don't know Phil. I told you there are some who are beginning to ask questions. Our internal auditor asked me about the new car this morning. I'm a little nervous right now," Jean tried to reason with her husband.

"Too late to be nervous. In for the penny, puts us in for the pound. Now re-write those specs and get them out today. Use the ones I gave you," Phil's tone was demanding.

"We will talk about this tonight," Jean said and hung up the phone.

'You just don't get it Phil. Even these rubes in Plano will catch on if we keep cooking these specs. The smart thing to do is ease off and let someone else have this bid, but I bet he is going to make me do an addendum to this bid,' Jean sighed and hurried out of her office to the meeting with the managers.

"Wait Jean. I know you are in a hurry, but there are two things I have to talk with you about, in your office," Robbie said striding into the office without waiting.

Jean stomped in after her and closed the door, "This had better be life and death," she was seething.

"First, you have calls from five principals wanting to know when you are going to get back with them on the refreshments for their holiday parties. Next, the warehouse in Garland called and said that a city inspector was in there yesterday.

He saw all of the government commodities in your freezer units and asked who owned them. They told him, and he asked to see the records of the rentals.

Lonnie Watkins, the manager, said to tell you that the inspector asked a ton of questions and was most curious about how you had managed to stockpile so many government commodities. Lonnie expects you or someone with the district will be hearing more from this," Robbie said.

Jean felt her legs grow weak. She walked behind the desk and sat down. "Robbie, who else, besides you and me, knows about those freezer units?" she gasped.

"I don't know, Jean. The invoice for the rental payments come through here, whoever is working the payables on that day reviews it, puts the payment code on it, makes a copy and sends it up for payment.

Whoever is working disbursements in finance sees the invoice and enters it on the list for payment in the next check run. Then someone puts the check in the envelope and mails it out.

When the check is cashed and returned, someone has to record and reconcile it. So you see, there are any number of people who can know about them," Robbie said.

Jean leaned back in her chair and thought a minute. "Robbie, go tell Abbey to run the meeting for me. Tell her to follow the agenda we put together yesterday and leave it at that. Nothing else is to be discussed. Close the door behind you as you leave," Jean said.

CHAPTER 34
FILTER DUMP

Darrell Trenton leaned against the locked door and released a frustrated sigh. "This door is locked, and I don't have a key. That means we can't turn the record feature off on those security cameras," he said looking at Roger Morris.

"So what now? Do you want me to force it open" Roger asked.

"Are you serious? Is that all you Marines know how to do, use brawn? Think Roger. Breaking the door down would alert the first person that saw it.

Now, look at that monitor. Camera number three has a clear line of sight to the dumpster and will record us dumping the filters. Since we can't turn the camera off, we have to cover the lens long enough to get the job done without being seen. Let's walk to the back and take a look see," Darrell said.

Darrell opened the back door just enough to allow him to see the cameras mounted above the door. He followed the line of sight from the camera to the dumpster. "This is camera number three. That dumpster is setting in the middle of its' field of view," he said releasing the door.

Darrell saw a long handled broom sitting in the corner of the room. "Roger, bring me that broom," he said while taking his jacket off.

"What are you going to do boss?" Roger asked.

"I'm going to show a Marine how the Air Force uses brain rather than brawn to get the job done," Darrell said winking at the retired

Marine sergeant.

Darrell draped the jacket on the broom handle and opened the back door. He pushed the broom handle out and up until it was at the same height and alongside the camera. Then he moved it around in front of the lens and hung the coat over the camera housing.

He allowed the door to close and said to Roger, "Trot up to the front office and look at that monitor. See if the coat has covered the camera and blocked its' view of the dumpster and the parking lot around it."

Roger came hustling back with a smile on his face, "The Air Force scored again. The screen for camera number 3 is dark, totally dark."

"Good. Now get on the radio and tell the guys that we are at Davis. Tell them to kill their lights and come around to the back of the building.

You get out there with them and put those filters in the dumpster as quickly as you can. The PTA meets here starting at eight. It is seven-thirty now and we have to hustle if we are going to be out of here before they show up.

Make sure they have enough room in that dumpster to get all the filters inside and still be able to close the lid. We don't want them showing.

The dumpster will be emptied tomorrow, and the evidence will be gone. Go. Get it done," Darrell said pushing Roger out the door.

•　　　•　　　•

Lightning streaked across the North Texas sky, turning the purple darkness into a brilliant flash of power. Sam Turner sat hunched over the steering wheel of his Chevy Suburban while waiting for the thunderclap that was sure to follow.

The eruption startled him, even though he knew it was coming. The rain was hammering down with violence that matched the thunderous display he had just witnessed. He glanced at the sky once more and realized that there was no let up in sight. Sam grabbed his hat, pulled it down tight and jumped from the truck.

The flooding waters swirled over and into his shoes, turning his socks into squishing sponges. *'I'm swimming not running,'* he thought as he struggled to keep his hat on his head. He pushed the door open and stepped quickly inside.

"Well, good morning Sam. I rather enjoyed watching you battle your way across our flooded parking lot," Phyllis said.

"Yeah, well I'm glad I could provide the entertainment, Phyllis. I'm here to take Darrell and Roger to lunch," Sam snapped.

"Well, don't be such a grouch. I didn't mean to upset you," Phyllis said as she punched in the number for Darrell Lynch's office.

She looked at the dripping salesman while waiting for Darrell to answer. *'I didn't like that SOB the first time he came prancing in here, and I like him even less now,'* she thought to herself.

"Darrell, Sam Turner from Southwest Filters is here to see you," she spoke into the phone.

"He said for you to wait here. He and Roger will be right up," Phyllis said.

She turned her back to Roger and started to type. He didn't know it, but she could see him in the reflection off of the glass in a picture hung on the wall in front of her.

She watched now as he glanced at her back and then lifted his middle finger and mouthed, *'You Bitch.'*

Anger rushed through her. She struggled to control her emotions. She kept typing until she heard the footsteps of her boss coming down the hall. She then turned to face him and smiled, "Joe Sims called just before Sam came into the office. He wants to talk with you. Should I call him back and tell him it will be after lunch?" she asked.

"What in the hell does that bean counter want?" Darrell glanced at Roger.

"He's the internal auditor, so I would guess it has something to do with invoices, purchase orders or such," Phyllis had not missed the concern that flashed across the faces of Darrell and Roger.

"Call him and tell him that I am going to be out this afternoon and I will call him tomorrow morning," Darrell said.

"Oh, are you not coming back this afternoon?" Phyllis asked.

"No. Sam is taking Roger and me to lunch. After that, Roger and I are going to conduct the monthly safety meeting for the HVAC supervisors. We will finish up around three-thirty and then Sam will do a product presentation, explaining how to get the best use, the longest life out of our HVAC filters. That will take the rest of the afternoon.

Sam will bring us back here to our cars, and we will go home without coming back inside the office," Darrell said while looking out the door at another bright flash of lightning.

The three men rushed out of the door, and Phyllis watched as they splashed across the parking lot and got into Sam's Suburban.

Phyllis glanced at the clock on her desk and saw that it was eleven thirty-five, *'Hmmmm, I smell something fishy. If these guys take a full hour for lunch that will mean that the Safety Meeting will start at twelve-thirty or thereabouts. Those meetings never take more than forty-five minutes, but let's give them an hour. That would mean that the meeting would be finished at half past one at the latest.*

Sam is a blowhard, but even he won't take more than an hour and a half for a product presentation. That puts him finished at three o'clock. And that's too early to leave work, even on a Friday.

Darrell is lying. They are going to the bar at the Outback Steak House and drink all afternoon. That's my bet. I do believe I will make a record of this event. A girl can never tell when such a record might come in handy,' she mused.

She walked back to her desk and adjusted the monitor for the parking lot cameras, turning it so she could watch it as she typed. She checked to be sure that both Roger's and Darrell's vehicles were visible. She checked to be sure the time, and date display was correct; then she pushed the record button.

Phyllis dialed Joe Sims' office and waited for him to pick up. "Joe, this is Phyllis at the facilities service center. I gave Darrell your message, but he said to tell you that he was going to be out the rest of the afternoon and would call you first thing tomorrow morning," she said.

"Tomorrow is Saturday Phyllis," Joe said.

"Wow, I never thought of that. Well, that's what Darrel said, so I guess it will be Monday," she said.

"Okay, thanks, Phyllis. Oh, where did you say the safety meeting was going to be conducted?" Simms asked.

"I didn't say Joe," Phyllis said and then waited.

"How would you get in touch with Darrell in the event of an emergency, say a school's HVAC system shut down?" Joe asked.

"I would probably look for him in the bar area of the Outback Steak House on Fifteenth Street. But I sure would appreciate not being quoted on that," Phyllis said.

"No quotes and I'm grateful," Joe said and broke the connection.

The auditor sat chewing his lip for a minute. *'I wonder if I should drive by the Outback and catch these guys drinking on duty? '* Joe thought.

His office exploded in light as a bolt of lightning danced across the sky. *'Well, that settles that. I am not going out in this storm,'* Joe mumbled as he picked up the phone and dialed.

K.W. had just walked into his office and was shaking the rain off of his coat. The phone rang followed by a crash of thunder. He hung his raincoat on the coat rack and sat down, picking the phone up.

"Bangs," he spoke.

"Ken, this is Joe Sims. I need to come down there and talk some business. Can you see me now?

"Sure, come on," K.W. said and hung up.

Sims came into the office and said, "Do you mind if I close the door?"

"Not at all," Bangs said.

"I have to talk with you about some district business, but first I want to be sure that I know what your position is here. My understanding is that you are the District's cop, is that right?" Sims asked tersely.

Bangs noticed that Sims had a pronounced twitch. The man's head would jerk down and to the right, while his right shoulder would heave upward to almost touching the right side of his face. *'Is this man under a lot of stress or what?'* he asked himself.

"No, I am not the District's cop. I am a licensed and certified peace officer of the State of Texas. My position with the District is rather complicated but suffice it to say that I am the contact for law enforcement needs within the District," Bangs said.

"Good enough. I am the internal auditor for the District. I was out at Davis Elementary last night to talk with the PTA about the proper way to account for the money they raise for all their parties and so forth.

As you might expect, the parking lot was filled with cars, and I had to park around back, next to the dumpster. I got there about a quarter to eight, and it was dark, but I noticed that the dumpster was overstuffed with something that was spilling out and had collected on the pavement. I walked over and saw HVAC filters, new and still in the factory wrapping. I stopped counting at 125 filters.

When I got into the office this morning, I ran a quick audit on the number of filters we are buying. The numbers staggered me.

My curiosities ratcheted up another notch. So I called the lead custodians at five other elementary schools. I choose these campuses carefully in order to get a sample from schools all across the District.

I asked the same question at each campus; "Have you been finding HVAC filters, new HVAC filters, in your dumpster?

Five out of five said yes. Now, understand they were skittish about answering me and I had to coax, cajole and threaten, but each custodian answered my question by saying yes, that they had been finding new, unused filters in their dumpsters.

A composite of my conversations with them leads me to believe that this started right after school was out last year and went on all through the summer. It has continued in this current school term, and the number of filters dumped is constant.

From a quick look at our purchases, I can say that so far this year we have purchased nine thousand new filters. That comes to an average of just over twelve hundred and eighty-five filters a month.

Annualize that, and the number becomes fifteen thousand four hundred and twenty nine units a year. Paying two dollars and ninety cents for each one will cost us forty four thousand, four hundred and forty four dollars for the year.

Now consider this, we have sixty-one facilities in the district with HVAC systems. The total number of HVAC units in those sixty-one facilities is one hundred and eight.

Each unit's system uses six filters. That means we need to have six hundred and forty eight filters in use at any one time. Each one of those filters has a service life of ninety days, so they have to be changed four times a year. Six hundred and forty-eight filters replaced four times a year means we need two thousand five hundred and ninety two filters each year.

Again, we pay two dollars and ninety cents for a filter, so our budget on filters is seven thousand five hundred and seventeen dollars, rounded up, a year.

So far this year we have purchased seven thousand four hundred and eighty-eight more filters than we need. We have spent twenty six thousand one hundred dollars or some eighteen thousand five hundred and eighty-two dollars more than we budgeted for or need to have spent. Annualize that, and the overage becomes thirty seven thousand two hundred and twenty two dollars.

The contract is for two years. If this pattern repeats next year, double the cost, and we will end up spending eighty nine thousand four hundred and eighty-eight dollars or eighty one thousand nine hundred and seventy one dollars more than necessary.

Split that three ways and each crook is reaping a twenty seven thousand three hundred and twenty-eight dollar windfall.

K.W. picked the printout up and scanned it. He looked at Joe and said, "All of these purchases are made from Southwest Filter Manufacturing, Incorporated. I take it you have a contract with that firm and that you know who the Southwest representative is."

"Southwest gained the contract, a two-year contract, in a competitive bid process. The Southwest representative is named Sam Turner. His bid of two dollars and ninety cents per filter was the low bid received.

I also found a complaint contesting the bid process. A separate bidder, HVAC Service Company, Inc., complained that it costs Southwest more to manufacture and deliver the filters than the price for which they were offering them to the District. They requested that the contract not be awarded until an investigation could be completed.

Our manager supervising the HVAC Department is Roger Morris. His boss is the Director of Facility Services, Darrell Trenton. Both Morris and Trenton appeared before the Board of Trustees and testified that they agreed with HVAC Service Company.

The quoted price seemed impossibly low. They stated that they had asked Southwest's representative Sam Turner to accompany them to the meeting so the Trustees could hear his explanation directly from him.

Turner stood up and told the Board that his company had purchased a complete warehouse full of the filters, some one hundred thousand of them, in a bankruptcy sale. Under questioning from the Board, Sam identified the bankrupt manufacturer as Air Services, Incorporated of Macon, Georgia.

Sam said that Southwest had bought them for pennies on the dollar. He declined to provide the exact amount claiming it was proprietary. His pitch was that Southwest could offer them at the quoted price and still make a decent profit.

The Board asked about warranty if the filters were purchased out of bankruptcy.

Mr. Morris testified that he was a retired Marine Gunnery Sergeant with a thirty years experience in managing HVAC services. He told the Board that these filters met all the requirements of our systems and that Southwest offered the same warranty as the original manufacturer.

The Board overruled the complaint, and the deal was done," Sims said.

"So, tell me what you want me to do about this?" Bangs asked.

"I want you to find out who is tossing our filters away and why, " Sims answered.

"Joe, it is not a violation of the law for the owner, or their agents, to throw their property away. But it would be a violation of the law if these agents entered into a conspiracy to steal from or defraud the taxpayer.

The question then becomes, is there a fraud being perpetrated on the taxpayer and if so by whom and in what manner. The answer to that question lies at the end of a formal and rather complicated investigation.

Before we go any further, let me ask you this question. Does the District receive federal funds that are used in the HVAC operations?" Bangs asked.

"Yes, we do receive federal funds. Those funds are used in every part of our operation, from the classroom to food service, to transportation and certainly in facility management and services," Sims replied.

Bangs nodded and said, "I figured as much. That means the feds, in this case, the FBI, would have jurisdiction in any investigation related to the fraudulent use of those funds.

I will notify my supervisors here in the District and if they approve I will make a referral to the FBI. They get the first bite out of this apple, so to speak."

"Will you allow me time to tell Dr. Henderick about this before you make a referral?" Sims asked with a series of twitches that made K.W. wince.

"Relax Joe. We need to take our time and be sure of our facts before we start accusing these men of engaging in nefarious behaviors.

I need you to submit a written summary of what you have seen, what you have found in your review of the records and then formalize your request for law enforcement to make an inquiry into the matter. Once I have that in hand, I will contact my superiors and follow their instructions," Bangs said.

"I will do that as quickly as possible, but I want you to know that I am going to give a copy to Dr. Henderick," Sims said.

CHAPTER 35
THE SAFETY MEETING

The traffic was at a total standstill and had been for some three minutes. A gust of wind rocked the pickup, and the rattle of rain against the metal roof intensified for a few seconds.

He glanced at the clock on the dash of the Ford and winced. He was now officially late for the Departmental Safety meeting. Attendance was mandatory, and his boss was not happy when his men were late.

Jason sighed and picked up the handheld radio out of the front seat. He keyed the mike and spoke, "Facilities fourteen to Facilities three."

He released the transmit button and waited. The silence grew deeper and deeper. *The meeting has already begun, and Darrell has made them turn off their radios,'* he was thinking.

He tossed the radio back onto the seat and opened the door of the truck to step out and onto the raised median next to where he was stalled. As far as he could see the traffic was jammed, bumper-to-bumper, with no movement. Now soaked, he sat back down on the vinyl seat covering and reached into the glove box for a rag to wipe his face.

"Facilities thirty-four to Facilities fourteen," the radio squawked.

Jason grabbed the radio and said, "Go ahead to Facilities fourteen."

"The boss wants to know why you are not here?"

"I am stuck in traffic on Fifteenth just west of Custer Road. I have been here for about three minutes now without moving. There is no way for me to get out of this until the police get things moving again," Jason replied.

He sat and waited for the next transmission. He knew that his message was being relayed to Roger and he knew that Roger was steaming.

Finally, the breaking of squelch split the silence, "Fourteen, the boss says that if you miss more than fifteen minutes of the meeting, you will not receive credit for the month, will not be safety certified and will not be qualified to lead. Get here or pay the cost of poor planning."

Jason was shocked. *'That pompous ass! He is just trying to degrade me in front of my crew. He knows I can't get there. What goes around comes around, and I want to be there when he gets his,'* he pounded the steering wheel of the truck.

Jason groaned and leaned forward, resting his head against the steering wheel. The inside of the truck lit up with a flash of lightning as the storm continued its' savage sweep across North Texas. He heard a car horn and raised his head to see that the traffic was moving. Five minutes later he had parked his truck and was splashing through the flooding parking lot and into the Outback Steak House.

He hurried past the receptionist and into the conference room in the back. Every face turned to look at him as he opened the door. Some had smiles on their faces, some smirked, and some looked away quickly.

He sat down and glanced at the clock on the wall. *'Meeting started at twelve forty-five and it is now nine minutes after one. I am four minutes late. I missed his deadline by four minutes. He will chew on me but surely he will won't disqualify me over four minutes,'* Jason mused.

The big boss, Darrell, was still opening the meeting with some stats on vehicle accidents and or damage since the previous meeting. He was stressing the importance of driving defensively, and Jason allowed his mind to wander.

He looked around and noticed that the attendance sheets had not yet been collected and were still lying on the tables in front of each attendee.

Darrell finished up and said, "Roger, why don't you come on up and while he is coming, pass the attendance sheets toward the aisle end of your table and we will collect them before the Roger starts."

The men started shuffling papers down toward the aisle. Jason stood and said, "Boss, could I get a sheet and fill it in while Roger is getting ready to start the meeting."

Darrel turned to look at Roger. Roger said without looking up, "No. I told you if you were more than fifteen minutes late you would not receive credit. I looked at the clock when you came in. You were nineteen minutes late, so you will not receive credit."

"But Roger, the meeting hasn't even started yet. That doesn't seem fair," Jason said.

"Life is not fair Jason. I made you a team leader. Team leaders should be responsible enough to be on time for meetings. You failed, and now you will pay the price. I don't want to hear any more of your whining," Roger said.

The room was quiet, and Jason felt as though he was sitting under a spotlight. Every eye was on him. His face was burning with embarrassment, and he suddenly felt nauseous. He sat back down, and someone behind him snickered.

Jason pushed back from the table and stood. Roger looked at him, and Jason turned and stepped away from the table.

"Where are you going, young man?" Roger barked.

"No need for me to sit through this meeting if I am not going to get credit. I've got things I can be doing," Jason replied.

"I tell you where you are to be and when you are to be there. Obviously, we have a failure to communicate in that regard. But now that you are here; sit down and be quiet," Roger bite the words off in his best Marine Corps command voice.

Jason sank into his chair and looked at the table. He didn't want anyone to see the glistening of his eyes.

"Levi Valance, stand up," Roger barked.

Jason raised his head and turned to look at Levi who was looking back at him. The stricken look on Levi's face told Jason that he didn't want to be part of his humiliation. But he stood and faced Roger.

"Eli you are now the leader of team six. Jason, you now work for Eli. Are there any questions?" Roger asked.

Eli looked at Jason again and said, "None from me boss."

Jason stood and said, "No. None from me either."

"Good, both of you sit down and let's get this meeting started," Roger said.

Jason sat still for the first few minutes and then glanced at Darrel. He was surprised to see that Darrel had been staring at him. Jason looked back down and then raised his head to watch Roger make his presentation but inside he was burning, '*Eli is the youngest, most junior member of the team. Roger made him lead just to humiliate me even more,*' he thought.

Fifty minutes later Roger ended his program and sat down. Darrel stood and introduced Sam Turner as the sales representative for Southwest Manufacturing.

Sam spoke for forty-five minutes on the new filters the District were using and how to get the best service and longest life out of them. When he sat down, Darrel stood and dismissed the men telling them to return to work and to be careful on the wet streets.

As Jason waited at the door with the crowd of men preparing to make a dash through the wind-driven rain, he felt a nudge on his right hand. Looking down he saw another hand, a black hand holding a wadded up piece of paper. He took the paper and sprinted for his truck.

Once in the truck, he strapped his seat belt on and started the engine. Rain flooded in waves over the outside of the windows. His body heat caused the inside of the windows to fog over, effectively blocking any view into the truck.

Jason opened the wadded up note and saw Elvis Mims neat handwriting, "I saw something before the meeting started that you might find useful one day. Meet me in the overhang behind Williams High School."

Jason turned the wipers on, flipped on the lights and drove out of the parking lot. He turned east on Fifteenth Street, toward Williams.

He drove into the back lot at Williams and saw a District truck backed in and parked under the overhang next to the auto mechanics shop. He parked next to the truck and rolled his window down. The drumming of the rain on the metal overhang was loud, so he stepped from his truck and leaned in so he could hear what Elvis had to say.

"Jason, I am so sorry about what Roger did to you in there today. That man just made you his bitch in front of the whole shift. But, I got something that might get you even. That is if you're interested," Elvis said with a tight smile.

"Why Elvis? Why are you willing to help me?" Jason asked.

"Because Roger is a racist. He gives me every dirty job that comes around and is always calling me 'his boy.' I can't file a complaint because I need this job. I would be labeled a troublemaker, and that would destroy any possibility of building a future in this job.

I like working for the District. I want to make this my career, but I don't see that happening as long as Roger and Darrel are here. What I am about to tell you just might solve the problem for me and get you even with Roger," Elvis said.

"I'm listening," Jason replied.

"I decided to eat my lunch at the Outback just to be sure I didn't get hung up in this storm and be late. That's what you should have done too, Jason.

Anyway, I ask the girl for a seat in the back, away from the front door. She seated me in the last booth on the wall opposite the bar. As you know, there is a half wall with columns separating the bar from the dining area. That makes it almost impossible to see out of the lounge if you sit at the bar.

Well, I'm sitting there eating my steak lovers' salad when Roger, Darrel and Sam Turner come hustling in. They stand there at the door shaking rain off, and I notice that this guy Sam has a long carrying case in one hand and a smaller compact case in the other.

I don't know if you know it or not, but I was an armorer in the Army. So I knew that the long case was for a rifle and the compact case was for a pistol.

That made me curious. So, I waited until they are seated, and then I eased up and stood in a spot where I could see and hear them without their being able to see me.

They ordered beers and burgers, and then Sam turns to Darrel, hands him the long case and said, *'I know you like to hunt and that you are headed to Alaska to take a Big Horn next month. I also know how hard it is for you left handed fellows to find a rifle that fits you. So, I had this one made up for you.*

This is the best rifle available for hunting Big Horns in the Alaskan mountains. It is a Winchester Model Seventy, Extreme Weather Stainless Steel in .308 caliber. And, like I said, it is made for lefties.'

I had to see it, so I craned my neck around and there it was, a left-handed rifle gleaming in stainless steel. I tell you, Jason, that rifle in a standard model will cost twelve hundred dollars. I have no idea what a custom made one, with the bolt on the left, costs.

Then ole Sam handed the smaller case to Roger. *'Roger he said, being a Marine myself I know that every Marine wants a Model 1911. I got this John Wayne commemorative model for you. Once this rain lets up, we will have to go out to my place and burn some powder.'*

I peeked at the pistol too and saw that it is engraved with a gold hammer and trigger, all fancied up. Must be a thousand dollar pistol.

Darrel and Roger stammered around some, and finally, Darrel said, *'I sure appreciate this Sam, but you know if anyone found out we were taking gifts from a vendor it might open up an inquiry. We cannot afford to take that chance. I don't want to risk big money for a couple of nice but minor gifts. Know what I mean?'*

I could see Sam's face in the mirror. He didn't blink an eye. He just smiled and said, *'Why don't you put those in the Suburban before the crew starts to arrive and we can talk about it later. Once things settle down, I think you will see that there is no harm in taking them. We have this thing by the tail with a downhill drag Darrel. No one is going to find out what we have going. No one. Just relax and let's make some money.'*

I scooted back to my table and watched as Darrel ran his rifle out to the car. Roger put his pistol in that big satchel he was carrying around today and stayed at the bar with Sam.

As soon as I saw Darrel exit the door, I moved back to my listening post. I heard Roger say, 'Sam, don't push Darrel. He can't take the strain. Let's keep this a Marine operation. What we need to do now is get that connection in Allen finalized so we can move some filters up there.

I am taking our man in Allen out for steaks tomorrow night. He is recently divorced, and the ex-wife cleaned him out. He needs money badly. I am going to give him a grand tomorrow just to whet his appetite.

I know he happens to like red heads too. I have arranged for a lovely young red-haired lady of the evening to join us for dinner. She is going home with him afterward.

I might even slip this .45 you just gave me to him if I think he is wavering on us. By the way, where did you get these weapons? Are they safe, no way we are going to get burned on them is there?'

Sam shook his head and said, 'No way. I bought them just like any other Sears and Roebuck Joe. I ordered them both from Extreme Outfitters in Arlington. A Marine I was in Nam with is the firearms manager there. The weapons are new, and the serial numbers are legit. I paid with cash and used a bogus id, so there is no trail to be followed.'

I was watching for Darrel as I listened and had to hustle back to the table when he came to the door. But there it is, a vendor giving gifts to those who recommended his bid and something that just might explain why we are using so many filters."

Jason leaned back against his truck before remembering it was wet. He pushed off and stood to stare at Elvis. Then he asked, "Elvis, are you sure about all of this?"

Elvis smiled and nodded, "As sure as I am that I am black and you are white. The crux of this matter is that these three are crooks and we have to get this information to someone who will know what to do with it."

"I know the man," Jason said.

"Who is that?" Elvis asked.

"The new cop. Bangs is his name, and he has an office at the administration building. I will get this to him and let's see what happens then," Jason said.

"Good. Do you want me to call Bangs or do you want to?" Elvis asked.

"Why don't we go to see him together? Are you willing to testify if it comes to that?" Jason asked.

"Absolutely. I would love to sit in the witness chair and watch Roger's face as I tell it all," Elvis nodded.

"Okay, meet me at the office and let's get on the same page before we go see Bangs," Jason said.

•　　　•　　　•

Jason and Elvis ran through the flood and into the front office of the Facilities Service Office. They stood in the lobby, looking back out at the parking lot where Darrel and Roger's cars were parked.

"Hey, look at the water dripping off of you two and pooling on the floor? I don't want you to walk away and leave that mess for me to clean up. Both of you grab a mop and get that water off of the floor," Phyllis demanded.

"Okay, okay. There is no need to bite our heads off," Elvis said.

Phyllis smiled and said, "Sorry guys. It's just that Roger and Darrel will yell at me if they come in and there is water on the floor."

"Come in? Their cars are parked out front. Aren't they here already?" Jason asked.

"No, they rode to the meeting with Sam Turner. Darrel said the meeting would take the rest of the day and that they would not be back," Phyllis was watching the impact of her message on Elvis and Jason.

"So, then you haven't heard about what happened at the meeting today?" Elvis asked.

"Happened, is the meeting over?" Phyllis asked glancing at the clock.

"Oh, it's over alright. It ended about forty-five minutes ago," Elvis said.

"So what happened?" Phyllis asked.

"I got hung up in traffic and was late for the meeting. Roger reamed me in front of everyone and then removed me from my team leader position. I have to clean out my office before I leave today," Jason said.

"He is the most arrogant, hard-hearted man I have ever known. He will get his someday. Do either of you know where Sam, Roger, and Darrel went after the meeting?" Phyllis asked while glancing at the monitor to ensure that both cars were still in the parking lot.

"They didn't go anywhere. They are sitting at the bar, drinking beer and talking," Elvis said.

"You saw them sitting at the bar and drinking beer?" Phyllis asked.

"I did too," Jason said looking pointedly at the clock that showed the workday had not yet ended.

Phyllis looked at the monitor again, and Elvis asked, "Why do you keep looking at that monitor?"

"Because I have it set to record with the date and time stamp engaged. I knew they were lying about this being an all day meeting and I want to get on record the time that they return to their cars," Phyllis lifted her left eyebrow.

Elvis leaned in and lowered his voice, "Listen Phyllis, as long as you are making a record, Sam gave both Roger and Darrel firearms as gifts before the meeting.

They don't know that I saw and heard the whole thing, but I did. Right now it would be my word against theirs. But if you get them on tape taking those firearms from Sam's car and placing them in theirs, it will help our cause."

"I will have it on tape, but what do you intend to do with it? You both better think this through because it is a violation of the bid laws for a public employee to accept gifts from a vendor," Phyllis said.

Elvis and Jason looked at each other and smiled. Then Jason said, "Maybe that someday is coming quicker than we thought."

CHAPTER 36
WHITE HATS ~
BLACK ROCKS

K.W. sat waiting outside the Colonel's office. He thought back over the developments of the *'filter caper'* since his conversation with Special Agent Jim Zarriet.

"The Bureau appreciates your bringing this matter to our attention but, after consulting with the Special Agent in Charge, we have decided to cede jurisdiction in this matter to your agency. Please feel free to call us for any assistance you might need during the investigation," the FBI agent had said.

K.W. glanced at his watch and saw that he had been waiting twenty minutes. He stood and walked to the receptionist desk. "Does the Colonel know that I am waiting to see him?" he asked

"Yes sir, he does. But you did not have an appointment and he is with his staff officers. He will be finished in another fifteen minutes. I am sorry for the delay but ..." her voiced trailed off as the phone began to ring.

Bangs returned to the bench seat and opened the investigative file. He began to review his notes.

He looked again at the diagram of the timeline and the information Sims had given him, the comparison of that information with the printout detailing the number of filters purchased year to date and then cross referenced them with the number purchased during the same period the year before. The numbers validated Sims' concerns.

He had followed up the interviews Sims had with the custodians and was able to obtain affidavits from each attesting to the fact that new, unused filters were being deposited in the dumpsters at their assigned schools on a regular basis.

Then he had gone to the first school on the list and checked the security tape for the day in question. He found that the screen had suddenly gone dark. He backed the tape up and played it forward in slow motion. He could see what appeared to be a pole or rod lifting an object up beside the camera and then over the lens.

He saw the dumpster before the view was blocked sitting with the top and side gates closed and nothing protruding. But in the next frames, when the obstruction was removed from the lens, the dumpster was stuffed to overflowing with filters.

Since the office staff had not yet arrived, he took his time and made meticulous notes on what he had observed, the time the blackout started, and the time it ended. He then reviewed the rest of the cameras and saw that District vehicles had arrived at the front of the school before the blackout and were seen leaving the school after the dumpsters were filled.

The camera in the front office had recorded Darrell Trenton and Roger Morris entering and leaving the office before and after the events were recorded.

A review of each of the schools tapes revealed a repeat of this action. He had taken the tapes into evidence and now had them tagged and locked securely in the bottom drawer of his desk, which was serving as his temporary evidence locker.

And then there were the affidavits from Jason and Elvis detailing the bribes giving to Roger and Darrel by Sam Turner. *'But the piece de resistance is the tape showing Roger and Darrel transferring their gifts from Sam's Suburban to their cars,'* K.W. smiled.

The door to the Colonel's office opened, and the staff officers filed out. K.W. closed his file and stood to wait for the receptionist to announce him. He saw her pick up the phone and punch in the extension. He heard the phone ring and the Colonel say, "Yes?"

The Colonel hung up the phone and stepped to the door. He looked K.W. over from head to toe, and K.W. felt himself involuntarily coming to attention.

"I am Colonel Beaty. Come in," he said.

"Thank you, sir," K.W. replied as he stepped into the Colonel's office and stood in front of his desk.

The Colonel walked behind his desk and studied K.W. for a few seconds, "Are you a veteran?" he asked.

"Yes, Sir. Army, Military Police Sir," K.W. said.

"Your rank?" the Colonel asked.

"Sergeant, E-five Sir," Bangs replied.

"Good, sit down sergeant. By the way, what is your name?" the Colonel asked.

"Sir, I am K.W. Bangs. I am here today in regards to a criminal investigation I am conducting," Bangs said.

"Very good sergeant. How can the Marine Corps help the Army?" the Colonel asked with a slight smile.

"Sir I need your assistance in checking the military history of a District employee, a retired Marine, who is a suspect in the case I am working," Bangs said.

"You drove all the way from Plano to Fort Worth to ask this question? Why didn't you call or submit your request through channels?" the Colonel asked.

"Sir, you are the Provost Marshal for the only active duty Marine law enforcement unit in North Texas. The case I am working is ongoing and involves the theft of public assets.

I have been through this drill before Sir. If I called, the message would have been taken for someone to call me back. If I had submitted my request in writing and sent it through channels, the wait would have been even longer.

Even coming here has been somewhat challenging Sir. You desk sergeant sent me to the first sergeant, and he sent me to the duty officer, who sent me to you Sir.

I am trying to stop the loss of thousands of tax dollars and time is of the essence Sir," Bangs said.

"And you think I can and will do this for you?" the Colonel asked staring at Bangs.

"Sir, you are a full Colonel. There is no question that you can. The question is will you?" Bangs asked.

"What is it that you want to know about this Marine?" the Colonel picked up a pen.

"Sir, his name is Roger Morris. He put on his application for employment with the District that he is retired after thirty years of honorable service with the Corps. He lists his final rank as Gunnery Sergeant, E-seven.

He applied for the position of the Director of HVAC Services. His application states that his entire career was spent in that field. He listed his MOS as eleven sixty-one.

I need to verify this information, Sir. I also need to know if there are any indications of criminal activity in his file, any record of misconduct resulting in disciplinary action and if he indeed he is retired with an honorable discharge," Bangs said.

"That's it?" the Colonel asked.

"For now, yes Sir," Bangs responded.

"I am going to have my First Sergeant work with you on this," the Colonel said as he picked up his phone and punched in the extension.

"First Sergeant, come to my office," the Colonel said and hung up the phone.

A knock on the door and the First Sergeant reported to the Colonel. "Sit down First Sergeant. This is K.W. Bangs. He is a former Army M.P. Sergeant and needs our help with an investigation he is working.

Most of the information he needs will be in the subject Marine's personnel file stored at the National Personnel Records Center in St. Louis. Any records related to criminal activity will be stored at Marine Headquarters in Quantico, Virginia. I want you to provide Sergeant Bangs with all the information he needs.

Then I want you to prepare a memorandum from you to him listing what you have given him with a notation that this is for official use only. Have him sign it and return it here to me," the Colonel said and stood to indicate the meeting was over.

"Thank you, Sir," K.W. said and followed the First Sergeant out of the office.

•   •   •

K.W. worked his way through the early morning traffic. Cars were lined up, bumper to bumper on East Randol Mill Road. Seeing an opening, he moved to the right lane in preparation for his exit onto Six Flags Drive. An angry horn commented on his quick move, and he smiled.

The traffic came to a standstill, and his mind wandered as he sat in the idling vehicle.

'All the records verify the unnecessary increase in the purchase of filters by Darrel and Roger. The surveillance tapes and affidavits prove up the dumping of the filters, and the information from the Marines proves that Roger lied on his application for employment with the District.

He did spend thirty years in the Marines, but his MOS was thirty fifty-one, not eleven sixty-one. He was a warehouse manager, not an HVAC Specialist. He also lied about his rank.

He put on his application that he retired as Gunnery Sergeant, which is an E-seven. But he was a Staff Sergeant or an E-six.

His discharge was not honorable originally. It was listed as Other Than Honorable and converted to Honorable one year from the date of his retirement.

The truth is he retired rather than face an inquiry regarding a shortage of boots, fatigues and web gear at the warehouse he managed.

I can prove all of that. But all of those facts together do not provide probable cause sufficient to support a criminal charge in regards to the filters. What I need is some corroborative evidence showing that Roger, Sam, and Darrel have entered into a conspiracy to defraud, by theft, the government. Then, I can introduce the act of removing and dumping the filters to facilitate the purchase of replacements. That will complete the act of theft.

I also need to prove up the allegations made by Elvis Mims and Jason

Berber that a vendor had bribed Roger and Darrel to obtain favoritism in the awarding of the bid. Then I will follow up by interviewing the HVAC Director of the Allen ISD. My bet is that he will fold and roll on Sam.

If he does, and all of this other comes together, I can stop the theft of tens of thousands of tax dollars. Dollars that should be used for the benefit and welfare of kids,' K.W. knew.

He saw the exit sign for Six Flags Drive and flipped his turn signals on. The traffic was sparse on Six Flags, and he quickly found his destination. He pulled onto the parking lot and parked in front of Extreme Outfitters.

"Can I help you, sir?" the greeter asked as K.W. walked in.

"Yes. I have an appointment with the firearms sales manager, Mr. Ricks," K.W. replied.

"I'm Ricks. Are you Bangs?" came a voice from behind K.W.

K.W. turned and saw a large, square-jawed man. The look on his face told K.W. that Mr. Ricks was not happy to see him. *'Okay, so we will play the official game, Mr. Ricks,'* K.W. thought.

"My name is K.W. Bangs. I need to talk with you relative to a criminal investigation I am conducting. My understanding is that one of the suspects may have purchased a firearm from you. You are not a suspect at this time but should your answers during the interview indicate that you do have culpability relative to the criminal matters I am investigating, I will stop and make sure you understand your rights under Miranda," K.W. said.

"What the hell are you talking about," Ricks growled.

K.W. took his time before answering. He was thinking, *'this man is not going to be cooperative. I am going to proceed like I know what I say to be true and see if he buys it.'*

"On or about November 26 of this year a man named Sam Turner took possession, from this store, of a Winchester Model 70 Extreme Weather Stainless Steel rifle in 308 caliber. He had ordered it some time before and had it custom made for a left-handed shooter.

Mr. Turner used a false name and identification. He paid in cash. I need to examine your records to find the particulars of that sale. I will also need to photocopy the record," Bangs said tersely.

Ricks was shaking his head no before Bangs finished telling him what he needed. "Do you have a subpoena?" Ricks asked with a smirk.

"No Mr. Ricks, my thought was to obtain the information I need while causing as little disruption to your business as possible. However, out of an abundance of caution, I called Special Agent Toby Short in the Arlington field office of the Alcohol, Tobacco and Firearms Agency. I explained to Agent Short what I need and why I need it.

He agreed that the easy way was to give you the chance to cooperate. But he said that he would be in the office all morning and for me to feel free to call him if I needed any assistance. Am I going to need the ATF to come down here and assist me in reviewing your records?" Bangs asked.

Ricks laughed, "Call the ATF. I will tell them the same thing I'm telling you. Bring a subpoena if you want to see my records. Until then, I have work to do." Ricks turned on his heel and stomped off.

Bangs picked up the phone sitting on the front counter and dialed Agent Short. "Toby, just like we thought. This Ricks guy will not cooperate. He says it does not matter who it is asking. No one sees his records without a subpoena. Can you help me?" Bangs asked.

Bangs nodded, hung up the phone and walked over to where Ricks stood. "Special Agent Short and his team will be here in a few minutes. He says to tell you that he has called for a temporary suspension of the Federal Firearms Dealers License for all Extreme Outfitters locations nationally pending his audit of your records.

Since I am a Public Safety Official of the State of Texas, my informing you of that suspension serves as official notice that any sales out of this location will be in violation of Federal Law. His office staff is informing the cooperate office of Extreme Outfitters as we speak."

The color left Ricks' face. Then he collected himself and looked at Bangs, "I don't believe that."

The office phone rang, and Ricks lifted the receiver and said, "Ricks speaking. What, are you sure? Well, yes. I told him he has to have a subpoena to look at and copy our sales records. But…but, yes, sir."

Ricks hung up the phone and said, "Call off the ATF. You can look at my records if you want. But I remember that left handed hunting rifle and can find it quickly if that is all you want."

"Show me," Bangs said.

"Call the ATF first. My boss is hot and corporate is hot. This can get me fired," Ricks said.

Bangs shook his head no; "You got yourself into this mess. The only way you are going to get your way out is to show me what I need. If we get that done before ATF gets here, then I will call their office and tell them."

Sweat had beaded on Ricks' forehead. He wiped it away with a cloth and realized the cloth was soaked in gun oil. He sighed and laid a large ledger on the counter.

"This is the quickest way to get you the information you need. I know that he did not use the name Sam Turner, but I swear his identification looked legit to me.

Here it is, Colby Johnson. That's the name he used. He has a Texas Drivers license, here is a copy of it, with his picture and that name on it," Ricks said turning the ledge and pointing to the transaction.

"Copy that for me," K.W. told Ricks.

Ricks brought the copy back, and Bangs asked, "Did you know that this was a scam? If you did, fess up now, and we will work with you on it. But if you don't and we find out later, we will file on you."

"I knew something was wrong because the guy was paying cash and offered me a *'little extra'* if I could make the sale off of the books. I know that's a federal rap, so I said no," Ricks stuttered.

K.W. laid his notes on the counter and looked at the clerk who had joined Ricks behind the counter, "I am about to discuss some issues with Mr. Ricks that will probably have to be repeated on a witness stand. If you are here during that conversation, I will list you as a witness, and you will be required to attend the trial and testify. Do you want to stay or would you rather step away?" K.W. said.

The clerk said nothing but moved to a position where he could not hear the conversation between Bangs and Ricks.

"Mr. Ricks, I have been doing this job for some 12 years now. In that time I have come to recognize when a man is lying to me. You, sir, are lying to me.

I am going to give you one chance to come clean. After that I am going to treat you as hostile. Do I make myself clear?" K.W. said in a soft voice.

Ricks sighed deeply and nodded. "Look officer. I have a wife and kids. Let me help myself as much as possible. Ask your questions, and I will give you straight answers," Ricks pleaded.

K.W. pulled a cassette tape recorder from his briefcase and laid it on the counter in front of Ricks. "I will give you that opportunity. But you have to be truthful, answer my questions fully and allow me to tape record our conversation for use in court.

This is the way it works; I will turn the recorder on, give our names, the date, the time and where we are. I will state that this is an interview against your penal interests. I will then recite your Miranda rights and ask if you understand those rights and agree to the interview being recorded. Are you ready?" Bangs asked.

Ricks nodded, and Bangs flipped the recorder on. After the preamble Bangs said, "Mr. Ricks you have shown me the records reflecting the sale of two firearms on or about November twenty-sixth to a man who identified himself as Colby Johnson. One of those weapons was a Colt 45 model 1911 John Wayne Commemorative pistol, and the other was a Winchester Model 70 Extreme Weather Stainless Steel 308 caliber rifle that was custom made for a left handed shooter. Do you remember that transaction sir?"

Ricks nodded his head, and Bangs said, "Mr. Ricks I saw you nod your head, but for the tape, I need you to give me an oral answer."

Ricks said, "Yes, I do remember that transaction, and I have given you copies of our records on it."

"Thank you, Mr. Ricks. Now, those records identify that man as Colby Johnson, and you have told me that you do not know him. Is that correct?" Bangs asked.

"Yes, that is what I told you. But, I lied to you. I do know who he is. His real name is Sam Turner. We were in the Marines together in

Vietnam," Ricks replied.

"Are you now telling me that you sold him these firearms allowing him to use a false name and Identification?" Bangs asked.

"Yes, I did that," Ricks answered.

"Mr. Ricks you knew that was against the law, but you did it anyway?" Bangs bored in.

"Yes sir, I did," Ricks was crying now.

"Why are you crying, Mr. Ricks?" Bangs asked.

"Because I have been so stupid and I am thinking now of what that stupidity on my part is going to do to my family," Ricks said.

"Why did you do that, Mr. Ricks, why did you so willingly and knowingly violate the law? Tell me also, why did Sam Turner want to use a false name to complete the purchase?" Bangs asked.

"I did it because Sam pays me well for doing it. And, yes we have done it several times. I feared we would get caught, but I needed the money.

Sam uses a fake name because he gives the guns to decision makers in companies where he is submitting bids for the sale of his products. He sees it as business. A tactic that it gives him a leg up on the competition," Ricks said.

"Do you know who these particular weapons were going to be given to?" Bangs asked.

"Yes, he said he was in a real money making deal with another Marine and his boss out in Plano. I think it was at the school district out there. He wanted to keep them happy and said the weapons were a drop in the bucket compared to the money he would make on the deal," Ricks said wiping his eyes on his shirtsleeve.

"Do you have a flyer or a picture that will accurately represent these two firearms? I will need one that will aid me in identifying the weapons in a group of other similar weapons," Bangs said.

Ricks laughed and said, "Sam is an egomaniac. Nothing pleases him more than to have his picture taken. He had me photograph him holding both of them. I have a copy of that picture if you want it."

"Yes, I do want all of those pictures. Do you know where he got the fake driver's license he used in this transaction?" Bangs asked.

"He has a whole bag full of them. He makes them himself. He got into that in the Marines, selling underage Marines identification cards so they could go off base and drink. I used to deliver some of them for him. He made a ton of money off of that," Ricks had control of his emotions now.

"That's it for me, Mr. Ricks. But I am going to give a copy of this tape to the ATF, and I'm sure they are going to have questions for you," Bangs said and flipped the tape recorder off.

K.W. settled into his car and sat a minute thinking over the last two days investigative efforts. He ran through an inventory of what he had.

He smiled to himself and started the car, 'It has been a good two days of getting the goods on these crooks. I want to interview both Darrel and Roger, but I don't have to. I can direct file this with what I have and let a grand jury make the decision. Either way, it is a win for the white hats and a bad day at black rock for the crooks,' he smiled as he turned East toward Plano.

CHAPTER 37
THE LIE

Joe Bates sat in the stands and watched the Plano Wildcats race up and down the court. Their sprints were governed by the coach's whistle. He would blow it, and they would race away. He would blow it again, and they would stop and drop into a three-point stance. Another blast and they were away again.

On and on it went. Sweat was dripping from their faces and naked chests. Their shorts were soaked through and were clinging in such a way to deny any modesty.

He felt the surge deep within his loins as he watched their muscles rippling across the taught stomachs and down their stout legs. He realized he was panting and looked quickly around to see if any of the other observers had noticed his arousal.

Shame flooded him. He knew his reactions were wrong. They violated the ethics of his chosen profession. He was their teacher. His was a position of trust, and his passions had led him to violate that trust. He had tried to change. He had dated many women, even been engaged a couple of times. But he just couldn't go through with it.

He had also visited some gay bars and attempted to date other men. He was sexually attracted to other males, but not adult males. Finally, he accepted that he preferred kids. He was not gay. He was a pedophile.

Joe was ashamed. But even in the midst of this introspection, his passions ruled his behaviors. *'Look at that Billy Weems. What an Adonis. I bet he is going to be sore after this workout. Maybe a full body massage is what he needs,'* his gaze was locked onto the team captain.

Billy Feems stopped and bent over with his hands on his knees. His heart was pounding, and he was sucking in air to meet the demands of his oxygen-starved lungs. There was a roaring in his ears, and his vision was blurred.

"Everyone circle up and take a knee," Coach Williams said.

Billy looked around and saw that his teammates were in the same shape he was. *'Why do we put ourselves through such torture?'* he asked himself.

But Billy knew why. He had grown up watching the mighty Wildcats win state championships in football. His sport was basketball, and no Plano team had ever won a State Championship in basketball. *'We will be the first,'* he promised himself as he kneeled with his teammates.

"Okay, guys listen up. I told you back in the summer that physical conditioning would be essential to our winning. You have just won the district title because you had more left in the fourth quarter. Now you are ready to take the bi-district crown.

Your opponent is Duncanville. They are big, they are fast and they will come to play. The difference is that you will be stronger in the fourth quarter. You are in the best physical condition of the season.

I have pushed you hard. I know you are tired. I know your legs are spent. But I also know you are ready.

Today is Friday, and you have two days off. Rest, relax and let your body recover. I want you to stay away from the sweets and the junk food. No pizza. No burgers. No greasy foods at all.

I will see you all on Monday, and we will start working on our game plan to beat those Duncanville Dragons. Okay, put your hands in here on mine and break on the count of three. One, two, three, *Wildcats!*" Coach Williams said, and they broke the huddle.

Eric Williams stood and turned toward his office. "Hey Eric, hey coach," he heard the call from the stands.

He turned and saw Gene Scott hustling toward him. He noticed that a second man carrying a camera was trailing along behind Gene. "Hey Gene," Coach Williams answered.

"Do you have time for a couple of questions from your favorite sports writer?" Gene said.

"Sure thing Gene. Always have time for the Plano Star Courier," Coach smiled at Gene.

"Coach this is my photographer. He took some pictures during the workout. Do you mind if we run them with this weekend's story on the playoffs?" Gene asked.

"Not at all. We worked on conditioning today, so there is nothing that will hurt us with any opponents," Williams said.

"Good, thanks Coach. Duncanville is the defending state champions. What do you think about drawing them for the first game in the playoffs?" the reporter stood with pen poised over his notepad.

"The UIL alignment means that Duncanville will always be our bi-district opponent. They are a great team, well coached and beating them is going to take a total team effort. But if we can get past them, we will have taken a giant step toward that Championship game," Williams answered while noticing that Joe Bates was walking out of the gym with Billy Weems.

"Excuse me a minute Gene. I need to say something to Billy before he gets away," Williams said as he stepped toward the door.

He watched as Weems and Bates walked through the exit. Bates put his hand on Billy's shoulder and then let it slide down and rest on his belt. After a few seconds, Bates dropped his hand even lower and slapped Billy lightly on his butt.

'That guy gives me the creeps. There is something wrong with him, but he is so popular with the administration that it is almost suicidal to suggest his interest in these boys is abnormal,' the coach thought.

"Hey Billy, wait up. I need to talk with you a minute," the coach called.

Weems turned toward his coach and stopped. Bates did too and remained standing beside Billy. *'Go away you pervert,'* the coach thought.

"Hey there Joe. I heard you are writing children's books now. How is that going?" Williams asked Bates.

"Oh, it is fairly slow right now. I need a publisher, so I don't have to put all the money up front. But that will come if I can get some sales," Bates replied, shuffling from one foot to the other.

"I'm sure those sales will come. Just give it some time. Hey, I need to talk with Billy a minute. Do you mind stepping away and let us discuss some team stuff?" Williams asked with a smile.

"No, not at all. I will wait for you in the car Billy," Bates said and walked to his car which Williams noticed was parked in a Coaches Only parking slot.

"Billy, what's up with all the time you are spending with Mr. Bates? I noticed him putting his hands on you. I saw him patting you on the bottom. That doesn't look good. Is there anything you need to tell me about this relationship?" Williams came right to the point.

Billy was looking at his feet and shrugged.

"Look at me, Billy. Shrugging your shoulders does not answer my question. Is there anything you need to tell me here? Has Mr. Bates ever touched you inappropriately?" Williams asked.

"He is my mom's friend, coach. They date some. They started dating about a year after dad died. I was in the fifth grade then. He gives mom money. He helps buy me clothes and stuff. I don't think mom likes him, but she needs his help. She doesn't make much money teaching, and there are three of us kids. You know what I mean?" Billy said.

"Okay, so he is your mom's friend. I understand that he helps the family out, but that does not mean he has a right to touch you or to abuse you. You didn't answer my question. Has he ever touched you inappropriately?" Williams asked.

"Not yet, but there have been a couple of times when I thought he was going to. I don't know Coach. Maybe I am just imagining things. I know that he is friends with a lot of guys and none of them have ever said that he did anything wrong," Billy said.

"What do you mean he is friends with a lot of guys Billy? What does that friendship consist of?" Williams asked.

"Well, you know. He takes guys camping. He has sleepovers, and sometimes he will tutor guys at his house. Like I said, he has never tried anything with me but...," Billy's voice trailed off, and he looked toward the car where Bates waited.

"But what Billy? What were you going to say?" Williams pressed.

"Well coach, I have heard that he sometimes gives guys a massage. You know like a full body massage. Rumor is that he rubs a lot of oils and stuff all over you and that he comes awfully close to touching the privates. He keeps asked me to let him massage me, but I always tell him no, that I don't like guys touching me," Billy was almost mumbling now.

"Billy, I don't want you being alone with Mr. Bates. I don't want him touching you the way he did coming out of the gym.

I am going to call your mom and talk to her about this, and if you want me to, I will tell Mr. Bates right now. Why don't you let me do that, and I will get another coach, and we will drive you home? Is that okay Billy?" the coach asked.

"No, sir. Please don't say anything to Mr. Bates and let me talk to my mom. I will be careful and if he does try anything I will tell you first," Billy said.

"Okay, Billy. I don't want to embarrass you. I won't say anything to Mr. Bates, but I am going to call your mom. You go on home and get some rest. Monday is the first day in our playoff drive, and you are our leader. I am looking to you to lead us all the way to Austin and that state championship trophy," Williams said and walked away.

Billy stood looking at his coach walking away. *'I just lied to you, and I am sorry. But my mom needs his help. Now it's time to entertain mom's friend,'* he sighed as he turned and walked to the car where Joe Bates sat waiting.

CHAPTER 38
FREEZER RUN

Joe Washington wrestled the big truck through the gate, past the parked buses and into his assigned slot next to the frozen food lockers. He switched off the ignition, gathered his clipboard, opened the door and stepped down on the running board.

He closed and locked the cab of the truck and climbed the steps onto the loading dock. He walked through the door into the lobby and over to the time clock. He grabbed his card and clocked out, noting that it was now fifteen minutes after five. *'Fifteen minutes past quitting time means they will have to pay me overtime. The boss man will be fussing at me about that,'* Joe chuckled.

He signed the card and laid it on his boss's desk. He walked to the dispatcher and handed her his delivery slips for the day's work.

"Here you go, Helen. The Plano ISD got their nickel's worth out of ole Joe today. I had ten stops scheduled and made every one of them. All ten schools have freezers full of meat and poultry for use on Monday.

By the way, the freezer unit on that truck is in dire need of cleaning. Someone needs to get in there with a steam hose tomorrow, after it defrosts overnight, and give it a good going over," Joe said as he handed Helen the keys to the truck.

"All the vehicle maintenance crew is off tomorrow Joe. If I get Elmer to approve the overtime, will you be able to do it?" Helen asked.

"That means giving up my Saturday. I had better call the wife first and be sure she is okay with it. I'll be right back," Joe said and headed toward the employee's lounge.

'Got to make this look good,' he thought as he sat his lunch pail down and picked up the phone. He punched a made up phone number and waited.

He turned and surveyed the room, waving to a couple of his fellow drivers who were finishing up their logs. Then he turned back to face the wall and said, "Hey sugar. Helen just asked if I could work tomorrow. It would mean about six hours of time and half, and we know that would come in handy with Christmas coming up.

What? No I don't have to, but again that overtime will be sweet this time next month. But I will tell her you have plans, and it's a no on the overtime. Be home soon," and he hung up.

He looked at the grinning faces and said, "Hey if the boss lady ain't happy you know Joe ain't going to be happy," he winked and walked out.

"Sorry, Helen. The wife said no. He parents are coming for dinner tomorrow night, and she has a full day of cleaning and straightening the house planned for me," he said with a sigh.

"That's not good. It's a definite no then?" Helen asked.

"My brother works at Duck Creek Cold Storage in Garland. They have a complete set up for the cleaning of their freezer trucks. I live about fifteen minutes from there, and I know they will let me run my truck through the steam station.

I will be happy to do that if Elmer wants to let me drive the truck home. But I don't want to do all the driving back and forth. Know what I mean? If it makes any difference, I won't ask for overtime," Joe said.

"What a deal. Do it," Elmer spoke from behind Joe.

Joe turned with a smile and said, "Dang boss. You startled me. I didn't know you were back there."

"One never knows when ole Elmer is watching and listening. Just get it done Joe and don't be running all over Garland in that truck," Elmer said and waved goodbye to his staff as he left for the weekend.

Helen handed him the keys to his truck, and Joe turned to go. He stopped at the door. He walked back to the dispatcher's office and looked at her desk, then the counter and said, "Helen, did you see me with my lunch pail?"

Helen nodded, "Yes I did. You had it with you when you went to call your wife."

"That's right. Thanks, Helen," he said and headed to the lounge.

He pushed through the door and saw that the lounge was now empty. He stepped quickly to the phone and dialed a familiar number. The phone rang once and was picked up.

"Hello."

"Jean, this is Joe. I got the truck. Give me the scoop on tonight's freezer run," Joe spoke in a soft voice while watching the door.

"I have called Duke. He knows what the load is and will have it ready and on the dock at eleven forty-five. You must be there no later than that because his shift ends at midnight and they lock the place up.

I need you to deliver the load Sunday afternoon to Sigler. I will have my staff ready in the kitchen, and we will help you unload.

Also Joe, you need to know that Lonnie called today. He said a City of Garland Inspector had been in there asking a lot of questions about all the commodities we have stored off site there. So I want you to keep a sharp lookout for cops or inspectors. If anyone asks you any questions, tell them that you are working late to get supplies to the schools in preparation for the holidays.

You don't know anything about where the stuff came from or why it is stored in Garland. Got it?" Jean asked.

"Got it," Joe said and hung up.

He climbed back in his truck and drove out of the parking lot and headed home. As he drove, Joe was thinking. He had come up hard. He and his family lived in the projects in *old town* Garland.

Necessities had been lean and life was cheap. The violence, the poverty and the lack of hope had driven Joe to enlist in the Army. That's where he had learned to drive the big rigs. He had vowed to use his skill to lift his family out of the poverty and to escape the projects.

Soon as he was discharged from the Army, he had taken a job driving cross-country. The money was good. But Joe missed his family. He wanted to be home, to watch his kids grow up. Joe wanted to be the father that he had never had.

So he walked away from the big rigs and hired on with the school district. The work was steady and secure, but the pay was not sufficient to support his wife and three kids.

Then he met Jean Steeps. He knew a shyster when he saw one, and he made Jean the first time they met.

He let things rock along and then one day she asked him if he would like to make some extra money. That had been three years ago now.

'This has been a sweet deal for me, and I know Jean is making some major money. She has me skimming eggs, butter, flour, sugar, powdered milk, cheese, meat, poultry, and fish. All of that has been going into these off-site cold storage units. I know the District is paying for the rent on the units, but I also know that no one has snapped on what she is doing.

Then that woman uses all this stuff in her private catering business. Hellfire, she even uses it to cater school district events and charges the district for feeding them with their food,' Joe had to chuckle.

Then the sobering thought of what it would mean to his family if he got caught and locked up. 'It is time for me to start making me a record of what has gone down the last three years. When the policeman shows up, he is going to find Joe ready to roll for the right deal. Truth or Consequences is the name of the game, and I have a whole lot of truth about the 'freezer runs' as Jean calls them to help me avoid those consequences,' Joe would start writing a history of the past, for his future, tonight.

CHAPTER 39
THE LEFT HANDED RIFLE

Phyllis turned at the sound of the office door opening. "Well hello, Sam Turner. What brings you to Plano this fine November day?" she asked with a smile.

"I need to see Darrel and Roger," Sam said.

"They are drinking coffee in Darrel's office. Go on back," Phyllis said.

Sam grunted, "Thanks," and stomped down the hall toward Darrel's office.

'Something is up,' Phyllis thought. She picked coffee cup up and followed Sam quietly down the hall. She stopped at the coffee bar, just three steps from Darrel's open door.

She stood listening and heard Sam say, "That K.W. Bangs has been nosing around. He went out to the gun shop in Arlington and got the records on those guns I gave you two."

"What? How in the hell did he know to go there? What did you friend out there tell him? What do we do now?" Phyllis could hear the panic in Darrel's voice.

"Calm down Darrel. I don't know how he knew about the guns or where I bought them, but he does. He also knows that I used a bogus name in the purchase. He knows all of that because my so-called 'friend' rolled on me. He sang like the stool pigeon he is and Bangs has it all on tape," Sam said.

"So, what does that mean?" Darrel asked.

"What it means is that he has Sam on a federal firearms violation.

That is a felony. He has nothing on us, even if he can prove that we accepted the guns. All that proves is that we have violated District policy by taking a gift from a vendor. The District might take disciplinary action. But unless he knows about those filters, he can't prove that the guns were more than a gift. He cannot prove bribery," Roger said.

"Okay, what do we do now?" Darrel asked.

"Well Darrel, the first thing is for you to stop pissing your pants. Just sit tight and wait. If Bangs has a case made, he will show up with arrest warrants. If he doesn't, he will come asking questions," Sam said.

That's right Darrel. Calm down and keep your mouth shut. I will call a lawyer that I know. We will visit with him and tell him the whole story. That way he is on board to represent us when Bangs makes his next move.

Sam and I have been through all of this before. The most important thing for you to remember is to keep your mouth shut. Got it, Darrel? Say nothing to anyone.

What are you thinking Sam?" Roger asked.

"I'm thinking you call your lawyer and I'll call mine. We need to do all we can to make it harder for them to link us together in a conspiracy.

I figure my lawyer will snoop around with the Collin County District Attorney to see if Bangs has filed a case. If so, he will evaluate the evidence and then we will make a decision on which way to go.

Once he has the state case settled, my lawyer will call ATF and see if I can cop a pre-indictment deal on the federal firearms violation. We will try to trade some information I have for a probated sentence or at least a reduced sentence," Sam said.

"So, you think the feds have made a case on you?" Roger asked.

"Hell yes. They got pictures of me holding the guns, the sales records with the serial numbers and a copy of the fake driver's license I used. Then they have the taped testimony of my Nam buddy. But the key to this is that *left handed rifle*.

Somebody knew about me giving that gun to you, Darrel, and that information led Bangs right to the transaction records. From there it is going to be easy to tie it to the three of us. Especially to you Darrel because you are left handed. There is no escaping that left-handed rifle.

Yep, I have been here before. Time to cut my losses. I will see you later," Sam said and stood up.

"Okay, but you are not going to roll on Darrel and me the way your buddy did on you. Are you Sam?" Roger asked.

Phyllis hurried back to her desk but heard Sam say, "No. I will take my lumps and let you take yours. It was sweet for a while, but now it's over. See you down the road."

Sam walked out of the office without a glance at Phyllis. She looked toward Darrel's office and saw him step into the hallway. "Hold all calls for Roger and me. We have some business to discuss, and I don't want to be interrupted," Darrel said.

"Right," Phyllis said. But she was thinking, 'so it is the guns Sam gave them that the tape shows being transferred from Sam's Suburban to their cars.'

Darrel refilled his coffee cup at the bar, turned to stare at Phyllis a minute and then walked into his office and closed the door. He looked at Roger and held a finger up to indicate he should remain silent. Darrel picked up his cap and motioned for Roger to follow him.

Phyllis heard the door open and saw Darrel walk out of his office and turn toward her. Roger was right behind him. Both men had put their hats on, and Darrel was fishing in his back pocket for his truck keys.

"I changed my mind, Phyllis. Roger and I are going to visit the schools as we discuss next year's first quarter projects. We will be on the air, or you can page us," Darrel said as they exited the building.

Phyllis smiled. 'Darrel is concerned that I will eavesdrop or that his office is bugged. I bet those two rats are about to abandon their sinking ship. But they aren't going to find it that easy to walk away.

I knew that tape would come in handy. Now it's time to drop a dime on the high rollers,' she thought. She reached for her phone and punched the number for K.W. Bangs.

CHAPTER 40
CULTURE CHANGE

"Good Morning Mr. Bangs. Dr. Henderick came by earlier. He wants to see you," the receptionist said.

"Do you know why Edith?" K.W. asked.

"No, sir. He just said for you to come to his office as soon as you got here," she said.

K.W. climbed the stairs and walked into the Superintendent's office suite. "Good morning Ms. Haun. Dr. Henderick wants to see me?" he asked.

"Yes, he does Ken. He said to send you straight in, so just knock and go on into his office," she replied.

K.W. knocked on the door and walked in. Dr. Henderick looked up and said, "Come in and sit down Chief."

K.W. smiled and sat down. "I am a one man crew Dr. Henderick. Exactly what am I chief of?" he asked.

"Well, that is what I want to talk with you about. The City Manager came by to see me late yesterday.

It seems that Chief Kinsey is not happy with the arrangement the manager and I have made regarding your assignment to the District. In fact, he is insisting that you resign your commission or return to work full time for the police department. Dr. Henderick paused and looked at K.W.

"So, that ends my assignment here then. I will gather my stuff and report to the Chief's office tomorrow morning," K.W. said.

The superintendent leaned forward, rested his chin in his right hand and began to twirl a glass paperweight on his desk. He was silent a minute and then looked up and said, "I'm afraid it is not going to be that easy. It seems that Chief Kinsey has taken offense with our arrangement.

He has said some things to the manager that indicate he doubts your commitment to the police department and told the manager that it might make things easier for him if you were to voluntarily resign your commission as a police officer. He hinted that you may have effectively surrendered your commission when you signed our oath of office and accepted our payroll check. The manager has consulted his legal staff and they tell him that the Chief has a point," I discussed the issue with Mr. Turley, our lawyer, and he agrees.

So now here we are. It appears that your days with the City of Plano are numbered and that your best interest may lie with the District.

Ken, we are growing and I need people I can trust to put in position to help us shape that growth. We need more than the day-to-day job done. We really need to have our own people in positions of authority and influence.

I talked with the mayor at Rotary yesterday. You know that Joe Steenbergen used to work for him selling insurance before he became the Justice of The Peace here in Plano. Joe is going to run against Jerry Burton for sheriff. The mayor suggested you might be a good fit to take Joe's place. We checked with the lawyers and you could work for us and hold that position at the same time. I like that idea.

You are one of ours. Your family, Trudy's family are all Plano folks. This can work out well for the District and for you. What do you say?" the superintendent asked.

K.W. sighed and said, "Wow, that's a lot to think about Dr. Henderick. What I want to do first is go talk to my boss. I want to see where I am with him and if he truly thinks it best for me to move on then I will.

But I want to be clear with you Dr. Henderick. I would insist on being free to do the job without regard of who is involved. The law is the law. Policy is policy. They apply equally to all. No one would be exempt, not even you.

I don't do investigations with a directed outcome and I don't allow my findings to be compromised. Would you accept those conditions?"

The superintendent squirmed in his chair and then said, "Yes, I will and I will see to it that all of my staff understands as well. All I ask is that you keep me informed."

K.W. nodded and then asked, "Who would I report too?"

"Ray Hopper. He is currently the Assistant Superintendent for Business Services but I am about to expand his role significantly. Ray is a steady man, level headed and will not chafe at your needing a free hand," Dr. Henderick said.

"When do I have to give you my answer?" K.W. asked.

"I would think tomorrow by noon would be about as long as we can keep the manager waiting to hear from us," Dr. Henderick replied.

●　　　　●　　　　●

K.W. left the superintendent's office and walked downstairs to his office area. He sat for a few minutes going over all he had just heard from Dr. Henderick. His head was swimming and he felt pressure building in his chest.

'How did I allow myself to get in this position. I should have never let Pete Barnes talk me into that lunch meeting. Now I may well be out of a job,' he sighed and reached for the telephone.

He punched in the number for the Chief's office and waited. "Chief Kinsey's office, Kay speaking," came the response.

"Kay, this is K.W. I need to see the Chief. How soon can you get me in," K.W. asked.

"Where are you K.W.?" Kay asked.

"I'm at the school administration building," he replied.

"Give me that number and wait until I call you back," Kay was speaking in a low voice.

K.W. gave her the number and hung the phone up. 'What is up

with that,' he wondered.

The phone rang and he grabbed it. "This is K.W.," he said.

"I'm going to tell you something and you have to promise not to burn me," Kay said.

"I promise," K.W. said.

"The City Manager came by here yesterday. He met with the Chief behind closed doors but I could hear because they were speaking in raised voices.

The Chief told them that you worked for him and he made the decision on where you were assigned. The manager tried to calm him down and told him that the arrangement he had made with Dr. Hendrick was good for both the city and the district.

Chief was having none of it. Then they called the captain into the meeting. I heard him say that he thought that you had effectively resigned your commission as soon as you signed the oath of office for the district and accepted their paycheck.

He went on to say that the City was exposed to lawsuits by allowing you to continue functioning as a police officer with arrest powers. His suggestion was to call you in, take your credentials and terminate your employment with the City.

The Chief agreed with him. The manager finally agreed also. He told the chief that he would talk with Dr. Henderick and then get back to him.

Captain Dan came out and had me type up a letter of resignation for you to sign. It is on my desk now.

I think it is over for you here K.W. I'm sorry it has worked out this way," Kay said.

K.W. sat in a stunned silence. Then he stood up from behind the desk and said, "It is what it is. I will be over there in a few minutes and sign the letter."

"Do you still want to see the Chief?" Kay asked.

K.W. smiled at the stress in his friend's voice, "No Kay. Let's just get this over and done with," K.W. said.

• • •

K.W. walked into the superintendent's office and said, "If that job offer is still open, I will take it."

"It is indeed. I will get you down to see Dr. Dunlap in few minutes and he will get you signed up. We have to run it by the board but I have already cleared it with Rutledge and it is a go.

But come in and sit down for a few minutes. Ray and I were just talking about the losses we are experiencing as a result of criminal activity. What can we do to stop them?" Dr. Henderick asked.

"We average a burglary a day Dr. Henderick. Then there are the criminal mischief, the vandalisms, and the internal thefts. One reason is that we have no burglar alarms and no cameras in any of our buildings.

Add to that the fact that our unwritten policy against prosecuting employees and students who we identify as responsible for these offenses and you can see that we have created a culture where there is no fear of being caught. The result is the loss of resources and revenues. We have to change the culture.

The way to address this trend is to install alarm systems and cameras. Inventory and track our equipment requiring employees to sign for anything they remove from the building and prohibit the non-official use of that equipment.

The second part of the answer is just as important as the first. We must send the message to all and any who commit criminal offenses against our students, staff or resources that we will find them and we will prosecute them to the fullest extent of the law.

Give me the money, and I can take care of the first part. But that second part is going to require you to put out the message that we will prosecute. I can catch them, but if you don't back me up it is all for naught," K.W. said.

Dr. Henderick sat looking at K.W. for a few seconds and then said, "Give me an example of a case that you would have us prosecute."

K.W. pointed to a file lying on the Superintendent's desk. "There is a prime example right in front of you. Two District employees and one vendor, acted in concert to steal tens of thousands of dollars from the District.

My investigation shows that our employees provided the vendor with the bids submitted by other vendors thus enabling their friend to submit a lower bid. When the bid was contested, the favored vendor stated that he was able to offer the low bid because he had purchased the filters from another firm in bankruptcy.

That is a lie. The firm he identified has never filed bankruptcy. But they did report a burglary of their warehouse and the loss of 100,000 filters, exactly like those the favored vendor submitted for bid.

He and our employees then proceeded to throw thousands of our unused HVAC filters into the trash, so they could replace them with his new ones.

The Georgia State Police are following up on the burglary of the warehouse and using my investigative findings. The evidence I gave them is circumstantial but still strong enough for an indictment.

However, we do have a solid case against all three actors for violation of the State Bid Law. The aggregate totals in value bump the charge up to a third-degree felony.

Additionally, during my investigation, I developed evidence of a violation of the Federal Firearms Act. That occurred when the vendor purchased firearms to be used in bribing our employees. The vendor has waived indictment, pled to a felony and will serve five years in a federal correctional institution. Part of the plea deal requires him to testify against our employees should they plead not guilty and go to trial.

Filing these cases will put criminals on notice that we will prosecute them. That is the first step in turning the district and our losses around," K.W. said.

"What other investigations do you have ongoing?" Dr. Henderick asked.

"Well, as you know Dr. Hendrick in addition to my role as a police officer, I have also been working for the District, sorting out and making recommendations on those issues and behaviors that violate District policy. That is why you had me sign the oath of office. It was for this work that I accepted that paycheck.

That has increased my caseload considerably and I currently have several active investigations and or inquiries in progress. They range from personal misconduct to violations of the criminal code.

For example, I received a call from an anonymous source telling me that her principal leaves the building every Thursday at noon. She reports that the principal goes to have her hair done and then spends the rest of the day at a local bar drinking. This past Thursday I went to the bar identified by the caller and found the principal there. She was fairly non-pulsed by my appearance and readily admitted that she had been engaging in the behavior for some time. In fact, she told me that she was one of your favorites and was not worried about what you might say. I have completed an information report and given it to personnel for their action.

The next misconduct involved two staff members engaging in sexual activity at school. My information was that the female staff member would visit the male staff member; one of the campus coaching staff, in the training room after the kids had left for the day. They would then engage in sexual intercourse on the training table.

I visited with them both on campus. At first they denied the allegation but then the woman broke down and started crying. It turns out that she is pregnant. I referred the whole issue to their principal for his action.

The next misconduct case I have right now involves another coach. I got a call from a lady who says she lives next door to him in Allen. They have been having an affair for some time. She states that she wants to end the affair and has told him as much. She told me that he refuses to accept her decision and is stalking her. She says that he leaves school during the day and sits across the street watching her home.

She says that he telephones her six to ten times a day and calls her a whore, slut and various other disparaging names. Well, the back-story is this; it seems that when she ended her affair with the coach she started a new one with the mail carrier who delivers to her home.

The coach has found out and confronted the mail carrier telling him that he was going to kill him.

I interviewed the coach and he basically told me to go to hell; that this was the woman of his dreams and he was going to do any and everything necessary to have her. I interviewed the mailman and he refuses to prosecute or give us statements fearing that his wife will find out.

Because the coach threatened to kill the mail carrier and because he continues to stalk the woman, I made a referral to the Allen Police Department and informed the coach's principal.

There is one more misconduct case that I am just about ready to wrap up. It involves two staff members using the teacher's lounge at their school for midnight liaisons. That one is clear cut and will be resolved administratively," Bangs said.

"What do you mean the staff members were using the lounge for midnight liaisons?" the Superintendent's face showed that he feared the answer.

"The night shift custodians at that school are married to each other. They walked into the lounge to eat their meal and caught two teachers having sexual intercourse on the couch.

The husband wanted to keep quiet, but the wife knew the male teacher's wife and said no way. She called the wife and told her. The wife called me the first thing next morning," Bangs said.

"What do you intend to do with that information?" Dr. Henderick asked.

"I have interviewed both of the teachers, and they admit their conduct. I have made a referral to their principal, and he will make the decision on what to do with them," Bangs said.

Now for the criminal cases I have going. I had a call from a Health Inspector with the City of Garland. He was conducting a routine inspection at a freezer facility and found several lockers containing government commodities. He was curious and asked to see the records for those lockers. It turns out they were leased by our food service director and has been used to store government commodities for the past three years.

I visited the facility, and the first thing the manager said to me when I identified myself was, "I wondered how long it would take for you to show up."

I sat him down for a full interview, and he showed me film footage of a District truck delivering and removing product from those lockers. The interesting thing is that most of the deliveries were made during the daytime, but all of the removals were after hours, just before the facility closed at midnight.

He gave me the name of the District employee making those deliveries and removals. I have interviewed him, and he sang like a bird. He told me that he skims the commodities out of the District's allotment and takes them to the storage facility. The food service director and a 'selected staff' then uses those commodities in her private catering service.

It appears from the interview that there may also be some bid law violations with her providing insider information to her husband who is the Vice President of Institutional Sales with North Star Foods. Our records show that North Star is the odds on favorite to win every bid on meat, poultry, and fish. I am still working on that case, but it is coming together nicely.

Then I have a call from the basketball coach at Plano Senior High School. He is concerned that one of our staff members is involved in an illicit relationship with a student. I am going to interview the student and his mother tomorrow.

If I find credible evidence to support a concern, then I will make a referral to law enforcement as required by law. "

"Is that it, do you have anything else going on that I need to know about?" the superintendent asked.

"Not at this time," K.W. replied.

"Okay, here's what I want you to do. Go ahead and file the case against those conspiring to trash our new filters to replace them with the new ones.

Interview the student and his mother about the illicit or possibly illicit conduct between him and a teacher. After the criminal issues are settled, I want the teacher in my office.

I agree with your decision to let the principal make the decision on the teachers engaging in sexual relations at school. But I want to know what he does.

But now on the food service issue, I don't want you to file that case. Let me handle it," the superintendent said.

"There is a problem with that Dr. Henderick. The theft of government commodities makes it a federal case. We don't have the option on that.

The issue of bid rigging is a State Law violation. I believe that it should be filed to help establish the pattern of zero tolerance for such conduct," Bangs said.

"You have mentioned making a referral? What is the difference in that and this direct filing you are talking about?" the superintendent asked.

"A referral means that I take what I have to the District Attorney and he makes the decision on how to proceed. A direct filing means that I file the case, and the grand jury decides if there is enough evidence to indict," Bangs said.

Hendrick looked at Hopper and then turned back to Bangs and said, "Make a referral on the food service case, but do not make any suggestions regarding prosecution.

Ray, I want you to work with the Chief on developing an addendum to the next bond election addressing the purchase of burglar alarm systems, cameras and anything else he needs to develop his department.

Chief, do you have a priority list?" the superintendent asked.

"Yes, sir. I need to start hiring officers to provide traffic control, police security and District patrol at the campuses and across the District on a twenty-four seven basis.

I also want to tell you that I have thought about running for Justice of The Peace as you suggested. I like the idea and will do it if you still want me to," K.W. said.

Dr. Henderick stood and said, "I do indeed. I have talked with Board and they have all agreed it is a good idea. Welcome aboard Chief."

Ray and K.W. walked out of the office, and neither man said anything until they reached Hopper's office. Bangs sat down and looked at Hopper, "The superintendent said I was going to reporting directly to you. Did he explain that I was to have a free hand?" K.W. asked.

"Yes, and Yes. Dr. Henderick told me earlier this morning that he just doesn't have time to help you with all that you are involved in. So from now on, you will be reporting to me," Ray said.

"Suits me. Let me ask you what you think about what you just heard me tell Dr. Henderick?" Bangs asked.

"Dr. Henderick and I both want you to do your job. I want you to treat everyone courteously but I also want you to treat everyone the same. Do not have favorites. We must have an understanding within the District that the good ole boy days are over.

I also like the idea of you running for Justice of The Peace. We want our employees to be involved in civic endeavors, to serve their communities and this is a great example of that.

The final thing I want to say is that I've suspected for a long time that we had real problems in the Food Service Department. Now that you have uncovered this information, I know Dr. Henderick will clean that Department out starting with the Director.

The same goes for that Service Center. In fact, he has told me that those folks will report to me from now on also. I am going to put James Noel in charge out there. James will not stand for any nonsense.

What happened today will go a long way in establishing your office. When these cases hit the Grand Jury or District Attorney's office, the message will be heard loud and clear. From now on, we prosecute.

To put it another way, working together we will change the culture," Hopper said.

CHAPTER 41
COMING OUT DAY

Billy Jack Edwards had slept fitfully. Now he was awakened by the noises that had grown to be such a part of his life.

The buzz of the ballasts as the big vapor lights at the end of each cellblock clicked off, and the overhead tubes flooded the cells with fluorescent light. Then there were the sounds and smells of 300 men attending to their biological needs as they rose to start another day.

Normally he would be joining them, moving quickly to prepare for breakfast and then to his job in the prison farm shop. But this morning he rolled over to face the wall and blot out some of the light. He allowed himself a smile. Today was his release date.

"Time to hit the floor Billy Jack, that is if you want one more breakfast on the good people of Texas," the corrections officer had stopped when he saw Billy Jack lounging on his cot.

"I think I will pass boss. If it all the same to you I will just hang out here in my cell until time to start the paperwork. I don't want to go down into the population and have something go wrong, get into it with some inmate and end up catching a case," he responded.

"There is a lot of wisdom in that Billy Jack. You sure as hell have not gone out of your way to make friends. I will tell my relief to keep an eye on your cell just to be sure no one comes by to settle any old scores before you leave," the officer said.

Billy rolled over, so he was facing the wall. The officer was right, he had made enemies, and some would not hesitate to stick a shank in him on the day he was to gain his freedom. He lay there thinking.

What an absolute mess he had made out of his life.

He had beaten a whore half to death, broken her neck and left her paralyzed for life. A nosy neighbor had called the police to report the sounds of violence coming from the whore's apartment. The cops had arrived just as he walked out of the building into the parking lot. The blood all over his shirt had attracted their attention, and that was that.

He coped a plea for fifteen to do and today marked the end of the sentence. He had done every day of it, rejecting parole in favor of a straight release. Billy lay still a minute and then rolled onto his side to face the bars. *'Not smart to lay here with my back to these bars,'* he thought.

The cell doors slid open, and the prisoners marched out toward the cafeteria. The cellblock was now quiet. Billy lay still and began to drift into sleep. As he did, he dreamed.

He was nine again. He and his twin brother, Jimmy Joe, were standing in the front yard of the family house; it was never a home, southeast of Enid. The hot August sun had baked the red clay soil. Billy Jack and Jimmy Joe danced back and forth from one foot to the other in a vain effort to stop the super heated clay from blistering their feet.

Their grandfather sat on the porch in his rocking chair staring at the boys. He took a long pull from his bottle of Old Crow and coughed a bit as the whiskey burned its' way down his throat and into his belly. Billy watched as the old man stood and pointed to the tub full of water. *'That rope has soaked long enough. Go and get it and bring it to me, Billy Jack,'* the old man said.

He remembered running to get the rope while Jimmy Joe begged their grandfather not to whip their mother, Louise, with it again. Billy knew that the begging was not going to change the old man's mind. He was a mean-spirited man. But when he was drunk he became violently mean, and he was drunk now.

He didn't care if the old man whipped his mother. But experience had taught him that once the old man started beating someone, everyone was at risk. Billy Jack was tired of the beatings.

Billy Jack knew that his grandfather hated him and Jimmy

because they were bi-racial. Their father was Cherokee, and to his grandfather, that was a shame too great to bear. He refused to let them use their father's last name, Ship. He demanded that they use the family name, Edwards.

Billy knew that his grandfather was mad at his mother because she had slipped out of the house after he had fallen into a drunken stupor the night before. She had gone to town to be with their father, Pawnee Ship, who was home on leave from the Navy. His grandfather hated Indians and considered it a slight on his *'good name'* that his daughter would *'lay with one like a bitch in heat.'*

He ran up to the edge of the porch and dropped the wet rope at his grandfather's feet. *'Hand the damned rope to me boy,'* the old man demanded.

Billy Jack shook his head no and started to back away from the porch. He didn't know when, but a plan had begun to form in his mind. He knew the old man would have to get down on his knees to pick up the rope. He also knew that once he was on his knees, he could not get up without something to hold onto. So he stood still and watched as his grandfather pushed the rocking chair forward and worked his way down onto his knees. Seeing his chance, Billy Jack darted up the steps and grabbed the rocking chair. He pulled it back out of the old man's reach and then pushed it off of the porch.

"Damn you to hell Billy Jack," the old man roared. "You are as worthless as that sorry bastard whose spawn you are," he said as he crawled toward the post at the far end of the porch.

Billy turned and ran into the house. The single shot ten-gauge shotgun was sitting in the corner behind the wood-burning stove. Billy Jack grabbed it and ran back to the porch.

His grandfather was pulling himself up with the aid of the porch post when Billy Jack leveled the shotgun and pulled the hammer back. His grandfather turned at the click of the hammer locking into place, and Billy Jack could feel the hate flow from his eyes, reach across the space between them and lash him just as cruelly as the wet rope.

"Why you little heathen! Give me my gun. Boy, when I get

through with your mammy I am going to take the hide off of you," his grandfather shouted.

The old man lunged forward, reaching for the gun and Billy Jack pulled the trigger. The recoil pushed Billy Jack against the wall, and the big gun leaped from his hands and slid down the steps.

The buckshot hit the old man in the center of his chest, blew him off of the porch and rolled his body across that hardpan clay into a giant red anthill. The ants boiled out of the violated mound swarming over his grandfather's face and into his gaping mouth.

Billy Jack heard his mother screaming and turned to look at her. Fear filled her eyes as she backed away from her son. "What kind of monster are you?" she asked.

•　　　•　　　•

Billy Jack awakened with a start and sat up on the side of his bunk. He stood and walked to the sink. He turned the water on and held his cupped hands under the faucet, allowing the cold water to fill them.

Bending forward, Billy Jack splashed the water across his face and then bent to allow it to run over his head. A sob escaped, and hot tears poured from his eyes. The prisoner turned his face up into the flow, and the little boy let his past spiral down the drain with the cold water.

Gaining control of his emotions, Billy grabbed a towel and rubbed it over his dripping face and head. He sat down on the side of the bunk, and the memories came again.

The sheriff had taken him to the reform school until a judge could decide what to do with a nine-year-old that had just killed his grandfather. Billy Jack remembered standing in the judge's office and hearing him say, "Louise can you handled this boy if I release him into your custody?"

His mother said to the judge, "Lord knows I have tried, but I just can't do anything with that boy. His brother is different from Billy. He is gentle while Billy is wild. I can handle Jimmy but to tell you the truth Judge, I am afraid to lay down and close my eyes at night with

Billy in the house. I am afraid his grand daddy's blood rules his mind and emotions. That boy is just mean."

Billy still felt the sting of those words. His eyes filled with tears again and he wiped them with the towel. The judge had sent him to live full time in a foster home until his tenth birthday. Then he was sent to a Residential Treatment Center in Oklahoma City.

It didn't take Billy long to realize the RTC, as the kids called it, was nothing more than a prison for kids. It was the survival of the fittest during the day and a fight to keep your body from being penetrated once the lights went out.

Jimmy went home with their mother. Billy had not seen nor heard from them until his eighteenth birthday. On that day he had been *'emancipated'* and released from the Oklahoma Child Protective Services. Discharged with a change of clothes and two hundred dollars.

His first stop had been the Sheriff's office in Garfield County. There he learned that his mother had turned to drugs and then to prostitution to support her habit. The drugs and venereal disease turned her from a beautiful young woman to a bent and diseased old hag. She had been found dead behind the Cherokee Strip Club on First Street in Enid. No one claimed the body, and she had been buried in a pauper's grave by the county.

The Sheriff told him that Jimmy had been placed with the preacher at First Baptist Church and then transferred to the Buckner's Orphan Home in Dallas. That is where Billy found him.

Jimmy was excited to see Billy. But Jimmy had changed. He was truly a Baptist. He didn't smoke, he didn't drink, and he would not allow Billy to cuss in his presence. Jimmy tried to get Billy to accept Jesus, but he could not answer Billy's first question, "If God is real why did He let all the bad things happen?"

Billy and Jimmy agreed to disagree. But they were still brothers, and the pain they had suffered bound them together. Billy left Jimmy in Dallas and started back North, toward Oklahoma.

Billy Jack sighed thinking, *'If only I had listened to Jimmy.'* But he hadn't.

Billy had left Buckner's when the Dorm Manager had called *'lights out'* at ten o'clock. He traveled north on Buckner Boulevard. At the intersection of Samuel Boulevard and Buckner he saw a flashing neon sign advertising *"Jolene's Asian Massage."*

Billy remembered slowing and looking at the sign and realizing it was just ahead on his right. He had pulled into the parking lot and sat looking at the barred windows and cinder block walls. He looked around and saw that there were only two other cars in the parking lot. *'What's up with this'* he remembered thinking.

As he sat there, the front door opened and a young woman wearing what looked like a short, silk wrap beckoned him in. Billy switched the car off and fished around in his pocket to see how much of his *'emancipation money'* he had left.

He counted out a hundred dollars and pushed it deep into the front pocket on his new jeans. That left him with fifty dollars, and he figured that would be plenty to get him back to Oklahoma.

Stepping from the car, Billy swaggered forward. "Hey handsome," the young lady cooed. "Come on in and let me take all that stress away," she said placing one slim hand on Billy's arm.

Billy followed her into a small room. She closed and locked the door and Billy did a quick survey of the room. There was a massage table for the customer to lie on and a roll away cart covered in oils and creams.

The girl turned from the door and said, "My name is Jasmine. What is yours?"

"Billy, my name is Billy Jack," he was wondering if her name was really Jasmine.

"Well Billy Jack, have you been here before?" she cooed while loosening the belt holding her thin wrap in place.

"No, I have never been in a place like this before," he stammered.

"What kind of place do you think this is Billy?" she asked.

"I think it is a whore house," Billy said.

"And you think I am a whore?" Jasmine asked with a slight smile.

"Yep, I do. At least I hope you are," Billy was grinning.

"Okay, so let's say this is a whore house and that I am a whore.

Why are you here Billy Jack?" she was grinning right back at him.

"Because I just got out of lock up and I need a whore," he smiled right back at her.

"How old are you Billy Jack?" she asked.

"I just turned eighteen. How old are you?" he asked.

"I am supposed to tell you that I am nineteen, but the truth is that I am just sixteen. Does that bother you Billy?" he could tell from her eyes that she was telling him the truth.

"Nope. I don't care at all. I have fifty dollars, and that's it," he said reaching for his money.

"Whoa, hold on cowboy. I am a whore, but I am not a cheap whore. Fifty dollars won't get you anything but a thirty-minute rub down here. Make it an even one hundred dollars, and you will get one hour of what you came here for," she was cinching the wrap to close the view he had been enjoying.

"Make it seventy-five dollars for an hour and a half, and we can stop all this talking," Billy had counted out the money and pushed it toward her.

Jasmine looked at the clock and then at Billy Jack, "Monday's are slow, so you have a deal." She took the money from Billy's outstretched hand and said, "I have to give this to the front desk and tell them how long you are on the clock. I will be right back."

Jasmine returned quickly and walked into the room, locked the door once more and turned to switch off the overhead lights, leaving just the dim glow of a lamp to light the room.

She pointed to the clock on the wall above the door and then a switch next to the doorframe, "Just so we are on the same page Billy, it is now ten thirty. That means your time will be up at midnight. When I flip this switch, it turns a red light outside the door. The manager then knows that your time has started.

In exactly one and one-half hours, at midnight, a buzzer will sound in here. Ten minutes later, the manager will knock on the door, and you have to leave or give him more money. Is that clear, do you have any questions?" she asked while removing the wrap and tossing it onto a chair.

"Nope, that works for me," Billy Jack said.

It seemed that only a few minutes had past when the buzzer sounded. Billy Jack thought, *'Hell no, I have not had all my time.'*

He rolled onto his back and looked at the clock over the door; it read twelve o'clock straight up and down. Jasmine jumped from the table and grabbed her wrap.

Billy Jack reached for her saying, "Come on back, I still have ten minutes before the manager knocks."

She backed away laughing, "Listen, Cowboy, you got your money's worth and then some. How long was you locked up?"

"Nine years," Billy Jack said as he caught his jeans that Jasmine had tossed at him.

He reached into his pocket and pulled out the last fifty dollars. "How much longer will another fifty get me," he asked.

Jasmine looked at the clock again and said, "We close at two o'clock. That is just under two hours now. Add another twenty-five to that fifty, and I will see if the manager will let you stay until closing."

"I don't have another twenty-five. This is the last of my 'liberation money'," he said.

"He won't do that. But here's what I will do. You leave now and wait for me at the

7-11 on the corner of Samuel and Buckner. I will leave here when we close. I will be driving a gold Honda with a Jack In The Box ball on the radio antenna.

When you see me come by, just follow me to my place. I will let you stay another hour for that last twenty-five if you promise to be my regular customer and send me more business," Jasmine whispered.

"You are a whore, aren't you," Billy said.

"Yep, you called it. I have one thing going for me, and that's my body. I am trying to break away from the club and get into business for myself. I don't see why I should let them get half my money when I'm doing all the work," she said pushing him toward the door.

Billy saw the gold Honda turn the corner at five minutes past two. He flashed his lights at her, and she honked her horn in response.

Billy followed her to the East Gate Apartments, and they parked in front of building C. She stepped from her car and waited as he looked cautiously around the area and then joined her in front of unit one twenty-three.

"What you looking for? Are you afraid I have a pimp or someone hiding in the bushes to jump you for your money?" Jasmine teased.

"Naw, just nervous or careful I guess," Billy smiled.

Jasmine hesitated to look at Billy and then asked, "Billy Jack, you aren't some freak that's going to beat me, take my money and leave me bleeding on the floor are you?"

"No, I wouldn't hurt you, Jasmine," Billy Jack blurted out.

Jasmine believed she had become a pretty good judge of men and she tended to believe him, "Okay. So tell me, cowboy, what were you locked up for?"

"I killed my grandfather," he said.

"Wow. What was that about?" Jasmine asked.

"He was mean as a snake. He hated my brother and me because our daddy was Cherokee. He made a habit of beating us with a wet rope. One day he got drunk and was going to beat my momma. I didn't care about that, but I knew he would beat my brother and me after he got through with her, so I shot him," Billy Jack said.

Jasmine opened the door, and they walked into her apartment. She tossed her purse and keys on the table and said, "I'm going to freshen up a bit for you. Grab yourself a coke out of the fridge."

Billy sensed that the mood had changed and asked, "What's wrong. You seem down all of a sudden. Did I do or say something wrong," he asked.

"Not really. It's just that when you talked about your grandfather, it brought back memories of mine. You see my grandfather was also my father. He raped my mother, who was his daughter, and here I am. Does that surprise you?" she turned to face Billy Jack.

"Yep, guess so. I've never heard that one before. Did he rape you too," Billy asked.

"He started molesting me when I was five. By the time I was ten, he was having sex with my momma and me. Sometimes he would make us both get in the bed with him. He was one mean man. It seems as if we have had some of the same life experiences Billy Jack," she smiled.

Billy grabbed a cola while Jasmine took a quick shower. He sat thinking about the girl and what she had shared. He was beginning to feel something for her, and he figured she did for him also.

An hour later Jasmine pushed him away and said, "Time's up Billy. Give me the money, and I need to get some sleep."

Her words and sudden coldness hit Billy hard. "Wait, Jasmine. I have to tell you that I have thought a lot about what you said earlier. We do have a lot in common, and I think we could be good for each other.

I'm eighteen; your sixteen and we have our whole lives to change our luck. I have to tell you that I like you and I think you like me. What do you say, let's see if we can make a go of it together?" Billy said.

Jasmine had been pulling on her sleeping gown and now looked up with a smile on her face and said, "Hey now. This is business remember? I'm a whore, and you are my customer."

"But you don't have to be a whore Jasmine. We can live here together. I will get a job, and you can get a job, and we can make a home together," Billy said.

"What kind of job Billy? Washing dishes, waiting tables, pole dancing? And what will you do? You have no skills and no education. No, I like being my own boss, and I like the money I make.

So you just go on now and come back to see me when you have more money. Go on now Billy Boy; I need my beauty rest," Jasmine said placing one hand on his chest and pushing his gently toward the door.

Billy leaned forward to kiss her, and the gentle push turned into a shove. "Get out now," Jasmine spat.

Billy felt the blood rush to his face. He did not realize that he had slapped Jasmine, but she was suddenly stumbling backward and into the wall.

Jasmine struggled to her feet and wiped the back of her hand across her mouth. Jasmine looked at the blood on her hand and then ran her tongue over her broken lips. She felt her mouth filling with hot salty blood. Pursing her lips, she spewed the blood out and over Billy.

Billy slapped her again, and she screamed. The scream seemed to release the pent-up anger in Billy. He slammed a fist into her belly and shouted, "Whore."

He lifted Jasmine from the floor and threw across the kitchen table. The table splintered and crashed into the wall shared with the next apartment.

Billy tossed the mess aside and reached for Jasmine. Then he saw that her head was resting at an odd angle on the floor. *'Her neck is broken,'* he realized.

He kneeled beside her, and her eyes turned to look at him. Fear filled them. He saw that she was breathing but that she could not move. *'Damn it, I paralyzed this girl,'* he mouthed to himself.

The neighbor next door pounded on the wall, and Billy jumped. "I am sorry Jasmine, I didn't mean to hurt you. I just lost it," Billy said.

He saw that her lips were moving and dropped down lower so he could hear what she was saying. "Kill me, Billy. Don't leave me paralyzed like this," she pleaded.

"I can't Jasmine. I just can't take the chance of falling behind a murder rap," he replied and ran for the door.

As Billy walked out of the apartment, he saw the flashing lights of a police car turning the corner and driving toward him. He walked slowly toward his car and kept his head down.

"Sir, stop right there," the officer said as he stepped from the car.

"Why? What do you want with me?" Billy asked belligerently.

"What I want to know first, is where did all of that blood on your shirt come from," the officer replied reaching for his pistol.

•　　　•　　　•

"Get up Billy and grab your stuff. It's time to go," the voice pushed its' way in and pulled Billy Jack back from the past. He looked at the bars and saw Captain Curtis Green standing there.

Billy stood and pulled the denim shirt on. He buttoned it quickly and then shoved the tail into his waistband. Billy ran his hand over this closely cropped hair and grimaced at his image in the polished steel over the sink. "You know Captain, I've aged since the first time you locked me up in this cell," he smiled at the Captain's image over his shoulder.

"Yeah, well Billy we were both kids then. You were just eighteen, and I was just twenty-one. Now here we are fifteen years later.

We have seen a lot happen in those fifteen years, and it has put some wrinkles in our brow. But that's over for you now. Grab your valise and let's get you checked out of here. Today is your coming out day. Your brother Jimmy is already downstairs waiting to drive you home," the Captain said.

Billy picked up the valise and said, "I'm ready boss."

Captain Green nodded and lifted the microphone from the clip on his belt, "Boyd Six to control, open cell Twenty-One B," he spoke into the microphone.

The cell door slid back with a whisper, and Billy stepped forward and then stopped. "It is going to be hard to put my hands behind my back and carry this valise boss," he said.

"Don't worry about putting your hands behind you Billy. Just come on out and walk alongside me," Captain Green said.

Billy stepped out, and the two men turned toward the stairs. "Why did you come to get me, boss? Why didn't you send an officer?" Billy asked as the started down the stairway.

"I figured since I was the first to lock up here at Boyd Prison Unit that I should be the one to take you out for the final time," Green said.

"Well, thanks, Captain. Say, when are you going to make warden? You have been a Captain nearly five years now," Billy asked.

"Awe Billy, if you make Warden, they move you. I've lived here in Teague all my life. My family and my friends are here, and I just don't want to leave. So I won't bc taking that test for Warden," Green said opening the door with "*Release Processing*" painted on the glass.

Billy stepped in and up to the counter. He saw Jimmy waiting just the other side of the wire.

The paperwork was completed quickly, and a buzzer sounded to open the door for Billy to exit the unit.

He held it open a minute and turned to look at the Captain. Green extended his hand and said, "Don't take this wrong Billy Jack Ship, but I hope I never see you again."

Billy grabbed the hand and said, "Not in here Boss, not in here."

He turned and walked through the barrier and Jimmy was there. They hugged each other and Billy said, "Get me out of here."

They passed through the last gate and into the parking lot. Jimmy stopped, and Billy looked back, "What's up. Why are you stopping?" Billy asked.

Jimmy smiled broadly and tossed a set of car keys to Billy. Billy caught them and gave Jimmy a questioning look. Jimmy pointed to a yellow Mercury Cougar. "We took up a collection at church and bought it for you," Jimmy said.

"What? Jimmy, I've been locked up for fifteen years. I don't even have a driver's license," Billy said.

"I didn't think about that. Okay then, I will drive us home and then take you to get your license tomorrow," Jimmy said.

Billy tossed the keys back to Jimmy and said, "Wow, that's taking things a little fast bub. Let's just get out of here and stop at the first burger joint you see. I am dying for a greasy cheeseburger and fries," Billy tossed his valise in the back seat and settled in the front passenger's seat.

Jimmy drove from the parking lot and turned east on Spur Thirteen heading for I-Forty-Five. "We will go to Dallas where you will spend the night with me.

Then after we get you a driver's permit, or whatever, you can take head north to Enid. But for the life of me Billy Jack, I don't know why you want to go back to Enid. There is nothing there for you and me except bad memories," Jimmy said.

Billy didn't answer. He reached over and switched the air conditioner off and rolled the window down. "Sorry, Jimmy. I know it's hot, but I just want to feel the wind on my face for a while. Then I will roll the window up, and we can turn the air back on," Billy said. They rode in silence, and the roar of the engine lulled Billy to sleep.

"Billy, wake up," Jimmy was shaking his sleeping brother gently. Billy sat up and rubbed his eyes, "Where are we?" he asked.

"We are just coming into Dallas. I know you wanted a burger, but I figured you needed the sleep more," Jimmy replied.

"Yep, for sure," Billy nodded.

"I have a small apartment at the church. The church is right downtown. We walk a couple of blocks to a burger shop on Commerce. It is a hole in the wall, but they have the best, and greasiest burgers, in Dallas," Jimmy laughed.

"Sounds good to me," Billy said and sat back enjoying the skyline of Big D.

Jimmy pointed to a cross extending far into the darkening skies and said, "That's First Baptist Church. My apartment is in the back. It's perfect for me and saves me a great deal of money. In exchange for the free use of the apartment, I am on call for any emergency on the property after regular hours," Jimmy said.

"Why did you never marry, Jimmy," Billy asked.

"I just never wanted to be tied down. I enjoy my freedom," Jimmy smiled at his brother.

"Are you gay Jimmy?" Billy asked.

Jimmy roared with laughter, "No, not at all. It's like I said. I like my freedom," Jimmy said.

"So, do you ever need a woman?" Billy asked.

"Sure I do. But I don't want one with strings. I deal only with professionals Billy. Then I go home," Jimmy said.

"Okay, I totally understand that. Speaking of which, I might need to step out a little tonight," Billy said.

"Whatever, just let me park this car and then we will put your valise in my apartment and walk around to Zube's and grab a burger," Jimmy said as he piloted the Cougar into a spot marked reserved for pastoral staff.

The burger was hot, greasy and took both hands to hold. Billy had ordered a cold beer and fries to go with his and Jimmy had the same except he ordered a chocolate malt rather than a beer. "Baptists don't drink beer, at least in public," Jimmy laughed.

"Or patronize whores?" Billy smirked.

Jimmy let that pass, and they watched the people pass by as the night claimed downtown, Dallas.

Walking out of Zube's with a full stomach and a toothpick stuck in his mouth Jimmy said to Billy, "Let's go this way. The Baker Hotel is just a couple of blocks down. I know a lady that you might want to talk with. She will be in the lobby or just outside. She is clean, she is safe, and she won't put your business on the street. How does that sound to you Bro," Jimmy asked?

"Sounds good, if the price is right. Remember all they gave me at the release was two hundred dollars, this suit of clothes and that valise with some new underwear. I just spent twenty on supper. That leaves me one hundred and eighty," Billy answered.

"I told you to let me buy supper. Anyway, she will charge you fifty dollars an hour. I can give you some money to get you home if you need it," Jimmy said.

"I won't need it. I got my Indian Papers while I was in the joint. I am going straight to the reservation and check in.

They will give me a place to stay until I can get all the paperwork finished for my monthly allotment. Our daddy is Cherokee Jimmy. We have benefits coming, and I am going to get mine," Billy Jack said.

They walked on in silence and Jimmy pointed to a woman sitting just inside the front doors of the Baker. "That's Charlene. Be cool when you approach her. The bellhop is on board but the night manager is not. He won't say anything as long as you are discreet.

Just walk in and sit down beside her. Tell her that you are my brother. She will get up and go to the elevators. Wait until she has gone up and then you get an elevator and go to the third floor.

She will be in room three-thirteen. Knock, and she will let you in. She will want to be paid in advance. Enjoy, and I will see you back at the apartment. You do know how to get there?" Jimmy asked.

"Yep. See you in a couple of hours," Billy said.

"Okay, remember she charges fifty an hour. Two hours is going to eat up a hundred bucks. Be wise brother, not lustful," Jimmy said.

Billy walked out of the Baker two and one-half hours later. He stretched and then stuck his hands in his pocket.

Looking to his right and up he saw the cross in the church. Billy ambled in that direction, taking his time and enjoying his freedom. He window-shopped along the way and suddenly found himself in front of the Commerce Street Package Store.

Billy stood in front looking at the massive displays of beer. One caught his attention, '24 *pack of Budweiser $19.99 plus tax.*' The display was set right at the open door of the store, and Billy found himself wondering, '*Could I grab that and run?*'

"Can I help you, sir?"

Billy looked at the speaker and said, "The price on that Budweiser seems awfully high to me."

The man laughed and looked Billy over. "When did you get out?" he asked.

Billy looked at the man's name badge and saw that his name was Cecil. "Well Cecil, since you asked, I got out this afternoon," Billy smiled right back at him.

"How long were you locked up?" the man asked.

"Fifteen years," Billy frowned.

"Listen, don't get sore now. I got out two years ago after doing eight on twenty-five. I remember how shocked I was at how things had changed in just eight years. I can't imagine how it is for you," Cecil answered.

Billy nodded and said, "All I have left of the walking money is thirty dollars. Would you let me have this on a special for fifteen of that? I have to make it all the way to Enid on the rest, and I figure that I will need every bit of the fifteen for gasoline."

Cecil looked around and said, "Gasoline has gone up too Billy. Fifteen dollars will not get you to Enid unless you are driving a VW Bug."

"Nope, a Mercury Cougar with a high performance three ninety," Billy replied.

Cecil shook his head and looked over his shoulder. "Sonny Boy, you will need all of that thirty and then some the way that engine will suck gasoline.

Tell you what; I am going to stand here in the door. You ease up here and see how quietly you can lift a case of that Bud and get gone. If anyone sees you set the beer down, do not drop it, and run. Got me?" Cecil said.

Billy nodded and eased up a step. Cecil acted like he was enjoying the night air and whispered, "Enjoy the beer on me and take some advice. Try to get that first tank of gasoline on the glam. You will need that thirty dollars before it is over."

Billy smiled and lifted the case of beer. He shuffled sideways until he was away from the store and then lifted the beer onto his shoulder and headed for the church. He walked straight to the Cougar and set the beer on the floor on the right side of the car. Then he knocked on Jimmy's door.

Jimmy opened the door and said, "Hey there you are. I'm bushed from that long drive and going to bed. I've made the couch up for you. Watch television or whatever and then bed down when you're ready. I will see tomorrow, and we will get those license for you."

"No, listen Jimmy. I slept all the way home. Man, I am awake and restless. I think I am going to head out and drive through the night. It will be cooler, and I will be careful to watch the speed limits. There will be less chance of getting stopped at night, and I will get my license in Oklahoma. That's where I'm going to live anyway," Billy said as he grabbed his valise.

"Okay, if that's what you want to do. Remember that I am here if you need me," Jimmy yawned.

Billy hugged his twin and walked away. The Mercury was old, but it was in good shape. It fired as soon as Billy hit the starter. He eased out of the parking lot and turned north on US Seventy-Five.

Billy popped a top on the Budweiser and took a long pull. *'Damned beer is hot,'* he gagged. He looked in the rearview mirror and tossed the beer onto the median and accelerated to stay in the flow of the late night traffic.

He made it to Plano before the car coughed and he realized the gas gauge was not giving him an accurate reading. Billy looked up and saw an exit sign reading Parker Road.

He exited the highway and coasted into the parking lot of a Gulf Magic Market. He parked the car at the gas pump and walked into the store. As he entered, he noticed that there was no traffic on Parker Road and that there was but one attendant in the store. Billy Jack knew he was going to rob the store, but how? He had no weapon.

"Good morning sir," the attendant called from the cooler where he was stocking the soda supply.

"Morning," Billy Jack replied.

He walked around behind the counter like he owned the place. The surprised attendant rushed toward him shouting, "Sir, you can't go behind the counter."

Billy Jack waited until the attendant was in range and then launched a vicious right jab that knocked the attendant backward into a display of tobacco products.

Blood poured from the dazed man's mouth, and Billy Jack could see his eyes glazing over. Billy hit him again, this time with a left hook. The man fell to one knee, and Billy hammered him with a sweeping roundhouse right that knocked the man onto his back.

Billy leaned over and saw that the man was unconscious. He looked at the nametag pinned to the man's vest and saw that his name was Jimmy Olson.

"Hey, Jimmy. I have a brother named Jimmy. Sorry bub but it doesn't look like this was your day," Billy said.

Billy dropped to his knees and crawled to the register. He half stood and looked out the big front windows. There was no traffic on Parker Road, and he and Jimmy were all alone in the store. Billy looked at the cash register and realized that a key was required to open it. He heard Billy stir and glanced at him.

Billy dropped back to one knee to remain out of sight of anyone passing by and started to crawl toward Jimmy. Then he saw it. A pistol lying half hidden under the bags used for customer's purchases. He grabbed the pistol just as Jimmy slammed into him.

The force of Jimmy's charge bowled Billy over onto his back.

Jimmy pounded Billy in the face with a fury.

Billy cocked the pistol and pushed it up into Jimmy's left armpit. He saw Jimmy's eyes widen as he realized that Billy was about to shoot him, and then Billy pulled the trigger. The explosion was muffled as it pushed into and through Jimmy's chest.

Billy pushed Jimmy off and kneeled over him. Flecks of blood covered Jimmy's lips. Billy could hear the gurgling as the stricken man was drowning in his own blood. Jimmy opened his eyes and looked at Billy. He reached for and grabbed the collar of Billy's shirt.

Billy wrapped his left hand around Jimmy's wrist and gently pulled it down, breaking the hold on his collar. Jimmy's gasped one more time and was still.

Billy found the register key on Jimmy's belt. He removed it and opened the register. He removed the till and dropped back down below the counter to count the money.

"Sixty dollars, are you kidding me? I killed this man for sixty dollars?" Billy whispered to himself. Then he remembered that the bigger bills were often kept under the drawer in the register.

He eased himself back up and looked into the open register. He saw one fifty-dollar bill and several twenties. He scooped them up and dropped back out of sight. He counted all the money and found that he had a total of two hundred and ten dollars.

He stuffed the money into his pocket and pushed the drawer closed. He looked at Jimmy and reached down to close his eyes. He straightened Jimmy's legs putting his feet together. He then crossed Jimmy's arms over his chest and spread his hands to show the wounds from where he had hit Billy.

He noticed that Jimmy had a wristwatch with a Dallas Cowboys logo on the face of it. "Dang, Jimmy ole pal I'm going to take that. You won't mind cause time don't mean anything to you anymore," he chuckled.

Billy eased the watch off of Jimmy's arm and placed it on his own. "Man, it is already four thirty. I've got to go, Jimmy, lots of miles ahead of me," he grinned and patted the stilled chest of Jimmy.

"You were a fighter hoss and damned sure worth more than this two hundred and ten dollars. Rest in peace. I would like to say that I will see you on the other side, but you won't be where I'm headed," Billy looked at Jimmy a few more seconds and then stood.

He stuffed the revolver into his waistband and walked to the back row of coolers. He grabbed an R.C. Cola and then a couple of packages of peanuts. He strolled from the store and calmly filled his gas tank with premium. Billy waved bye at the storefront and settled down in the seat of his car. He drove out of the parking lot and turned north.

Billy popped the top on the can of R.C. Cola and lifted it to his mouth. He took a long pull from the can and then reached for the peanuts. He tore the top off and lifted the bag to his mouth. He tilted his head back and let the salted nuts pour from the bag. He winced as the salt settled into the open wound on his lips. "*Darn Jimmy, you broke my lips open hoss,*" he whispered.

Billy Jack glanced in the rear view mirror and saw Jimmy's dead face staring back at him. A cold chill ran down his spine, and he squirmed in his seat. '*What a coming out day this has been. Texas is just not good for me. Oklahoma is where I belong. Maybe I can get lost on the reservation,*' Billy thought as he looked into the rearview mirror once more.

Jimmy was no longer there, but he saw red lights flashing. He pulled to the right lane and watched as an ambulance raced by. He looked into the rearview mirror once more for the red lights that he knew would come for him, sooner or later.

CHAPTER 42
DEADLY DAWN

There was a clanging in his head. He rolled away, but it persisted. K.W. lifted his head and stared at the clock, "Who in the hell is calling me at this hour of the morning?" he asked.

"I don't know but answer it," Trudy said.

K.W. sat up on the side of the bed and lifted the receiver. "Hello," he said.

"Judge Bangs, this is Tiffany in Plano Police dispatch office. We have a dead body found behind the counter at the Gulf Magic Market at the intersection of Parker Road and the US Seventy-Five service road. We need you there for the inquest," the caller spoke.

K.W. grimaced and said, "I'm on my way. Be sure they do not move the body before I get there."

"They know not to move the body, but I will tell them anyway," Tiffany responded.

Flashing red lights bounced off of the building and skipped past the gas pumps streaking through the early morning darkness. A uniformed officer waived K.W. past the barricades and onto the side of the parking apron. He stepped from his car and the officer lifted a hand saying, "Good morning Judge Bangs. We have a real nasty one here."

K.W. nodded. He had seen it all before, the broken bodies lying in the tangled evidence of life and death struggles. He stood on the driveway looking at the concrete for any evidence of who had been here and how they left. But there was nothing, no tire marks, no cigarette butts, no shell casings, nothing.

He turned to look at the door and across the canopy to see if there were any cameras. He saw one, positioned to cover the pumps. '*Yep, they put that one there to make a record of anyone filling up and driving off without paying. Be interesting to see what is on that tape,*' he thought.

He walked to the pumps, pulled a pen from his pocket and recorded the numbers on each pump so he could compare them with the store's records on gasoline sales. '*Maybe he fueled up before or after. If we know how much he got, and when he got it maybe we can figure how far he can go before stopping again,*' K.W. mused.

He pushed open the door, and the smell of death hit him. '*I smell gunpowder, so this is death by firearms. I smell blood but not brain blood so it must be a torso wound. I don't smell urine or a bowel release so the death was not instant and the victim had not had a meal or drink for a while,*' his mind was recording these impressions.

A uniformed officer stood at the end of the counter and greeted K.W., "Sorry to start your day this way, Judge Bangs. The victim is here behind the counter."

"Don't worry about it, Larry. Who called it in, how did we know about this?" he asked as he stepped around the counter and saw the body.

"A customer came in at five o'clock to get a coffee and donut. He saw the tobacco display on the floor and looked over the counter. He saw the body and ran back outside and called us from the payphone in front," the officer replied.

"Who is the detective that will be working the case?" K.W. asked.

"Ken Walker is the detective on call. He lives in Little Elm, so it will take a while for him to get here," Larry said.

K.W. kneeled beside the body and surveyed the scene. '*There is the till from the register pushed into the corner. He took all the money, even the change. That means he came in here broke. That increases the odds that we will have him on tape pumping gas.*

The body has been posed, almost as it will appear in the casket. The killer took some time, and that shows that he is pretty cool and it also shows that he had respect for this man.

There are scuffmarks all over the polished concrete floor. They struggled here and the shooter crawled around tying to stay out of sight.

There are no shell casings so either he picked them up or the weapon was a revolver. Those bags under the register are out of order, wonder if that was where the victim was keeping a pistol and the killer found it. Bet he got killed with his weapon.

There is blood on his hands, and the skin on his knuckles is broken open, he fought this guy, and that blood on his hands will belong to the killer. But look, there is also blood on his wrist, bet that blood is the killer's also and that would mean he was...yep, there is a piece of cloth and a button in his hand. Bet you a dollar that came off of his shirt,' K.W. mused as he made his notes for the inquest report.

He stood and looked around the usual pathway to be followed when leaving the counter and walking to the door. He turned to Larry and asked, "When you came in did you see any blood before you looked behind the counter?"

"No, sir. I didn't know what I was walking into so I had my weapon at the ready and came in slowly. I wasn't paying a lot of attention to the floor. Why are you asking?" the officer responded.

"Kneel right where you are and bend over so that your head is parallel to the floor. Shine your light along the plane of the floor and tell me what you see just in front of the door. Then turn and do the same thing from the edge of the counter to those coolers in the back there," K.W. said.

The officer did as K.W. suggested and said, "I seen what looks like dried blood that has been tracked to the coolers and then to the door exiting the store. I don't know how I missed that," the officer said.

"You missed it because you were making a tactile entry. I don't blame you at all. But the other thing is that it was the killer who tracked that blood. That tells us that this is one cool dude. He killed our victim in what looks to have been a violent struggle and then walked back to the cooler and grabbed a drink before he left.

Go ahead and have your crime scene crew come out to process the scene. After they finish up, have the dispatcher call Dallas County and request a unit to transport our victim for an autopsy," K.W. said.

K.W. signed the order directing the Dallas County Medical Examiner to perform a forensic autopsy on the body, handed it to the officer and said, "Give this to the field agents when they arrive. They will report their findings to me, and I have ordered them to provide a copy to the department. Let me know if the detectives have any questions from me."

The sergeant came through the door and nodded to Judge Bangs. "Morning Judge. Is there anything you need from us or that you need to tell me before you leave?" he asked.

"Yep, Smitty. There is a camera in the corner of the outside canopy watching the pumps. There is also one right there in the middle of the store, concealed in that black dome and there is a third one directly over the register.

I'm hoping the cameras were on and recording. We need to find the VCR and look at the tape. But I'm going to leave that for the detectives," K.W. said as he finished up his notes.

Smitty had stepped to the doorway of the office that was located directly behind the cash register. "The VCR is here on the desk, and there is a monitor sitting on top of it. Do you want me to rewind the tape so we can look at it?" the sergeant asked.

"No, I still think it is best to leave that for the detective assigned. I've signed the order and given it to Larry. He has ordered the crime scene unit, and they should be here anytime now.

I have all I need for the preliminary inquest report. I will do the final after we get the autopsy results and see what's on that tape.

For the time being, I am going to enter a finding stating the cause of death as a gunshot wound to the upper body and the manner of death as a homicide. Please give Ken these observations about the inquest finding," he said as he jotted down a copy of the notes he had made.

"I will give these to Ken. Thanks, Judge," Smitty said as K.W. walked from the store.

The Judge stood on the curb just outside the door and let the scene play out in his head. A flash of sunlight reflected off of a car turning from the service road onto Parker.

He looked at the Eastern sky and was amazed at how beautiful the sunrise was. He walked toward his car thinking, *'Yep, this is going to a beautiful day, but a deadly dawn.*

Somewhere out there is one who has stolen life from Jimmy. He is running, and he will try to hide, but my guess is that he will never be able to hide from the look on Jimmy's face as he took his last breath.

That will haunt him right up to the time the executioner pulls the switch on him. Bet you a nickel that Jimmy Olson's face will be the last thing he sees before hell's fires consume him.'

CHAPTER 43
REVENGE SHOOTING

"Hey Billy, give me another Bud," Frank was having trouble speaking, but he knew the bartender heard and understood what he wanted.

Billy was talking with Ed Bradley at the far end of the bar. He heard Frank and said, "Just a minute Frank."

"Damn your eyes, Billy Combest. Bring me another Bud," Frank became belligerent and mean when he was drunk, and he was definitely drunk.

"Who is that loudmouthed drunk?" Ed asked Billy.

"That is the one and only Frank Browning. He comes in here every Friday after work. He always wants me to cash his paycheck, and then he will sit there on a stool and drink until he gets to thinking he is the world champion eight ball shooter. Then he pushes his way into the game and gets cleaned out." Billy replied.

"Is he married? Does he have kids?" Ed asked.

"Yes and No. He has moved in with Doris Shaw, Bernie's widow. She has a trailer out on County Road Forty One Sixteen where she lives with her six kids.

Bernie bought six acres from old man DuBois a couple of years back. He used his Texas Vet Land Board privileges and was able to buy the land and a double wide that he and Doris set up on the land.

They were planning on building a house and raising their kids out there. Then he found out that he had colon cancer. Got it from all that Agent Orange they were spraying in the Nam when he was with the

Twenty-Fifth Infantry back in the day.

He had enough life insurance to pay off the note on the land and trailer, but not much was left to help Doris in raising those kids.

Frank and Bernie had been best friends in high school. They enlisted on the buddy plan and both shipped over to Viet Nam with the Twenty-Fifth.

After they had been in country six months, they got leave for R&R. They choose Hawaii, and the army sent them for a two-week break from the combat they had been in.

Frank got drunk one night and as always when he gets drunk, he became mean. He muscled his way into an eight-ball tournament, and an eighteen-year-old airman cleaned him out. Words were exchanged, and Frank decked the kid with his cue stick.

The Military Police showed up and tried to take Frank into custody. He hit one of them with the stick. Knocked the M.P. silly and then tried to grab his pistol out of the holster.

Well, if you know anything about M.P.'s you know they keep their weapon secured by a lanyard that is clipped to the butt plate. That lanyard probably saved the cops' life because Frank couldn't get the pistol away from him.

The second M.P. arrived and laid his baton upside Frank's head and turned his lights out. Frank woke up in the stockade. He was court-martialed and sent back home to Ft. Leavenworth, Kansas where he served a three-year sentence.

When his sentence was up, the army gave him a dishonorable discharge, and he came home. Went to work at the mill and here he is," Billy said.

"So, how did he end up with Doris?" Ed asked.

"Well see, Frank and Doris were sweethearts in high school. We all figured they would get married and raise a family. But Frank got his draft notice and decided he didn't want to leave his future up to the army.

So, he went to his best buddy, Bernie, and they made the decision to get in, get it over with and come on home. Then when things went they way they did, Bernie came home and married Frank's girl while

Frank was serving time in Leavenworth.

Frank got all liquored up one Saturday afternoon and waited for Bernie and Doris over at the Brookshire's. He knew they would be coming in to buy a bill of groceries and he figured to have his say. He did, and Bernie whipped his tail for him. Right there in the parking lot with all the Saturday grocery buyers watching.

Somebody called the Sheriff and Will Banks answered the call. He rolled up in his county car and beeped the siren a couple of times. That broke the fight up and Will took Frank and Bernie aside to figure out what was what.

Of course, he saw right away that Frank was drunk and as always mouthy. So he locked Frank up. Frank never let it go. He would come in here and get too many beers in his belly and start talking about how he was going to catch Will alone and get his revenge.

Then Bernie caught the cancer and died. Frank waited about six months and then drove out to see Doris. By that time she was broke and had just about given up all hope of keeping the land.

Frank convinced her that they could make a go of it. He promised her he would quit drinking so much and work on holding his temper. I don't think she believed him, but like I said, she was desperate and let him move in.

It didn't take but a couple of months until ole Frank was back on that favorite stool of his, drinking all the grocery money up. Doris came in here to get him one Friday night.

One of the kids, her and Bernie's youngest girl, was sick. She had the kid in the car and started pleading with Frank to go home and take care of the other kids while she carried the little girl into the emergency room.

Frank was drunk and mouthy. He told her that he didn't give a tinker's damn about Bernie's kids. She said something to the effect of *'Frank honey you don't mean that.'*

Frank laughed right loud and said, "The hell I don't and while I'm at it, I might as well tell you that I'm tired of taking Bernie's leavings."

The room got kind of quiet when he said that. Doris was crying and slapped him on the shoulder. Frank came up off that stool in a rage and backhanded Doris across the mouth.

A couple of the boys from the Bar T were in here and they didn't take kindly to a man hitting a woman like that. They whupped poor old Frank like a rented mule.

Then those boys told Frank that if he ever hit Doris again, they would strip him naked, hang him from a tree and horsewhip him.

They took Doris under their wing and drove her and the little girl into town. They paid the bill for the doctor and then took Doris home.

By the time Frank got home, Doris had thrown all of his clothes into the front yard. She told him he could stay in the tack room off of the barn, but could not come back into the house. That is where he lives today," Billy said as he moved down the bar to where Frank was mean-mugging him.

"Give me a beer Billy," Frank demanded.

"Nope. You've had enough Frank. Go on home and sleep it off," Billy said.

Frank stared at Billy a minute and then stood up off of the stool. He hefted the mug and drained it of the last swallow of beer. Then in one smooth motion, he launched it into the long mirror on the wall behind the bar.

The mirror shattered and began to fall. It fell in a wave from the middle outward in both directions until only the frame was left on the wall. There was a dead silence in the tavern.

Billy stood looking at his ruined bar, the shattered glass and the broken bottles of liquor that were spilling their contents onto the floor. He placed one hand on top of the bar and vaulted up and over.

Frank was backing up and bumped into a pool table. Billy shrugged out of his vest and balled his hands into fists. He stepped toward Frank and saw him pulling a something out of his back pocket. He stopped as Frank leveled the pistol at him.

Frank sneered at Billy and said, "What's a matter, Billy? Don't you want any of me? Come on if you do and let's see if you are bullet proof."

Billy raised his hands and backed away. Frank moved toward the door and sprinted across the dark parking lot to his car.

Billy yelled to a group of cowboys who had started to follow Frank, "No, don't. He is drunk and mean. He will shoot you. Just watch which way he goes and I will call the Sheriff."

"He's head out toward Doris' place and he doesn't have his headlights on," one of the cowboys answered.

Frank was smiling as he pushed the old Ford down the dirt road. *'Guess I showed them by God. Bet those hotshots won't be so quick to mess with Frank Browning next time I walk into that joint, if I ever go back,'* he mumbled.

Frank heard a horn, then a siren and looked into his rearview mirror. Red and blue lights were barely visible through the wall of dust the Ford was raising as he sped along County Road Forty-One Sixteen. *'So they called the Sheriff on me. What the hell, I will take care of that punk too,'* Frank said and pulled the car to a stop on the side of the road.

Frank watched the mirror as the sheriff's unit stopped behind his Ford. He saw the officer lift the radio and speak into it. A smile came across his lips as he saw that it was Will Banks who stepped from the cruiser. *'Well, well. Deputy Will Banks. What goes around comes around and I am going to get my revenge tonight,'* he said as he stepped from the Ford.

Will had been walking toward the car when Frank opened the door and stepped out. Frank watched as the deputy stopped in his tracks. He could tell that Will recognized him. He saw the officer drop his right hand to rest on the pistol at his belt. He heard Will say, "Frank, please get back into your car and keep your hands where I can see them."

Frank stood staring at Will. *'He has the drop on me,'* he thought. He turned and sat down in the car. Frank felt the bump of the pistol in his back pocket and smiled. *'I have one too big shot,'* he thought as he exited the car reaching for the pistol.

CHAPTER 44
PROBABLE CAUSE

"Cause number ET- 5001-JCD 3-1. The State of Texas versus Robert Browning," the clerk called out.

"Mr. Browning is present and represented by Frank Jinks, Judge," the defendant's attorney answered.

"The State is present, ready to proceed and represented by Howard Hamilton," your honor.

"Arraign the defendant, Mr. Hamilton," the judge said.

"Judge we waive arraignment and announce ready," Jinks said.

"Very well. For the record, this is a hearing to determine if there is probable cause for the defendant to be bound over for trial on the charge of Attempted Capital Murder. The court will limit the hearing to that purpose. This hearing will not be used as a vehicle of discovery. You each know the law and your options in that regard.

Are we clear on that gentlemen?" the judge asked.

"The State understands you instructions, Judge Bangs," the assistant district attorney said.

"Yes your honor, the defense understands," the attorney said.

"Thank you, gentlemen. Mr. Hamilton, call your witnesses to be sworn. Mr. Jinks, will you call witnesses?" Judge Bangs asked as the state's witnesses filed into the courtroom.

"Only the defendant judge. I have explained to him his rights to remain silent, but he insists that he wants you to hear what happened out there on County Road Forty-one Sixteen," Jinks said.

"Fine, we will handle that at the appropriate time. You have waived arraignment, do you now wish to stipulate, on the record, that this court is the proper venue and that the alleged offense occurred within Collin County Texas?" the judge was anxious to move the hearing along.

"We do, your Honor," Jinks said.

"Call your first witness Mr. Hamilton," the judge said.

"The State of Texas now calls Deputy Sheriff Will Banks," Hamilton said.

"Raise your right-hand deputy. Do you swear or affirm that the evidence you will give in this matter now before the court will be the truth, the whole truth and nothing but the truth?" Judge Bangs asked.

"I do your honor," the deputy answered.

"Have a seat in the witness chair. Mr. Hamilton, you may proceed," the judge said.

"Thank you, judge. State your name for the record deputy," Hamilton said.

"My name is Will Banks," the witness answered.

"How are you employed, Mr. Banks?"

"I am a Deputy Sheriff for Collin County, Texas," the officer replied.

"How long have you been so employed?"

"Since November 1, 1979," the deputy answered.

"Were you so employed and on duty as a Deputy Sheriff for Collin County on or about August 1, 1983?" Hamilton asked.

"Yes sir, I was," the officer answered.

"Did you in the course and performance of your duties on that day have an occasion to make contact with Mr. Robert Browning?" Hamilton asked.

"Yes, sir. I stopped Mr. Browning for driving a motor vehicle during the evening hours of darkness without his headlights illuminated," the officer pressed forward with the answer.

"Thank you, officer, but please give me answers to the question I ask without adding information," Hamilton directed the officer.

"Okay," the officer answered.

"At the time you initiated the traffic stop on Mr. Browning, were you wearing a uniform that clearing identified you as a police office?" the prosecutor asked.

"I was wearing this same uniform, or one just like it, with my badge on my shirt and patches on both shoulders identifying me as a Deputy Sheriff.

I was also driving a vehicle bearing markings identifying it as belonging to the Collin County Sheriff's office. That vehicle had a bar with red and blue lights which I activated to make the stop," the officer was clearly agitated with the progress of his examination.

Hamilton paused then asked the next question, "Deputy Banks, you have testified that the vehicle you stopped did not have the headlights illuminated. And you said this was during the hours of darkness. By that did you mean that the vehicle was being operated on a public roadway more than thirty minutes after sunset and more than thirty minutes before sunrise?"

"Yes that's right," Banks answered.

"Deputy was the sole reason you initiated the stop the failure of the driver to have the vehicle's headlights on?" Hamilton asked.

"Yes. It turns out that the suspect had been involved in a disturbance at a local tavern a few minutes before I saw him, but I did not know that at the time I stopped him," the deputy said.

"Thank you. Where was the defendant operating the vehicle without the proper illumination of the headlights when you first observed him?" Hamilton stammered some as he asked the question.

"On County Road Forty-one Sixteen approximately two and one half miles north of its' intersection with State Highway Sixty-seven," the officer answered.

"And was that location you just described in Collin County Texas?" Hamilton seemed to have forgotten that the defense had stipulated that the alleged offense would have occurred in Collin County.

"Yes, it was," Banks twisted in the seat and folded his arms across his chest.

"Tell the court in your own words what you did after making the traffic stop," Hamilton was shuffling through his file, and the judge knew he was stalling.

"Just a minute Mr. Hamilton. The court, as the finder of fact, will ask a couple of questions to move this along," Judge Bangs said.

"Officer, did you make contact with the driver of the vehicle you saw driving without the headlights on, and if you did is that driver present in the courtroom today?" the judge asked as Hamilton sat down.

"Yes I did, and yes the operator of the vehicle is sitting at the defense table with his attorney," the officer replied pointing at the defendant.

"Let the record reflect that the officer has identified the defendant named in the charging instrument," the judge said speaking to the reporter.

"What if anything happened after you made contact with the defendant Deputy Banks?" the judge asked.

"I exited my vehicle and started walking toward the defendant's vehicle. Just as I got about halfway there, he opened the door and stepped from the vehicle. I told him to return to his vehicle and remain seated. He turned as if he was going to comply and then turned back toward me and I saw a pistol in his hand.

He leveled the pistol at me and told me to get on my knees. I started backing up because I figured that if I got down on my knees, he was going to execute me right there.

He started advancing on me, and I saw him pull the hammer back on the gun. I turned to run, trying to put the patrol vehicle between him and me. I had taken maybe two steps when he shot me.

The bullet hit me on the lower left side of my back, just above my gun belt. The impact pushed me into my patrol vehicle, and I fell to the roadway. He fired again and that bullet hit me in my upper left arm.

I rolled under my car but before I could get all the way under he fired again and this time the bullet hit me in the left foot.

I could hear him running toward the car and figured he was going to stick that pistol under the car and finish me off. So, I got my pistol out of the holster and started shooting at his feet as soon as I could see them. That spooked him I guess because he ran back to his car and took off.

When I was sure he was gone I crawled out from under my patrol vehicle and called for help," Banks said.

"Mr. Hamilton you may resume your direct examination," the Judge said.

"I understand from your testimony that the defendant shot you three times. How badly were you injured," the prosecutor asked.

"The bullet in the back traveled forward and struck my ribs breaking three of them. One of the broken ribs punctured my lung and caused it to collapse. The bullet then was deflected downward and exited my body through my abdomen.

The bullet that hit my left foot shattered the heel and ruptured my Achilles tendon. The bullet that struck me in the left arm broke the Humerus.

I had lost a lot of blood by the time help arrived and had to be flown to Baylor hospital in McKinney by helicopter," the officer was staring at his shooter.

"Tell me this officer. How far where you from the defendant when he first exited the vehicle?" Hamilton asked.

"About fifteen feet," the officer replied.

"You have already testified that it was dark enough to require illumination to operate a motor vehicle safely, so how were you able to see the defendant well enough to say definitely that Mr. Browning is the man who shot you?" Hamilton asked.

"I had my flashlight in my hand, and I directed the beam onto his face when he exited the vehicle. I could see him clearly and besides that, I recognized him from an arrest I had made on him two years ago," the officer said with a shrug.

"Without going into the past arrest, is it your testimony that you are certain that this defendant is the person who shot you on the night in question; and that you base that identification on what you saw out there that night and not on the previous arrest you alluded to?" the prosecutor had hit his stride now.

"Yes, that is my testimony," Banks answered.

"Do you know how the defendant came to be arrested?" Hamilton asked.

"Yes, I do. I had given the dispatcher a description of the car and the license plate number of the vehicle when I checked out on the traffic stop. I told the first units that arrived to help me that it was Robert Browning who had shot me.

Mr. Browning is well know by local law enforcement and the officers on duty knew where he lived. Several units converged on that location, saw his vehicle parked in front of the barn and called for him to come out. He did and they were able to take him into custody without any trouble," the deputy said.

"One final question Deputy, do you believe that this defendant knew you were a peace officer for the State of Texas at the time he shot you and that his intention was to kill you?" Hamilton asked quickly.

"We object to that last part of the question judge. It calls for speculation on the part of the witness. He cannot possibly know what my client's intentions were," Jinks was standing.

"The objection is sustained. Do not answer the question Deputy Banks," the judge ruled.

"The state will pass the witness judge," Hamilton said.

"We have no questions for this witness, your honor," Jinks said.

"The State rests judge," Hamilton said.

"Mr. Jinks?" the judge looked at the defense counsel.

"Judge I would like for the record to reflect that I have cautioned my client against testifying in this matter and that I have in fact advised him not to testify. I have told him that once he testifies the State can cross examine him and that anything he says can and will be used against him when this case is tried on its' merits. But, he wants to testify judge," Jinks said and sat down.

"Mr. Browning, I understand that you want to tell your side of this event. But this is a probable cause hearing. It is not a trial on the merits. The sole purpose is for the court to determine if there is probable cause to apprehend that you should be bound over to the District Court for trial.

Given the testimony offered before the court, I now find that Probable Cause Does Exist to support binding the defendant over to the District Court of Collin County, Texas for a trial on the merits as outlined in the charging instruments, in this case, an Information.

The hearing is hereby severed, and the defendant is remanded to the custody of the Sheriff of Collin County, Texas who is ordered to safely keep the defendant until he has posted a bond of $250,000.00 or until he is to be presented before the District Court for trial.

We are adjourned. Thank you, gentlemen," the judge said as he left the courtroom.

Judge K.W. Bangs walked into his chambers. He was tired from the long day's docket but knew he had duties as the Director of Police for Plano ISD waiting on him.

He moved behind the desk and sat down to review his schedule for the remainder of the day. The phone rang behind him. He picked the phone up, and his clerk said, "Judge, a detective named Beth called from Plano P.D. She said to tell you she needs to talk with you about a sexual assault case. She asked that you call her as soon as you got off of the bench," the clerk said.

"Okay. What about any other calls that came in while I was in court? Can they wait," he asked.

"Yes, Judge. A couple of them are from folks wanting to get married. But one is from the owner of a car dealership in Farmersville. He said to tell you that he is a lodge brother and needs to talk with you.

I checked his name against our dockets and found that he has been sued in our court. His case is set for next Wednesday," she said.

"Debra, I need you to call that gentleman back and tell him that I cannot engage in an Ex parte conversation with him once the case has been filed," the judge said.

"I told him that Judge. He said that tell you a lodge brother called and that he expects, as a lodge brother, for you to return his call. I got the feeling he was expecting favoritism as a brother and that he is going to cause you trouble if he does not get it," Debra said with a sigh.

"Do you still have that note?" the judge asked.

"Yes sir, it is here with all of your other notes," she said.

"Throw that one in the trash and then get Beth on the phone for me," the judge said and hung the phone up.

CHAPTER 45
MR. POPCORN

Abe lifted the five-pound bag and poured a pound of popcorn into each of the four commercial poppers. He topped off the cooking oil and closed the glass doors on each machine. He flipped the power switch to the on and moved back a couple of steps to lean against the stainless steel table.

He pulled the kitchen towel from his back pocket and wiped the excess oil from his hands. Glancing up, he saw his reflection in the polished surface of the metal framing of the machine immediately in front of where he stood. He grimaced at the image of a forty-four-year-old man staring back at him. He looked away, but the image was still in his mind.

He shook his head and looked up at the ceiling and then forced himself to confront the image. *'Look at yourself, Abraham Cobb Jacobs. Here you stand, forty-four years old and working for your parents.'*

Abe as he was sometimes called or Cobb as he liked to be called, was a miserable man. He had married his high school sweetheart, Rene, as soon as they graduated.

Two kids later she had filed for divorce citing his insatiable gambling habit as causing irreparable harm to the viability of the union. What she didn't put in the petition to dissolve the marriage was that his continued presence in the family unit presented a danger to her and the children.

But she did tell his parents, Carter and June Jacobs, that Cobb's gambling debts had outstripped his ability to meet his losses. The collectors had begun calling the house demanding payment and threatening dire actions against him and his family if he did not come up with the money quickly.

Now here he stood, dressed in white from the cap on his curly red hair to the white shirt emblazoned with the yellow 'Mr. Popcorn' logo over the left chest. His white pants were stained with the greasy residue that came from working with the oily corn.

'What the hell am I going to do? I can't stand this damned popcorn much longer, and the bank and the bill collectors have now joined Ricco's collectors demanding money. I don't have any money, and I am not going to have any money. Maybe I should file bankruptcy. That will get the bill collectors off my back, but what about Ricco and his goons?

One stupid bet and here I am facing dudes who want to break my legs or worse. But if I had hit, the payout would have cleared the board for me. If only…

The only answer seems to take off, maybe to Alaska, and disappear. That would give me a chance to start over and put all this behind me,' Cobb mused.

The corn was cooking now, popping out its' staccato rhythm that fascinated Cobb. The beat was broken yet the rhythm was consistent. *'How can four different machines keep such perfect rhythm with a broken beat?'* he wondered.

The jangling of the phone interrupted his train of thought, and he pushed away from the counter and shut the power off on the machines. He opened the doors and stepped aside as the superheated steam flowed from the cookers.

Cobb grabbed the handle on the built-in butter cauldrons and pulled the stop back so that the melted butter could be drizzled over the corn. Once he had the corn covered in butter, Cobb reached for the rod protruding from the salt bins and shuffled the rod back and forth pushing the salt through the filters to settle over the now buttery corn. The butter and the salt became one, and the corn was now ready to be scooped and packaged.

Cobb had just shoved the corn scoop into the first machine when his mother called from the front counter, "Son the phone is for you."

He dropped the scoop, wiped his hands again and sidled over to the extension mounted on the wall of the kitchen. Lifting the receiver, he said, "This is Cobb."

"Cobb, you welching son of a bitch, the boss wants his money, and he wants it now," he recognized the voice as that of Tony Capricio.

"Tony, you know I'm not a welcher. It's just that I am in a bind. My wife just filed for divorce, and her lawyer took every penny out of our joint account. I don't even have the money to hire a lawyer. Every one of those bloodsuckers I talk with wants fifteen hundred up front.

Look, here are the facts. You can't get blood out of a turnip. I'm totally tapped out. I can't pay, and all the threats won't change that. You tell Ricco that," Cobb said.

There was silence for a few seconds, and then Tony said, "Hold the phone a minute Cobb while I tell the boss what's going on with you."

Cobb could hear the muffled voices, and then Tony said, "The boss is going to check your story. You had better be telling the truth, Cobb. Just remember this Sport, that turnip may not have any blood you sure as hell do. Follow me?"

"I know what you are saying, Tony. I am telling you the truth. How can I give you what I don't have?" Cobb asked.

"What if we had a way for you to work your debt off? Would you be interested in doing a couple of jobs for us?" Tony had lowered his voice to almost a whisper.

"What kind of jobs?" Cobb asked.

"Let's not talk about it over the phone. You know the place where we met the last time we talked? Can you meet us there tomorrow at noon? We will eat a little pasta and talk a little business," Tony said.

"Do you mean the place across from the Dr. Pepper plant?" Cobb asked.

"You stupid fag! Why don't you give the address to whoever might be listening? Yeah, that's the place. Be there at noon," Tony growled.

"I am not a fag. I swear that guy looked like a woman and a good-looking woman at that. Did you know she was a he Tony?" Cobb was sore.

Tony laughed and said, "Yeah we knew. The boss had a line on whether or not you would realize it before you took off to the back room. The longer you danced with and kissed on that bozo the better the action got. The boss made nearly four grand off of that deal. Hey get over it, see you tomorrow."

Cobb hung up the phone and stood leaning against the wall wondering if he could work his gambling debts off. If so, he would file the bankruptcy and walk away from the business debts.

• • •

Cobb drove south on Greenville Avenue until he saw the Dr. Pepper plant. He knew that the restaurant where Ricco and Tony wanted to meet was nearby, but he did not know exactly where. He turned onto Mockingbird and crept along until the guy behind him grew impatient and started honking his horn and waving his hand out the window.

'Where is this place, what did they call it? Something odd, ah there it is, Campsi's Egyptian Room. What an odd name for a pasta and pizza joint,' he said as he parked. Cobb sat in his car a few minutes looking around at the cars parked nearby and the men lounging around the front door. Why was it that they liked this place so much?

He had seen these men before, *'oily looking gents and every one of them are carrying a gun,'* he remembered. He knew they were the first line of defense for Ricco and that there would be more scattered throughout Campsi's. The men were looking at him now. One of them opened the front door of Campsi's and motioned to someone inside.

'Spotted me,' he said under his breath and stepped from his car. Two of the men turned to him, and one motioned for him to keep his hands out of his pockets. Cobb walked slowly forward until the man told him to stop.

The second man was smiling and clapping his hands as if he was greeting an old friend. He slapped Cobb on the shoulder and shook hands with him. The 'handshake' was an immobilizing grasp, holding Cobb in place while the first man did a quick pat down. As soon as they were sure he was not armed, the first man dropped the handshake and patted Cobb in the chest with his open hand.

Still smiling and laughing, the bodyguard ran the hand across Cobb's chest and down around this waist. Convinced that there was no wire or other listening device, they walked him to the front door where Tony waited.

Cobb stepped through the doorway and Tony said, "Follow me."

Cobb followed Tony past a group of men sitting at a table with Ricco. Tony led Cobb down a short hallway and then pulled a curtain aside to reveal a small utility room.

Cobb looked inside and saw that it was where the brooms, mops and other cleaning equipment were stored. He also noticed that there was a door on the opposite wall.

'Bet that door leads to the alley between this and the next building,' he thought to himself. Tony motioned Cobb inside. Cobb hesitated and asked Tony, "What's up with this? Why do you want me to go into a broom closet? I thought I was here to talk with Ricco."

Tony didn't bother to answer; he just shoved Cobb through the doorway and into the room. "Get in there welcher," Tony growled. He stood outside a few seconds and then stepped inside and closed the curtains.

"What are you doing Tony?" Cobb asked.

"Shut your pie hole welcher," Tony said.

The curtain parted, and a swarthy man stepped in. He turned to draw the curtains and said to someone Cobb could not see, "Nobody comes in."

The swarthy man turned to look at Cobb and then said to Tony, "Check him again, all the way down including his ankles."

Tony ran his hands down both of Cobb's legs, then grabbed his crotch and around to his buttocks and all the way up to the back of his neck. "He's clean," Tony said.

Cobb saw that the second man was wearing a dark blue Khaki

uniform. There was a logo of what looked like a cigarette machine over the left shirt pocket. Under the logo were the words, '*V&R Vending*.' Over the right pocket was a white patch with the name '*Vinny*' in red script.

"So Cobb, I understand you owe some money that you don't have and probably are not going to be able to raise. Is that right?" Vinny asked.

Cobb nodded but said nothing.

"Okay, so here are your options. Either I take you out that door; down the alley and stuff you into the trunk of my car for a one-way ride, or you work your debt off by doing some odd jobs for us. You got one minute, which is it going to be?" Vinny asked.

Cobb looked at Tony and then at Vinny. "Easy decision. I am not ready to take that ride. But I want to be sure that doing these jobs squares me with the man," Cobb said looking at Tony again.

Vinny said, "This is between you and me. But yes, you do this, and you are square with the house."

"That works for me. So tell me what, when and where," Cobb said.

"We understand that you drove big rigs in the Army. Can you still drive an eighteen wheeler?" Vinny asked.

"How did you know that?" Cobb asked.

"You don't ask questions, welcher. You are not in any position to ask questions. You answer yes or no, and we will react accordingly. Now, can you still drive a big rig?" Vinny was surly.

"Sure," Cobb said.

"Have you ever driven one with tandem trailers?" Vinny asked.

"Yep," Cobb nodded.

"Okay, so here's the setup. Tonight at ten o'clock you drive the same car you came here in into the employee's parking lot across the street at the Dr. Pepper plant. Just drive in and park.

Stay in your car and wait. One of my men will contact you. You go with him. He is going to take you to a truck stop where you will see a driver get out of a Peter Built truck pulling tandem trailers. He will be wearing a Texas Tech baseball cap.

That driver will walk toward the truck stop café. As soon as he enters the café, my man will pull his car alongside the truck. The truck will be unlocked. You get into the truck and follow my man.

We have told him where to go. When he gets there, you put the truck where he tells you and then get back into the car with him. He will take you to your vehicle, and run number one is behind you.

Do this five times over the next three months, and we will be slick. Got it?" Vinny asked.

"Okay, Vinny. But as you are talking, I'm thinking that those trailers are going to be filled with cigarettes. That kind of rig will easily hold eighty thousand pounds of cigarettes. That dollars up to a hell of a lot more than the ten thousand dollars I owe Ricco.

Stealing those loads is a federal offense, doing it five times in three months is asking to get caught. It seems to me I am assuming a lot of risk with little return," Cobb was shaking his head.

"Think of it this way welcher. Say you do this and get caught? You do a two to five year stretch in a federal joint.

Now let's say you don't do this. You do forever at the bottom of the closest lake. Follow?" Vinny was already turning away.

"Wait. Okay. I'm in. Five times and we are slick, right?" Cobb asked.

"Yep, five times and we are slick. By the way, you are right about the Feds being all over this after we steal a couple of loads. So, we will change things as we go. Don't worry about that. Just keep showing up, and all will be well.

But the final word for you is this. You screw us over, and we will waste you *and your entire family*. You have my word on that Cobb," Vinny said and walked away.

"He's not kidding Cobb. Do not think for one minute that he will not kill you and everyone dear to you," Tony said.

"Oh, I believe him. But look here Tony. I sure would appreciate your talking to Ricco about cutting me in on some of this action after I pay my debt. Think about it Tony, five of these gigs will bring in four hundred thousand pounds of cigarettes. That is a lot of profit, my man. Shoot, I want in on this setup," Cobb said.

Tony laughed and said, "Abraham Cobb Jacobs, Jr., is that your full name?"

"Yeah, that's right. Cobb was my mother's maiden name, so my parents used it as my middle name," Cobb said.

"But Jacobs is your father's family name and Jacobs is Jewish, right?" Tony asked.

"Are you anti-Semitic?" Cobb asked.

"No. We are pro-Italian, and you are not Italian," Tony said and walked Cobb to the front door.

CHAPTER 46
TRAVEL AMERICA

Cobb parked in a spot under the big Dr. Pepper logo and switched his engine off. As he did, a black Ford stopped behind his car. Cobb got out of his vehicle and walked to the pickup.

The driver rolled the window down and said in thick Italian, "Get in and don't talk."

Cobb walked around the front of the truck and sat down in the passengers' seat. He buckled his seatbelt, and the driver exited the parking lot and turned right on Mocking Bird driving toward Central Expressway.

He crossed over the freeway and turned south on the service road and then merged into the southbound traffic. The clock on the dash of the truck read ten minutes after ten. Twenty-five minutes later they exited Inter-State Twenty at Bonnie View Road and entered the parking lot of the Travel America Truck Stop.

At ten-fifty a Peter Built tractor pulling two pup trailers bearing the Campbell Freight logo pulled into the lot and parked. The driver got out of the cab and walked around his trailers thumping the tires with a weighted club. He tossed the club into the cab and slammed the door.

Cobb watched as the driver removed his Texas Tech cap, rubbed his head and strolled into the café. The driver spoke for the first time since he had picked Cobb up, "Go get into the truck. Follow me. If you get stopped, you are on your own. Keep your mouth shut if your family means anything to you."

Cobb didn't even look at the man. He walked around the truck checking the air brake hoses, looking at the lights and then he stepped up into the cab. The diesel was running, and Cobb couldn't help but admire how smooth it sounded.

He shifted into first gear and followed the Ford pickup out of the parking lot and turned north on Interstate Twenty. Traffic was thin this time of night, and they made good time. Cobb saw the black Ford slow and turn into the parking lot of V&R Vending Warehouse at Lancaster and Ann Arbor Road. Billy made a note of the address; *'Forty-three zero two South Lancaster Road.'*

The driver of the pickup stopped and walked back to the big rig. Cobb rolled down the window, and his mysterious escort said, "Unhook the second pup and then back into one of those slots just like you were making a drop here."

Cobb unhooked the pup and backed the rig into an unloading lane and eased it back until he felt contact with the padded bumper on the loading dock. He switched off the engine, climbed down from the cab walked to the back of the truck. A dock-worker was clipping the seal and raising the door on the trailer. Another worker drove up on a forklift and said, "We have it from here."

Cobb heard a horn honk and walked to the pickup and settled in. "What about that rig? What if it has a GPS tag on it and the cops find it here? Shouldn't wait until they unload it and then drop the rig somewhere else?" he asked.

"That's not your concern. Next time, just get out and come to the truck. You don't need to be seen, and we don't want you talking to anyone," the driver said.

Twenty minutes later Cobb was headed to his parents' house on Eighteenth Street in Plano. *'The first run is done. Only four more and I will be even with the house. This is easy money, and I want some of it.*

From what I saw on the manifest, this load was headed for Houston. No one will expect to hear from the truck for at least four hours. That gives the driver some time to report the theft but not more than an hour. With the crew they have working I can see them unloading both trailers in an hour. Then they will hook up that extra trailer and move the rig but where?

Do they dump it to be found or do they change the numbers on the frame and fence the whole rig? They might even drive across into Mexico. There is a big market for these rigs down there. That would add about a hundred thousand to their profit. Bet that is what they are doing,' Cobb was thinking about all that money.

•　　　•　　　•

It was early April, and Cobb was about to make his fourth run in payment of his gambling losses. The night had started like all the others. He had parked under the giant Dr. Pepper logo, and his ride pulled up behind him. He jumped from his car and ran around the front of the truck wanting to get inside out of the heavy rain as quickly as possible.

He settled in and reached for his handkerchief to wipe the rain off of his face and dripping hair. Tonight there was a different driver, but Cobb knew the routine would not change. The driver would not speak unless it was necessary or if Cobb irritated him in some way.

Which was the case now. "Stop looking at me. Look out of the window on your side or straight ahead out of the windshield," tonight's' driver said without turning his face toward Cobb.

Cobb decided not to respond but took a long look at the man before turning his face away from him. He made a mental note as he had on all these drivers, *'He is about forty years old, he has his hands at the two o'clock and ten o'clock position on the wheel, he put the turn signal on even to exit the parking lot, he is unshaven and smells like one who has gone without bathing for a while. He is a driver, probably a union man, right off of a run,'* Cobb thought as he scooted down in the seat and laid his head back against the rest pad and closed his eyes.

The driver had turned north onto US Highway Seventy-Five and was traveling at a steady fifty-five mph with the flow of the traffic. The slapping rhythm of the windshield wipers and the hum of the tires on the wet pavement put Cobb into a deep sleep. A sudden jolt woke him, and he sat up to see the driver's hand on his arm. "Wake up, we're close," he said as Cobb shook the sleep out of his head.

Cobb glanced at the clock in the dash of the truck and saw that it was now eleven thirty. They had been driving for an hour and a half.

They passed a roadside sign that declared they were entering the city limits of Denison, Texas. Just past that sign, he saw a big billboard advertising the State Line Truck Stop. *'Nearly in Oklahoma'*, he mused as the driver took the exit and parked just outside the apron of the fueling area at the State Line Truck Stop.

The driver left the engine running on the pickup but turned the wipers off. Rain quickly covered the windshield effectively blocking the view of the pump area.

Cobb had not been given the description of the truck they were meeting since that first run. He figured it was a safeguard against him snitching the operation off. He didn't care, two more runs and he was going to find a way to cash in on this operation.

He glanced toward the driver and said, "I've got to pee. I am going to walk into the café and take care of that and grab me a cup of coffee for the drive back. Do you want anything?"

The surly man didn't even look at him. Cobb shrugged, pulled the collar up on his jacket and ran for the canopy covering the pumps. Reaching the dry area, he stomped his feet to rid them of the excess water and walked into the café.

Cobb noticed a man follow him from the parking lot into the café. He was dressed in gray pants, a white shirt and a dark blue sports coat.

'He is not the typical truck stop customer. His type does not eat in a truck stop café. Wonder if he is just an average Joe stopping for the restroom or what?' Cobb looked at the man out of the corner of his eye.

Cobb realized the man was watching him in the mirror. Cobb walked on into the men's room, took care of his business and then walked out. The man was leaning against the wall with his back to the men's room door. But he was watching its' reflection in the rain-spattered windows.

A bulge at the man's waistline caught Cobb's attention, *'that looks like a pistol on his belt. The dude is a cop. But why is he following me?'* Cobb forced the panic down and calmly walked to the counter and ordered a tall black coffee to go.

Cobb walked outside and stopped. He took a sip of the coffee and looked around as if he was just stretching some before climbing back into a rig. He could see the front door of the café in a reflection off of the gas pump. His shadow had moved toward the door but stopped when Cobb did.

Cobb watched as the man turned away. The man dropped his head with his mouth moving as if he was talking into his jacket. *'Son of a bitch! He is a cop, and he is wired. He just updated his partner that I am outside the café. Where is his partner?'* Cobb looked at the vehicles parked nearby as casually as possible.

He couldn't see anyone that looked like a cop to him. He moved toward the edge of the canopy and reached up to flip his collar up and then trotted toward the truck. *'Should I tell the driver, or should I just let this play out and see what happens? Why is this even a question, what am I thinking?'* Cobb wondered.

He opened the door and started to get in. "Don't get in. Your ride is that Central Freight rig sitting off to the left of the pumps there. The GPS is already programmed. Just follow it until it says you have reached your destination. There will be someone to meet you when you arrive," the driver said looking at Cobb for the first time.

Cobb saw that the man had a deep and ragged scar running from the tip of the left eyebrow all the way past his jawbone. It continued down the side of his throat to disappear into his shirt. *'That's why he didn't want me to look at him. It looks like he has been in a knife fight. I wonder what the other guy looks like?'* Cobb thought.

"What do you mean? I have always followed my driver back to the drop location. Why the change, where am I going?" Cobb felt danger in this change.

"You are asking questions that I don't have answers to. But I do know that as soon as you fire the engine up the GPS map will pop up and you will know your destination. I don't need to know, and I don't want to know. Close my door," Scarface said.

The pickup was already rolling forward when Cobb slammed the door. He circled the Central Freight Rig checking tires, hoses, and lights. He walked up to the driver's side door and stood looking at the tractor. *'Ken Worth, a brand new Ken Worth; bet this rig doesn't have a hundred thousand miles on it. Wherever I'm headed, this new truck has something to do with it,'* he mused as he climbed into the cab.

Cobb settled his coffee in the console and fired the engine up. The big diesel was so sweet sounding to him. He smiled and thought, *'Man, I would love to own this rig.'*

He watched as the GPS flickered on and the route planned became clear. *'Laredo, Texas! What the hell? I guess V&R Vending has filled the warehouse with cigarettes and have sold this load to someone in Mexico. They probably sold the whole rig too.*

Okay, they will get theirs, and I have another job out of the way. But damn this run will take seven hours and fifty-two minutes. I guess I am about to drive from the Northern line of Texas to the Southern line of Texas. I better run back inside and call dad to tell him I will be out a couple of days,' he said to himself as he ran for the café.

CHAPTER 47
THE SILENT MAN

Cobb looked at the clock as he exited the parking lot and turned the big rig South toward Laredo. *'It is now midnight. I should pull into Laredo about eight o'clock tomorrow morning. Better add an hour or more for comfort stops and to eat,'* He was looking forward to the open road. He loved driving at night, especially in the rain.

He followed U.S. Highway seventy-five south to Dallas and then cut over to Interstate thirty-five. The traffic was heavy as he circled Dallas but thinned once he was outside the city limits. He moved to the center lane and pushed the Ken Worth to seventy miles an hour. He set the cruise control and settled back in the big seat for the long ride.

As he neared Austin, Cobb glanced in the right side mirror and noticed that the tan Chevrolet was still there; about four cars back. He smiled to himself. He had seen them follow him out of the State Line Truck Stop in Denison and guessed that they would trail him all the way to Laredo.

He could see two men in the car. *'Who are they? They might be the new owners of the rig, but if so why didn't they drive it? Playing it safe against getting stopped with a stolen shipment? Or could they be cops?'* Cobb sat thinking about this as the miles fell away. *'If they are cops I'm busted. Then what? Theft of Interstate Shipment brings federal time, a lot of federal time. Maybe I can cut a deal. I can give them Ricco, Tony, and Vinny. But if I did that, I would need protection. If the feds want me to testify, they are going have to put me in the witness protection program and give me a new identity, a new life.'* The more he thought about it, the better it sounded. His mind made up, Cobb relaxed and the time flew by.

The sun was up now, and he saw the big green sign 'Laredo City Limits.'

The GPS screen was flashing, and then Cobb heard the message, *"Take Exit Thirteen two miles ahead and keep to the right on the service road."*

He saw a sign advertising the Pilot Truck Center at Exit Thirteen and thought, *'Bet a dollar this GPS takes me right into that parking lot.'* He moved to the right lane and glanced in the left side mirror. The tan Chevy changed lanes to fall in behind him.

Cobb guided the big rig off of the highway and onto the service road. The truck stop was now in sight. *"Your destination is on the right, four hundred feet ahead. You have arrived,"* the GPS spoke.

Cobb was watching in the side mirror as he slowed the Ken Worth and then turned onto the ramp for entrance into the truck stop parking lot. He followed his usual practice and parked close to the service road so the new driver would be able to make a quick and easy exit. As he shut the rig down, he saw the tan Chevy drive past the truck stop and turn right onto the next cross street and then into a Cracker Barrel Restaurant.

'Okay, whatever,' Cobb said and swung down from the cab. He stretched and ambled toward the café.

Just before he reached the pumps, a red Toyota Tundra stopped beside him. The power window on the passenger side slid down, and a Hispanic woman wearing a Red Ball Express cap said, "Get in."

Cobb nodded toward the café and said, "Got to go pee first."

"No, get in. You don't have time to pee," she said.

Cobb shrugged and opened the door to the truck. The first thing he noticed was chrome plated pistol lying in her lap. "Whoa, what's up with that?" Cobb asked pointing to the pistol.

"Shut up and get in the truck," she said.

He looked into the woman's eyes and what he saw there convinced him that she was not one to be argued with. He stepped onto the skid bar and into the truck. He slammed the door, and the woman said, "Put your seatbelt on and keep your mouth shut."

Cobb did as she said and the window next to him rolled up and the door locked with a click. The woman pulled away from the truck stop and into the parking lot of the Cracker Barrel Restaurant across the cross street. But rather stopping in the parking lot, she pulled around behind the building. The tan Chevrolet followed.

The woman stopped the truck and said, "Get out."

Cobb stepped out and was pushed against the side of the truck by two men wearing dark glasses. One leaned close and said, "We are federal agents. You, Abraham Cobb Jacobs, Jr. are under arrest for theft from Interstate Commerce. Stand still and keep your hands on the truck while I check you for weapons."

Cobb sighed and said, "Thank God it is over."

After a quick pat down, the agents handcuffed Cobb and sat him back down in the Toyota. The taller of the two males fastened the seat belt around Cobb, nodded toward the woman driver and said, "This is Special Agent Patrice Gomez. I am Special Agent Frank Dodd, and my partner is Special Agent Felix Roddy.

Agent Gomez is going to transport you to our office downtown. My partner and I will be following. Don't give us any trouble Cobb."

"Aren't you going to read me my rights?" Cobb asked with a smile.

"Not here. Not now. We want to clear this scene as quickly as possible. We will not ask you any questions until we get to the office," Dodd said.

Dodd slammed the door, and Gomez pulled away from the building, turned right on the service road and headed south. "What about the truck?" Cobb asked and turned to look at the rig.

He almost gasped but was able to control his surprise. Walking past the rig and into the café was the Scarface man who drove him to Denison. Cobb sat back and said nothing.

"Be quiet," Gomez said without taking her eyes off of the road.

"Okay, let me say this one last thing, and then I will be quiet. I want you to tell Dodd that I can give him the entire story and all the players in this deal. All I want is protection. That's it," Cobb said and sat back.

Gomez slowed the pickup and signaled for a right turn. '*What is she doing, we are mid-block. There is no place to turn,*' Cobb was thinking. He saw the sloping drive. It dropped quickly from the sidewalk and disappeared into a black hole that was the entrance to a subterranean parking garage.

The garage was bright with florescent lighting. There were no police vehicles and Cobb knew that this was not a jail. '*They aren't taking me straight to lock up, so they are looking for more information,*' Cobb reasoned.

He smiled as he realized that the ball was soon going to be in his court. '*Bring it on G-Man. I am ready to trade the past for the future,*' he was feeling better about his situation.

Gomez led Cobb up a ramp and into a basement lobby. The elevator ride was completed in silence. As the doors opened, he saw that the whole fourth floor was filled with men and women wearing guns.

Gomez led him down a long gray hallway and into a suite of offices. "Walk straight back to that office marked Conference," Gomez told him. She steered him to a chair in the middle of the table with his back to the wall. "Sit down and remain quiet. My partners will be here shortly," Gomez said and moved to exit the room.

"Wait. How about taking these handcuffs off?" Cobb asked.

"Nope," Gomez said as she left the room and Cobb heard the door lock.

Fifteen minutes later Dodd walked into the conference room carrying a tray with coffee and an Egg McMuffin sandwich. Agent Gomez and Agent Roddy followed with a video camera and audio recorder.

Dodd sat the tray down in front of Cobb and said, "Lean forward and let me take these cuffs off."

He leaned forward, and the cuffs were quickly removed. Dodd stepped to the end of the table and pulled a chair out to sit in.

"We followed you all the way in from Denison. You didn't stop to eat so I figured you would need a little something before we get started.

Gomez and Roddy are going to set the recording equipment up while you eat. Then we will let you tell us your story," Dodd said.

Cobb nodded his thanks and reached for the sandwich. "Why not sign the Miranda warnings first and then we can talk as I eat?" he asked.

Dodd opened his folder and pushed the warnings across the table. He laid a pen on top of the sheet and said, "We need to do that on tape. Go ahead and eat and then we will get started."

Cobb swallowed a gulp of the hot coffee and said, "I am glad this thing has ended without me getting hurt. There are some bad folks that are going to be looking for me after this. I am going to need protection if I am going to remain safe," Cobb said.

"The Witness Protection Program is reserved for those who are willing to testify against criminals engaged in major crimes, usually those engaged in organized crime. Are you suggesting this theft ring you are associated with is part of an organized criminal enterprise?" Dodd seemed surprised.

"Yep. That's what I am saying," Cobb said.

"Okay, stop. Roddy, are we rolling on camera and tape?" Dodd asked.

"Rolling on both boss," Roddy answered.

"Okay Cobb, listen carefully to what I am now going to tell you. I need you to understand that you transported stolen property that was part of an interstate shipment before your participation in the event. That means the products traveled through more than one state. By transporting the product, you are just as guilty of the theft as those who took the product in the first instance.

You are under arrest and will be charged with Theft From Interstate Shipment in violation of Section Eighteen of US Code Six Fifty Nine. That is a felony, and if convicted you could be sentenced to a Federal Prison for up to ten years and or fined up to ten thousand dollars.

You have a right to remain silent..." Dodd was saying.

Cobb interrupted him and said, "Save it. I know it all by heart. Just give me the waiver to sign."

Dodd pointed to the waiver in front of Cobb. Cobb signed it and pushed it back. He took a swallow of coffee, wiped his mouth with the back of his hand and sat back in the chair.

"Here is the Reader's Digest version of the story. I got into a jam behind some gambling debts; you know playing the numbers. I was getting pressure to pay from a guy named Tony Capricio who works for Ricco Baroffio.

This was at the time of the Super Bowl. Oakland was the odds-on favorite, so I took Philly hoping they would upset the Raiders and I would score enough on the thirty seven to one odds that I could pay everybody off and have a little left. The Eagles lost, and suddenly my debt mushroomed from a couple thousand to over ten thousand dollars. I could not pay of course and the threats started to come in.

Then I get a call from Tony. He wants to know if I would be willing to work my debt off. I tell him sure as long as I don't have to commit murder.

He sets up a meet at Campisis' in Dallas; it is their favorite hang out. Do you know the place?" Cobb asked and chewed while watching for the reaction on Dodd.

Dodd smiled at the obvious ploy and nodded, "We know it. Go on with your story."

Cobb slurped some coffee and said, "I met Tony there. As I walked in, I saw Ricco sitting at a table in the back with some older guys. Tony took me into a back room, and this guy wearing a V&R Vending uniform comes in. The name of his shirt was Vinny. I later found out that his full name is Vinny Rossi and that he and Ricco are partners in the vending machine business."

Dodd interrupted, "Wait. What is Vinny's last name?"

"Rossi," Cobb said.

"Are you sure that this man is the Vinny Rossi?" Dodd asked.

Cobb said, "Yeah. Positive. The phone rang while Tony was setting up a run for me. The guy who took the call yelled out that it was for Tony. Tony wanted to know who it was. The guy said it was

Vinny Rossi and he had some information for Tony on the night's run."

Dodd said, "Okay, go ahead with what you want to tell us."

Cobb studied the agents and could tell that they were anxiously waiting what he had to say. ' *What they want to hear is what I know about Vinny and V&R Vending,*' he guessed.

"Like I was saying; this guy named Vinny Rossi came into where Tony was holding me. He had this V&R Vending uniform on, and he started telling me that I was going to be carried to a truck stop where the driver of a Peter Built pulling a tandem hook up would stop, get out of his truck and walk away. He said the driver would be wearing a Texas Tech baseball cap.

I was to wait until the guy was in the café and then walk over to the truck. Vinny said it would be unlocked and running. I was to climb in and drive it out of the parking area where I would see the same guy who carried me down to the truck stop. I was to follow him with the truck.

I did what they told me to and dropped the truck at the V&R Vending Warehouse at Ann Arbor and Lancaster Road in Dallas. I made a note of the address; it was Forty-three zero two South Lancaster Road.

I got into the pickup with my escort, and he took me back to my car.

The plan was to do that five times, and then I would be even with the house, debt free. I complained about the deal because just one run would net them eighty thousand pounds of cigarettes, plus what they would get for the truck and trailers. Do the math, and that comes out to a hell of a lot more than what I owed.

Tony and Vinny showed me the error of my thinking. They told me that my choice was to spend a few hours doing these jobs and walk away free or cross them and spend eternity at the bottom of the nearest lake.

There you are. That's their deal. They steal truckloads of cigarettes and put them in their warehouse. Then sell the equipment. They are making a killing!

One more thing, I overheard Tony and Vinny talking about some guy at a club called the "It'll Do" who refused to allow V&R to put their cigarette machines in his joint.

Tony told Vinny that Vegas had given him the green light and he had two torches set to handle the problem that night. The next morning I read that the place had been bombed and burned to the ground.

These guys mean business. They are also organized. I think you made a real mistake to pop me the way you did and leaving that truck sitting at the pumps. I figure you planned to try and grab whoever picked it up.

These guys are too smart for that. That truck and its' load were sold before I ever left Denison. Just before Gomez drove out of the parking lot, I saw the guy who took me to Denison.

I call him Scarface. He is an ugly dude with a scar on the left side of his face that runs from the temple down across his throat. He was staring right at me.

That means they saw Gomez pick me up, they saw her pull behind the restaurant, and they saw you two follow us out from behind the building and head downtown. They probably followed.

Odds are this whole thing has been compromised. I bet the call has already been made to Tony and Vinny that I am in custody. They can't take a chance that I will talk. A contract will be out on me before dark. That's why you have to put me in witness protection,"

Cobb sat back and looked at the agents. He saw how what he said impacted them. *'Yep, I'm right. They thought this was just a small time theft ring and now realize what they have stumbled into. Abraham Cobb Jacobs is a dead man, that is why he has to be reborn as someone else,'* his mind was made up.

"That's all I am going to say until I have a signed agreement for the protection program," he said and crossed his arms over his chest.

"How many runs did you make for them Cobb?" Dodd asked.

Cobb shook his head and smiled at Dodd, "Think of me as the silent man from whom you get nothing more until I have that written agreement."

CHAPTER 48
THE SHADOW

Campsi's was packed with the early evening crowd celebrating Friday and the end of another workweek. Tony was working the crowd, shaking hands and slapping backs while making sure that there were no infiltrators in the mix. A clap on the shoulder ended with a casual run of his hand down and across the back checking for a wire.

Ricco and Vinny were watching Tony. Each time he would 'clear' a table they would signal the waiter to serve the occupants a complimentary beer or glass of wine. The guests would then turn and pay their respects to Ricco.

As they did, Vinny made a note of the look on each face. Anyone who failed to present the brightest smile or in whom Vinny detected a trace of rancor would be politely but firmly removed from the table and escorted to the side room.

Vinny would check them for weapons and question them to determine the reason for their less than a full appreciation of the largeness of Ricco.

Tony saw Benito, the maître d', discreetly wave to him. Tony nodded and finished his conversation. Then he walked over, and Benito said, "I am so sorry Mr. Capricio, but Mr. Conti is in the side room and says he must speak with you on a matter of the upmost importance."

Tony patted Benito on the arm and said, "I didn't see him come in. But no matter I will speak with him now. Ask Mr. Rossi to join us please."

Tony stepped down the hall, parted the curtains and stepped into the room. Cicero Conti was pacing back and forth and had a deeply furrowed brow. He looked up at Tony and started to speak. Tony interrupted him saying, "Wait, I have asked Vinny to join us."

Vinny came through the curtains, and Tony nodded to Cicero, "Now, what is so important that you risk coming here?"

"The driver on the Laredo run has been arrested. Our shadow dropped him off in Denison and then drove ahead and waited. He picked him up as he passed through Austin.

As he followed him south, he realized that there was another car, a tan Chevrolet, with two men in it watching the truck. He dropped back and followed them both all the way into Laredo. Once our driver pulled into the truck stop, the tan Chevrolet passed by and parked across the street at a restaurant.

Our shadow pulled up to the pumps and acted like he was getting gasoline. The driver of our truck got out and was immediately approached by a woman in a pickup.

He got into the truck with the woman, and she drove into the same parking lot where the tan Chevrolet was sitting. But then she drove past the Chevrolet and behind the restaurant. The car followed her, and a few minutes later both the pickup and the car drove from behind the restaurant and headed downtown.

Our shadow says that Cobb was leaning forward in the seat and it appeared his hands were handcuffed behind his back. They drove downtown and into a parking garage under a building.

We have checked the address and find that it is leased to the United States Department of Justice. We ran the license plates on both the pickup and the Chevrolet. The registration is not reported.

It is safe to assume that our driver is in the custody of the FBI and they are interrogating him even now," Cicero said and fell silent.

"What about the truck and cigarettes?" Vinny asked.

"The buyers arrived while our shadow was putting gasoline into his vehicle. They saw him and parked at the pump next to him as if they were buying gasoline. As they stepped up to remove the hose from the pump our man told them that the deal had gone bad and to stay away from the truck. They finished gassing up and left.

The truck is still sitting at the truck stop. I would guess the feds are waiting nearby to arrest whoever comes for it," Cicero said with a shrug.

Vinny looked at Tony and asked, "What now?"

"Wait here," Tony said and walked from the room.

He gave Ricco a quick update and then waited for the old man to tell him what he wanted to do. Ricco sipped his wine, puffed on the cigar a couple of times and then motioned Tony to lean down so he could speak confidentially to him.

"Leave the truck, count it as a loss. Tell the buyer we will refund his money. Figure Cobb to talk. If he does, they will send him back and put a wire on him. Stay away from him.

I want you to put a watch on his house. Have a team ready to move as soon as he is seen. I want this mess cleaned up. Follow?" Ricco asked.

"I follow Mr. Baroffio. He lives with his mother and father. If they are in the house when our team arrives?" Tony knew the answer, but he wanted to be covered on the deal.

Ricco puffed the cigar again and said, "Clean the house."

Tony nodded knowing that he meant to leave no witnesses.

CHAPTER 49
DEATH WARRANT

Cobb read the contract through two times and then nodded his agreement saying, "This has everything I asked for. I see the signature block for the Assistant U.S. Attorney, Diane Bagwell, but she has not signed it.

Without her signature, this is just a bunch of words on paper. Why hasn't she signed it?" he asked.

Dodd glanced at the young woman sitting across the table from Cobb and said, "Her boss has told her not to sign it until she hears from him. We are just waiting for him to give her the go ahead."

"So, why is he hesitating? I know a curve ball when I see one, and I think I am about to see one. Let me think this through now; you show me this great offer of a new name, a new identification, relocation, lifetime support and even plastic surgery if necessary.

I get all excited about the possibilities, and then you throw the curve. This document goes away, and a new one is substituted. Only the next one will have a requirement that you didn't want me to see at first. But what could it be? Is it a wire? Is that it? Do you think I am stupid enough to believe that Ricco does not know I have been arrested?

I can assure you that his crew had eyes on that truck the minute we pulled into the truck stop. I have already told you about Scarface.

They know I have been popped. If I show up for a meeting with them, the first thing they will do is check me for a wire. If they find one, Abraham Cobb Jacobs, Jr. returns to the dust from whence he came. No way. Forget it. I am not wearing a wire," Cobb said.

"We know that Mr. Jacobs. We are not that stupid either. Here is what my boss is trying to get approved.

We take you to the jail and book you in, charged with Theft From Interstate Shipment. We walk away and leave you just like any other case we work.

A friendly reporter from the Laredo Morning Times will run a small piece from the police blotter along with your mug shot.

Then in two to three days, you make your first appearance before a Federal Magistrate. He will inform you of the charges against you, appoint you an attorney and set bond. Our reporter will run that story also.

In about three weeks, we will arrange for a bond reduction hearing, and you will be released. You will buy a bus ticket and return to Dallas. You will go back to your normal routine.

They will wait for a while, and then they will contact you. When they do, you act frightened and tell them you are finished. Do not agree to meet with them.

They will keep working you. You reluctantly agree to meet them in a public place, say the library downtown Dallas.

They will check you for wires and find none. You will continue to meet with them whenever they ask. They will check for wires each time but will find you clean. You tell them exactly what happened and that we tried to flip you.

Then you remind them of your previous conversation about becoming part of their operation. They will eventually trust you. We are in no hurry, just let this thing take its' course.

Then you will tell us where you are going to meet the next time. We will try to bug the place. But the odds are we will not be able to. So we will set up with a parabolic microphone and try to record the conversation from outside the meeting place.

If we get enough on the tape, you might not even have to testify. You will just disappear without a trace. How does that sound?" Ms. Bagwell asked.

"What if I say no," Cobb asked.

Dodd started to say, "Look Cobb…"

"Wait a minute Agent Dodd. Let me tell you *what if* Cobb. If you refuse this request, we will prosecute you to the fullest extent of the law, and I promise you that your sentence will be ten years in each case we have.

I will ask the judge to run the cases consecutively, which means that you will serve all ten years in the first case before you serve one day on the next. We have three solid cases. That means you will do every day of the next thirty years locked up.

That's what if, Mr. Jacobs. Take it or leave it. I don't care," Bagwell reached across the table and withdrew the first agreement.

She then took a second contract from her briefcase and slid it across the table. She dropped a pen on top of the contract and looked at Cobb with an arched eyebrow and said, "Try hitting that curve ball, Cobb."

Cobb sighed and said, "I find myself between the proverbial devil and the deep blue sea. I can say no and rot in hell. Or I can make a deal with the devil and hope to float.

I think I will hope to float." He signed the contract with a flourish and pushed it back to the lawyer.

She picked the pen up, signed Diane Bagwell in bold letters and said, "Smart move Mr. Jacobs because we hold all the cards." She looked at Dodd and said, "Lock him up and let's get this gig underway."

Cobb stood, and the agents handcuffed him. Gomez took him by the arm and led him toward the elevators. He looked at her and said, *"I feel like I just signed my death warrant."*

CHAPTER 50
CLEAN THE HOUSE

Tony had just sat down for lunch when the phone rang. He took a bite of his sandwich and stared at Benito.

Benito turned to look in his direction and raised his shoulders in a questioning shrug. Tony nodded, and Benito walked over with the phone. "It is New Orleans," he whispered.

Tony grabbed the phone and said, "Yes sir?"

"Cobb has been released on bond. He caught a cab to the Greyhound bus station where he bought a ticket to Dallas. He will arrive at nine tonight. We expect a call no later that three, tomorrow morning. See to it," the caller said and hung up.

Tony wiped his mouth and tossed the napkin aside. He called Benito over to the table and said, "Keep everyone away from me until I say different." He waived Benito away and dialed Ricco.

"Yes?" Ricco answered.

"Just got a call from New Orleans. Cobb has been released on bond. He is riding a Greyhound back to Dallas. He gets in at nine tonight. The boss wants a call no later than three o'clock tomorrow morning. What do you want me to do?" Tony asked.

"Take care of it," Ricco said.

"But I thought we had said that it looked like he was keeping his mouth shut and that we should wait and see what he can tell us," Tony said.

"That is what Vegas wanted to do. New Orleans overruled them. This is Dixie business. So do it," Ricco said and broke the connection.

Tony sighed deeply and dialed Alberto. "Cobb is headed to Dallas on a bus. He should be here by nine. I expect to hear that the house has been cleaned."

Tony hung up the phone and waved Benito back over, "Bring me a fresh sandwich, a cold Bud Light and see to it that I can eat in peace."

Aberto pushed the button down on the hook and immediately released it. He dialed the number for Lucio and waited. On the third ring, he heard the connection made and then, "Si?"

"We have a house to clean. I will pick you up in fifteen minutes," Aberto said.

"Si," Lucio replied, and the connection was broken.

Aberto had been expecting the call. He stepped into the bathroom, pulled a plastic shower cap over his hair and walked to his hall closet. He grabbed his "go bag" and walked out the door.

There was no need to check the bag; he knew what was in it. But still, he went over it in his mind, *'The sweeper loaded with Buckshot, a five round box of twelve gauge slugs, the Berretta nine loaded with fourteen rounds of hollow points and an extra magazine with thirteen more. The plastic gloves, the mask, the tape and the soft cloth are there. But I probably won't need anything except the gloves. Yep, I have all I need to clean the place. Lucio will have his stuff ready too.'*

The drive was a short one. Lucio lived just six blocks from Aberto, close enough for support but far enough that it would take a coordinated effort to catch them both in the same net.

He parked as close to Lucio's garage door as possible. He saw the door opening even before he had the car stopped. *'Lucio is so dependable,'* he thought.

Lucio tossed his bag in the back and settled in the front with Aberto. "Ready?" Aberto asked. Lucio nodded.

Aberto backed the car out and turned it toward Central Expressway. Neither man spoke until Aberto had turned north and merged with the traffic.

The wind and rain were savaging the streets and traffic was almost non-existent. There were a few cars pulling off of the roadway, seeking shelter beneath the overpasses. Aberto moved into the center lane and set a slow, but steady pace toward Plano.

Lucio shifted in the seat so that he was partially turned toward Aberto. "Mi brevi," he said.

"I will brief you but in English. I want you to practice your English, it is important," Aberto said.

"Okay, I will try," Lucio, stammered.

"The one that we have been waiting for will arrive in Dallas at nine. We will set up outside his house and wait until they are all inside. Then we will make entry and clean the house.

There will not be many people on the streets in this storm. But still, I have changed the plates on the car and we will drive it straight back to the warehouse afterward. It will be chopped and scattered by the time the sun comes up. Do you have your hair net on?" he asked.

"Si, I mean yes," Lucio smiled.

"Good, very good Lucio. Now, where were we? Ah yes. The storm will reduce the traffic in the neighborhood thus the number of potential witnesses.

Once inside the house, we will take command of all the subjects. We will wait for a flash of lightening and time the crash of the thunder. Once we have the timing down, we will use the thunder to cover our shots. The shotguns will be especially loud and tend to attract attention in a residential neighborhood.

We will walk through the house to be sure we are not missing anything and then leave quietly and quickly. Any questions?" Aberto asked.

"Why are we killing them all? Why not just the snitch?" Lucio asked.

Aberto had thought about that a lot. He was a professional killer, but he did not consider himself a cold-blooded killer.

He was a man of honor. It is what his father had taught him, *'to kill one who needs to be killed can be done honorably. Treat the target honorably and kill them quickly.'* But this job requires the killing of the target and his parents. Simply because they will be witnesses and there can be no witnesses. The stakes are too high for the organization. He understood it, but it still had the stench of dishonor about it.

"We are killing them all Lucio because we do not know what Cobb has told his parents. There is just too much risk, so they must die. We will treat them with honor, but we must kill them," Aberto said.

Lucio stared straight ahead for a long while. Then he said, "I will follow your lead as always. But I want to go to confession afterward. Father Nazario can be trusted. He will hear my confession and grant me absolution."

Aberto shook his head back and forth slowly, "You cannot go to the priest Lucio. Father Nazario is a compassionate man, but he is still a priest.

He will not grant you absolution for this thing unless you assure him that you will return to the Church and not engage in such activity again.

If you do that and Tony or Ricco find out, they will kill you. No. You listen to me; go to Mass if you must. Confess to God and ask Him to forgive you. But do not tell the priest."

Lucio said nothing but Aberto could not press the matter further because they had arrived at the Fifteenth Street Exit for Plano. He took the exit and drove through the intersection and turned right onto Eighteenth Street.

"I have driven this several times Lucio. The target will be in the house at Seventeen Twenty-Four Foreman Court, which sits on the corner of Foreman Court and Eighteenth Street. We are four miles from that location. There is a church half a block west of the house. It sits on the corner of Avenue P and Eighteenth Street. We will park on the side of the church.

We can find cover in an unlighted part of the parking lot. The house has a front entry garage, so we have a perfect view of their arrival.

After they are in the house, we will drive past the house and turn onto Avenue R. That will take us to Willow Lane. Willow is a circular street that comes back out onto Eighteenth Street next to the side yard of the target house. There is a house for sale on the corner. We will park in the drive of that house and walk to the target house.

A privacy fence runs alongside the target house and joins the house at the front bedroom window. We will go over the fence and walk up to the window. The telephone wires are right beside the window. We will cut them and then we will force the window and make our entry into the house.

Once inside, we take command. You will hold the mother and father in their bedroom. I will escort the target into the front bedroom and execute him.

I will join you in the master bedroom, and we will execute the parents. Do you have any questions?" Aberto asked while parking the car next to the church.

"How long before they are here?" Lucio asked.

Aberto pulled the sleeve of his jacket up and looked at his wristwatch. "It is nine twenty-five p.m. so they should be on their way here. Give them forty-five minutes in this storm, and they will be in the house by ten-fifteen say ten-thirty at the latest. We will make entry twenty minutes after that and by eleven o'clock we will be on our way back to Dallas," Aberto said and settled back for the wait.

•   •   •

The wind caught the bus and pushed it toward the bridge railing. There was a gasp from the passengers and Cobb looked toward the driver. He noticed that the driver was leaning forward trying to see through the driving rain. *'He is gripping that steering wheel so tightly that his knuckles have turned white,'* Cobb thought.

Another rogue gust hit the bus, and the passengers gasped again. The driver looked into the big mirror over his seat and said in a loud voice, "It is okay folks. Once we cross this bridge, we turn into downtown Dallas, and the station is two blocks straight ahead. The tall buildings will keep this wind off of us, and we can pull in under the covered parking and get away from the rain. Just hold on now, here we go."

The driver eased the big Greyhound into the center lane and made a sweeping right turn into the terminal. "Here you are, folks, safe and sound in Big D. You can always take our bus and leave the driving to us," he said with a huge smile and lots of relief showing on his tired face.

Cobb was the first one to step down off of the non-stop from Laredo. His mom stepped up and grabbed his arm. "Oh son, we were so worried. It is a blessing from the Lord Himself that you all made here in this storm," June Jacobs stood on tiptoes and pecked her son on his cheek.

"Where is dad, mom? I am so ready to get home," Billy said.

"He is waiting in the car around the corner. The depot manager has reserved a lane on the other side to serve as a pickup lane. Come on, let's get out of here," she said leading the way through the press of people.

Cobb saw the black Lincoln drive into the pickup lane and pulled his mother in that direction, "Here he is mom, back this way."

Abe Jacobs saw his son and wife and drove the car into the inside lane and stopped. June opened the front and Cobb the back door. They settled in, and Abe piloted the big car through the mini traffic jam and out from under the cover into the flooding streets.

"I am going to take it slow and easy in this storm, but we will be home soon. Why don't you tell us where you have been son?" he glanced back at Cobb.

"Dad, I'm too tired right now. Let's just get home and get a good nights' sleep. I will fill you guys in tomorrow," Cobb said as he laid his head back against the leather headrest.

"Fair enough son. Next stop Plano," Abe said and focused on driving through the rain and the wind.

CHAPTER 51
THE NIGHT WALKER

Billy Jack drained the last drop of Old Crow. He savored the harshness of the bourbon, relished the burning trail it left as it flowed down his throat and into his stomach. The more it hurt, the more he wanted.

He tilted the empty bottle, hoping for one more drop. It was dry. He slammed it against the far wall. The bottle shattered sending glass bouncing across the wood floor and under his bed.

He lifted himself from the chair, staggered across the room and fell onto the bed. Fatigue overcame his fear, and he fell into the swirling darkness. From out of the darkness there came a face and then another.

'You sorry little bastard! That is what you are, the bastard issue of heathen scum. It was your heathen blood warring against your white blood that led you to kill me. I am taking my name from you. No longer will you be an Edwards. You are a Ship. I am waiting for you here in hell,' the old man laughed and faded.

Billy Jack rolled onto his belly and buried his face in the pillow. But still the face of Jimmy Olson floated in, *'my spirit cannot rest as long as you are free. Your grandfather cannot cross over, but his spirit has assisted me in making a deal with the evil that resides within you. I will have my rest soon.'*

"No, get away from me," Billy Jack stood beside the bed. The burn had gone from his belly, and the cramping was beginning.

Billy Jack grabbed his hat and the keys to his truck. He staggered across the yard, stumbling over objects hidden by the dark. The clouds blew over, and the dull light of the moon directed him to the truck. He felt something crawling over his legs and then the pain hit.

Billy Jack turned the interior lights of the truck on and looked at his legs. Giant red ants were swarming up and over his boots, inside his pants and attacking his exposed skin.

Billy screamed as the first of the invaders found his crotch. He bolted from the truck and peeled his pants off. He sat on the ground and began to push the ants off of his legs.

He kicked his pants away and sprinted naked from the waist down to the faucet outside of his trailer. He grabbed the water hose and opened the tap as far as it would go.

The cold water jetted forth blasting the ants from his rapidly swelling legs. He moved the stream to his testicles and penis. The ants were everywhere, and the relief of the cooling water disappeared as soon as he moved the stream to another area demanding relief.

Another break in the clouds allowed the moon to light the yard. Billy looked back to where he had seen an ant bed yesterday. The mound was broken and scattered. Thousands of soldier ants were swarming, looking for the one responsible for the destruction of their home.

He could feel a change in the atmosphere; he knew that he had passed from one dimension to another. He had traveled back to that day of his boyhood when he had used the ten-gauge shotgun to blow his grandfather off of the porch. His body had landed on a mound of giant red ants just like the ones devouring his flesh now.

He watched as the ants covered the dead body of his grandfather, filling his gaping mouth. Billy remembered that there were so many climbing over and into his grandfathers' staring eyes that his eyeballs appeared to be moving. Billy heard his grandfather's cries as the ants invaded his body through the gaping wound in his chest.

The water was no longer helping his pain. He dropped the hose and made for the truck. He crawled in and fired it up. One thing was on his mind as he drove out of the yard, '*Big Tree Liquor Store. Got to get me some whiskey. That will take the pain away and make the memories fade,'* he whispered to himself.

The lights of the crossroads stood out in the distance. Billy pushed the gas pedal all the way to the floor, and the old red truck flew down the road. He raced through the flashing traffic signal and stood on the brakes.

The truck started to slide. It left the roadway and slid down the slope of the graveled shoulder. Billy could feel the wheels loose traction, and then the truck went over and began to roll.

Billy fell into the roof of the tumbling truck. He heard voices singing; it was a chant. Then he saw them, the ancient ones gathering around a figure. He looked closely and saw that he was the one they were gathered around.

Billy looked back at the truck and saw his body being ejected. He watched as the bouncing truck rolled over him. He felt the crushing pain, and then it was gone. He watched as his spirit left his body, flowed out from under the truck and lifted up from the ground to join the council of ancient ones.

'This is not so bad. The pain is gone, and I am with my people,' was the thought racing through his mind.

The chant stopped. No one spoke, but in his spirit, he heard, *'You have dishonored our blood. You owe much for the evil you have done. Your destiny is to be an outcast; you will walk these hills alone. You will never again walk in the sun. Darkness will be your abode. Depart from us now Night Walker.'*

CHAPTER 52
KILLING WITH HONOR

Aberto shook the slumbering Lucio, "Wake up, they are here."

Lucio sat up in time to see the taillights of the big Town Car disappear inside the garage of the house across the street. Neither man said anything until the garage door had gone down and they saw lights come on inside the house.

Aberto looked at Lucio and said, "Here we go. Be ready."

He started the car and allowed it to roll slowly away from the church, out of the shadows and onto the street. Alberto followed his planned route and cut his lights as he approached the vacant house.

He drove into the driveway and cut the engine. They sat still for several minutes watching for any sign that their arrival had been noted by anyone. All the houses remained dark with the only illumination coming from the streetlights and the bright flashes of lightning.

Aberto reached into the back seat and grabbed his go bag. He pulled the wool cap down over his face, turned the collar of his jacket up and stepped into the storm. Lucio followed and they were soon running between the houses, making their way to the target's home.

Aberto dropped his bag beside the stockade fence and settled his foot into the clasped hands of Lucio. He pushed himself up and grasped the top of the fence. He swung himself over and dropped quietly into the yard.

Aberto moved to the front gate and lifted the latch. He pushed the gate open, and Lucio slid through with both go bags. The men flattened themselves against the brick wall of the house and listened.

Aberto took the knife from its' sheath on his belt and prepared to slash the window screen. A flash of lightning illuminated the entire yard, and Alberto saw the phone lines. He grasped them in one hand and cut them with his knife.

Aberto crept up to the window and leaned over to look in. To his surprise, the window was unlocked and hand been raised a few inches. '*An open window, good for us and bad for them,*' he mused.

He could see that there was no one in the back bedroom. He slipped his knife into the screen and whipped it across. He sheathed the knife and placed his hands through the long slit in the screen. A quick tug and the screen popped out. Aberto sat it on the ground beside the air conditioning condensing unit. He placed one foot on the condenser and hoisted himself up and through the window.

Lucio handed him his go bag, and Aberto sat it on the bed. He pulled Lucio through the window and then kneeled beside the open door to peek down the hallway. He saw no one but could hear voices at the end of the hallway. '*The voices are coming from the kitchen,*' he reasoned.

There was no need for talk; each man recognized that the plan had to be adjusted to meet the circumstance. They unzipped their bags, removed their weapons and moved down the hall toward the voices.

Aberto stopped just outside the kitchen door. He looked down and saw that the carpet where he was standing was wet. '*My shoes are wet. I have to be careful they don't slip on that tile floor,*' he thought.

He listened carefully and could tell that there were only two people in the kitchen. One voice was that of a young man, and the other was a woman.

He looked back and saw Lucio watching him. He held up two fingers and pointed at the kitchen. He then pointed across the living room toward the closed door that he guessed was the master bedroom.

Lucio nodded and started creeping that way. Aberto slung his shotgun over his shoulder and pulled his Colt Commander forty-five from his belt. He looked up to see Lucio standing outside the closed bedroom door and nodded. Lucio opened the door, and Alberto stepped into the kitchen.

Cobb saw him first. He jumped up from the chair he had been sitting in and screamed, *"Run mom."*

The woman looked over her shoulder and bolted for the door leading from the kitchen into the garage. She placed her left hand on the refrigerator door and her right hand on the doorknob. She managed to open the door before Aberto clamped his left hand around her wrist. He pulled her back, away from the door and she stumbled, losing her balance.

Aberto waited until she had regained her balance and was facing him in an upright position. Then he shot her through the heart.

The heavy slug pushed her back against the door, and she slid down it to sit on the floor. Blood spread across her chest and dripped onto the nightgown covering her legs.

Aberto turned the pistol on Cobb just as Lucio's pistol exploded. Aberto looked into Cobb's eyes and saw that the man knew he was next.

"Please, let me pray first," Cobb asked.

Aberto nodded, "Of course," he said.

Lucio stepped into the kitchen, and Aberto asked, "Is the old man dead?"

"Yes. His hearing aids were on the table beside the bed. He did not hear your shot. He never woke. I put a pillow over his face and fired one round through it into his brain," Lucio said.

"Did you check for a pulse?" Aberto asked.

Lucio nodded and said, "Yes, he is dead."

"Did you leave him in an honorable composure?" Aberto asked.

"Yes, I placed his hands on his chest, pulled the covers up to rest just below them and turned the bedside lamp on. He does not rest in darkness," Lucio said.

Aberto pointed to Cobb and said to Lucio, "Take him to the back room and wait for me.

Lucio walked Cobb down the hall, and Aberto kneeled before the mother. He saw a gold bracelet on her left wrist and bent to look at it.

'*June,*' he read.

He gently eased her body down to lie full length on the floor. He placed her legs together so that they were resting ankle to ankle.

He pulled her gown down and arranged it, so she was covered from the knees up. He lifted her hands off of the floor and folded them over her chest. He then stood and crossed himself. He turned to walk from the room and said silently, '*May your rest be peaceful, June.*'

Aberto walked into the back room and found Billy on his knees beside the bed. He had placed a black Yakama on his head and had a prayer shawl draped over his shoulders. He was holding a bible in his hands and rocking back and forth as he read the twenty-third Psalm.

Aberto motioned to Lucio to pick their bags up and then to move out of the way. Lucio lifted the bags and moved into the corner behind Aberto.

Aberto pushed the forty-five into his belt and brought the shotgun down off of his shoulder. He placed the barrel of the shotgun against the base of Cobb's bowed head and waited.

A flash of lightning filled the room. The roll of the thunder began, and Aberto pulled the trigger.

Blood, bone and brain spewed out of Cobb's opened skull. It bounced off of the ceiling and covered the walls.

One of Billy's eyes landed on and stuck to Aberto's gloved left hand. The eye seemed to be staring at him, carrying conviction and a measure of condemnation.

Aberto shook the eyeball off of his glove and watched as it bounced once on the carpet and came to rest in the corner of the room. The eye rolled over in a half turn, so the pupil was again fixed on him.

He turned away and grabbed his bag from Lucio. He stripped off his gloves, the mask and his jacket now splattered with Cobb. He stuffed them into the bag.

Then he placed his weapons on top of the jacket and zipped the bag closed. Aberto turned to Lucio and said, "Let's do a walk-through of the house and be sure we are not leaving any evidence.

I noticed that our wet shoes left some prints on the tiled floor in the kitchen and on the carpet in the hallway. Grab a mop and clean those prints up in the kitchen, I will get a towel and wipe down the carpet. Be sure to check the old man's room."

Lucio pointed at Cobb who was now slumped forward with the bloody stump of a neck resting on the floor in front of his knees and asked, "Do we leave him like this or do we arrange him in an honorable position?"

"Leave him as he is. He is responsible for the death of his parents, and he snitched us off to the feds. There is no honor in that," Aberto said and turned away.

Twenty minutes later Aberto walked down the hallway and out the front door. Lucio followed.

They settled into their car and drove away. They passed the Plano City Limits sign and stopped at the next gas station. Aberto dropped a coin into the slot of the phone and dialed slowly.

"The house has been cleaned," he said and hung up the phone.

CHAPTER 53
THE GUARDIAN

The judge walked from the courtroom and hung his robe in the closet. "What a docket! I just want to sit quietly for a few minutes. Hold all of my calls please," he said as he dropped into his chair.

"Sorry Judge. But the Plano Police dispatcher is on the phone. They need you at a house out on Eighteenth Street," the clerk said.

"What do they have out there?" he asked.

"Three dead bodies. Lieutenant Johnny Mock is the commander on the scene, and he is asking for you. He said it looks like a father, mother and son have been executed. He thinks it is a professional hit," Shelia said.

"Johnny Mock is one of the best. If he says it was a hit, then I am willing to bet it is a hit," the Judge said standing and reaching for his briefcase. He started for the door, and the phone rang. He stopped and looked toward Debra, his clerk who had answered the call. He heard her say, "I will tell him."

"That was the superintendent's office. A man called the office to report that a teacher molested him when he was a student in the District. The superintendent wants you to meet with the man at two o'clock this afternoon," Debra said and hung up the phone.

The Judge sat back down in his chair and dialed the number for the Detective Division of the Plano Police Department. When the phone was answered, he said, "This is Judge Bangs. Let me speak with Detective Beth Chaney."

"Hey Judge, this is Beth. What can I do for you?"

"Beth, remember our conversation and suspicions about Joe Bates and his relationship with kids?" he asked.

"Yep. I still believe that with that much smoke there has to be some fire," she said.

"Me too. I just got a call from the superintendent's office that a former student wants to meet with me a two o'clock to talk about a teacher who molested him when he was a student in the District. I'm willing to bet it is going to Billy Weems and that he wants to talk about Bates.

I would like for you to be there too. Can you meet me in my office at the administration building about one-thirty so we can talk about how we want to handle this?" the Judge asked.

"Yes, sir. I remember Billy Weems. He was a basketball star, and Bates was dating his mother. I knew that the kid was lying when he said Bates was not abusing him. I've been waiting on this for a long time. I will see you at one-thirty in your office Judge," Beth said and hung up the phone.

The Judge sat for a few seconds thinking, '*I had a full docket this morning, applying the law to the evidence as a guardian of justice.*

Now, an entire family has been murdered in their home. Their spirits cry out for justice and it is our responsibility as guardians to find those who have done this and bring them to justice.

Next, one who has suffered abuse by a wolf in sheep's clothing waits for his justice. We will hear him out, he will have his justice and the wolf will be removed from the flock.

There was urgency in his stride as he hurried from the office. The flock was at risk, and he was a *GUARDIAN.*

THE END

EPILOGUE

The Cloud of Witness

The arrest of Issac Newton completed the '*round up*' of the vicious gang who were responsible for the killing of Garth Binkle; the 66 year old security guard who confronted the gang as they stormed the Big World Liquor Store.

Newton and his gang had a modus operandi that included the use of white medical tape to bind the hands and feet of their victims. The non-adhesive side of this tape has a smooth surface.

Criminals always make mistakes. The gang failed to wear gloves when wrapping one of the victim's hands with the tape. The smooth side of the tape held Newton's fingerprints. Because he had a criminal record we were able to identify him as being one of the armed robbers.

He was convicted and sentenced to death for the murder of Mr. Binkle. After he had been sentenced and was serving his sentence, the death sentence was declared to be unconstitutional (The United States Supreme Court decision in Furman v. Georgia (408 U.S. 238 (1972)) and he was resentenced to life without parole.

The Beast Gets Loose

Benny McBay was sixteen years old at the time Tyree killed Jaylee and Perry Ray. He was certified as an adult and tried for the theft of the money from the Burger King and as being an accessory to the murder of Perry Ray. He was not charged in connection with the abduction, rape and murder of Mary Lynn. He was sentenced to not less than five or more than 99 years in the Institutional Division of Texas Department of Corrections.

Tyree used the money from the Burger King to make his way to El Paso, Texas. His first thought was to cross into Mexico but changed his mind when he saw the Mexican Immigration officers questioning and checking the identification of those crossing the border.

He was wandering through the downtown section when he saw an Armed Forces Recruiting Center (an area containing the recruiting offices of all branches of the military) and remembered what Benny had said about his father. He tried to enlist in the Air Force and the Navy but both refused him because he did not have sufficient identification or a high school diploma.

A recruiter for the Army had watched Tyree and hailed him as he left the Naval recruiting office. Tyree told the recruiter he had been turned down because he did not have a high school diploma. The Navy's recruiter verified this but failed to mention that Tyree did not have the required birth certificate and that his driver's license was suspect.

The army recruiter listened to Tyree's life story and felt compassion for him. After much string pulling and waivers, Tyree was able to enlist, using Perry Ray Gholson's name and date of birth and was assigned to a transportation unit in Italy.

His intention was to fashion a new life with a new identity and to never return to Texas. However, while the *beast* was suppressed, it was not dead. It escaped again when an Italian girl refused Tyree's advances. He waited for her to leave the bar where he had seen her, followed her home and waited until she had turned all the lights out in her apartment. Believing her to be in bed and asleep, he broke the glass in her front door and reached through to open the dead lock.

But she had not been asleep. She heard the glass break and called the police. They arrived while the *beast* was attacking the girl. Tyree was arrested and convicted of criminal sexual assault.

After serving his time in the Italian penal system he was surrendered to the United States Marshal Service and brought home to face murder charges in Texas. Benny McBay agreed to testify against Tyree in exchange for being released on parole. He had already served six years.

Tyree was convicted of three counts of murder, abduction and rape. He was sentenced to life on each of the counts. The judge stacked or required that one sentence be completed before the next began. Tyree Dobbs will die in prison.

Taken

Linda Sweat recovered and was able to testify against Le Roi Reneau. He was convicted of Aggravated Kidnapping and rape. He was sentenced to 40 years in the Texas Department of Corrections. He was denied parole three times and served every day of his sentence. Le Roi was released three days short of his seventy-fifth birthday. His records reflect that he intended to return to Dallas, but nothing is known of him after he left prison.

The LampLighter Inn

The murder of Joram Amine is the only murder case that K.W. worked that he was never able to solve. All of the evidence pointed to Joram's *'summer wife'* Fadilah Diveck being complicit in the murder.

K.W. chose not to file the case on circumstantial evidence. Murder has no statute of limitation. That means that should evidence sufficient to convict be discovered at a later date, the case can still be filed. But because of double jeopardy, if the case was filed and Fadilah was acquitted she could never be tried again.

Before leaving the scene, K.W. had laid hands on Joram's body and promised him justice. For years afterward K.W. would have dreams in which Joram's head would float up beside the bed and say, *"You promised me justice."*

These dreams became so disturbing that K.W. sought spiritual relief and sat in a session where the contract he had made with the dead was cancelled and deliverance from the dreams was prayed for. The connection with Joram was broken and the dreams have not returned.

Lemonade and Omelets –

K.W. advised his superiors that the payroll robbery in France had all the earmarks of an inside job. After consultation with the FBI and the United States State Department the French government directed the French National Police to investigate that possibility.

After interviewing the former Maritime Police officers working for

TI Security in France, the National Police broke the case. The payroll money was recovered. It is unknown what if any actions were taken against the Officers involved in the robbery. TI France fired all the security officers involved.

Lubbock International –

The arrest of Cisneros, Pete and Willis by K.W. and Special Agent Charlie Tulling at Lubbock International Airport broke the smuggling case wide open. Faced with federal smuggling charges, the three suspects flipped and gave the government the names of those involved domestically.

Working those individuals and the undercover agent within the TI plant, U.S. Customs agents were able to identify and arrest those involved in Taiwan.

After this event, all TI products entering the US from Taiwan were quarantined until agents inspected them with dogs trained to detect narcotics.

Back To The Badge ~ The Plano Police Department

Being promoted to sergeant and returning to patrol division was a major turning point in K.W. 's life as a *guardian*. He was deeply conflicted.

His major function as a patrol sergeant was to provide supervision for officers in the field. If performed properly these duties would preclude his pursuit of his passion to seek out and bring to justice those who worked the streets seeking to kill, steal and devour.

After much prayer and consultation with his wife, K.W. resigned his commission as a Dallas Police Officer and moved into a role of Investigations Management with Texas Instruments, Incorporated.

He enjoyed the work but there was an empty space, a constant ache in the center of his being. The payroll robbery in France accentuated his yearning to return to the public sector.

K.W. applied for and was hired by his hometown police department. He was once again a commissioned peace officer with the primary function of being a *guardian*.

The Cold Case –

The murder of Shirlene Minkus has never been solved. Her spirit asks for justice and the *guardians* will continue to look for those responsible.

The Skull ~ The Rolex ~ The Ring

Bobby Atkinson, also known as Bobbie Allen, strangled Jeremy Spurgeon during their sexual liaison. He put the body into the Lincoln and drove to the projects, dragged the body into the wooded area and dumped it into the creek.

He sold the Lincoln to a chop shop on South Oakland Avenue for five hundred dollars. Bobby used the five hundred to travel to St. Louis where he knew a former prison cellmate, Damien Seals, would welcome him.

Damien introduced Bobby to Walter Teats; a pawnshop owner who Damien knew took stolen goods. Walter bought the Rolex from Bobby for fifteen hundred dollars.

Bobby used the money to rent an apartment and remained in St. Louis. During the warm summer days Bobby worked for a swimming pool service company. He worked the streets as a male prostitute during the evening hours. When the weather turned cold the pool service let him go. The cold natured *Bobbie* could not stand to work the streets and began burglarizing houses.

He sold the jewelry taken form the baseball player's house to Damien. He took the Ring to Walter.

Walter recognized the ring as the one on the flyer as soon as he saw it. He wanted the five thousand dollar reward and called the greater St. Louis Crime Stoppers. For some unknown reason, Walter failed to elect the option to remain anonymous.

St. Louis detectives contacted Walter at his pawnshop. They became suspicious of his story and conducted a routine inventory of his shop. They found several items that had been reported stolen.

The officers arrested Walter for receiving and concealing stolen property. He had two prior felony convictions. A third conviction would result in him being classified as a habitual offender; and receive an automatic life sentence with no possibility of parole.

In an effort to avoid being charged as a habitual offender, Walter began giving the officers information on numerous crimes and those who had committed them. Included in that spill of information was the Rolex that Bobby had sold him. He told the officers that he believed Bobby had murdered the owner of the watch. He also told the officers that Bobby had told him that he was headed back to Dallas.

The detectives ran Jeremy Spurgeon's name and the information on the Rolex through the NCIC. They found the listing and called the Dallas Police Department.

After receiving the call from the St. Louis Police, Dallas officers began looking for Bobby. They found him working the streets, as a male prostitute, around the bus stations in downtown Dallas.

Bobby was arrested and during interrogation confessed to the murder of Jeremy Spurgeon. He pled guilty to Capital Murder in exchange for the State not seeking the death penalty.

He is doing life without the possibility of parole. He told the Judge at his sentencing that prison posed no threat to him. It was, he said, *'like casting Br'er Rabbit into the briar patch.'*

The Plano ISD -

After a year with the Plano Police Department, K.W. was recruited by Dr. H. Wayne Henderick to become the first police/security specialist for the Plano Independent School District (District).

Plano ISD is a large District, with some 56,000 students, 7,500 employees and facilities in five cities of the Metroplex (the greater Dallas area). The vast majority of the employees are dedicated to education and the welfare of kids. However, as in any large organization there are those who violate the policy, break the law and take advantage of the most vulnerable in our society. The men and women of the Plano ISD Police Security Services were their guardians.**

The cases recounted herein are a mere fraction of the cases K.W. worked during his years with the District.

The Filter Dump -

Those involved in the scheme to defraud the taxpayers with the theft of the HVAC filters waived indictment and pled guilty in State District Court. Each received a probated sentence that included fines and restitution.

Violations of the Federal Firearms Act of 1938 charges were filed against Sam Turner and Shelton Ricks. They both pled guilty and received probated sentences.

The Freezer Run –

Plano ISD (District) like all public school districts participates in a federal program to provide food for low-income children. The District received both money and food commodities from the United States Department of Agriculture. Those commodities included such things as meat, powdered milk, eggs, butter, flour, sugar, etc.

Jean Steeps rented cold storage units in Garland and charged the cost of the rentals to the District. She was able to justify this because the District lacked the facilities needed to store the commodities and there were no such commercial facilities located within the District.

She soon realized that no one was keeping an inventory of the products stored in Garland or of the products removed for use within the District. She then rented additional cold storage units but failed to make declaration of the additional rentals.

She then began to skim from the District's commodities and place them in her *'undeclared'* units. She used these commodities in the production of food for her private catering business. She was bold enough to fill orders for the District and charge them for the food made from their own commodities.

Recognizing the lax oversight in the food service, warehouse operations, Jean and her husband began to develop bid specifications that favored his employer. This was so successful that he was soon promoted to Vice-President for Institutional Sales.

This *'cooking of the specs'* and giving favoritism to her husband's employer netted Jean and her husband tens of thousands of dollars in sales commissions.

K.W. interviewed Joe Washington. Joe willingly told of the many 'freezer runs' he had made for Jean. During the interview K.W. learned that every run Joe made ended with him depositing the load at a campus of the District.

K.W. knew the evidentiary links were lacking so he made a referral to the District Attorney for their review and decision on how to proceed.

Jean was charged with violation of the State Bid Law and pled true. She escaped jail time because an error in the charging instrument presented by the District Attorney referred to a section of the law that had no penalty clause for the alleged conduct.

The Federal Department of Agriculture (FDA) declined to prosecute on her use of the commodities for personal gain. The FDA had no records indicating what or how many commodities had been delivered to the District and when. Thus they could not prove what was taken.

The District allowed Jean to resign her position. Her husband was never charged.

The Lie

The case involving Joe Bates came to a close when one of his victims came forward as an adult. He confirmed what the *guardians* had long suspected but had not been able to prove.

The District supported the Plano police detectives in their investigation of Bates. A warrant for his arrest was obtained and K.W. called him with instructions to report to the Police Security Services Offices at the District administration building.

Bates fled but later called K.W. using his cell phone. It was determined that the call had originated from a public park near Lake Lavon in Collin County, Texas. K.W. "*talked*" a Collin County Sheriff's unit to the location.

The Deputy saw Bates vehicle and initiated a traffic stop on him. Bates did stop his vehicle and sat quietly as the Deputy approached him. As the deputy stepped up beside his car Bates produced a firearm and shot himself in the head.

He was flown by helicopter to a hospital and survived his wounds. He was convicted and sentenced to prison for his years of sexually abusing young boys who were his students.

Clean The House

The murder of Cobb and his parents has never been solved. It is an open case and the *guardians* will never stop looking for those responsible.

Judge Bangs

K.W. ran for and was elected to the office of Justice of the Peace for Collin County, Texas in 1980. Texas law allowed him to hold the office of Justice of the Peace and Director of Police for the Plano Independent School District simultaneously.

The Justice of The Peace is an elected office created by the Texas Constitution. The elected official serves as a Magistrate of the State of Texas. The purpose of the office is to make a court of law available to the people on a local level. The elected official serves as the Presiding Judge for a court of General Jurisdiction. He hears cases involving civil law, criminal law, and administrative law.

He is also charged with the responsibility to conduct inquests into all deaths occurring within a jail or outside a doctor's supervision in counties that do not have a medical examiner. In this duty he determines the cause and manner of death and may enlist a licensed medical doctor to assist him in making that determination. He also determines who is responsible for a criminal or negligent homicide and makes the appropriate referrals for further investigation and or prosecution.

In Texas, all citizens have the constitutional right to an examining trial prior to charges being presented to a grand jury in any and all felony cases. The Justice of The Peace conducts these hearings.

K.W. served as Justice of the Peace for eight years, or two terms. He was defeated in his bid for a third term after his opponent and the local press mounted a campaign to challenge his ability to perform the duties of both offices.

K.W. continued to serve as the Director of Police, Security, and Student Safety Services for the District. He retired in 2002 after twenty-five years with the District and a total of thirty-five years in public safety and law enforcement.

But his call to be a guardian was still as fresh as the day he was called to duty with the Dallas Police Department. He and his wife answered that call by moving to Gateway Farm outside of New Boston, Texas. There they established Christian Ambassadors Gateway Farm.

They obtained a license from the State of Texas and for the next ten years provided a home, a hope and a future for abused and neglected children who were in the care of the Texas Department of Family and Protective Services, Child Protective Services.

Ken was fond of telling those who answered the call to love these kids that they were changing generations. They were true *guardians*.

ILLUSTRATIONS

WARRANT OF APPOINTMENT

No. 1657

The State of Texas
CITY OF DALLAS

KNOW ALL MEN BY THESE PRESENTS: That I, W.S. McDonald, City Manager of the City of Dallas, do, in conformity with the Charter of the City of Dallas, and the laws of the State of Texas, herby, on behalf, and in the name of the City of Dallas appoint Kenneth Wheat Bangs to the position of Apprentice Policeman in the Police Department of the City of Dallas for the fiscal year beginning October 1st, 1966 and ending September 30th, 1967, and empower him to discharge all, and singular, the duties of said position according to law, and subject to the Civil Service provisions of the City Charter, and provisions thereof, and the ordinances of the City of Dallas, and the laws of the State of Texas. This Warrant of Appointment shall be his commission, and is good only for the period named, in accordance with the City Charter and ordinances, and rules of the Police Department, and confers upon him authority to carry arms.

IN TESTIMONY WHEREOF: I have hereunto subscribed my name, and caused the corporate seal of said City to be affixed, this the 14 day of June, A.D. 1967.

City Manager, City of Dallas

ATTEST:

City Secretary, City of Dallas

THE AUTHOR'S FIRST WARRANT OF APPOINTMENT AS A
POLICE OFFICER FOR THE CITY OF DALLAS

CITY OF PLANO
POLICE DEPARTMENT
COMMISSION

Know Ye, That by virtue of the authority vested in me and that reposing special trust and confidence in the loyalty, patriotism, fidelity and prudence of **KENNETH W. BANGS** I Grant R. Kinsey, Chief of the Plano, Texas, Police Department do hereby affirm his appointment as a police officer in the Plano Police Department as of **August 23, 1977**, to have, hold and exercise under said appointment all of the power appertaining thereto, and to fulfil the duties thereof.

In Testimony Thereof, I do hereunto set my hand this 25th day of September Anno Domini One Thousand Nine Hundred and Seventy-seven.

Grant R. Kinsey
CHIEF OF POLICE

THE AUTHOR'S COMMISSION AS A POLICE OFFICER FOR THE CITY OF PLANO

THE AUTHOR AS A ROOKIE POLICE OFFICER

THE AUTHOR SOON AFTER BEING PROMOTED TO SERGEANT

THE AUTHOR'S PLANO POLICE IDENTIFICATION PICTURE

THE AUTHOR BEING SWORN IN AS A POLICE OFFICER FOR
THE CITY OF PLANO BY JUDGE RAYMOND ROBINSON

THE AUTHOR AS JUDGE BANGS

THE AUTHOR AND HIS BRIDE, TRUDY TURNER BANGS, AT
THEIR WEDDING

CAPTAIN TOMMY ASHLEY
PLANO POLICE DEPARTMENT
RECEIVING AN AWARD FOR VALOR

OFFICERS OF THE FRENCH NATIONAL POLICE

A PATROL BOAT OF THE MARITIME FORCES OF THE
GENDARMERIE

AEOPORT DE NICE COTE D'AZUR

**TEXAS INSTRUMENTS SITE IN
VILLENEUVE-LOUBET FRANCE**

TI-TAIPEI, TAIWAN
TI-TAIWANPLANT WAS COMPLETED
IN 1970 IN CHUNG HO

PRESTON SMITH
LUBBOCK INTERNATIONAL AIRPORT

FOUR KILOS OF COCAINE AS IT APPEARED IN THE SEIZURE
WHEN FOUND BY THE U.S. CUSTOMS K-9 AT THE AIRPORT
IN HAWAII.

COCAINE OF THIS PURITY WOULD
SELL FOR ABOUT $50,000 A KILO IN HAWAII,
PUTTING THE SEIZURE VALUE AT $200,000

FLEXICUFFS CARRIED BY POLICE

**THE ROSIE CLIFF SUPPER CLUB WHERE THE OFFICER FOUND
B.J. (BILLIE JOE) RING, A.K.A. THE RING MAN**

**A 1951 CHEVEROLET BEL AIR DELUXE COUPE
LIKE THE ONE OWNED BY
MISS GLADYS**

AN AMC HORNET
SIMILAR TO THE ONE
EVERETT KILLED JAMES
AND HIMSELF IN

1959 IMPALA 4DR HARDTOP LIKE THE ONE PERRY RAY AND
MARY LYNN WERE DRIVING ~ NOTE THE ANTENNA ON THE
FINS AND THE FENDER SKIRTS

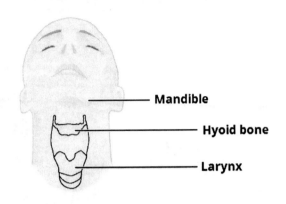

Mandible

Hyoid bone

Larynx

AN ILLUSTRATION OF THE HYOID BONE.
THIS BONE IS OFTEN BROKEN IN MANUAL STRANGULATION.
THE AUTOPSY SHOWED THAT SHIRLENE'S HYOID BONE
WAS BROKEN. THE ODD THING IS THAT THE AUTOPSY ALSO
SHOWED THAT SHE HAD BEEN ASPHYXIATED BY LIGATURE
STRANGULATION AND HER PANTY HOSE WERE FOUND
WRAPPED AROUND HER NECK.

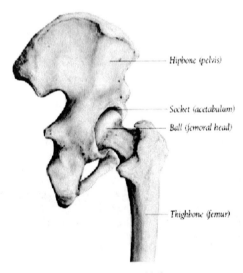

Hipbone (pelvis)

Socket (acetabulam)
Ball (femoral head)

Thighbone (femur)

Bones of the hip joint

**ILLUSTRATION OF THE FEMORAL HEAD (BALL) WHERE IT
JOINS THE HIP SOCKET AS DISCUSSED IN K.W.'S DREAM
ABOUT THE COMMACHE WARRIOR**

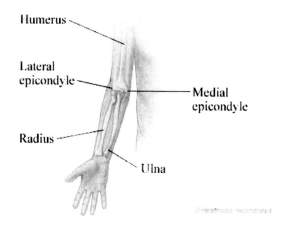

AN ILLUSTRATION OF THE HUMERUS BONE BROKEN WHEN FRANK SHOT DEPUTY BANKS.

A BERETTA .32 CALIBER "TOM CAT" MODEL PISTOL SIMILAR TO THE ONE JORAM WAS ARMED WITH DURING THE SHOOT OUT WITH JAVIER

SIG-550 (5.56 MM) RIFLE
THIS IS THE TYPE OF LONG GUN CARRIED BY THE ARMED
ROBBERS DURING THE PAYROLL ROBBERY IN FRANCE.
IT IS ALSO STANDARD ISSUE FOR THE
FRENCH MARITIME POLICE FORCES.

HK USP 9MM PISTOL
THIS IS THE TYPE OF SIDEARM CARRIED BY THE
ARMED ROBBERS DURING THE PAYROLL ROBBERY
IN FRANCE. IT WAS ALSO STANDARD ISSUE
FOR THE FRENCH MARITIME POLICE.

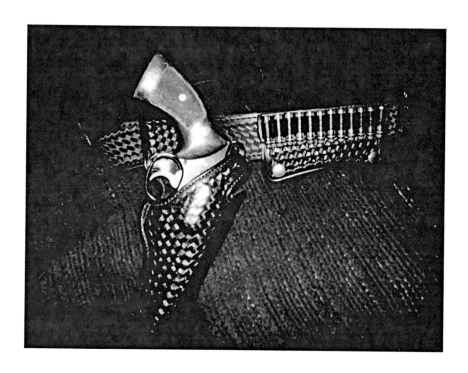

A SAM BROWNE GUN BELT, HOLTER AND AMMUNITION
HOLDER WITH A HOLSTERED .357 MAGNUM REVOLVER

A SUBJECT UNDERGOING A POLYGRAPH EXAMINATION

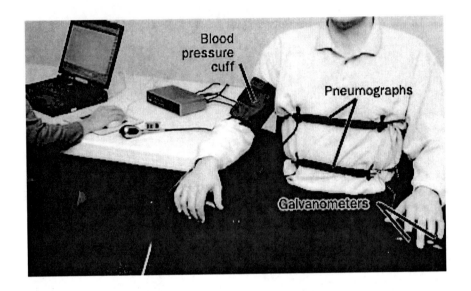

When you sit down in the chair for a polygraph exam, several tubes and wires are connected to your body in specific locations to monitor your physiological activities. Deceptive behavior triggers certain physiological changes that can be detected by a polygraph and a trained examiner. The examiner is looking for the amount of fluctuation in certain physiological activities. Here's a list of physiological activities that are monitored by the polygraph and how they are monitored:

Respiratory rate – Two pneumographs, rubber tubes filled with air, are placed around the test subject's chest and abdomen. When the chest or abdominal muscles expand, the air inside the tubes is displaced. In an analog polygraph, the displaced air acts on a bellows, an accordion-like device those contracts when the tubes expand. This bellows is attached to a mechanical arm, which is connected to an ink-filled pen that makes marks on the scrolling paper when the subject takes a breath. A digital polygraph also uses the pneumographs, but employs transducers to convert the energy of the displaced air into electronic signals.

Blood pressure/heart rate - A blood-pressure cuff is placed around the subject's upper arm. Tubing runs from the cuff to the polygraph. As blood pumps through the arm it makes sound; the changes in pressure caused by the sound displace the air in the tubes, which are connected to a bellows, which moves the pen. Again, in digital polygraphs, these signals are converted into electrical signals by transducers.

Galvanic skin resistance (GSR) - This is also called electro-dermal activity, and is basically a measure of the sweat on your fingertips. The finger tips are one of the most porous areas on the body and so are a good place to look for sweat. We sweat more when we are placed under stress. Fingerplates, called galvanometers, are attached to two of the subject's fingers. These plates measure the skin's ability to conduct electricity. When the skin is hydrated (as with sweat), it conducts electricity much more easily than when it is dry.

Some polygraphs also record arm, leg and other physical movements. As the examiner asks questions, signals from the sensors connected to your body are recorded on a single strip of moving paper.

VICTORY'S HAND

Into the valley strode the giant of Gath
Dressed for war and full of wrath

The mountains shook, as he spoke with a roar
No need for armies; one man, no more

Champion to Champion
Let this be the word

The winner will live
His people be served

None could be found who would answer the call
Each man was fearful afraid he would fall

Then up stepped a lad, fresh from the field
Ruddy of complexion with no sword to wield

Who is this giant defiling the land?
Where is the faithful, does God have no man?

If none other, then I will go
For my God is greater than this uncircumcised foe

His brothers chided and ridiculed with mirth
You're just a lad and this giant a warrior from birth

My king listen, let there be no fear
Your servant shall fell him as I have the bear

Out he stepped with no sword or spear
The giant was furious and cried, Who comes here?

What kind of army sends out the least?
You come with sticks, as at a beast

In the name of my gods, this I declare
I will take your head, feed your flesh to the birds of the air

Not so cried the lad
You've brought weapons to the fight
You boast, posture, and speak of your might

But my God is greater
I have no fear

I come in His Spirit
I need no spear

The battle is His, not yours or mine
This issue was settled before there was time

I heard your threat
The mountains echoed your boast
You have defiled the Lord of the host

God will not be mocked, there is a price to be paid
I shall take your head and send you down to the grave

It will be proof positive to all in these hills
That God is alive and rules as He will

All the words spoken
Nothing more to be said
Each faced the other
Knowing one would soon be dead

The lad stood still, so small, so alone
Then he ran to the giant reaching for a stone

With all of his strength, he let it fly
It sang to the giant as it sliced through the sky

I bring to you death, the penalty you must pay
By this all will know it was God who triumphed today

The stone found its mark and the giant fell dead
The lad picked up the sword and cut off his head

The invaders all fled
Not one to avail
Their lives forfeit to the swords of Israel

The battle was over, lost by the Philistine
The lad was anointed, soon to be King

Let all remember as we celebrate the lad
It is by the hand of God that all victory is had

Based on 1 Samuel 17 © Kenneth W. Bangs, all rights reserved

GLOSSARY OF TERMS USED IN *GUARDIANS*

A.S.A.P. – Acronym for as soon as possible.

Attempted Burglary – Texas law used to contain a statute that made it a felony to attempt to burglarize a building or vehicle. For the charge to be sustainable the prosecutor had to be able to prove that the actor did more than the mere preparation to commit the offense. The actor had to actually engage in activities that if successful would have resulted in him/her entering into or remaining within a building without the effective consent of the owner to commit theft or another offense. An example of preparing would be the gather of tools to be used in the burglary. An example of doing more than said preparation would be the prying on the lock of the door with one of the burglar tools.

Blow – Slang term for Cocaine.

Blue Warrant – A blue warrant is so named because it was printed on blue paper in order to alert officers serving it that it issued for the arrest of a felon who was wanted for the violation of parole or probation. Blue warrants had no bond amount set as it was assumed that the subject was a flight risk.

Burn – Police parlance that means to identify one who has informed on another or given protected information.

CAPERS – An acronym for the Crimes Against Persons Division. This division investigates crimes that are perpetrated against an individual, i.e. an assault, robbery, kidnapping, rape, murder.

Casing – The act of watching, studying or learning about a location or business in preparation for burglarizing or robbing.

C'EST la vie - a French phrase, translated as "That's life."

Charging Instrument - In a criminal case, the government generally brings charges in one of two ways: either by accusing a suspect directly in a "bill of information" or other similar document, or by presenting evidence to a grand jury to allow that body to determine whether the case should proceed.

Chop Shop – a shop, garage, were stolen cars are cut up and sold for parts.

Code 6 – means the officer has arrived at the location to which he has been dispatched.

Code two (2) - means that the dispatcher is authorizing the officer responding to a call to use the vehicle's red lights, siren when necessary to clear traffic and to exceed the posted speed limit no more than ten miles an hour.

Code three (3) – means the dispatcher is authorizing the use of red lights, siren and to exceed the speed limit by no more than ten miles an hour.

Coped A Plea – pled guilty to a criminal charge, usually in exchange for a reduced sentence.

Coke – Coke is a slang term for cocaine.

Cooter – This is a slang term for one with odd personality traits.

Crimes Against Property – a crime that is perpetrated against property rather than against the personage of an individual, i.e. burglary of a building.

Criminal Mischief – A criminal Mischief occurs when an actor intentionally damages the property of another. The penalties are graduated with the cost of the damage. See Texas Penal Code Section 28.03 for more information.

Douglas Community – an area of Plano that was historically populated by predominately by people of African American descent.

Fall On – to arrest, as in a raid or by surprise.

Fence – refers to one who knowingly buys stolen goods and then resale's them.

Flexicuffs – Plastic handcuffs (also called PlastiCuffs or FlexiCuffs, flexcuffs or Double Cuffs) are a form of physical restraint for the hands, using plastic straps. They function as handcuffs but are cheaper and easier to carry than metal handcuffs, but they cannot be re-used. The device was first introduced in 1965.

Flip – To convince a criminal to become an informant against those who he has engaged or is engaging in criminal activities with.

French National Police – The *Police Nationale*, formerly called the "Sûreté", is considered a civilian police force. It has primary responsibility for major cities and large urban areas. The *Police Nationale* is under the control of the Ministry of the interior. Its' strength is roughly one hundred and fifty thousand officers (150,000).

Galvanic Skin Response - a change in the electrodermal activity (EDA) of the skin in response to stress or anxiety; can be measured either by recording the electrical resistance of the skin or by recording weak currents generated by the body.

The traditional theory of EDA holds that skin resistance varies with the state of sweat glands in the skin. Sweating is controlled by the sympathetic nervous system, and skin conductance is an indication of psychological or physiological arousal. If the sympathetic branch of the autonomic nervous system is highly aroused, then sweat gland activity also increases, which in turn increases skin conductance. In this way, skin conductance can be a measure of emotional and sympathetic responses.

More recent research and additional phenomena (resistance, potential, impedance, and admittance, sometimes responsive and sometimes apparently spontaneous) suggest this is not a complete answer, and research continues into the source and significance of EDA.

Gendarmerie - The Gendarmerie is part of the French armed forces. It has the primary responsibility for policing smaller towns and rural areas, as well as the armed forces and military installations, airport security and shipping ports.

Today there are about 105,000 *gendarmes* in France.

Good Eye – a lookout or watchman in a criminal enterprise.

Guardian - a person who guards, protects, or takes care of another person and their property.

Harness – refers to working in uniform as a patrol officer as in, "*I worked that area in harness.*"

Iftar - the meal eaten by Muslims after sunset during Ramadan.

Jack or Jacked Up – A slang term used to refer to the act of altering, or addressing with force, violence or the threat of force and violence.

Joint – a marijuana cigarette as in "*he smoked a joint.*"

A reference to prison as in, "*he just got out of the joint.*"

Keepers – Keepers are strips of leather that wrap around a gun belt and waist belt and close with a snap. The purpose is to hold the gun belt in place, to prevent it from riding up or sagging as the officer goes through his/her workday.

Kidnapping – the taking or holding an individual against their will. The demand for ransom is not necessary for the offense to occur. The holding of an individual against their will is sometimes filed as "false imprisonment".

Kilo – 1,000 grams. Used in Guardians to refer to that amount of drugs.

Kipe – This is a slang term used by criminals to describe the act of stealing.

KKB-364 – the radio call sign of the Dallas Police Department. Federal Communications regulations require the identity of those broadcasting over the airways to give their call sign periodically.

KKZ-954 – the radio call sign for the Plano Police Department. Dispatchers gave the call sign on a time schedule to identify their base but would also give the time and call sign when engaged with a unit relative to a high priority call and or action.

Loot – A term used to describe articles of property taken as spoils or from a criminal enterprise.

Maritime Forces of Gendarmerie - The Maritime Gendarmerie is a component of the French National Gendarmerie under operational control of the chief of staff of the French Navy. It employs 1,100 personnel and operates around thirty patrol boats and high-speed motorboats distributed on the littoral waterways of France. Like their land-based colleagues the Gendarmes Maritime are military personnel who carry out policing operations in addition to their primary role as a coast guard service.

The uniforms and insignia of the Gendarmerie Maritime are very similar to those of the French Navy, but the ranks used are those of the rest of the Gendarmerie

Mass - The Mass or Eucharist is the central act of divine worship in the Catholic Church, which describes it as "the source and summit of the Christian life". In formal contexts, it is sometimes called the Holy Sacrifice of the Mass.

The term "Mass" is derived from the Late Latin word *missa* (dismissal), a word used in the concluding formula of Mass in Latin: "Ite, missa est" "In antiquity, *missa* simply meant 'dismissal'. In Christian usage, however, it gradually took on a deeper meaning. The word 'dismissal' has come to imply a 'mission'. These few words succinctly express the missionary nature of the Church"

Maui Wowie – refers to marijuana grown in Hawaii. It is generally regarded as more potent because the hot, humid growing conditions tend to increase the production of Tetrahydrocannabinol (THC) or more precisely its main isomer, tetrahydrocannabinol, the principal psychoactive constituent (or cannabinoid) of cannabis.

Maui Waui, sometimes called Maui Wowie, is a mostly Sativa hybrid that was considered a top of the line strain when it first appeared in the 1960s. The argument, *'pot wasn't as potent back then'* generally refers to a time before Maui Waui was developed.

Maui Waui was one of the first strains with greatly increased THC content. In the 60's, when Maui Waui was bred, the THC content of an average marijuana strain was quite low (almost always under 8%). Maui Waui featured THC content well into the teens and quickly became one of the most desired strains available.

Mi breni – In Italian this means 'brief me.'

Midnight Sales – refers to illicit transactions where all parties know that they are involved in criminal activity. In Guardians this refers to the knowing purchase of stolen goods, fencing, from the one who stole them.

Mike – the microphone of a police sending and receiving unit, i.e. radio

NCIC – An acronym for National Crime Information Center, which is computerized database, containing information on criminals across the nation. Only law enforcement can access this information and then for official purposes only.

Off – refers to the killing of a person as in, *"he offed him."*

Old Sparky – refers to the electric chair formerly used to execute condemned criminals.

Modus Operandi - a particular way or method of doing something, especially one that is characteristic or well established.

MOS – This is an acronym for Military Occupational Specialty.

Parabolic Microphone -A parabolic microphone is a microphone that uses a parabolic reflector to collect and focus sound waves onto a receiver, in much the same way that a parabolic antenna (e.g., satellite dish) does with radio waves.

Parabolic microphones have great sensitivity to sounds in one direction, along the axis of the dish, and can pick up sounds from many meters away. Typical uses of this microphone include eavesdropping on conversations, for example in espionage and law enforcement.

Parabolic microphones were used in many parts of the world as early as World War II. The Japanese used them extensively.

Polygraph Exam - A polygraph, popularly referred to as a lie detector, measures and records several physiological indices such as blood pressure, pulse, respiration, and skin conductivity while the subject is asked and answers a series of questions.

The belief underpinning the use of the polygraph is that deceptive answers will produce physiological responses that can be differentiated from those associated with non-deceptive responses.

The inexact science of "polygraphing" prevents the results from being acceptable as evidence in courts of law.

Probable Cause - A common definition is "a reasonable amount of suspicion, supported by circumstances sufficiently strong to justify a prudent and cautious person's belief that certain facts are probably true.

In United States criminal law, probable cause is the standard by which police authorities have reason to obtain a warrant for the arrest of a suspected criminal, for the searching of a person and or his property.

Probable Cause Hearing - Probable cause hearing" may refer to a preliminary hearing that happens well after the filing of charges, at which the court hears testimony in order to determine whether it's more likely than not that the defendant committed the alleged crimes. If the court finds "probable cause," then the case may proceed to trial.

Ramadan – refers to the ninth month of the Islamic calendar. Muslims, worldwide, observe it as a month of fasting to commemorate the first revelation of the Quran to Muhammad. This annual observance is regarded as one of the Five Pillars of Islam.

The month lasts 29–30 days based on the visual sightings of the crescent moon, according to numerous biographical accounts compiled in the hadiths.

Sam Browne – Sam Browne is a brand of leatherwear made principally for use of military and civilian officers. Pictured in the Illustrations section at the end of this book is a Sam Browne gun belt, holster and ammunition carrier.

Shoat – refers to a big car, liking it to a 'hog'

Shia – refers to one who follows the Shia branch of Islam. Shia (/ˈʃiːə/; Arabic: شيعة Shīʻah, from Shīʻatu ʻAlī, followers of Ali), is a branch of Islam which holds that the Islamic prophet Muhammad designated Ali ibn Abi Talib as his successor (Caliph). Shia Islam primarily contrasts with Sunni Islam, whose adherents believe that Muhammad did not appoint a successor. Instead, they consider Abu

Bakr (who was appointed Caliph through a Shura, i.e. consensus) to be the correct Caliph.

Signal – When referring to Dallas police communications the word signal is used to designate the type of call or incident an officer is being dispatched to handle. Any signal starting with the number forty-one (41) the officer knows is a felony in progress. For example, a signal 11 is a burglary. A signal 41-11 is a burglary in progress.

In *Guardians* there are references to Signal 27. A signal 27 refers to a dead person. Another used in Guardians is a Signal 19. A signal 19 refers to a shooting. A 41-19 refers to a shooting in progress.

Snitch – a criminal who gives information to the police concerning the criminal activities of others.

Snort – slang term for a drug that is inhaled.

Sunni – refers to one who follows the Sunni branch of Islam. Sunni Islam (/ˈsuːni/ or /ˈsʊni/) is the largest denomination of Islam. Its name comes from the word Sunnah, referring to the exemplary behavior of the Islamic prophet Muhammad.[1] The differences between Sunni and Shia Muslims arose from a disagreement over the choice of Muhammad's successor and subsequently acquired broader political significance, as well as theological and juridical dimensions.

According to Sunni tradition, Muhammad did not clearly designate a successor and the Muslim community acted according to his Sunnah in electing his father-in-law Abu Bakr as the first caliph. This contrasts with the Shi'a view, which holds that Muhammad intended his son-in-law and cousin Ali ibn Abi Talib to succeed him. Political tensions between Sunnis and Shias continued with varying intensity throughout Islamic history.

Summer Marriage – the practice, in some Islamic cultures, of women (usually under the age of 15) entering temporary marriages during the summer in return for money for their families. These unions, dubbed summer marriages, are not legally binding, and end when the term of the marriage has expired.

A recent US State Department report "Trafficking in Persons" found that wealthy men buy "temporary" or "summer marriages" with girls under 18, and that these arrangements are often facilitated by the girls' parents and marriage brokers. The report found that children involved in the temporary marriages suffer both sexual servitude and forced labor as servants to their "husbands".

Suhoor - is an Islamic term referring to the meal consumed early in the morning by Muslims before fasting, sawm, before dawn during or outside the Islamic month of Ramadan.

The Bitch – a criminal who has been convicted on two previous occasions for felony offenses can be deemed to be a habitual felon. The adding of this designation to a criminal charge is referred to as filing *"the bitch"*. When convicted as a habitual offender a criminal is not eligible for parole.

The Onion Field - is a 1973 nonfiction book by Joseph Wambaugh, a sergeant for the Los Angeles Police Department, chronicling the kidnapping of two plainclothes LAPD officers by a pair of criminals during an evening traffic stop and the subsequent murder of Officer Ian James Campbell. It was one of the most influential murder cases in U.S. history, as it forced the Los Angeles Police Department and other large municipalities to change some of their police tactics in the field.

To File Against – refers to the formal presentation of charges, alleging a specific violation of the criminal law, committed by a specified person, against another specified individual or property. The allegations are presented to an agency or authority authorized to 'prosecute' the allegations, i.e. a court of law or a Criminal District Attorney.

To Troll or To Drag – refers to the practice of driving back and forth in an area looking for an individual or to be seen.

Toke On A Number – This is a slang term to describe the act of smoking a marijuana cigarette.

UIL – The agency that governs high school sports in Texas is the University Interscholastic League. UIL is the acronym for that agency.

Voir Dire - a preliminary examination of a witness or a juror by a judge or counsel.

VIN – An acronym for Vehicle Identification Number. This is a number that is produced by the manufacturer and placed on all motor vehicles. It identifies the vehicle and is used to track its' history which includes the name and address of its' registered owner.

WASTE – When used in relation to a homicide this term defines a death as senseless as in a waste of a human life.

WEED – This is a slang term for marijuana.

Whup-Out Book – Slang used to describe a small spiral notebook carried by police officers for taking notes at the scene of crimes or incidents that they are dispatched to investigate.

ABOUT THE AUTHOR

KEN AND TRUDY BANGS

A native Texan, Ken was walking a beat in downtown Dallas at the age of 19. Within a year, he was drafted into the army and assigned to Ft. Polk Louisiana for basic training. Following basic training, he was assigned to the Military Police Corps and deployed to the Alaskan Command, United States Army Alaska.

At the end of his service, Ken returned to a career in law enforcement and public safety. He retired in 2002 having served the last twenty-five years of a thirty-five year career as the Director of Police, Security and Student Safety Services for the Plano Independent School District.

Ken earned a B.S. in Criminal Justice from Sam Houston State University, a M.S. in Human Relations and Business Management from Amberton University and a Doctorate of Ministry in Christian Counseling from Jacksonville (Florida) Theological Seminary.

Ken and Trudy (Turner) Bangs have been married 48 years. They have two children and two *perfect* grandchildren. They currently live in McKinney, Texas.

PUBLICATIONS:

Rosco Jack of Gateway Farm,
Black Rose Writing, May 15, 2014,
ISBN 978-1-61296-354-9

Arctic Warriors,
Black Rose Writing, April 16, 2015,
ISBN 978-1-61296-594-8

The Adventurous Travels of J-Dog and Miranda,
Black Rose Writing, October 18, 2015,
ISBN 978-1-61296-603-8

Guardians In Blue,
Black Rose Writing, May 2016,
ISBN 978-1-944715-01-4

COMING SOON FROM KEN BANGS

Out of Saul ~ Paul

This novel will be a creative fictional work telling the life story of the great Apostle.

The Return of The Pirate

This will be a Sequel to Rosco Jack of Gateway Farm.

The Levee

This novel will be a creative fictional work telling the real life story of the abduction and murder of Dallas County Sheriff's Deputies by a burglary suspect they had sought to arrest.

Once A Wildcat

This work will describe what it was like for boys growing up in Plano, Texas and how important it was for them to become members of the High School Varsity – a *Wildcat*.

View other Black Rose Writing titles at www.blackrosewriting.com/books and use promo code **PRINT** to receive a **20% discount** when purchasing.

BLACK✿ROSE
writing™

CPSIA information can be obtained
at www.ICGtesting.com
Printed in the USA
FFOW02n0114220118
44325905-43987FF